PRAISE FOR

I Am No One You Know

"These are small, hard gems, full of the same rich emotion and startling observation that readers of Oates's fiction have come to expect. . . . It is as if these pieces, by being smaller, are even sharper—as a small television's picture can seem unnaturally crisp."

—*New York Times Book Review*

"Joyce Carol Oates has done it again. Her newest collection of 19 previously published stories contains all the typical elements of her previous fiction: provocative characters, effective plots, variations in point of view, startling figurative language, and that deceivingly simple and matter-of-fact presentation that keeps many readers turning pages."

—*Philadelphia Inquirer*

"The beauty and tragedy of each of these short stories is that they are all lost chapters of novels begging to be written."

—*New York Post*

"*I Am No One You Know* is filled with stories that perfectly represent America's warped and undying [illegible]/repulsion with acts of violence and sex. In a single [illegible]00 pages, Oates says more about [illegible]u-thors can communicate in a lif[illegible]

—[illegible]*ost*

Recent Story Collections by Joyce Carol Oates

The Assignation (1988)

Heat and Other Stories (1991)

Where Is Here? (1992)

Where Are You Going, Where Have You Been? Selected Early Stories (1993)

Haunted: Tales of the Grotesque (1994)

Will You Always Love Me? (1996)

The Collector of Hearts: New Tales of the Grotesque (1998)

Faithless: Tales of Transgression (2001)

Joyce Carol Oates

I Am No One You Know

STORIES

An Imprint of HarperCollinsPublishers

 For information address HarperCollins Publishers Inc., 10 East 53rd Street, New York, NY 10022.

HarperCollins books may be purchased for educational, business, or sales promotional use. For information please write: Special Markets Department, HarperCollins Publishers Inc., 10 East 53rd Street, New York, NY 10022.

FIRST ECCO PAPERBACK EDITION 2005

Designed by Cassandra J. Pappas

Library of Congress Cataloging-in-Publication Data

Oates, Joyce Carol, 1938–

I am no one you know : stories / Joyce Carol Oates.—1st ed.

p. cm.

Contents: Curly Red—In hiding—I'm not your son, I am no one you know—Aiding and abetting—Fugitive—Me & Wolfie—The girl with the blackened eye—Cumberland breakdown—Wolf's Head Lake—Happiness—Fire—Upholstery—The instructor—The skull : a love story—The deaths : an elegy—Jorie (and Jamie) : a deposition—Mrs. Halifax and Rickie Swann : a ballad—Three girls—The mutants.

ISBN 0-06-059288-5 (alk. paper)

1. United States—Social life and customs—Fiction. I. Title.

PS3565.A8I13 2004

813'.54—dc22 2003061283

ISBN 0-06-059288-5 (HARDCOVER)

0-06-059289-3 (PAPERBACK)

---

04 05 06 07 08 BV/RRD 10 9 8 7 6 5 4 3 2 1

to Robert and Peggy Boyers

CONTENTS

PART THREE

PART FOUR

Part One

CURLY RED

I WAS DADDY'S FAVORITE of his seven kids, but still he sent me into exile when I was thirteen and refused to speak to me for twenty-seven years, nor would he allow me to return to our house on Crescent Avenue, Perrysburg, New York, even when Grandma died (though he couldn't keep me away from the funeral mass at St. Stephen's and afterward the burial in the church cemetery, where I stood at a distance, crying) when I was twenty-two. Only in the final months of his life, when Daddy was weakened with emphysema and the anger leaked from him, was I allowed to return to help Mom sometimes. Because now Mom needed me. But it was never the same between us.

Daddy was only seventy-three when he died, but he looked much older, ravaged. Always he'd driven himself hard, working (plumber, pipe fitter), drinking heavily, smoking, raging. He'd been involved all his working life with union politics. Feuds with employers, and with other union members and organizers. Every election, Daddy was in a fever for weeks. One of those men involved behind the scenes. "Delivering the Perrysburg labor vote." A hard-muscled man with a roostery air of self-esteem, yet edgy, suspicious. Daddy was a local character, a known person. He'd been an amateur boxer, light heavyweight, in the U.S. Army (1950–52), and worked out at a downtown gym, had a punching bag and a heavy bag in the garage, sparred with my brothers, who could never, swift on their feet as they were, stay out of reach of his "dynamite" right cross. When I was living with relatives across town, in what I call my exile, I knew my father at a distance: caught glimpses of him on the street, saw his picture in the paper. Then things changed, younger men were coming up in the union, Daddy and his friends lost power, Daddy got sick, and one sickness led to another. By the time I was allowed back in the house on Crescent Avenue, Daddy was under hospice care, and he'd turned into an old man, shrunken by fifty pounds, furrows in his face like you'd make in a piecrust with a fork. I stared and stared. Was this my father? That face I knew to be ruddy-skinned, good-looking, now gaunt and strangely collapsed about the mouth. Even his shrewd eyes were smaller and shifting worriedly in their sockets as if he was thinking, *Is it in the room with me yet?*

John Dellamora, who'd always been contemptuous of weakness in others and in himself, now dependent upon breathing oxygen through a nose piece. Watching me sidelong as I approached his bed bearing a bouquet of white carnations in my trembling hand.

"Daddy? It's Lili Rose . . ."

When the hospice nurse took me aside and said, If there's some bitterness between you and your father now's the time to make it up, later will be too late, I said right away, "That's up to my father, I think." Everything was up to him. God damn if I'd say I was sorry when I was not sorry.

I think Daddy knows me. Sometimes. Still he stiffens as if he's afraid I might touch him, and moves his head in a tight little nod when I speak to him, though I can feel him staring at me, at my back, when I leave the room, and always I'm thinking he's going to call me back in his old teasing voice—*Hey Curly Red, c'mon! Let's make it up.*

Curly Red. That name I haven't heard from anyone's lips in twenty-seven years.

I'm waiting. I'm certain that hour will come.

WE WERE MARIANA, and Rick, and Emily, and Leo, and Mario, and Johnny Jr., and Lili Rose. Daddy would stare at us in disgust, picking at his teeth with a silver toothpick. "Christ! Looks like a platoon." He was proud of us and loved us, though. Most of the time.

We lived in a large wood-frame house Daddy made sure was always painted and in good repair, front and back lawns mowed, sidewalk shoveled in winter. There was a tall red maple in front that turned fiery and splendid in October. Our house was at the dead end of Crescent Avenue, above the Niagara River. It was a steep dizzy drop to the riverbank. Cliffs on both sides were exposed shale that always looked wet, sharp. Beyond the dead end was a no-man's-land of scrub trees and thistles and sumac that flamed up in early autumn, where young kids played. It was a dangerous playing area, if you lost your footing. The view of the river from our house was beautiful, I guess. A river you see every day, from the window of your own room, you take for granted until one day it's gone from you. I cried a lot when I was sent away.

But the river got into my dreams. Wide, and glittery like fish scales, always choppy like a living thing restless beneath its skin. Miles away the thunderous Falls like a nightmare. Always there was a wind, and in winter the air could freeze your eyelashes together in a few seconds. There was that morning in December you'd wake to see the river had frozen, turned to black ice.

I had a happy childhood in that house. Nobody can take that from me.

THIS CLIPPING FROM the *Perrysburg Journal* I saved until it was so dry it fell to pieces in my fingers. An obituary beneath a two-inch-high photo of a shyly smiling black boy with a gap between two prominent front teeth.

> Jadro Filer, 17. Resident of Bayside Street, Perrysburg. Varsity basketball at Perrysburg High School. Choir, Bible Baptist Church. Died in Perrysburg General Hospital, April 11, 1973, of severe head injuries following an attack early in the morning of April 9 by yet unidentified assailants as he was walking on Route 11. Survived by his mother,

Ethel, his sisters, Louise and Ida, and his brothers, Tyrone, Medrick, and Herman. Services Monday at Bible Baptist Church.

Always people would ask if I'd known Jadro Filer. No! Or any of his family. It was only after his death I came to know him. It was only after his death we came to be associated in some people's minds. *Jadro Filer, Lili Rose Dellamora.*

Not that it did any good for Jadro Filer, who was dead. And it was the worst thing that could have happened to me.

WHEN WE WERE growing up my brothers were often in some kind of "trouble." I had four older brothers. All except Johnny Jr., the closest to me in age, had quick tempers. It's serious trouble I'm speaking of here. That time Leo and Mario got into their first "serious trouble" I was ten, and never knew what happened exactly. Nobody would tell me much. Mom kept saying, scolding, "Never mind!" The girl, Liza Deaver, was fifteen, with thick glasses, a splotched turtle face, a slow whiny insinuating manner of speech. She was as fattish and mature as a grown woman, in special-education class at Franklin Roosevelt Junior-Senior High School, where Leo, sixteen, was a sophomore and Mario, thirteen, was in eighth grade.

No news item would appear in the *Perrysburg Journal* about Liza Deaver. Only minors were involved, and the victim so young.

There were ten or eleven of them. They'd cajoled Liza into coming with them to Huron Park after school. They'd tramped through the muddy playing fields, past the skeletal trellises of the municipal rose garden to the swimming-pool area, to the old stucco building where refreshments were sold in summer and where there were foul-smelling rest rooms, changing rooms. In the off-season the building was deserted, dead leaves blew about the cement walks. But the rest rooms were unlocked.

The boys brought Liza into the men's room.

Questioned afterward by police, school officials, parents, the boys would claim, "Liza wanted to come with us." "It was Liza's idea." "Liza said she'd done this before, with her brothers." Liza would deny this, Liza's parents would deny it, strenuously. Liza hadn't been injured enough to require hospitalization, but her clothes had been torn, her nose bloodied, her body bruised and chafed. Still, the boys insisted it had been Liza's idea. They'd been "nice" to her, they said. Witnesses would corroborate that they'd given her presents she'd eagerly accepted: a Mars bar, a plastic pearl necklace found in the trash, a perfumy deodorant. (Liza Deaver was notorious around school for her strong, horsey odor.) The boys' fathers hired a single lawyer to represent their sons, a friend of Daddy's retained by the AFL-CIO branch union to which Daddy belonged, and a public hearing in juvenile court was avoided.

After the incident no one wanted to talk about it in our household, at least in my presence. Leo and Mario were subdued, respectful of our father, for weeks, like kicked dogs. They had 9:00 P.M. curfews; Leo wasn't allowed to drive for six weeks. My mother said, incensed, "Those Deavers better get her fixed, that one. Before it's too late."

I asked what "fixed" meant. It scared me to think that whatever the boys had done, Liza might need fixing, like a broken clock.

Disdainfully my mother said, "Like a cat, spayed. So it can't have kittens."

GROWING UP, we Dellamora kids knew that our daddy would die for us. We never had to be told. Of course the concept "to die for" was too extravagant to have occurred to us. Still, we knew.

Our father had fought in Korea, years before I was born. He'd tease me, saying it was lucky the shrapnel hit him where it did, in the ass, not in his you-know-what, 'cause maybe Lili Rose wouldn't have been born. (I knew this was a joke. But not very funny, to me.) Daddy was cited for heroism, saving several other soldiers, but he said he was twenty-three at the time—"Too stupid to know what I was doing." None of us believed this. Daddy was one who thought you should die for your friends, your brothers, your family. No questions asked. He lent money to all the deadbeat relatives, including his own heavy-drinking father. He was always doing favors for guys in the union, for "up-and-coming" boxers and for "over-the-hill" boxers—sometimes the same man, after a few years' interim. Daddy was fond of the cryptic remark *Revenge is a dish best served cold,* but we'd noticed how he was always making up with men he'd been feuding with.

Another remark he liked, from the boxing world, was *What goes around comes around*. Meaning not just bad but good, too. The good you do will be returned to you. Eventually.

IN APRIL 1973, when Jadro Filer was beaten unconscious and died, and the lawyer my father hired to defend Leo and Mario pleaded their case to prosecutors, the defense of impulsive, hot-headed boys didn't work out so well for them, or for my cousin Walt and a neighborhood friend named Don Brinkhaus. And this time I was involved.

Did I know Jadro Filer, or any of his family? Did I have Negro friends? ("Negro" was the polite, prescribed term.) There'd been a Negro girl in my fourth-grade class with the strange, beautiful name Skyla I'd been friends with, but not the kind of friend who invited you to her house, or vice versa. When Skyla dropped out of school I missed her, but never thought to ask where she'd gone.

Nigger lover, I'd be called. A girl of thirteen.

At this time Leo was nineteen, living in a walk-up apartment downtown and working for the plumbing contractor our daddy worked for; he'd been accepted into the union. (No Negroes belonged. This would come out later, the union thought unfairly, in the media coverage of the case.) Mario was sixteen, a sophomore in high school, big for his age, bored. Leo and Mario were together a lot, cruising in Mario's car, drinking beer with guys mostly Leo's age. Leo was discovering what Daddy called "fucking-real life." He hated working full-time. His girlfriend had broken up with him because of his drinking and general evil temper. He pissed Daddy off saying he wished to hell the Vietnam War hadn't ended so fast, he'd have liked to go over and "see what that shit was all about."

At Perrysburg High there'd be isolated incidents involving white and Negro boys, especially following Friday night sports events, but none of these had involved Jadro Filer. In 1971–72, his senior year at the school, Leo had known Jadro but there'd been no "bad blood" between them, he insisted. Mario would deny it, too. Certainly they were aware of Jadro on the basketball team, who hadn't been? Perrysburg wasn't a large school: fewer than five hundred students. Everybody knew everybody else, in some way. But whites and Negroes didn't mix much. On sports teams and in the school band and chorus, in a few of the clubs, maybe. But not much.

There wasn't "mixed" dating. Just about never.

Questioned by county prosecutors if they'd had any special reason to harass Jadro Filer, provoke him into a fight, Leo and the other boys said no. Had they attacked Jadro because he was a Negro?

Repeatedly they denied this. Four white boys, a solitary black boy. But they weren't racists, the attackers.

They'd been drinking since about 10:00 P.M. *We saw this guy walking by himself by the railroad track, cutting through a field and onto Route 11, it looked kind of weird, suspicious. We didn't know who it was . . .* Well, maybe they could see the boy was dark-skinned. Maybe one of them yelled out *Nigger!* Those skid marks in the gravel . . . Maybe Leo, who was driving, aimed the car at the kid just to scare him, to make him run. After that, things got confused.

It had been approximately 12:15 A.M. on April 9, 1973, when Jadro Filer left his girlfriend's house to walk back to his home, a ten-minute walk under ordinary circumstances, across the railroad embankment, along the highway shoulder past darkened gas stations, a Taco Bell, a McDonald's. It was 12:50 A.M. when an emergency call was made reporting a badly beaten young man lying in a roadside ditch near a railroad culvert. (No other call was reported that night. But the following morning, when news of the beating began to spread through Perrysburg, an anonymous caller would report to police that he'd seen what appeared to be a new-model Buick in the vicinity of the attack scene, parked off the highway shortly after midnight. The caller, slowing, then accelerating to speed past, had an impression of four or five young white men "involved in some activity like fighting." The caller would supply police with the first three digits of a car registered to Leo Dellamora.) By 12:50 A.M., however, Leo and Mario were back home. They'd dropped Walt and Don Brinkhaus off, and come directly to Crescent Avenue. At this time they hadn't known, would claim they'd had no idea, that Jadro Filer had been beaten so badly he'd never regain consciousness. They were aroused, excited. Maybe a little panicked. I overheard them speaking together in low, urgent voices. I heard "nigger" several times repeated. I heard their nervous laughter. I hadn't been asleep when they came home, and I'd noticed the time. And this was strange: no headlights sprang onto the wall of my bedroom, moving swiftly from one corner of the room to another as usual when someone turned into our driveway at night. Leo must have cut his headlights. Or he'd been driving without them.

My room was downstairs, toward the rear of our house; my single window overlooked the driveway and, beyond that, the river. I'd had to share this room with Emily for years, and now I missed her. Always I'd wanted a room to myself in our crowded household, but now I was lonely a lot, especially at night. When Daddy was out, which was often, or my brothers, I'd wait for them to come home. I missed them! Patiently I'd watch for headlights to flash onto the walls. That night I was waiting for Leo to bring Mario back home, and I was hoping Leo would hang out awhile. In the kitchen, having a beer or two.

Dad, Mom, and Johnny Jr. were sleeping upstairs. I left my room and entered the darkened kitchen, barefoot, to wait for Leo and Mario.

The back kitchen door opened out into the garage. It was rarely locked. I opened it just a little and listened. Often I eavesdropped on my brothers. I was never caught, they took so little notice of me. Tonight I couldn't hear clearly what my brothers were saying in the garage. I heard only lowered, isolated words, but one of them was "nigger." I heard the outside faucet being turned on. My brothers were doing something with the hose? Washing the car? I peered through the crack and saw them squatting close together on the floor washing a baseball bat. This was Leo's bat he carried in his car "for protection." Leo and Mario had rolled up their sleeves to wash their hands and forearms, cursing as water sprang up out of the hose onto their clothing.

I wanted to laugh, they looked so funny. They were only about ten feet away and unaware of me.

Why didn't I speak to them then? I would wonder. Any other night, I would have. Why not that night?

Not for a long time would I learn that my brothers were deliberating what to do with the bat during these minutes. *The murder weapon,* it would one day be called. They weren't thinking very clearly, but they knew they had to get rid of the bat, fast. They thought about throwing it into the river, of course—but what if it floated? Even weighed down, a wooden bat might somehow work loose and float.

And the river would be the first place Perrysburg cops would look. Finally they decided to bury it somewhere on the riverbank, in the underbrush. A few hundred feet away from the house. There was a lot of litter on the riverbank; this seemed like a practical idea. I saw my brothers wrap the bat in a piece of burlap and I saw them leave the garage, but I couldn't see them for more than a few seconds from my bedroom window. I was mystified. I had no idea what they were doing. I guessed they were drunk. Maybe it was some kind of joke.

ABOUT FORTY MINUTES later I heard them enter the house. The kitchen. I heard the refrigerator door being opened and shut, the sound of beer cans being opened. Eagerly I left my room to join them. I was a scrawny weed of a girl who adored her big brothers, basking in the most meager glow of their careless attention. And they loved me, I believed. I'd always believed. Calling me, like Daddy, "Curly"—"Curly Red." When they were in the mood.

"Hey guys! What've you been doing, fighting?"

They stared at me as if for a shivery moment they didn't know who the hell I was. What to do about me. They were both drinking beer thirstily. They were breathing through their mouths as if they'd been running uphill. I felt their excitement. Their jackets were unzipped, wet in front. Mario's big-jawed face looked raw; a small cut gleamed beneath his right eye. Leo was rubbing the knuckles of his right hand as if they pained him. But he'd taken time to dampen his longish, lank, sand-colored hair and sweep it back in two wings from his forehead. His skin, like Mario's, was slightly blemished, but he had a brutal handsome face. He had Daddy's young face.

Leo said, with his easy smile, "Some sons of bitches over at the Falls. But we're okay, see? Don't tell Mom."

Mario said, "Yeah, Curly. Don't tell Mom."

No need to warn me against telling Daddy. None of us would ever have ratted to our father. Even if we hated one another's guts, we wouldn't. That was a betrayal so profound and cruel as to be indefinable, for Daddy's punishment would be swift and pitiless; and for a certain space of time Daddy would withhold his love from the one he'd punished.

I asked who it was they'd been fighting. How badly I wanted to be like them: a brother to them. Though I knew it was hopeless; they'd shrug as they always did when I asked pushy questions. Leo said quietly, "You got to promise you won't say anything, Curly. Okay?"

I shrugged and laughed. "Gimme a sip of your beer."

Leo handed me his can, then Mario. It wasn't beer but Daddy's favorite ale. I hated the taste, even the smell, but was determined to keep trying to like it, until one day I would like it just fine. I swallowed, I choked a little. I said, "I promise."

NEXT DAY, news of the beating of Jadro Filer spread through Perrysburg. Even in junior high no one was talking about much else. I heard, and I knew.

A Negro boy, basketball player at the high school. Beaten by several not yet identified white boys. Left unconscious by the side of Route 11. Sometime after midnight. In critical condition in intensive care at Perrysburg General Hospital.

I was frightened for Leo and Mario, I was in dread of their being arrested. I would tell no one what I knew.

But already the Perrysburg police were making inquiries about Leo, Mario, Walt, and Don Brinkhaus. They had the first three digits of Leo's license plate and a partial description of his car. Leo was picked up at work. Mario had gone to school groggy and nervous, trying to behave as if nothing was wrong, but he was called out of third-period class and taken downtown to the police station. I would learn later that Daddy had accompanied Leo and Mario to the police station; he'd arranged for a lawyer to join them. My mother, at home, was agitated, preoccupied. I knew it was expected of me to ask, "Where's Mario, Mom? Where's Daddy? Is something wrong?" But my mother turned away.

In silence Mom and I watched the local TV news at 6:00 P.M. The lead story was the "severe beating" of Jadro Filer, a "popular basketball star" at PHS. I saw my mother's lips move wordlessly as sometimes in church, at mass, she knelt, shut her eyes, moved her lips as she said the rosary like an exhausted woman in a trance. Such public behavior embarrassed me now that I was a teenager. Everything about my mother embarrassed me. I hated her for her spreading hips and flaccid upper arms, the creases in her face, her scared shiny eyes. That night, seeing her praying as she stared at the TV screen, I was filled with raging contempt.

How much did my mother know? How much did she refuse to know?

That night I was wakened from exhausting dreams by voices. At first I thought it was the wind, then I understood it was Daddy talking with my brothers in the kitchen. His voice was low and urgent, and their voices were murmurs. Occasionally Daddy's voice would be raised, but I couldn't hear any words distinctly, and I didn't want to hear. I was sick with the knowledge of what Leo and Mario had done. I had no desire to eavesdrop. Never would I eavesdrop on anyone again. I lay in my room in my bed hunched beneath the covers. I knew that, if anyone questioned me as they'd been questioning my brothers, I couldn't lie. I could lie to my brothers and sisters but to no adult. I would have to tell the truth. In confession, I listed the sins I'd committed, which included sins of omission. Usually these were small, venial sins. But this was different. If the priest asked me . . . If one of my teachers asked me . . . All day I'd been thinking of Jadro Filer. His face on the front page of the newspaper. On TV. *I can't be like my brothers. I hate them.*

Daddy, Leo, and Mario were in the kitchen much of the night. I lay with my hands pressed over my ears. I seemed to know that, upstairs in her bed, Mom was lying awake, too, not-hearing. I seemed to know that Daddy was asking my brothers what they knew about the beating, and my brothers were insisting in hurt, aggrieved voices that they knew nothing. The police had questioned them for hours, and hotly and angrily, like the other two boys, they'd denied everything. My father must have been exhausted by the ordeal of the police station, and humiliated, because he was friends with a number of Perrysburg police officers. Each time he asked Leo and Mario, their replies were more vehement. Of the four boys under suspicion, Leo would probably have been the most convincing. Mario, the youngest, would have been least convincing. Mario with the scabby scratch beneath his right eye. Mario, shifting his shoulders, sweating as he lied to Daddy, yet like a tightrope walker venturing across the rope, in terror of falling, he couldn't walk back. *We don't know nothing. We didn't do it! They just want to arrest somebody white.*

I wondered: Did Daddy believe them?

JADRO FILER DIED in the hospital on April 11.

There was a rumor that Jadro had been "involved in drugs." He'd been beaten by "black drug dealers" from Niagara Falls. There was a rumor he'd been killed by his girlfriend's older brother. Or: it had been a random attack, white racist skinheads from Niagara Falls.

These rumors came to nothing. Leo, Mario, Walt, and Don Brinkhaus were summoned back to the police station. And Daddy went with them again.

The phone rang repeatedly, and Mom refused to answer. Finally I took the receiver off the hook.

But Leo and Mario weren't yet arrested. Their names had not been released to the media. Daddy insisted Leo move back into his old room; there'd been "racist" threats against him, and he wasn't safe in his apartment downtown. Mario was told by the high school principal he should stay home for a while, feelings were running high between whites and blacks at PHS and Mario's presence was "undesirable." Mom wanted to keep me home from school too, but I refused. I didn't care if my teachers and the other kids looked at me strangely. I needed to be at school. I loved school! The thought of being kept home panicked me. I couldn't bear to be trapped here where my parents and my brothers were waiting for—what? What would save them? For somebody else to be arrested for the crime? (As my mother said, "The people who did this terrible thing. The guilty people.")

There was the hope, too, never uttered aloud, that the evidence police were assembling would be only circumstantial, not strong enough to take before a grand jury. This was what the boys' lawyers insisted.

Neighbors, friends of Daddy's from work, relatives, dropped by our house to show their support. Rick, Mariana, Emily, came to supper. It was like old times: nine of us Dellamoras at the table. Mom's older, favored daughters helping her in the kitchen. There was no subject of conversation except Leo and Mario and the injustice of what the police were doing to them. The name "Jadro Filer" was never spoken, there was reference only to "the Negro boy," "the black boy." No more did my brothers refer to Jadro as "nigger." My brothers didn't speak of Jadro at all. It was the Perrysburg police who were reviled, held in contempt. And some of these men had called themselves friends of my father! There was the "anonymous" driver who'd supplied the police with Leo's partial license-plate number, to throw them off the track . . . Our household was under siege, the very walls and roof buffeted by ferocious winds. We Dellamoras huddled inside, clutching one another. Daddy would protect us, we knew.

With so many people around it wasn't hard for me to avoid my brothers. Still, they sought me out. "Hey Curly: what're you hearing at school?" Their eyes snatching at mine. *You promised, remember? Not to tell.* They had no idea that I knew about the bat. Only that I knew they'd been fighting that night, with some guys from the Falls. And I'd promised not to tell Mom. Meaning I'd promised not to tell anybody. I shrank from Leo's gaze. He saw something furtive and guilty in my face. *You wouldn't rat on us, right? Your brothers?*

Only years later would I wonder what Leo and Mario might have done to me if they'd guessed all that I knew.

I WAS THE girl who never cried, or rarely. But now I started to cry easily. My outer skin hurt like sunburn, my eyes filled with moisture. At school, at home. Watching TV and seeing Jadro Filer's mother and older brother interviewed, seeing Mrs. Filer clutch a tissue to her face, dissolve into tears, I began crying, too. *He really is gone. Somebody's dead. It's real.* The taste of it was like copper pennies in my mouth.

Angry, my mother switched off the TV. "They're just doing that for the TV cameras. All that attention, to make people feel sorry for *them*."

I followed Mom out into the kitchen. I said, "Mom? It was Leo and Mario. I saw them with the baseball bat. They were the ones." But my mother was at the sink, running water hard. She stood with her back to me, furious, shaking. Somewhere close by the telephone began ringing; we waited for Daddy to pick it up, in another room.

NEXT DAY IN homeroom I was crying, sniffling. Wiping my nose with my fingers like a small dazed child. This was the third day after

Jadro Filer's death. My homeroom teacher called me to her desk to ask cautiously, "Is there something wrong, Lili Rose? Are you upset about something?" She knew the rumor about my brothers. "Are you sick?" I shook my head no. But the woman peered at me worriedly, touched my warm forehead with her fingers, decided I had a fever, and sent me to the school nurse, who made me lie down on a cot, took my temperature, noted that my teeth were chattering. Gently she scolded, "Lili Rose, you're a sick girl. Your temperature is 101 degrees, that's *fever.* Your mother oughtn't to have let you out of the house this morning."

These words, like a curse, made me cry harder. The alarmed nurse called in the school principal, Mr. Mandell, who asked me what was wrong, why was I crying, and somehow it happened that I was telling him about Leo and Mario and the baseball bat; I was telling Mr. Mandell how afraid I was, how angry my father would be, I didn't want to go home . . . Within a few minutes plainclothes police officers, one of them a woman, had been summoned to speak with me.

That was how it began. And once it began, it couldn't be stopped.

It would become a matter of public record: the unsolicited, uncoerced, purely voluntary information provided police by the thirteen-year-old sister of two suspects in the Jadro Filer beating death.

I WAS MOVED across town to live with my aunt Bea and uncle Clyde, who hadn't any children. This was a practical move, better than a county foster home. None of the other relatives wanted me. My sister Mariana and her husband, my sister Emily. *Never want to see her face again. She makes me want to puke.*

I had to change schools, too.

I would live with my aunt and uncle for four years in their prissy little house on Pearson Street. Aunt Bea was my mother's older sister. Uncle Clyde was a bricklayer. So boring, my mind drifted out the window when they spoke to me. In the beginning my aunt hugged me a lot, mistaking my passivity for sadness. She told me I'd learn to be happy with her and Uncle Clyde, I'd get used to my new home, my new room, things would "settle down" and after a while my parents would forgive me—all of which, and I knew so at the time, was bullshit. The first few days I was stunned. I was too young to realize how the only life I'd known had been taken from me. Those swift uncalculated minutes in the school infirmary. The nurse gently scolding. *Your mother oughtn't to have let you.* In my dreams in years to come I would mistake the school nurse for my mother. And there was Mr. Mandell crouching beside me. *Lili Rose? What is it? Is there trouble at home?* I had to tell them what I knew. I had no choice.

In AA they tell you: nobody starts out thinking, as a kid, he's going to wind up an alcoholic or a junkie. Add to that an alcoholic twice-divorced with no kids, age forty-three and counting. Add to that a daughter denounced by her family for ratting to the police on two brothers. Nobody starts out thinking she'll be so defined, but there it is. Blunt and irrevocable as a headline.

13-YEAR-OLD SISTER OF SUSPECTS
PROVIDES INFORMATION TO PERRYSBURG POLICE
Filer Death Investigation Continues

So they moved me away. In an afternoon. I wouldn't speak with Leo and Mario; I was spared seeing the loathing in their faces. I wouldn't be informed but would read in the *Perrysburg Journal* that a police search team had found Leo's baseball bat, buried amid litter about two hundred yards from our house. The bat, its handle wrapped in black tape, had been washed to a degree, but bloodstains and partial fingerprints remained; most incriminating, wood splinters matching those in the bat had been embedded in Jadro Filer's scalp. I would read that, faced with this incontrovertible evidence, the lawyers representing my brothers and their friends advised their clients to plead guilty, not to murder charges but to manslaughter. The lawyers negotiated plea bargains with county prosecutors, first-degree manslaughter for Leo, who'd actually wielded the bat, second-degree manslaughter for Mario, Walt, Don. Because he was sixteen, Mario was sentenced to five years at a youth facility; he was released after three. Leo received the stiffest sentence, seven to fifteen years at Red Bank Correctional, a medium-security prison. The black community protested that these were overly lenient sentences, considering that Jadro Filer had been killed in an unprovoked attack; this was further evidence of racism and bigotry in Perrysburg. Some members of the white community denounced the sentences as too harsh, evidence of racism and bigotry in Perrysburg.

For a long time I'd wake in my new bed in my new room confused and hopeful. Thinking, *Maybe it hasn't happened yet?*

At least there was no trial. I was spared having to testify against my brothers in court.

NOBODY EXPECTED DAD to live to see the new millennium. But he did. So Mariana marveled, "He has so much courage."

They'd called me back, and like an eager dog I returned. On a windblown March morning, light flashing off the river like broken pieces of mirror, I brought my dying father a bouquet of white carnations from a florist in town. White carnations! As if Daddy had ever been a man to admire or even take notice of flowers, but what else? I could hardly have brought him a bottle of whiskey. I could hardly have brought a man dying of emphysema a handful of those fat foul-smelling Portuguese cigars he'd loved.

"Daddy, I'm Lili Rose. I guess Mom told you I was coming?"

Daddy nodded at me, frowning. It was all he could do, sucking oxygen through a plastic nose piece. His eyes careening onto me, and away. The truth was he'd never intended to get old like this. He'd been contemptuous of sickly, self-pitying relatives. I'd heard him say to whoever was listening, *Jesus! Take me out and shoot me, I ever get like that.*

Daddy had become a sunken-chested man with drooping eyelids and trembling hands. And the veins bulging in those hands, frightening to see. The hospice nurse had said, if there's bitterness between you . . . I wanted to lean close to Daddy to whisper, *Is there bitterness between us? After so long?* It was up to him, of course.

My mother had forgiven me, I guess. Those years she'd avoided me, saying her heart was broken. Well, what of my heart? I'd given up explaining. No one cared. *You made your choice, now live with it. Ruined your brothers' lives.* My sisters were the ones who'd urged me to return, now Daddy was sick. They'd told me it had come out just recently:

Daddy had given, over a period of years, more than five thousand dollars to Jadro Filer's mother. ("He wanted it anonymous. He didn't want it *known.*") They'd prepared me for the changes in our father, yet somehow they had not. This strangeness! Not just John Dellamora was an old, sick man but he was in a hospital bed in our house, in my former room. He hadn't been able to climb stairs in a while, so this was a practical solution. I wondered if he resented being in my old room. Or if he even remembered whose room this was. From the window, the river looked unchanged. It was slate-colored, so turbulent you couldn't have told which direction the current was flowing in. In a drowse of morphine Daddy's droopy-lidded eyes held more puzzlement than anger or judgment. He had trouble keeping them lifted to me, but I believed he was listening as I spoke of my life with the earnestness of one who must take it on faith that her listener cares for what she's saying. ". . . Teaching, in Boston. This summer I've been invited to Venice . . ." But there was the hospice nurse, Yolanda. She was cheerful, young. Half my age. I saw Daddy watching Yolanda, too. Possibly he thought that Yolanda was his daughter. His favorite daughter, who'd never left home. Never betrayed him. Never "ratted." The hospital had discharged him and sent him home to die. It wasn't just emphysema, it was heart congestion. Exhaustion. My father hadn't been a placid man, yet his ending would be placid, we were grateful for this. I was speaking softly. "Daddy? I had to do it. I didn't have any choice . . ." I wondered if this was true: don't we always have choices? Even a child of thirteen has a choice. I knew what was right, I did what was right, I'd do it again. I was stubborn, defiant. This was my truest nature. Maybe I'd ruined my brothers' lives and maybe even my own, but I would do it again.

I didn't tell Daddy this. His left eyelid drooped as if winking at me. He was trying to smile, was he? *Curly Red. How's my girl?* My hair wasn't red any longer, and it wasn't curly. I was a passionate AA advocate: one day at a time, the highest wisdom. You can eke out a life like that. Like Daddy's labored breathing, in which desperation was put to good use. When you have less than 40 percent of your lungs remaining, you use every cubic centimeter of those remaining lungs.

Of Daddy's seven children, Leo was the one who hadn't returned. Leo had served five years in prison, was released to parole at the age of twenty-four, choosing to reside in the Red Bank area; two years later he left New York State and never returned to Perrysburg. Where Leo was, somewhere on the West Coast, my mother and sisters knew, but I didn't dare inquire. *Why do you want to know? Why you?*

Mario had stayed away from Perrysburg for fifteen years, then he'd returned. He worked for a local construction company as a carpenter. He'd married twice, like me. Divorced twice. Like me, no children. I wondered if he'd given up drinking. He'd become a boneless-looking man of middle age, taciturn, purse-lipped, like an awkwardly hip high school teacher in tinted aviator sunglasses and suede leather jackets from Sears. We'd met on the front walk of the house on Crescent Avenue, by accident; Mario was leaving as I was approaching. I tasted panic seeing him, recognizing him immediately, my brother Mario I'd betrayed . . . I was frightened he might spit into my face. Or—the walk was slick with melting snow—he might kick my legs out from under me. My terror must have shown in my face. Mario laughed. He grinned, shaking his head, as if there was an old joke between us, moving past me on the narrow walk with no intention of speaking, certainly not of taking my hand, which I was holding out tentatively, but at the curb where his car was parked he called back, "Lili Rose, it's O.K. Only just too bad about the old man, huh? Seventy-three isn't old." I said, "Mario!" But he was in his car gunning the motor.

Now at Daddy's bedside I'm thinking, suddenly excited, I'll call Mario. Tonight. If he hangs up, I might drive by his place. I'll get the address from Mariana. I'll knock at his door, I'll see Mario again. God damn, I will.

I've taken Daddy's unresisting hand. I believe I can feel his fingers tightening. I'm thinking the wild extravagant thoughts you think at such times: the world is a hospice, we're all in it together. "Daddy, I love you. Even if . . ." Even if I've hated you. I lived with Aunt Bea and Uncle Clyde, who'd waited for me to love them like a daughter, but that hadn't happened; I'd broken their hearts too, moving out on the June morning following my high school graduation, living in a half-dozen cities, two husbands and more lovers than I can recall and no children, whether by design or chance I couldn't have said, but none of that sorry crap figures here. None of the rest of my life figures here.

IN HIDING

NOT THINKING *Is this a mistake, to begin?* nor *Will I regret this?* Normally a guarded woman, she'd given in to impulse. Hadn't considered any future beyond the gesture of an hour.

His name was Woodson Johnston, Jr.—"Woody." He signed this name with a thick-nubbed pen in black ink with a flair that suggested he wished to think well of himself.

Where'd he get her home address? A directory of poets and writers?

Please accept my poetry as a gift. I love your poetry truly. Even if you don't have time to read my writings. Even if you don't have a feeling for it. I understand!

He was an inmate at Kansas State Penitentiary for Men in Fulham, Kansas. His number was AT33914. He'd sent her a packet of poems and a few pages of a prison diary. She was a poet, translator, part-time college teacher, and divorced mother of a fifteen-year-old son. For the past seven years, since the divorce, she'd lived in Olean, New York.

A snowswept November. Swirling funnels of snow like vaporous human figures dancing across the snow-crust, then turning ragged, blown apart. She'd opened the packet, quickly read Johnston's poems that had been published in a small smudgily printed magazine with a clever name—*In Pen.* The diary had been photocopied from a laboriously typed manuscript without margins. There were frequent misspellings and typographical errors and Johnston had written in corrections in a neat, crimped hand. Her heart was moved to pity, seeing these corrections. As if they mattered! But of course they mattered to the author.

Quickly she read the poems, and reread them. She read the prison diary excerpt. Johnston was talented, she thought. Her pity became sympathy. Impulsively she wrote back to him, just a card. *Thank you for your intriguing, original poetry. And your disturbing diary with its vivid details.* Mailed off the card, and that was that!

EXCEPT: WOODY IMMEDIATELY wrote back. More poems, and more diary excerpts, and a snapshot of himself. A black man of about thirty-five, with faint Caucasian features, curly dark hair parted on the left side of his head, and plastic-framed glasses with lenses so thick they distorted his eyes. Woody was smiling hopefully, but his forehead was deeply creased. He wore a shirt open at the throat, and a jacket. On the back of the snapshot he'd written *In happier times—6 Yrs. ago.*

She hesitated, this time. But only for a few minutes.

She sent Johnston a package of paperback books including one of her own and one by a young black poet from San Diego. (Though afterward wondering was that a condescending gesture? perhaps even racist?) She didn't send him a snapshot of herself but there was one, blond-blurred and smiling, the poet at the age of thirty-nine, a few years back, on the back of her book of poems.

SOMETIMES, THESE LONG winters in upstate New York, she couldn't recall any previous life. Couldn't recall having been married, or before that. And her son Rick barely remembered a time before Olean. In her memory there'd been a young, wanly blond woman who might've been a next-door neighbor, a shyly smiling, self-conscious young wife secretly astonished that she was loved by any man, a man's wife, in time a young mother, all this blind-dazzling as winter sunshine on fresh-fallen snow and in truth in the deepest recesses of her heart (as she'd written in her frankest poems) she had never believed in such happiness; and so it had been revealed to her, in time, that her happiness was unmerited after all, the man who'd loved her had departed, withdrawing his love.

But leaving her with a son she adored.

A cheerful good-natured boy. A natural athlete, a smart if inconsistent student. Rick had friends, he didn't mope. His good luck, his acne was all on his back; his face was smooth. What an acrobat on a skateboard! Though sometimes when his mother happened to see Rick and he didn't see her, she was troubled at his boyish face so melancholy in repose. His mouth worked, with unspoken words. She loved her son, and her son loved her, yet it was all she could do to keep from begging his forgiveness. *I'm to blame. I must be. I couldn't keep him, your father. Try not to hate me!* Yet she knew that Rick was embarrassed by her sentimental outbursts. He liked his mom droll, wisecracking like a high-minded Joan Rivers. In sheepskin jacket, jeans, and hiking boots in winter. Chunky dark glasses obscuring half her face. The admiration of his teachers when she visited the high school. For she was something of a local celebrity, to her embarrassment. A poet published with a respected New York press, translator of slender volumes of German verse, Rilke, Novalis. She was a popular teacher of poetry and translation workshops at the State University of New York at Olean.

Since the divorce she'd been involved with few men. Her romantic liaisons flattened quickly into friendships. It was as if her sexual life, her life as a woman, had ended.

Rick's thoughts on the subject of whether his mom should "see" men, or remarry, were ambiguous. Of the sexual behavior of a parent, no adolescent can bear to speculate. If the subject came up, Rick winced, laughed nervously, rolled his eyes toward the ceiling. And blushed. "Hey, Mom. It's cool, O.K.?"

Meaning what? She had no idea.

She thought *Some illusions are too much strain to uphold, in any case.*

Olean was a community of married couples, many with young children. The divorced departed, or died. She was no threat to anyone's marriage. She was well-liked by both sexes equally.

Stalled in writing, she studied Woodson Johnston's snapshots. (He'd sent her several by this time.) In one, she saw a small vertical scar like a fish hook just above his upper lip. In another, she saw a curious asymmetrical alignment of his eyes, and the left eye just perceptibly larger than the right. (A trick of the camera?) He spoke of himself as a *lone soul.* Even before prison he'd been, he said, *condemned to solitary confinement.*

She didn't query Johnston about his personal life, nor did she answer his polite but persistent queries about her personal life. If he'd read her poems (as he claimed to have done) he would know a good deal about her. More than she was comfortable with him knowing, in fact.

Never did she reply to his letters immediately. Always she put them aside on a windowsill or on an edge of her desk.

He'd been sentenced to life in prison. He'd sent her printed information about his case, his appeals, a photocopy of a letter from his attorney. She'd glanced quickly through these. She did not want to discover, and to be embarrassed by, Johnston's inevitable claim of *innocence. Mistaken identity. Police coercion. False testimony.*

Did Rick know about his mother's prison admirer, as she thought of him? She'd mentioned Johnston to Rick only that first time, and then not by name or very specifically; since then, not a word. Nor had Rick the slightest interest in the treasures on her cluttered desk, whether hard-won drafts of poems, translation projects, or poems and letters from others. Now he was in high school, he rarely troubled to enter her study at the rear of the house, a winterized porch overlooking a shallow ravine. She'd glance around to see him leaning in the doorway—"Hey, Mom. I'm back." Or, "Hey, Mom. I'm out of here." She smiled and waved him away, pushing her glasses against the bridge of her nose.

Oh, she adored her son! Now he'd become untouchable.

THERE WERE WEEKS, even months, when she forgot Woodson Johnston, Jr. Or would have forgotten him, except Johnston didn't give up, and continued to write to her. *I wish to live through you! I see so much through your eyes.* It was a rainy spring, a heat-paralyzed summer. She went away, and Rick went to visit his father. She returned to Johnston's letters, packets of new poems and prose pieces. She read his poems guiltily. Was he improving? Had the man any talent, really? (But what did "talent" mean, wasn't this a middle-class, possibly racist supposition?) Johnston asked her for honest criticism but she shrank from remarks more specific than "very good!"—"excellent!"—"original image!"—"inspired!" Once, when she wrote "Unclear?" in the margin of a poem, Johnston fired back a two-page handwritten letter of defense and she thought, Never again. She had no right to interfere with the man's imagination, in any case. His use of black street talk, jazz and rap rhythms, obscenities, a zig-zag poetry she thought it, brash and childlike in its dramatic contrasts, innocent of poetic strategies.

She wondered if she was, unknowingly, a racist? Is this how a racist thinks?

She gathered Johnston's poems, some fifty new and printed, into a collection, and sent the manuscript to her New York publisher. She told Johnston nothing of this, but mailed to him, as if in parting, a popular paperback anthology, *These Voices: Black American Poetry & Prose.* She departed for three weeks in South America on a USIA reading tour, and when she returned letters from Johnston awaited her. She forestalled opening them. She forestalled replying. Her publisher declined Johnston's manuscript with regret—"No market for this, I'm afraid"—and she sent it out to another publisher, a small press specializing in quality poetry. Weeks passed, and months. There came an early autumn, a fierce, dry winter. At her desk, she observed the ravine filling up with storm debris and a thin crusting of snow. When she won a literary prize, Johnston wrote to congratulate her. When she lost another, he sent condolences. *You are a beautiful woman. A beautiful poet-soul.* She laughed, and felt her face burn. What kind of fool does he take me for? This letter of Johnston's she tore into pieces and threw away. What a horror if Rick should discover it. He'd be shocked, worse yet he might tease her. *Hey Mom—beau-ti-ful? Cool!* She hadn't been beautiful as a smooth-faced girl in her early twenties, she wasn't beautiful as a mature, rather worn woman in her early forties. She thought *I should break this off, with him. This isn't a wise thing.*

She ceased answering his letters. He continued writing to her, but at increasing intervals. (Had he found another correspondent? Another sympathetic white-woman poet? She hoped so.) The small press declined Johnston's manuscript with regret, explaining they were cutting back on poetry by unknown poets, however talented.

She made inquiries with other presses, hoping to send the manuscript out again, but weeks passed, no one was much interested, she began to grow tired of her own effort. She placed Johnston's papers in a closet in her study. That summer, she went to Ireland as a guest of the Aran Islands Literary Festival, taking Rick with her, and when she returned there was a letter from the American Innocence Defense Fund in Washington, D.C. A lawyer representing Woodson Johnston, Jr., was asking her, in what appeared to be a form letter, for a contribution to help in the man's defense. She thought, Am I surprised? No. She did feel manipulated. But why, manipulated? After all, a man is fighting for his life. Of course, she was sympathetic. Possibly he was innocent. Mistaken identity? Police coercion? False testimony for the prosecution? She made out a check for $500 and sent it to the fund and received a form letter thanking her for her generosity; she felt a wave of shame, for she'd given so little, and impulsively she made out a second check, for $1,500, and sent this to the fund; and received a duplicate of the previous letter, thanking her for her generosity. But nothing from Johnston. She realized she hadn't heard from Johnston in some time. Was he too busy for her, now? Had something in her last, rather brief letter offended him?

She thought, relieved *That's that.*

IN MAY, in the sudden warmth of a glowing mid-morning sun, she happened to glance out a front window of her house to see a car being driven slowly past. Out-of-state license plates. Was the driver looking toward her house? She watched as the car continued along the road, gathering speed, took a right turn and disappeared.

She lived, in Olean, in what was called a "development" at the edge of town, a suburban neighborhood now at least twenty years old, of medium-priced, attractive homes, split-level contemporaries, mock-colonials, with identical acre-lots and disfiguringly wide two-car garages and asphalt driveways. Her house was stucco and brick, somewhat shabbily overgrown with wisteria and English ivy. Forsythia bloomed in the front yard. Along the road were newly budded spruce trees planted at measured intervals. In the air was a heady fragrance of wet grass and sunshine.

She'd opened the front door, to look out. She closed it, and retreated to the living room, indecisively, watching through the plate-glass "picture window" (as the realtor had called it) without knowing what she was watching for. She saw herself, a figure in a split-level American house on a suburban street she could not have identified. She saw herself, a woman both girlish and middle-aged, straggling shoulder-length blond hair faded to a smudged-looking gray-brown, her face plain, shiny, with puckers beside her mouth and lashless eyes, her quite fit, healthy body grown thick-waisted, and her upper thighs disconcertingly heavy. She wore a soiled white Orlon pullover sweater, her usual jeans, and badly water-stained running shoes. She backed away from the window to observe, from a short distance, the out-of-state car, an economy Toyota, returning, this time parking at the curb. She saw a man climb out of the car, in a canvas jacket, a baseball cap, jeans, a lean dark-skinned man with glasses; his knees appeared to be stiff, he walked with a limp, self-consciously up the flagstone walk to the front door. His movements were deliberate and slow. He held his arms oddly, bent at the elbows, fingers slightly outspread. In the harsh sunshine, the lenses of his glasses shone. *See how I am being open about this? I am not dangerous. My hands are in full view. Unarmed.*

Quickly she retreated to the rear of the house, to her study. She shut the door. She was breathing with difficulty, a roaring in her ears. Morning light flooded the study, somehow she'd expected darkness, a refuge. On her computer, on her desk, a screen saver dreamily whirled pastel planets.

She heard Rick answer the door. Rick! She'd forgotten he was home, this was a Saturday. She heard no voices, only a murmur. Then came Rick loping along the hall. "Mother? Mom?" Without hesitation he pushed the study door open. She was standing very still. Not by her desk, nor by one of the crammed floor-to-ceiling bookshelves, but in an alcove of the L-shaped room, on the far side of the closet, where cartons and excess books had long been gathering dust. Rick stared at her. She saw the shock in his smooth boy-face. "Mom? Why are you hiding?"

I'M NOT YOUR SON,
I AM NO ONE YOU KNOW

DON'T MAKE EYE contact my brother warned.

They'll be waiting just inside. Don't look at them.

Deftly my brother punched in the code. Knew the code by heart. I had to be impressed, this was my younger brother and seemed possessed of a grim knowledge of which I was ignorant.

A hefty double door with inset wire-lattice windows. Overhead, a video monitor. As soon as my brother punched in the code, the doors slid open and we stepped inside and at once the doors slid shut behind us. Two, three seconds you were granted, no more. Like the sliding doors of airport trains. Like a maximum-security prison. For already the figures waiting just inside pressed forward. There were three of them. Dad won't be among them, my brother had promised. Yet my heart began to clamor, I felt sweat breaking out in all the pores of my clumsy body.

Hel-lo? Hel-*lo?*

Son? Son? Son? *Son?*

Sidelong my brother regarded me gauging how I was taking this, knowing me for a risk. His hand on my arm guiding me. He'd warned me not to look yet I could not not look. For the voices were calling to us, pleading. My instinct was to stop, to stare. An elderly woman with white hair lifting from her skull like electrified wire filings, a sunken-chested elderly man with a singed-looking face, a gnome-sized individual of no evident sex leaning on a walker and piping like an eager parrot, Hel-lo? Hel-lo? while the elderly woman began to scold, Dear? Dear? Here I am, dear! and the sunken-chested elderly man teetered forward on a cane managing to position himself in front of the others, blocking their entreaties pleading, Take me? Take me? Boys? Sons? I'm ready now. My things are ready. Take me with you? On his bony skull thick-lensed glasses were secured by an elastic band. The smell of them was acrid as goats. The befouled wettish-rotting straw in which goats dwell.

My brother yanked at me. Jesus! I told you come *on*.

Yet somehow in that instant I stood stone-still, unmoving. For these elderly strangers seemed to know me—how? They were pleading, scolding, bleating. Their faces were familiar to me in some way I could not comprehend. The white-haired woman had a fattish fallen body soft as a pudding but her eyes were vigilant, alert to insult. Here was a mother's voice—Dear? Dear? Come back here! Don't you walk away while I'm talking to you! Don't you walk away while I'm talking to you!—you could not ignore. And the others were crying to me, calling me Son. *Son!*

My brother pulled me away. Blindly we walked along the corridor. Even now I wanted badly to look back. I wanted to explain, apologize. *I'm not your son, I am no one you know.* My face burned, I was ashamed of myself. A deep visceral shame. To turn away unheeding from another who begs you. Those strangers with weirdly familiar faces. Ruins of faces. Desperation in those faces. It seemed to me that I did know, I'd once known, the sunken-chested old man with the singed face, but my brother was muttering in my ear, Keep moving. They won't follow us. They do this with everybody, I told you. It shook me up the first time, too. But you get used to it. They won't remember, see. They won't remember five minutes from now. Already they're forgetting. When we leave it will happen again, for them it will happen for the first time because they won't remember us. Just don't make eye contact with them and you'll be fine.

I pushed my brother's fingers from my arm. Coldly I said, I don't like to be rude to old people.

We're not being rude for Christ's sake! It's what you have to do.

I was pissed, my brother had put his hand on my arm.

I asked if the old people were anyone we knew.

My brother bared his teeth in a savage smile. Not really. Come *on*.

THE VISIT WITH Dad. My first at the Manor.

I'd stayed away for as long as I could but now I was here. Hadn't prepared for the visit beforehand and now it was too late, I was here. Of Dad I will not speak. Of Dad I refuse to speak. Of the visit I can say, yes it happened. On our way driving to the Manor my brother remarked casually that Dad had tried to escape, at first. This remark was met with silence. It might have been a sad, or a stunned, or a confused silence. It was not an indifferent silence and yet I didn't inquire how many times Dad had tried to escape nor did I ask what *tried to escape* literally meant. How much effort, with what emotion, cunning, desperation, force. Nor did I inquire with what force *tried* to escape was met by the staff.

Dad, hi! H'lo Dad.

Hi Dad! Hey. Looking good Dad . . .

Dad this is Norm, I'm Vince. You know . . .

Your sons. Hi Dad.

Your sons, Dad. Hey this is quite a place. Quite a . . .

In this way the visit with Dad began with ebullient spirits and raised smiling voices. Within seconds my mind detached itself from the scene. I was damned impressed: my brother who'd always been three years younger than me was now at least three years older. His eyes were older. The terror between us was *This isn't Dad. This elderly man. Not Dad any longer.* We could not look at each other, our eyes could not meet out of dread of *Then we are not brothers, either. For we have no father any longer.*

I went to the window to open it. Having trouble breathing suddenly. Like trying to suck oxygen through clots of greeny phlegm not your own. Help! Sweated through my fresh-laundered white cotton shirt, underwear stuck in the crack of my ass. The smell of wettish goat wasn't so powerful in Dad's room but there were other smells. Only one window, and it was stuck. My brother said, Hey: that window doesn't open. Grinning at me like it's a joke. I looked down and saw for Christ's sake the window is inset in the sill like concrete. You could rupture your guts trying to shove it open.

Where my brother and I were, we were in the E-wing. Visiting Dad in the E-wing of Meadowbrook Manor. From the two-lane country highway out front Meadowbrook Manor more resembled the campus of a well-financed community college than what brochures call an *assisted-care facility.* Seeing the Manor from the highway you wouldn't guess how certain of its wings were under tight security and guarded as a prison. You wouldn't guess how if any patient in these wings tried to escape confinement or through mental confusion appeared to be trying to escape alarm bells were triggered. E-wing patients like Dad were outfitted with unremovable bracelets around their left wrists with metal tags that, if brought through electronic detectors without clearance, set off alarms through the facility.

My brother had told me he'd heard the alarm once. Ear-splitting it was.

My brother had told me that Meadowbrook Manor was the best *assisted-care facility* within one hundred miles.

In fact my brother was saying now *Dad is a favorite here. All the nurses say what do the nurses say Dad the nurses say every time I come to visit what a sweet old gentleman your dad is.*

What I was noticing was the Manor was brightly lighted as a stage set. Furniture in bright pastel vinyl. Nurses and nurses' aides mostly black women in dazzling white uniforms smiling often at us who were visitors. My brother spoke of doctors, too. Of course my brother had met with doctors. This is the best place for Dad my brother said. His smile was a brave smile and infectious.

In my vinyl chair as we visited with Dad I was wondering how many times Dad had tried to escape, and when had been his last, or his most recent attempt. I was wondering how far the old man had gotten before the alarms went off. Before he was restrained. And how exactly was he restrained. Were *physical restraints* involved. Did *strait jackets* still exist. In his loud voice my brother spoke of the nursing staff. Very nice they were. Very sincere. Genuinely attached to their parents my brother said, then laughed at himself saying I mean patients: genuinely attached to their *patients.*

In his loud voice my brother asked me if he'd told me *Dad is a favorite here.*

At the highway beyond the wall, the unmovable window, the lawn greenly svelte as a golf course, a diesel truck thundered past.

I would not ask where Dad believed he was escaping to. The old house was gone. The past in which Dad had lived was gone. Nothing remained. An elderly doomed man might wish to escape to the years in which he was neither elderly nor doomed but those years are gone. You wake up one morning, those years are gone. There's a comfort in this fact perhaps. I want to think that there must be comfort in all facts we can't alter.

Shit, said the man with Dad's voice. Bullshit.

TIME FOR A walk?

My brother was on his feet. I saw that his jaws were stubbled and that the stubble glinted gray. My younger brother, no longer young! My own jaws were clean-shaven. Out of anxiety I shaved twice a day. I wasn't certain if Dad had spoken as I'd seemed to hear him. I wasn't certain if Dad had spoken aloud. In the Manor, voices tended to be louder and higher-pitched than normal. There were mirage voices, that possibly didn't exist, like upside-down and reversed images at desert horizons. And beneath these voices the murmurous quietly laughing TV voices. When I spoke, which had not been often in Dad's room, my voice cut the air like an awkwardly brandished blade, a machete perhaps. I was remembering who the sunken-chested man was, I thought.

Who the sunken-chested man had been.

Three of us on our feet. My brother led the way. We walked slowly. There was no hurry in the E-wing. In Meadowbrook Manor there was no visible hurry. My brother who knew the way led us past the TV lounge and the upright piano and the resident fat dog sprawled in sleep. My brother led us past a nurses' aide putting soiled diapers into a black plastic bag on a cart. The double door to the garden was unlocked. The garden was a secure place though you could not see the seven-foot chainlink fence through the dense hedge of wisteria. If there were video cameras trained upon every square inch of the garden you could not see them. My brother was saying in his loud cheerful voice, Dad is one of the best gardeners here. Dad, show us your tomatoes.

The tomatoes were indeed lush, staked to a height of four or five feet. There was really no need for Dad to show us, we were looking at them already.

Dad, show us which flowers are yours. Zinnias?

The word *zinnias* confused. The word *zinnias* met with no visible response.

We were circling the garden slowly. A graveled path, which we took counter-clockwise. Though we were on a more or less level plane it felt as if we were struggling against gravity on this path. For in this place time had virtually ceased. Perhaps between one heartbeat and the next time had in fact ceased. There was the danger of falling sideways in time, as when you pedal a bicycle too slowly, you fall sideways. In my right hand, somehow related to this strange cessation of time, was an elderly man's hand. It was a bony hand, unresisting. My brother gripped the elderly man's other hand in his left hand. A strange word, *zinnias!* I seemed to be hearing it for the first time. A combination of sounds like hot coiled wires that might spring suddenly out, and sting. *Zinnias.* There was a sound here too of wasps. I wished my brother wouldn't repeat in his unnervingly loud and buoyant voice *Zinnias! See the giant zinnias these are Dad's zinnias!* Almost, if you were wearing an electrically sensitive bracelet, you might think that *zinnias* was a code word or a means of torment.

Dad's hand trembled yet remained unresisting, like a hand made of slightly crumbling clay.

We were not alone in the garden. Other grown children were visiting with elderly adults. There were visitors, usually women, or couples. Never more than three individuals in a party, for too many visitors confuses the elderly residents of the E-wing. By chance we were all walking in a counter-clockwise movement on the graveled path. We did not glance at one another. An instinctive dread of glancing into a mirror. *We don't see you, you don't see us. We really have no idea what we look like.* Before my brother had punched in the code to open the E-wing doors, he'd told me that Dad no longer recognized himself in mirrors, so don't expect him to recognize you.

I had not that expectation.

I took my cue from my brother, I smiled. I had no expectations to be thwarted or mocked.

The season was fall. Yet hot as August. Air quivered in a sinister tangle of near-invisible filaments like those in a gigantic lightbulb. My eyes blinked, blinded. Yet I was calm recalling: the sunken-chested man with the singed face, Mr. M__ who'd taught junior high math. He'd taught me, he'd taught my younger brother. More than thirty years ago he'd taught us. Mr. M__ was not a name I wished to recall. Nor would my brother wish to recall Mr. M__. For Mr. M__ had graded my brother more harshly than he'd graded me who had been an honors student even in math which became my hated subject under Mr. M__'s instruction. Mr. M__ had taught at Yewville Junior High for a long time before they'd made him retire. That was the local story, Mr. M__ had been made finally to retire. Under threat of a lawsuit, or an arrest. He'd touched a boy too intimately, you had to surmise. Too lingeringly. He'd teased a boy to tears. He'd pinched, tickled, slapped a boy. He'd twisted the tender earlobe of a boy just a little too hard and left reddened prints in the flesh for an astonished parent to discover. Or he'd playfully locked a boy in his homeroom after school. Or not so playfully: "for discipline." The color rising in his face that had been fattish then, a moon face in which veins and capillaries glowed with an interior pulsing heat. During class you sat very still in your seat trying not to be seen by ever-vigilant Mr. M__. His eyes behind the black plastic teacher-glasses prowling the rows of desks. Eyes that were faintly bloodshot yet shone with a youthful vigor at such times. If you stared blinking down at your desk top Mr. M__ would see and know you were hoping to escape his scrutiny. If you dared to gaze at him guileless and unblinking Mr. M__ would see and know you were hoping to escape his scrutiny. For there was no escaping Mr. M__.

Certain boys were Mr. M__'s targets. You could see why certain boys were not Mr. M__'s targets for he never dared single out any strong-willed or defiant boy, or any boy from a prominent family, and boys of limited intelligence he ignored; but you could not always predict which boys, out of a number of possibilities, he would choose to torment. Vulnerable boys, shy boys. Shyly stubborn boys. Smart boys. Small-boned boys. Boys with girls' faces. Rarely homely boys. Never handicapped boys. Never Italian or Negro boys. First he'd call on you in class and if you gave the right answer he'd call on you repeatedly until at last you gave a wrong answer. You stood at the blackboard trying to solve a problem, chalk trembling in your fingers. Mr. M__'s scorn was so playful, his mockery so comical, you weren't always certain why you were being laughed at by even your friends. Your face burned, your eyes stung with moisture. You felt your bladder pinch with the need to pee. Once summoning me forward to his teacher's desk at the front of the room. Making of me a witness to his red-inked pen darting and swooping over my math test like a miniature deranged hawk. I had mis-numbered the questions! I was a careless boy! Might've had a grade of ninety-eight but now had a grade of forty-eight and this would be duly noted on my midterm report card to be sent home for my mother's signature. Tears welled in my eyes. My nose ran. Disgusted Mr. M__ tossed a tissue at me. It might have been a used tissue, out of his baggy pants pocket. Wipe your nose, Mr. M__ said. Stand up straight, Mr. M__ said. What a careless boy you are, not nearly so smart as you think you are, *I've got your number.* For it was so, there were boys (but never girls, and we never wondered why) of whom Mr. M__ could boast *I've got your number.*

Almost time for dinner, Dad. My brother spoke brightly as if he'd made a new discovery, and it pleased him.

Dad? It's that time.

We re-entered the E-wing. We'd circled the garden not once but twice, slowly. The *tomatoes* had been admired, and the mysterious *zinnias.* I had forgotten that time wasn't fixed like concrete but in fact was fluid as sand, or water. I had forgotten that even misery can end.

Got your number, got your number. Just ahead the sunken-chested old man with the singed face, the thick-lensed glasses taped to his head, was leaning on his cane. Again we must pass close by him. For he would not give way. For he wished to block our way. The white-haired old woman was gone. The gnome-sized individual was sitting, back against the wall. Here was Mr. M— wizened as a scrawny child. His face had lost its fat, his cheeks were papery thin and flushed as if with fever. I saw how, as his eyes lighted upon us, Mr. M—'s expression turned hopeful, shrewd. For the first time I saw how his dentures glared like cheap porcelain. Boys? Take me with you? Take me with you? He lurched near me, his palsied hand groped for my arm, and I shoved him from me. Mr. M—'s fetid breath in my face, that made me gag. Don't touch me, I said.

Shoving him from me I said, You're not going anywhere with anyone, you old bastard. Your place is here, you get to die here.

My brother turned an incredulous face to me. Yanking at my arm to pull me away from the tottering old man who gaped at me as if he hadn't heard a syllable of what I'd said.

Norm! For Christ's sake.

My brother was so rattled, he had trouble punching in the code to unlock the doors.

Second time, he got it. There was a bleating and pleading behind us we ignored. As soon as the doors opened we stepped through. We walked swiftly along the corridor to the lobby not looking back. My brother was cursing me under his breath. I'd never heard him so angry at anyone. God damn, God damn you, are you crazy, God damn you.

Why didn't you warn me, I asked my brother. You knew who he was.

Who who was? What? That pathetic old guy? He's nobody.

You knew. You know. God damn *you*.

We burst through the lobby doors. We walked to my brother's car in the parking lot without speaking. Without glancing at each other. Not a backward glance at the Manor. Inside the car it would be hotter than hell. My brother had insisted the windows be shut, the doors locked. At Meadowbrook Manor! Disgusted my brother threw himself behind the driver's wheel not looking at me and I had a choice, to climb inside that car beside him or to walk back to his house which was at least three miles, and along the country highway in the sun.

It wasn't much of a choice.

AIDING AND ABETTING

THERE!—THE PHONE is ringing.

The call usually comes between six and seven, weekday evenings exclusively. Steven will hear the phone and Holly, in the kitchen preparing dinner, will answer it quickly, before Steven or their eleven-year-old son Brandon can get to a phone. He'll hear his wife's urgent voice, an anxious hello and then subdued murmurs of sympathy or encouragement, finally silence, for the person on the other end of the line is doing most of the talking.

The conversation will never last less than twenty minutes. Once, Steven recalls, it lasted nearly an hour, and might have gone longer if Steven hadn't come into the kitchen to interrupt.

Tonight Steven is sitting in the family room adjacent to the kitchen with four-year-old Caitlin in the curve of his arm, listening to his daughter read aloud from one of her new, beautifully illustrated storybooks, a tale of imperiled but magically empowered talking animals, and he tries not to be distracted by Holly in the kitchen. He loves these reading sessions with Caitlin with a fierce, fatherly sense of privilege; he remembers with what stunning swiftness Brandon's early childhood passed, how abruptly his son became a boy, no longer a little boy, whose measure of self-worth is drawn from his boy-classmates and not from his adoring parents.

Steven resents this caller who interrupts Holly in the kitchen though she has asked him not to call her at that time; she loves cooking for her little family, as she calls the four of them; every evening for Holly means a serious, not elaborate but conscientious dinner, seafood, fish, omelettes, fresh vegetables, whole grain rice, thick spiced soups, her reward, she says, for a day of purely mental work performed for the benefit of strangers. But dinner will be delayed on those evenings when the call comes. The children will become hungry, impatient; Steven will have a second drink; when finally they sit down to eat he'll see his pretty wife's melancholy eyes, the downward cast of her smile, and feel rage in his heart for the person responsible.

By his watch, nearly thirty minutes have gone by.

As Steven enters the kitchen, Holly is just hanging up the phone. He sees her wiping guiltily at her eyes. "Honey, was that your brother? Again?" Steven tries to keep the exasperation out of his voice: in the little family Daddy is wise, compassionate, mature beyond his thirty-seven years, inclined to settle disputes with a laugh, a well-aimed kiss. Holly is the emotional parent, quick to laughter, tears, effervescence, worry. She says, taking up a spatula and stir-frying vegetables in a large aluminum wok, "Don't ask, Steven. Please."

"Of course I'm going to ask. Owen just called, didn't he, last Thursday?"

"Well, he's having a serious crisis. The anti-depressant his doctor has been prescribing isn't working out, he'll have to switch to another drug and he's anxious, insomniac—" Holly frowns at the simmering vegetables, avoiding Steven's eyes. "He's all right, I think. There's no talk of—you know. He's just lonely. He says he has no no one to talk with except—" Holly's voice wavers. She doesn't want to say *no one but me.*

"But why does he have to call at this time? He knows it's a difficult time. With dinner, the kids—" Steven is trying to speak reasonably. Holly stands silent, and he realizes that his brother-in-law has probably been calling her at other times, too; possibly he calls her at work. But Steven isn't supposed to know this.

Holly says apologetically, "Honey, I've tried to explain but Owen says, 'I don't know the time. It's a luxury to be conscious of clock-time.' "

"What's that supposed to mean? That gnomic remark?"

"He can't sleep at night, sometimes he sleeps during the day so it's 'night for day' for him, he says. He calls when he gets too lonely and can't stand another moment of himself. He isn't like *us*."

"Couldn't you explain that you're busy? You're tired, exhausted? You want to spend some time with your family?"

"But I'm his family, Owen would say. His only family." Holly speaks sharply, despairingly. The spatula slips from her fingers, falls clattering to the floor; Steven picks it up. "He says he's 'haunted' by our mother, hears her voice with some of the drugs he takes. I wish you could be more sympathetic, Steven."

"Honey, I am. I try. But it's been years, he's twenty-nine years old, he seems incapable of growing up. He has no self-respect, no shame, he's never paid us back that fifteen hundred dollars he borrowed for a down payment on—"

"Steven, you can't be throwing that back on him, on me. Not now. When you're doing so well. We're doing so well. When we have everything, and Owen has so little."

"I do feel sympathy for him, honey." Steven tries to stroke Holly's hair and like an offended cat she eases away. "I feel very sorry for him. But I feel sorry for you, too. He's eating you alive."

"What an ugly thing to say," Holly says, shocked. For a moment the lurid image hovers before them in their cozy, comfortable suburban kitchen: an enormous mouth devouring Holly. She says, tears in her eyes, "You just don't understand, Steven, how desperate Owen is. He has tried so hard with his art. He has tried to make lasting friends, he's tried to fall in love. Don't smile—he has! He's tried to be—well, normal. But ordinary life is like a maze for some people. It's biochemical, he's inherited it from our mother's side of the family. He was telling me just now he's terrified of the future. He feels as if he was born with a hole in him, in the region of his heart, he tries to fill, it's his duty to fill, and nothing will fill it."

"Nothing will fill it." It's a statement of Steven's, not a question. Nothing will fill the hole in his brother-in-law's leaky heart.

Even if Owen devoured Holly, and Steven, and their children—nothing would fill it.

But Steven doesn't say this, it's an insight he'll keep to himself. The last thing he wants tonight is to upset Holly further and ruin their family evening. Unlike his predator brother-in-law, he wants Holly to be happy as she deserves.

And now Caitlin comes bounding into the kitchen, eager to help Mommy. And Daddy has to deflect her with a task, setting the table. It's a game, but, for Caitlin, a risky one, for if she gets so much as a single fork in the wrong position, she'll be crushed with a childish mortification that touches Daddy's heart. No one wants so desperately to be perfect as a four-year-old girl.

Brandon too enters the kitchen, simulating casualness but glancing worriedly at his parents. "What're you guys fighting about?" It's a joke, Brandon is teasing, but beneath his teasing he's in earnest, anxious to know, so Mommy and Daddy protest in a single voice—" 'Fighting'?—*nobody's fighting.*"

THOSE EVENINGS WHEN Owen telephones are the only evenings when Steven and Holly, who have been married twelve years, come dangerously close to disliking each other.

Owen, all that remains of Holly's original family. The family that predates the little family.

Owen, Holly's younger brother by two years. As a child Owen was so much Holly's responsibility, in a household in which both parents were alcoholics, that he came to take for granted his sister's uncritical love, her indulgence, generosity, forgiveness. And blindness to his faults. He has grown into a snakily attractive young-aging man with lavishly blond-streaked hair trimmed up the sides, with a small pigtail at the nape of his neck. Though he's a clerk at the Green Earth Co-Op and complains of having no money, he wears black silk shirts that hug his narrow torso, stone-washed designer jeans, ostrich-hide boots. ("Gifts from friends," Owen explains with a droll smile, "—parting gifts.") He's shy, and cheeky; he's self-loathing, and self-absorbed; in profile he's strikingly handsome, seen head-on, he has a pinched, narrow fox-face with small features, a pouty mouth that breaks into a dazzling smile as if on cue. Owen's laughter is wild and extravagant. (Brandon has begun to imitate this laughter, unconsciously.) Owen's tears spill easily. His teeth are small and faintly discolored, the hue of weak tea. He's frightened of blood: and nearly collapsed once when Brandon, tumbling from his tricycle in the driveway, had a sudden nosebleed. In the final month of Holly's pregnancy with Caitlin, when Holly was grotesquely, comically swollen, like a boa constrictor who'd swallowed a hog, Owen was hardly able to look at his sister without flinching. "Owen, please understand: pregnancy isn't a medical pathology," Holly tried to tease him. When Caitlin was born, he sent flowers but avoided seeing Holly for weeks, on the pretext of illness; in fact, as he confided in Steven, as if man-to-man, he dreaded seeing his sister nursing the infant. "It's so atavistic. Primal. It must *hurt*. Ugh!"

Steven has to concede he'd been charmed by Owen until a few years ago. In his early twenties Owen had been a serious artist, a figurative painter. That he lived on scholarships, fellowships, art colony grants, and occasional loans from his sister made sense at the time. Owen was young, Owen was "very promising." If, in time, he came to rely upon these loans—of course, they were gifts—from Holly and her husband, this too made sense. (And he gave them paintings—not always his best paintings, perhaps.) He seemed perhaps bisexual, not exclusively gay; at least, he played at being attracted to the girls Holly introduced him to. If sometimes he stared long and longingly at Steven, Steven took care not to notice.

Once in their kitchen he overheard Owen say to Holly, "I love Steve. I love him as much as a real brother. Thank you for bringing Steve into my life."

Steven was suffused with warmth, tenderness. Though later he would wonder if Owen, who calculated so much, had calculated these words being overheard.

Though he drives a new-model Toyota (another parting gift from a friend?), Owen lives in a dismal rented apartment. He's a clerk at an organic foods co-op, a "servile, fawning" job he detests and will probably not keep long. His life appears to be cruising bars, sudden intense friendships, abrupt "misunderstandings" and dismissals. He'd been in and out of AA, rehab clinics. (At Holly's and Steven's expense.) Artist-friends have long since vanished. An MFA program at Temple

University in Philadelphia "didn't work out." Owen lives amid a shifting phantasmagoria of gay acquaintances, friends, lovers. Gary, Oliver, Mark, Kevin. If Steven remembers the name of Owen's new friend, by the time they speak again and he asks, "How's Kevin?" he's likely to meet with a stony silence from Owen, or a blithe, "How should I know, Steve? Ask him."

Yet Owen can be warm, charming. Steven tries to remember this. When Brandon was small he played with him for hours, filling in coloring books of his own invention with fantastical acrylic colors. For her third birthday he gave Caitlin a handmade painted book, *Frog & Beans,* one of Caitlin's prized possessions. ("Owen should have been a children's book illustrator," Steven said, "he has a real talent for this." Holly said, offended, "Don't you dare ever tell him that. He'd be *wounded.*")

What Steven fears in Owen is that he has the power of weakness: the power to set Steven and Holly against each other, the power to subtly erode the little family from within. Only recently has Holly confessed to Steven that when they were children in Rutherford, New Jersey, Owen set small fires in their neighborhood and at school. When he was sixteen, he and another boy parked in the boy's car, ran a hose from the exhaust into the car, and drank themselves unconscious, expecting to die of carbon monoxide poisoning; but they were found in time. And there had been other suicide attempts over the years . . . "Owen suffered from terrible nightmares as a child," Holly says. "He's never been secure. Our mother was sick so much, and sometimes deranged." Steven listens quietly, not about to say *Yes but you aren't suicidal, why's that?* "Our father died when Owen was eight." *Your father died when you were ten, why not see it from your perspective for once?* " 'Small mother with claws'—Owen calls her."

"Who?"

"I've been telling you. Our mother."

"I think the phrase is Kafka's. 'Small mother with claws.' "

Holly frowns, annoyed with Steven. "I guess we shouldn't discuss Owen. It brings out something petty in you."

Steven says, stung, "Holly, what's 'petty' to you is crucial to me. I hate it that you aid and abet your brother's weaknesses. He gets sympathy from you for being pathetic. If you'd encourage him to be strong, independent, to have some masculine pride—"

Holly bursts into incredulous laughter. "Steven, listen to you. 'Masculine pride.' I can't believe this, you sound like a parody. Owen *is* prone to illnesses, he *is* 'weak' compared to you. If that makes him less of a man, that's a pity."

Steven says, trying to keep his voice even, "Remember a few years ago, that Christmas we were snowed in, and Owen helped me shovel the driveway? He wasn't weak then, he surprised us all." It was true: Steven and Brandon had bundled up to shovel snow after a two-foot snowfall in northern New Jersey, and, after a while, as if reluctantly, Owen had joined them. He shoveled awkwardly at first, then got into the rhythm, cheeks flushed and nose running, joking with Steven and Brandon, quite enjoying himself. As if he'd forgotten himself. Steven had felt an unexpected bond between Owen and himself as the men shoveled the fifty-foot driveway, talking frankly of life, ideals, politics, family. He'd felt that he had established a new, significant rapport with his brother-in-law, of a kind that had made no reference to Holly. *I like him. And he likes me. That's it!* But the rapport hadn't lasted. What was genuine enough in the buoyant cold of a bright, dazzling-white winter day soon dissolved, and not long afterward there was Owen calling Holly to complain of his depression, his insomnia, "faithless" friends, yes and he needed money . . .

Holly says, annoyed, "Oh yes: the snow-shoveling. Fine. But my brother is a little more complicated than that, I hope."

Steven accepts this in silence. He has brought it on himself, he knows. It's pointless to argue with Holly about Owen: she loves him in a way impenetrable by Steven, in a way that pre-exists even her love for Brandon and Caitlin. You can call this love morbid, or admirable; a symptom of childhood pathology, or an expression of adult loyalty. But there it is.

Relenting, as if reading Steven's thoughts, Holly says gently, "You have to understand, honey: Owen and I were Hansel and Gretel together. Once upon a time."

This is meant to dispel tension, as a joke. Steven laughs, and Holly laughs. But is it funny, Steven wonders. It seems to him dangerous, treacherous. To perceive your childhood as mythical, out of a fairy tale.

THEN, ONE EVENING, when Holly is at the mall with the children, Steven has what will be his final conversation with Owen.

The phone rings, he answers, and there's his brother-in-law's reedy, drawling voice—"Is Holly there? Can I speak with her?"

"Holly isn't here, Owen," Steven says, more amused than annoyed that Owen hasn't bothered to identify himself, or to waste breath on a greeting to Steven. "What did you want with her?"

"I—don't 'want' anything. Just to talk to Holly . . ." Owen's voice is flat, disappointed.

"Talk to me."

Steven has been watching CNN and now he lowers the sound. He's in sweatshirt and jeans, drinking beer out of a can. Feeling good. Feeling generous. A productive day in his office in New York City and a warm cozy family evening coming up. He's possibly wondering if, with Holly out of it, he and Owen can re-establish their old rapport, speak frankly and from the heart. But Owen sounds as if he's been drinking, or is drugged. He's vague, not very coherent; lapsing with no preamble into a monologue of complaints—his disappointing job, his botched life, migraine headaches, insomnia—night sweats, fever—"And this new symptom like an elliptic fit that doesn't quite happen, a really weird sensation like phantom pain in a missing limb—an amputee? Like that?"

Steven guesses that Owen has meant to say "epileptic." Steven is distracted by jarringly close-up newsreel footage taken in the Gaza Strip where several rock-throwing young Palestinian boys have been shot by Israeli border guards. He raises the TV volume slightly, not loud enough, he hopes, for Owen to detect. Politely he asks Owen to repeat what he has said; which Owen does, at length. His voice drones on, a litany of physical maladies, psychological woe, despicable "malpractice-worthy" behavior on the part of a formerly trusted doctor. In his self-concern Owen has forgotten that he's speaking not to Holly but to Steven: he's alluding to *back in Rutherford, back there, remember when, dreamt about last night, O Jesus.* The Gaza Strip footage breaks off and an antic SUV ad comes on. Steven laughs.

There's a shocked silence. Then Owen says, in a small, hurt voice, "I'm sorry if I'm amusing you, Steve."

Steven will recall how easily he spoke, with no premeditation: "Owen, why be sorry to be amusing? I'd say, from you, that was a good thing."

Owen is silent for so long, Steven thinks he must have laid down the phone receiver. Steven has switched to NBC news, there's an exposé of deplorable conditions in the New Orleans Parish Prison which detains Asian and Haitian immigrants for the federal Immigration and Naturalization Service, interviews with visibly scarred, injured men, protestations and denials from prison authorities. Steven listens appalled as Owen resumes his monologue of complaints with renewed fervor, how hurt he's been, how depressed, the past six months have been hell, his thirtieth birthday is imminent and sometimes he wonders, with so much pain, his paintings rejected that are "every bit as strong" as Lucien Freud's nudes, Philip Pearlstein's overrated nudes, and friends letting him down, and the world so vicious, sometimes he wonders whether it's worth it to keep going. Steven, listening to the testimony of a hospitalized Asian detainee who'd been beaten nearly to death by Caucasian prison guards, says vaguely, "I suppose so, Owen." Owen says, "What?" Steven says, "Or—maybe it isn't. It's your call." Again there's shocked silence.

Then Owen says quietly, "You're saying, Steve, I should—give up?"

"From your perspective? Maybe."

There. Steven has said it.

Breathlessly, almost eagerly Owen says, "You think—? In my place—? You'd—"

"Owen, yes. Frankly, I would."

Steven switches back to CNN. The President stepping out of Air Force One somewhere in Europe. Steven's heart is beating quickly, as after an invigorating sprint. But he's frightened, too. Uttering words he has only fantasized. *Die, why don't you. You pathetic loser. Put yourself out of your misery. Give us a break.*

Of course, in the next moment Steven regrets what he's said. He's been blunt, cruel. Owen must be crushed. Quickly, he says, lowering the TV volume, "Owen? Maybe not. No. I'm sorry I said that."

He can hear Owen's humid-sounding breathing. Then Owen says, in a strange, elated voice, "Steve, thanks! You're the only person in my entire life who has ever spoken to me *the truth.*"

This forced, phony circumlocution. Steven perceives that his brother-in-law is posturing, taking on a role. He hates Owen with a pure scintillant savage hatred.

Owen is saying, "—the only one who has ever done me the honor of taking me seriously, not humoring me. Taking me as a man and not a, a cripple. *Thank you.*"

Steven has turned away from the TV. He's on his feet, suddenly sober, repentant. "Owen, hey: I didn't mean that the way it sounded. I was just—"

"—speaking from the heart, Steve! Yes. And I appreciate it. From you—I know you hate my guts, I admire you for that!—from you, my sister's husband and the daddy of her children, I've just had the best f-fucking advice of my life."

"I only meant—"

"Believe me, Steve, I've been thinking of killing myself for a long time. I mean *seriously.* I mean—the real thing. Not bullshitting." Owen pauses dramatically. He too is breathing hard as after a fast hard sprint. "I can't discuss anything serious with Holly, she's too emotional. She's too close to the edge herself. She tried some little-girl stuff, in high school, 'slashing' her wrists—but not too deep. Bet she never told ya, Steve! What I need to decide is how."

Steven is stunned. "How—what?"

"Not pills, not carbon monoxide," Owen snorts in derision, vastly amused, "not a razor blade—ugh! I was thinking of—in my car? Driving?"

Steven says in a lowered voice, "Driving—would be good. An accident."

"Steering my car into a, what do you call it—abutment? On Route 1, by an overpass—"

"That would do it."

"That would! That would do it! And nobody would freaking fucking *know.*"

Abruptly the line goes dead. Steven, on his feet, not knowing where he is, colliding painfully with a chair, cries into the receiver, "Owen? Owen? Owen!"

But he doesn't call Owen back.

"DADDY, SEE?"

When Holly returns with Caitlin and Brandon and their new purchases, Steven hugs them eagerly as if they've been gone for days. As if they've been in danger. His little family! He would die for them, he knows. Yet for their sake he must hide the ferocity of his love. Caitlin is wearing a new purple quilted jacket with a hood, peeping out at Daddy as he lifts her in his arms to kiss her. And Brandon is sporting new hiker's boots—"Look, Daddy. Cool, huh?"

Through that evening, through the mostly sleepless night that follows, Steven relives the remarkable exchange between his brother-in-law and himself, disbelieving his own words. Did he really say such things? He's astonished. He's sick with apprehension. He's elated, exhilarated. *Die, why don't you. Give us a break.*

A terrible thing to say to another person. Especially your own brother-in-law. "Family."

Steven smiles. Maybe the truth is terrible? And someone must utter it for once.

It's Holly's custom to take the phone off the hook each night when she and Steven go to bed, not wanting a ringing phone to wake the family, and in the morning when Steven checks, with some apprehension, he hears only a dial tone. No messages recorded during the night.

He's relieved. It hasn't happened yet. Holly is Owen's next of kin, named in his wallet identification in case of accident. But there has been no "accident" involving Owen during the night, evidently. Steven tells himself that Owen will probably just forget their conversation. Probably he's already forgotten. The man is too narcissistic, too shallow and cowardly for suicide.

Days pass, and a week. And no word from Owen. And no word of Owen. And no emergency call from a medical worker or police officer. Casually Holly mentions that Owen must be away, he hasn't called in a while. Her dinner-hour preparation isn't interrupted, she's relieved and yet, Steven knows, she's beginning to worry about Owen.

He tells her that Owen is fine, he's spoken with him recently, briefly. And remember the numerous times when Owen has ceased to call? Once he'd gone to Morocco with a friend, away for a month without a word to Holly.

Then one evening when Steven returns from the city, Holly tells him happily that Owen finally called, and dropped by the house; in a "very upbeat mood"; he stayed for only a few minutes because he was driving to see a friend in Manhattan. Fine, Steven says. Didn't I tell you nothing was wrong. Steven isn't disappointed, in truth he's relieved. Of course he hasn't wanted Holly's brother to die . . . But then Holly goes on to say, "Owen volunteered to drop Brandon off at Scott's house, he's staying the night," and now Steven stares at her, for a stunned moment unable to react. Then he says, choosing his words with care, "You let Brandon ride with Owen? In his car?" Holly says, "It's just across town, honey. You know where Scott lives." Steven says, dry-mouthed, "Alone with Owen? In his *car?*" Holly says uncertainly, "Well—why not? I mean—"

Holly sees a look in Steven's face he can't hide. She says:

"But—what is it? Do you—know something about Owen? *What do you know about Owen?*"

A moment's panic. Holly is thinking: pedophilia?

Quickly Steven assures her it's nothing. Only just that he's disappointed—Brandon won't be with them at dinner.

THERE!—THE PHONE ringing.

But it's only a solicitor. Steven hangs up rudely.

Now he's waiting for the phone to ring. Or waiting for the phone not to ring. Without Holly overhearing, he has called Scott's parents, who tell him that Brandon hasn't yet arrived. It's been forty minutes since Owen left, and Scott's house is a ten-minute drive from theirs, but Steven tells himself there's no need for alarm, yet. Owen and Brandon might have stopped at a video store, a McDonald's . . . Holly is in the kitchen preparing dinner. Steven sits in the family room, the portable phone at his elbow, Caitlin in the crook of his arm reading from *The Wind in the Willows;* the TV's on, CNN with the sound nearly inaudible; Steven's thumb on the remote control, poised and ready to strike.

FUGITIVE

CRAZY IN LOVE with the man. Such a man! She laughed shaking her head in wonderment: her luck he was crazy in love with *her.*

So they were married. In quick succession she had his children who were beautiful like him, though lighter-skinned, the girl, the youngest, nearly as light as she, the mother. He'd warned her in the early giddy days of their love (it was one of many jokes between them: his pretending to think that she might require such a warning) that most of his family was dark-skinned, very dark, black you might say, tarry-black, up from Georgia in the 1950's and settled in and around Detroit, Michigan. It wasn't until the wedding that she met his mother, two older sisters, and three brothers of whom one, D., was a child of eleven, his family smiling but stiffly silent in her presence; not out of resentment, she believed, of her creamy pale skin and wheat-colored gold-glinting hair but out of their sense of being alien to her, and she to them, a difference so profound it might have been molecular, cellular. Afterward in his arms hearing herself say almost in self-pity, hurt, "I'm afraid your family doesn't like me," and her husband said, laughing, teasing, "Never met anybody before who didn't fall all over you, eh girl?—that's the problem?"

He was joking, of course. Teasing. His playful sometimes rough manner. So she'd catch her breath, almost frightened. But only almost. Knowing he loved her, adored her. Their souls merging like flame in flame.

Must not make others envy us. Her Quaker modesty checked her gloating pride.

It was not the color of her husband's skin that had so powerfully attracted her to him, she was certain. Except of course it was *his* skin, *his* color; and all that was *his* was exalted, ennobled in her eyes. His maleness, his blackness. His "personality" like no other. Because as the daughter of white liberal Quakers (wealthy Philadelphians, a family history dating to pre-Revolutionary times) she was truly without prejudice. No longer a practicing Quaker (as he, her husband, was no longer a practicing Baptist) but retaining the old Quaker principles of respect for others, common decency, fair-mindedness, the interior light; perhaps in her heart she did still believe there existed a secret flamelike luminosity inside her she would have named, had she been sentimentally inclined, *my soul.* Or was it rather, simply *soul.* The divine essence, breath of God, sacred radiance—whatever. You knew somehow it did exist, does exist. And love, physical love, love between a man and a woman—in their fierce lovemaking sometimes especially in the early years of their marriage it seemed to her the *soulness* of their beings merged startling and incandescent as flame in flame.

It surprised no one, least of all her who loved him, that the man was such a success. In college, in graduate school. In New York City where he rose rapidly through the ranks of quality publishing, a black intellectual who was also an athlete (tennis, golf) and an amateur jazz pianist and handsome and *kind*. And when at the age of thirty-two he left his New York job to accept a position as director of a university press in California, a very good but not yet distinguished press, she, his wife, understood what none of his puzzled friends and acquaintances understood: it wasn't New York he was leaving, but a proximity to Detroit. For often there were calls from his mothers, his sisters. Requests for money (which, so far as she knew, he usually sent: rarely did he confide in her about his family and never did she feel comfortable about inquiring), appeals to him to come visit.

He was too busy, he had his own life. He'd been gone from Detroit since the age of seventeen and didn't even, he claimed, dream about it any longer.

So they moved across the continent to northern California, twenty-five hundred miles from Detroit. In their new community which was mainly white, Asian-American, and affluent they were an attractive, popular couple, as they'd been in New York. *Two such special people* they were spoken of, sometimes even within their hearing. And she thought *Yes. I've become special as his wife.*

Yet that was to underestimate herself, surely? For she, too, had an advanced degree. She published poetry, essays in first-rate literary magazines. She taught a poetry workshop at the university, was active in parent-teacher events at the prestigious day school their children attended. Not a beautiful woman (she knew) yet in her husband's company she became beautiful, her face shining, exalted. Sometimes by chance she glimpsed her husband at a distance striding along a sidewalk, entering a public room, her breath caught in her throat, she felt a sense of unreality sweep over her, a vertigo. It was love, it was terror of the man—his maleness, his blackness. For perhaps without her understanding it, his maleness was his blackness, and his blackness his maleness.

She was not a vain woman so she did not think, seeing him, *Can I keep him? A man like that?* for in her innocent egotism she retained unexamined the secret knowledge *He is black, and I am white: no black woman can take him from me because no black woman is so attractive to him as I am, and another white woman would be frightened of him.*

And then one night, when they'd been married for nine years, a call came.

AND VERY LATE that night, at 2 A.M. while the children were sleeping, her husband's brother D. arrived, now twenty years old and unrecognizable to her, who had not glimpsed him nor heard his voice since the day of the wedding; unshaven, disheveled, smelling of his body, driving a car with Ohio license plates which would turn out to have been stolen, in Toledo; his eyes dilated, snatching at her for a moment without recognition. As if he'd forgotten his brother was married to her, a white woman. As if he'd forgotten her existence.

The call, the arrival of D. had not been entirely unexpected. He'd been missing from home for five weeks, wanted by Detroit police for questioning in a nightclub shooting-murder. And her husband had not turned D. away, could not turn him away, how could he? Saying to her *You know white cops are after a black kid's ass, he wouldn't have a chance back there.*

She would prepare a meal for D. She would not object to him sleeping in the family room for how could she who was the wife of D.'s older brother, the mother of his beautiful children, object. Her husband was angry with D. and frightened for D. and bitter and protective, the brothers shut in together in the family room talking in subdued, rapid voices until past 4 A.M. while she cleaned up in the kitchen rinsing plates to set in the dishwasher, carefully wiping with a sponge the Formica-topped breakfast table where D. had ravenously eaten without a further glance at her, hunched over his plate, young-looking for twenty, scared. And afterward quietly slipping from the house, descending the grassy slope to the river; her breath quickened, shallow; her feet in open-toed sandals wet from the grass; sitting then at this undefined twilit hour of early morning on the lowermost, just slightly rotted wooden steps leading to the dock. (Their house was a handsome multi-level structure with numerous plate-glass windows, sliding doors, and decks, built at the top of an incline above a narrow, deep river; in a residential area of tall trees, two-acre lots, a rural-suburban neighborhood.) Staring at the dark water lapping against the dock, the pebbly shoreline. Thinking *I am his wife, I love him. What his life is, it's mine.* Except when he came to her, she flinched at his footsteps above her, steeled herself against his voice though she knew it would be a voice of calm, of control. He said, quietly, "Come back to the house, he'll think you don't want him here." She was shivering, she drew breath to reply yet could not, so he said, "Should I send him away?" and still she could not reply, seeing how across the river the treeline was dense as a single tarry substance, thickly smudged as with a trowel. Above the Mendocino mountains miles away heat lightning was pulsing forked and silent. "All right, then," her husband said, "I'll send him away," and now she spoke, her voice hoarse, "No. You can't do that," and affably he said, "No. That's right, I can't," not ironic, or not ironic in such a way she would be left with no choice but to register as ironic; for always at such moments, such was her husband's subtlety, his kindness and tact, he would allow her a margin of not-knowing, not acknowledging; and she said, not wanting to sound as if she were begging, "I love you," and he said, "But I could go away, if you'd like that," and she said quickly, in pain, "No," and he said, patiently, as if addressing a frightened or intimidated child, "Then come back to the house, now." She was staring at the slow-lapping shadowed water that might have been not water at all but molten lead, waves of whatever minor and inconsequential river flowing to what destination she could not, in the exigency of the moment, have named; understanding how it might be dangerous in this man's presence to seem not to have heard when in fact one had heard but she still could not speak, nor did she glance back as with an exhalation of breath and a muttered inaudible expletive her husband ascended the steps, and was gone. She saw herself climbing up the steps, hurrying after him, *Wait! I'm coming!* clutching at his muscled forearm *Yes of course I'm here* yet she remained sitting on the steps, motionless, paralyzed, as if lost in a dream, in that suspension of volition and even thought between sleep and waking, staring at the river waiting to understand what she would do, or had already done.

ME & WOLFIE, 1979

FUCK I'M THINKING, Me is cracking up again.

This season I was 13 yrs old & Me began to be paranoid about staying in our new rented bungalow in Olcott, New York by herself. Or through the night even with her dog-devoted son Wolfie on the premises. It had to do (was Wolfie's theory) with the wind blowing thin & whistling across wide choppy bruised-blue Lake Ontario & the fact, Me didn't discover till she'd signed the lease for 12 months, that the lane leading down to our bungalow was mostly sand and mud and at night black as pitch, no street lights. Me'd stuck us at the edge of a broken-down lake-resort town, signed the lease in a 100-watt mood *(100-watt mood* was what Me called her happy-craziness, & this term was apt) & all to escape the enemy.

What enemy? (Wolfie didn't ask.)

Me was in a habit of raking her nails through Wolfie's tender feelings saying in her I-just-thought-of-this-shit voice how'd she know Wolfie wouldn't side with the enemy if, in the night, the enemy suddenly showed up?

Enemy was Me-code for *them* as in (for instance) *us* vs. *them* but mainly Wolfie's ex-father whom we'd managed to elude for at least two years by the time of Olcott. (Can you have an ex-father? The guy who was Me's ex-husband is what I'm saying.) Says Me, "I wouldn't trust a kid your age, wolf-eyes & wolf-habits, sticking his big toe in the muck of male puberty, as far as I could toss him."

"Fuck you, Me."

Wolfie'd mutter under his breath. So Me could hear or not-hear, her choice.

It was typical of Me, that manic-depressed year on the southern shore of Lake Ontario, to lapse into a silence of hours & no more speech communication than grinding her teeth (you could feel more than hear, a brooding vibrating noise like a train passing), then break the silence with such harsh pronouncements. Sometimes Me positioned herself in doorways, for instance the doorway of my room at the cobwebby rear of the bungalow, backs of her slender veiny hands resting on her hips, & beautiful steel-eyes glaring, & sometimes (the weirdest times!) Me spoke with her head turned away, as if thinking out loud, private thoughts suddenly bursting out of her crammed head like a radio turned up so that Wolfie (who happened to be present) was privileged to overhear. The cruellest was a flung-in-the-face remark as Wolfie, sleep-deprived & cursing, stumbled out the door to tramp through sand to the Newfane Central Schools bus the color of a demon pumpkin & spewing exhaust at the top of the lane, "Wolfie! It's school you actually go to? All day? How can I trust a kid won't look me level in the eye?"

"You can't, Me. You're fucked."

It was like tickling Me, with rough fingers. Get her to laugh when she wasn't expecting to.

"Where'd you acquire such a foul mouth, mister? Not from *me.*"

"Exactly that's who: Me."

By instinct I knew that the best defense against Me's *bruise-mood* meanness (*bruise-mood* was what Me called her depressed state, & this term was apt) was a fast & unrepentant offense. Like a boxer who doesn't wait for his opponent's jab but goes for the head pronto.

"Bye, Me! See ya later."

"Fuck *you.*"

Most mornings even if Wolfie was a few minutes late the bus was waiting for him, & the other kids staring out the windows like by himself he, Wolfie, is a spectacle not just a scrawny long-haired 13-yr-old with shadowy doom eyes & sullen mouth like a girl's, & the reason was (Me's paranoia, but Me was accurate) that the bus driver was a true mother-type, all smiles & sympathy, who pitied Wolfie as a child-with-a-problem-mother. Olcott was a small town where rumors & gossip (not all malicious) were like radio waves continuously bombarding the air. Within a few days of Me & Wolfie moving into the bungalow on Seaview Lane with rusted screens & fake-brick asphalt siding & that weedy yard with a look of things buried in it, it was known through the neighborhood that this wasn't your normal American TV family.

No dad, for instance.

"See what I say? People spying on us."

"But not the *enemy,* Me. Not here."

If Me flashed a little crazy after a restless night of smoking & prowling the darkened house with owl-eyes alert to suspicious noises outside & on the roof, it didn't inevitably mean she'd still be in such a state when the schoolbus deposited Wolfie back home at 3:35 P.M. In fact it could mean Me'd taken her meds & calmed her mind by working at collage-sculptures of "found objects" (which Me never finished out of superstition) & having a vitamin-enriched midday meal (yogurt, wheat germ), & possibly she'd take a miles-long hike on the windy beach & even a nap curled up like a cat among the dunes, & return refreshed & invigorated & maternal. All this was a possibility. In the universe in which Me & Wolfie dwelled, each hour was a new toss of the dice. Heads, tails. You don't always lose.

So possibly Me'd be awaiting her only child home from school, a tray of peanut butter cookies (only slightly scorched) cooling on the kitchen counter, smiling & attentive like any Olcott mom. Teasing, "Oh hey: back so soon? Guess I gotta let you in, huh?"

(Not like any mom, maybe. Me'd have the screen door latched & within grabbing range, on a counter, one of her razor-sharp knives.)

"Guess so, Me."

"Well, I love ya, dummy. C'mere."

At 13-going-on-14 you're expected to shrink from a mom's kiss but I never did. Couldn't take a chance it wouldn't be the last.

WOLFIE THE DEMEROL kid. Me reminisced.

Meaning she'd had me by way of that "heavenly" drug. & other drugs keeping sanity afloat. Lithium, Dilaudid. Valium no more exotic than aspirin. If you grew up with them you saw them as greens, blues, whites, big-capsule, medium-size capsule, square-cut, pumpkin seed & clamshells. Some of the pills were manufactured with X's imprinted on them, almost invisibly, & others were indented with lines at the meridian so, if you wished, you could cut the pill neatly in two with a knife & it wouldn't crumble. Wolfie'd learned to split pills at a young age. When Me's hands were shaky.

Wolfie was the Demerol kid but in fact that was Ralphie. Little Ralph, Jr. God damn what a name for a sweet innocent guy, Me said. She'd repented not having the kid but the circumstances. Except if you subtract the circumstances, where's the kid? We'd ponder such riddles of metaphysics on our long drives in the ditchwater-color Chevy van Me'd borrowed (from a man friend in Stanley, Montana, who must've never seriously expected to get it back). Me was susceptible to *bruise-moods* when pondering how we're essentially determined by our genes, locked into patterns of behavior rigid as ants if you had the perspective to judge, yet Me could be lifted suddenly into *100-watt moods* by a vista of beautiful mountains, cloud-formations, rolling hills, farmland & dairy cows & horses grazing in fields, & the realization that mankind is essentially free, there's free will for all, since we can't foresee the future & strictly speaking there is no future until we make it. "See what I'm saying, kiddo?"

Wolfie grunted sure. By age 11 he'd become a metaphysician.

Figuring it's only words Me batted around like Ping-Pong balls. But words with a certain power to pierce the heart.

Wolfie, the weird name, was Me's compromise of Ralphie. She'd been pressured (not just by the baby's father, but by the baby's father's mother) into agreeing to that name. Ralph, Jr. For the father was Ralph, Sr. He'd had his proud-father way with naming & baptizing as well in that long-ago time. Baptizing! In 1966! Me was disgusted. You'd think by then the Christian religion would've gone the way of the dodo & the duck-billed platypus but it just hangs on, fumed Me, & Wolfie interjected with wiseguy pickiness is the duck-billed platypus extinct, I don't think so.

Me ignored this. If you hoped to correct her when she was slipshod, she had a queenly way of not-hearing.

"Those Christians! All they want is to gobble up our hearts."

Me was Wolfie's version of Mommy. Mom*mee.* Me liked to tell how I was a breathless butterball-baby squealing & lunging for attention already in the cradle, & snatching at words but able to grasp, as with pudgy butter-fingers, only syllables. Coaxed to say Mommy, the best I could do was *Meee* even as a toddler. Daddee came out *Du-ud* (as Me told hilariously) & naturally that pissed the guy off. Even an asshole has feelings.

Wolfie, who was Ralph in school records, tested out high on I.Q. exams (not genius like the 160's but pretty smart like in the 140's), & this was actually held against him by Me in her down moods. Me believed that the smarter you are, the more you suffer. The more developed your brain, the more there's to go wrong, like a high-speed computer. Me had a girl cousin in Geneva, New York, who'd had a Down's baby & was that little boy sweet! Wolfie said sarcastically he was sorry he wasn't brain damaged & Me said that's typical of a bright boy, sarcasm & irony as bad as me. Me seemed to mean it saying over the years she'd have preferred a sweet dumb child of either sex, not brain-damaged of course, just normal, what passes for normal in America, boy or girl wouldn't matter so long as this child didn't inherit her tendency to malaise, mope & metaphysics & yanking out eyelashes in idle times.

Actually, neither Me nor Wolfie'd succumbed to this bad habit for a while. Our sloe eyes were thick-lashed like dolls'.

Me said a high I.Q. is like a laser beam, peering into cavedarkness where you don't really want to go. She liked to retell Plato's parable of the cave which was more than 2,000 yrs old & which Wolfie thought was overrated. Me said, "There's two species within Homo sapiens, the illusioned & the disillusioned. You can begin as the first & end up as the second but not the other way around. You can be born either one & never budge an inch. Who knows why?"

Me had that teacherly way & with her icepick eyes was compelling.

Except in her own eyes where she was ugly & a scrawny blond

broad Me was a good-looking woman, & Wolfie'd seen how men stared at her in the street & sometimes followed her on foot or in their vehicles. That was how some mistakes were made, Me conceded. There were times she'd gone to a male barber & had her hair trimmed to a butch cut out of meanness to herself & whoever might've wanted to contemplate her, & there was her thin whiplash body & the scary glisten of her eyes & it was true Me had a scar on the underside of her jaw like a centipede (caused by tripping & falling on black ice Me insisted but Wolfie seemed to recall years ago the ex-father shoving Me down face first on a gas stove burner which lucky for Me's looks hadn't been turned on, Oh yes Wolfie recalled the blood & the crazed screaming & shouting of those lost days), still Me was a goodlooking woman & would retain her looks for another ten years at least. At 34, which was Me's age in 1979 in Olcott, New York, in T-shirt & khaki jodhpurs & baseball cap & sandals she looked so young, the schoolbus driver had to ask Wolfie is that your sister & Wolfie blushed grunting a reply that might've been *yeh* or *naw* stomping on to the back of the bus so the goddamn question couldn't be repeated.

The move to Olcott, like previous abrupt moves, had been an impromptu decision on Me's part. Departing one place of residence for another, & leaving no forwarding address, gave Me a quick high. (Wolfie grooved on it, too. No need for this kid to sniff airplane glue like his white-trash classmates, with such a mom as Me!) In Olcott, population 1,600, there'd been a period of peace & calm of approximately five weeks as in the aftermath of a hurricane & tidal wave. Olcott was a "resort" town of which Me claimed she'd heard, & must've confused with somewhere else. Cheap lakefront rental cottages & bungalows, bargain-rate motels, a tacky boardwalk & amusement park including a neon-pink Ferris wheel visible from their bungalow a mile away—Romantic, huh? Me asked, late summer nights. But summer ended. Half the population departed after Labor Day like robots & businesses shut down & immediately the air turned chill. Lake Ontario was a bitch, Me admitted, so fucking *big*. A harsh wind blew from the distant Canadian shore, an odor of rotted clams & fish. The tide began (as Wolfie knew it would!) to seep back into their lives. The *bruise-mood* tide. Me began to brood on death again & asked such questions: "Maybe we're actually dead & don't know it? Like you're dreaming, & don't know it? For the essence of the dream is to hypnotize you, right?" Me locked doors & windows in the five-room house when Wolfie was away at school & sometimes doubted he was at school & not elsewhere, kidnapped by the enemy. Or plotting with the enemy.

The lake winds brought hellish nights when Me's adrenaline level was such she couldn't sleep & her hunger for metaphysics kept her awake. But she was too excited to read, too. Her consciousness was piercing through to a higher level—"Beyond linear, man!" She worked with 25-lb dumbbells lifting & swinging the black weights for hours. Her biceps swelled like breasts. In Eagle Falls, Minnesota, she'd taken karate lessons with an ex-Marine instructor, a guy with thinning black hair in a ponytail who'd fallen in love with her (was Me's account) & given her gifts she hadn't wished for including money. & with this money, Me & Wolfie'd made their middle-of-the-night departure. If only the high could last forever! "Like those renowned rats," Me told Wolfie, "they implanted electrodes in their brains & the rats could stimulate 'pleasure zones' & grooved on that & forgot to eat, & died of starvation."

Wolfie said dubiously, "That's cool, Me? I don't think so."

"That's Nirvana, baby. You'll wish for it too, one day."

Not long afterward, one windy Olcott night Wolfie woke hearing mutterings & soft laughter through the plasterboard wall of his room. He recognized the symptoms. Crept out to see what the hell the woman was doing. Off her meds (that was obvious) & her skin smarting & burning & he dreaded to think that in a mutinous gesture she'd flushed every capsule & pill down the toilet. That shit's expensive, Me, Wolfie'd tell her. There Me was naked, splendid & naked, skin glittering like mica from the manic sweat, & eyes glaring fierce & scared. Her slender muscled legs covered in filmy blond hairs & the hair of her skull, Wolfie noted, grown now to several inches, floating & blond-filmy in lamplight. Oh, Me was a beauty! Quick, Wolfie ducked back into Me's bedroom to hunt up something for her to wear, returned to toss a rayon robe at her, his face heated with embarrassment. Saying, "What if somebody's looking in the window for

Christ's sake! Always you're worrying people are looking in our windows!" Wolfie raged & fumed (it pissed him off, the inconsistency of the paranoid) & Me laughed at him. Not that Me's nakedness, the dazzling milky skin of her breasts, belly & upper thighs in contrast to the tanned skin of shoulders, arms & legs, was a great surprise to Wolfie. Not that the staring breast nipples & the blond swath of pubic hair was a wholly fantastic sight to him. They'd been together, Me & Wolfie, for 13 yrs. Me laughed crudely at the kid's face. "Wolfie's a prude, I guess. How'd I give birth to a prude?" But she took the robe & struggled vaguely with the sleeves, got it on partway though unbuttoned & the belt not tied. On the shadowy living room floor—Wolfie'd stumbled against them—were cardboard boxes from their move, only partly unpacked, & on the ratty rattan sofa were a half-dozen of Me's knives, long gleaming blades & tooled handles, Me's so-called knife collection she'd inherited from a grandfather who'd been a major in the U.S. Army (Wolfie took this on faith, he'd never encountered grandparents let alone great-grandparents) & her Samurai puppets & aged rag & porcelain dolls she'd collected in a time preceding Wolfie, & old framed lithographs ("The Skaters," "The Engagement," "Three Little Kittens") that revived sharp memories in Wolfie. Those faded & dreamlike drawings Me & Wolfie'd tried to copy in crayons, rainy days, snowbound days & nights, in remote places they'd lived & had one day fled. Wolfie rolled his eyes at this corny old stuff but there'd been a time not too long ago when he was fascinated by the lithographs, like Me. Seeing that in olden times, in the 1880's, life was different. People were happier then. Their faces were less complicated. Their bodies were like mannequins, carefully dressed. Kittens had a way of smiling with upturned whiskers that brought tears into your eyes, almost. In pictures of families in horse-drawn buggies, even the horses smiled.

Me was smoking her goddamn cigarettes Wolfie hated, so to piss Me off he'd snatch the pack from her & light one himself & take a few drags with a practiced air. Tears in her eyes Me demanded to know if Wolfie was in touch with you-know-who. Wolfie exhaled smoke & smirked. Like a kid with a secret. Me said, touching one of the stainless steel blades with just her fingertips, lightly as if it was burning hot,

"You don't want to test me, kid. You or that fucker." Wolfie said, "What fucker? This is news to me." Me asked if he'd come to the school & that was how he'd traced them? Wolfie registered under that other name. A name Me wouldn't utter. Wolfie said shrugging, "Think any shit you want to think, Me. You're gonna think it anyway at 4 A.M." At this, Me had to laugh.

Wolfie sat on the floor looking through the boxes he'd helped to pack & Me smoked her cigarette & was drinking from a smudged glass just water from the faucet (Wolfie thought) & there wasn't going to be much sleeping that night. Tears in her eyes Me asked why she'd lost her illusions so young? She was only 16 when the craziness first began, not so bad as it'd be later, but the start of it was hearing voices, & mostly they were reasonable voices, & the surprise of it wasn't the voices themselves but the revelation she had at about age 19 that other people didn't hear them in their heads the way she did, & it was a sign of craziness to answer back.

Me said, pleading, "How the fuck would you know? That everybody else wasn't hearing them, too?"

Wolfie had to concede, "You wouldn't, I guess."

Incensed, Me said, "It's like a dream. You hear voices in a dream. Why'd you doubt they were real?"

Wolfie was thinking the weirdest voices he heard were real.

"I'm responsible for it, though, huh?" Me said. "For both of us, I guess." She sounded broody & speculative. Now running a fingertip along the sharp-honed edge of a twelve-inch blade with a carved wooden handle. Steak knife? A cigarette between her lips dropped hot ash, undetected, onto her milky-skinned little belly. "How long am I responsible for you, kid?"

Wolfie said, "Till I'm eighteen, man. That's the law."

Me said, "Maybe you won't live to be eighteen. Wise-ass."

THE CHILD SQUEEZES out of the mother's body. How you could get so small & like a fish, was hard to comprehend. Me'd explained in a crayon drawing. A long time ago. She'd drawn a woman with a small head & smiling mouth & mostly the woman was a belly & in the belly was a little thing coiled like a fish, with shut eyes. Me saw his face &

laughed tenderly saying, We were all little fishes once. Don't be afraid to think it. Some of us stay fish, & some evolve onward into standing upright & being human. It can be fun, darling! Don't look so glum.

She'd kiss & tickle him till he laughed, & shut his pudgy fingers in her hair. Their happiest time.

OUTSIDE A WAWA MARKET in Newfane, twelve miles south of Olcott where we'd go for groceries & gas, there's this tattoo freak sitting on the front steps about 30 yrs old & good-looking in a down-dirty way in sleeveless undershirt to show off his muscles & tattoos, smoking & drinking from a can of Budweiser. This guy with sideburns, long greasy tangled hair, a three-day beard like black spikes & he's got a crammed duffel bag so I guessed he was a hitchhiker. Not from around here I guessed. Unless just sprung from prison & on his way home. Taking up space on the Wawa steps so Me had to practically step over him, & Wolfie with her, & in that instant vigilant Wolfie saw *the look* pass between Me & the tattoo freak.

The look. In theory Wolfie's too young to know what it meant but practically speaking he knew it meant SEX.

Inside the store Me was breathless & talking fast in her scattered distracted way not seeing where she was headed, & Wolfie said severely, "We came in here to get tomato soup & ice cream & soap & toilet paper don't forget, Me!" & Me said quickly, "Hell I'm gonna forget." She was licking her lips like they were dry but she never once glanced toward the door.

Me's weakness was a certain breed of man. Where the ex-husband at least had a job, selling cars & making good money (at least when not drinking), these others were worse off than Me herself, & a few of them on the wrong side of the law. In her sane state Me knew these guys were losers & bad news for one with her special problems but in her other state Me was what you'd call susceptible. 'Cause she was so fucking lonely, that's why, she told Wolfie, just a single mom & a 13-yr-old headstrong kid & no friends or relatives to give a God-damn if they lived or died. Wolfie told her with a smirk more like it was a classic death wish.

Me flared up, "Lonely, or death wish, what's the difference?"

Wolfie had to concede, Me had a point. For a woman, maybe the two went together.

Being lonely was a female sickness for which the cure was the tattoo freak & the tattoo freak was also the sickness.

That Saturday in early October Me drove them in the borrowed van on the lookout for old cemeteries which sometimes they visited, & flea markets & auctions which were places of treasure where Me's face brightened like a little girl's & she could squander $5 on an armful of old needlepoint cushions, jars of buttons, bald-headed dolls & cracked china & rusted old jackknives. Evidence of lives lived! Me declared, as if some strangers' lives, no matter who, were more important than our own.

Wolfie shook his head, all this escaped him. Who gives a damn about such crap?

The open-air flea markets were jammed with customers on Saturdays, mostly women. There was a brisk trade in junk & you could see in certain faces that expression of tenderness & shrewd bargain-hunting combined.

Me poked Wolfie in the ribs. "Where's your air of romance? wonder? *hope?* Not just you're a prude, kid, you're a miser, too."

It was true, Wolfie obsessed about finances. Wasting even $5 made him cringe. In both Montana & Minnesota, Me'd had to borrow emergency cash & hadn't been proud of her transactions.

When they left the Wawa, where Wolfie'd kept them as long as he reasonably could, the tattoo freak was gone from the front steps but there he was a half-mile up the road, which was a country highway amid cornfields, squinting in the sunshine & raising his thumb for a ride. Farmers in pickups rattled past. Who'd stop for *him?* You'd have to be crazy Wolfie was thinking, with a sinking heart.

"No, Me, come *on!*"

"Why're you so uptight, you? Think there's danger, like on TV, in broad daylight on Route 78?"

Sure enough Me brakes the van to a skidding stop & calls out the window, "Hey, where ya going?" The tattoo freak (who's possibly a little younger than 30) blinks & grins like he just won a lottery he hadn't known he was entered in, & says, "Hell, it don't matter, anywhere north, closer to the lake." This guy would've climbed into the back with our purchases & accumulated junk except Me said quickly, all urgent & courteous, "Wolfie, hon, you crawl over the seat & let this man sit up front here? He's got *long legs.*"

Wolfie was so disgusted, he turned speechless. Did what Me said without a single-word commentary.

So the tattoo freak rode to Olcott with us! This stranger who might've been carrying knives of his own in that duffel bag, if not guns. This guy who might've been just released from prison or worse yet a psychiatric hospital. A Mongol type Me picked up for the hell of it & would claim afterward it was *doing a good deed.* Shit! Wolfie had to listen to Me asking this character questions like a girl TV reporter & this guy saying he used to live right on Olcott Beach where his dad had a concession a while back. Me in her freaky 100-watt mood, Wolfie knew! Her faded-gold hair matted & flattened down by a grimy baseball cap, & she's wearing a T-shirt of Wolfie's & her sexy jodhpurs & she's kicked off her sandals to drive barefoot. What the tattoo freak makes of Me, Wolfie has to wonder. The guy's got to think, for one thing, she's this kid's mom! From the rear the guy's got a muscled neck the color of grime & his profile shows a melting-away chin & coarse-pored nose & on his knotty left bicep a cobra tattoo quivering with slimy intentions only a few inches from Me's right, bare bicep. But the more Me talks & the more excited in her 100-watt way telling the guy about our place in Olcott by the lake & the wind at night & the Ferris wheel lights in summer, the quieter the guy is, & subdued, & by the Olcott town limits he wants to get out. "This is great, ma'am. Right here."

Me says, disappointed, "Don't you want me to drive you home?"

"Naw, ma'am, thanks, this is great."

So that's it. Wolfie doesn't know whether to be relieved as hell, or let down. He guesses that Me was debating asking the guy to stop in for a drink, or God knows, it's a sunny autumn day, in the 60's, a picnic on the beach. A nude swim! But the tattoo freak climbs out of the van hauling his duffel bag & you can see he's a youngish guy eager to escape & Me's got no choice but to continue on driving just her & the kid, the kid-that's-proof-she's-no-kid-herself, & now Me's subdued too, like a life-size balloon deflating, & chewing her lower lip,

Wolfie'd like to tease her about "ma'am" but won't, they're bumping down the sandy rutted lane to the dead end, to the asphalt-sided bungalow we'd gotten in the habit of calling *home.*

Life is to be LIVED.
But not in the HEAD.
& above all not FEARED.

Life is to be LOVED
& remember: YOUR SON.
In a dark time remember
YOU MUST LIVE FOR HIM.

This note, printed in green ink in Me's schoolgirl block letters, Wolfie was once shocked to discover taped to the inside of one of Me's bureau drawers. He knew it was a message from Me in a state of radiant revelation to Me in a state of despair.

He knew it was the reverse of a suicide note.

He shut the door as if shutting it on a snake. Hid his eyes, & ran to hide. If he was the only reason Me stayed alive, was her life his fault?

THERE WERE SECRETS Wolfie kept from Me.

He'd known from an early age he had to protect her.

True, Wolfie sometimes showed up bruised at school. (Or, bruised, didn't go to school that morning.) But Me bruised herself, worse. For every hurt dealt to her son she loved, Me dealt herself a dozen.

"Baby, it won't happen again. I swear!"

Always, Wolfie knew this statement to be true.

Another secret was how in Coldwater, Minnesota, in fifth grade he (Ralph L—) had been called out of class, & in the principal's office there was a whiskery-cheeked man in a soiled camel's hair coat who stooped & tried to grab him in his arms, & he backed away, & the man was his ex-father who'd tracked them down across three states as he said excitedly, & more loudly than the principal was accustomed to hearing. Mr. L—, the principal said, you led me to believe this was a family emergency? Wolfie stood like a stone boy. Even his heartbeat stony. Thinking how *Ralph* was their name & it was not a name Me would utter. *Ralph, Jr.* & *Ralph, Sr.* If Wolfie was surprised & even interested seeing at last *Ralph, Sr.* who was his ex-father he gave no sign for Me'd coached him strenuously, the enemy can appear at any time, don't allow the enemy to intimidate you & especially don't allow the enemy to touch you.

This dialogue, like TV:

"Hey, little fellow, y'know me, eh? Your dad."

(Not a glimmer of recognition. Wolfie's mouth shut tight.)

"You know your dad, Ralphie, don't you? C'mon!"

(Wolfie was backing up, though. Against the woman-principal's knees.)

"He knows me, ma'am. Sure he does. Ralphie, you're getting to be a *big boy.* How old?—ten? Oh Jesus."

(Stony Wolfie like a graveyard angel. Unsmiling & staring.)

The principal was saying to the ex-father that she was afraid he'd have to leave. The child didn't appear to know him.

The ex-father exploded, "Fuck he doesn't know me! His bitch of a mother who's a certified nut has poisoned him against me."

At this cue Wolfie spoke. In a small-boy earnest voice as Me'd coached him to remain calm in the presence of the enemy. "I don't want to be here. I don't know him. I want to go back to class."

The ex-father was getting excitable. Others entered the office to subdue him. In that flushed face emerged the rage that had been hidden. Wire glasses with smudged lenses & behind these the eyes glistened bloodshot. If somebody hadn't prevented this desperate man from stooping & lunging he'd have grabbed the child in his arms & run with him. It might've been like TV, cops shooting rounds of ammunition.

Wolfie laughed to think how mean a kid he was, not to know his own father. & before witnesses! It was of a meanness you couldn't explain, like grinding a tiny featherless fallen bird on the sidewalk beneath your heel, or smashing a window with your fist just to smash it & instead of crying because it hurt, laughing like a hyena.

Such were the secrets Wolfie kept from Me.

THAT SATURDAY NIGHT in Olcott there was a strong wind & pelting rain & Wolfie was awakened at about 2 A.M. by a sound of broken glass & his mother screaming. "Get away! God damn you! Get out of here! You fucker!" Wolfie thought: It's a man. The tattoo freak. There'd been a signal between them Wolfie hadn't comprehended, the guy must've come after Wolfie was in bed & Me had let him inside, in secret, as sometimes Me did with guys, & Wolfie stumbled in pajamas into the hall outside his room, already he was smelling whiskey, spilled whiskey, this was a smell he knew though he hadn't smelled it yet in Olcott. Wolfie heard a sound of struggle, another scream of Me's, & a deeper angry voice he believed he heard, & heavy footsteps, & more breaking glass, & standing in the doorway of her dim-lighted bedroom there was Me naked holding a sheet against her sweat-gleaming body. Me's hair was disheveled & her mouth appeared to be bleeding. Seeing Wolfie she screamed, "No! Don't come in here! It isn't safe in here." Wolfie was so scared the hairs lifted at the nape of his neck & his bladder pinched but he couldn't see any figure other than Me, unless the guy was hiding in the closet or bathroom? In Me's room lamplight spilled strangely against the ceiling & walls, the lampshade was knocked askew & still trembling. It looked as if a wind had blown through the room churning bedclothes & dragging the mattress partway off the box springs. There was an overturned whiskey bottle amid the sheets, & the smell of whiskey was sickening to Wolfie's nostrils, it had associations of which he didn't want to think & would not. He saw that the closet door was wide open, & nobody inside. Me's clothes on the floor looking as if they'd been yanked off hangers. Where was the guy? *Was there a guy?* He might've escaped by the broken window, maybe he'd climbed into Me's room through the window? (But why wouldn't Wolfie have heard anything until now?) Me was sobbing angrily & bleeding from cut fingers & cuts on her face & her eyes were so dilated Wolfie thought she must be blind. Staring at him & stammering words he couldn't comprehend. He saw, on the floor by the bed, a long-bladed knife glistening with blood. Me'd been stabbed! Wolfie tasted panic. Me was furious & not seemingly in pain & when he approached her she screamed at him to stay away, it was dangerous to touch her. "Call an ambulance! Call the cops! I've been attacked for Christ's sake! The fucker tried to kill me!"

Me tripped in the bedclothes & threw the sheet down in a rage & Wolfie saw to his horror that she'd been cut, stabbed, in her breasts, her belly, her thighs, & narrow rivulets of blood were running swiftly down her body. Wolfie was in terror that Me would die, & ran to the telephone to dial 911 but Me changed her mind & rushed at him & knocked the phone from him saying it was nobody's business but her own, she didn't want fucking cops barging into her home, rather bleed to death than invite cops into her home. Wolfie managed to walk Me into the bathroom & with badly shaking fingers dabbed at her wounds with a damp bath towel & Me sobbed quieter now, breathing swiftly & shallowly as if she'd been running, & her hair dark with sweat. Seeing that Wolfie was scared, his face pinched & dead-white, Me grabbed the bloody towel from him & tended to her own wounds, impatient, cursing. Wolfie tried to ask was it the guy they'd given a ride to? the guy with the tattoos? & Me said, "Who the fuck d'you think it was? That bastard, I'm gonna get a warrant for his arrest. I saw his face. I can describe him to a T. I can sketch his likeness." But Wolfie had to wonder: had there been a guy? Any guy? An intruder? The knife on the bedroom floor was one of Me's knives from her collection, & how'd a stranger get hold of it? Unless Me flashed it, first? & he got it away from her?

Wolfie wasn't going to ask.

Me was bleeding from a dozen knife wounds. Most were just surface cuts, though they bled a lot. The deepest were in the fingers of both hands as if she'd shut her fists hard around the blade and squeezed. By this time, now the worst was over, Wolfie'd begun to cry, nervous & scared, for if there'd been a man in Me's bedroom, & a man who'd beaten & cut her, & Me wouldn't call the police, what was to stop this from happening again?—& if there hadn't been a man, that was worse, Wolfie'd have to wonder if Me would be hospitalized to prevent harm to herself & others, & where would that hospital be? & where'd Wolfie be, then?

Even beyond 18, he could foresee he'd be responsible.

OR, MAYBE, NO: he'd hitch-hike West. Soon as Me was stable again. He'd seen photos of the Rockies, the Grand Canyon & Zion National Park & Yosemite. He'd get a job with the National Park

Service he'd been reading about, maybe as a fire ranger. Emergencies that had nothing to do with *him*.

AT AGE 13 Wolfie was too young for even a driver's permit in New York State but he could drive any reasonable vehicle, & had driven, spelling Me in the Chevy van on their long, mostly nighttime drive from Minnesota, & so that morning, a few hours later, Wolfie drove Me to a hospital in Newfane where in the emergency room, nearly deserted at 6 A.M., a young doctor treated her wounds & stitched the deep cuts in her fingers. The doctor was shocked & suspicious asking what had caused these cuts? & Me shrugged & murmured what sounded to Wolfie, some feet away, like "Life." Wolfie came quickly to join Me. He was anxious, protective. He'd talked Me into coming to Newfane for medical treatment (he knew about infections) & now he was worried that even in her moderately subdued state, not exuding the actual stink of mania, Me yet gave off an odor any professional could detect, as dogs are trained to sniff out illegal drugs. Wolfie said, "My mom's a sculptor, she carves things & cuts things up, like driftwood & metal & stuff like that. Sometimes she hurts her hands." This was such an inspired answer, & even proud, & that word *mom* at the core, Me brightened & smiled at Wolfie, & Wolfie saw that it would be O.K. The dice were being tossed again, & it would be O.K. "What about these other lacerations, on your body & face?" the doctor asked, & Me said with her most winning smile, like even with her stitched & bandaged fingers she was stroking this guy's thigh, "These're the hazards of being an artist, doctor. But I could use some painkiller." A nurse completed Me's treatment, putting gauze & bandages on Me's wounds, four on her face alone, & giving Me a tetanus shot, & Me insisted that her son be given a shot, too—"There's so much danger for kids these days. Even good, normal kids."

The hitch-hiker from the Wawa store was never mentioned again between them. Calling the police, or not-calling, was never mentioned again. Though in one day in November they'd see a motorcyclist on Route 78 who resembled the guy, straggly hair & sideburns, but it wasn't him, & both Me & Wolfie would glance away, wordless.

AFTER THE EMERGENCY room & the stitches & bandages that made Me laugh when she looked at herself in the mirror, it was a double 100-watt mood, Me & Wolfie both. Now she doesn't have to hurt herself for a while, Wolfie reasoned, & not me, either. A few days later driving along the windy lakeshore they discovered an old cemetery behind a stone church, in a place called Heartwellville, & as usual at such times Me was interested only in the more neglected graves, some of them covered in tall grasses & weeds & if there were flowerpots set before them, the flowers were long dead & the pots were cracked. Me could work herself up to actual tears at such sights amid rows of well-tended graves. "You never think of it. How you die twice. Once when you're dead, & then when nobody remembers." Wolfie laughed & said, "Oh, how d'ya know, Me? Some dead person told you?" Me said, "*I* wouldn't want to be forgotten." So Me knelt in the tall grass & stuck herself with prickles, clipping weeds with a rusty shears at the gravesite of Sarah Eliza Burd born 1891 & died 1946, & the grave overgrown & the pink marble marker badly cracked, a melancholy sight Me said. Wolfie got drawn into it, too, tearing out handfuls of weeds, & seeing that no one else was in the cemetery he prowled about the rows of gravestones & came back with a pot of real-looking pink geraniums to place by Sarah Eliza Burd's grave. There was justice to this: you had to figure that the tended graves would go on being tended for a while at least, but the untended, no. Their time was past. Me'd get worked up at such labor & would come almost to think that the dead knew of our effort & were grateful & who's to say they were not? Wolfie sneered, but that was Wolfie's way, Me expected it of him. "Of us two, I'm the idealist. That's 'cause I look oblivion in the face & make a choice: to persevere." Me & Wolfie were intrigued that in cemeteries there are family gatherings, sections of the cemetery like little neighborhoods, as in Heartwellville there were numerous Blackhulls, Dykemanns, Lindemanns, Epps. Yet, after a certain date, no more, as if the family'd died out, or the young ones moved away. This was sad, huh? Or was it? Me, wiping her forehead with her baseball cap, smiled at Wolfie, struck by a revelation. Despite her face-bandages that made her look like a car-crash victim. No matter that what she said now contradicted what she'd been saying a few minutes before. "God, Wolfie, doesn't it make you feel good, that we don't have some massive 'extended family' spying on us? All these people! Every one of them with their idea of *you*. Thanksgiving & Christmas & goddamn presents to wrap & unwrap. Just you & me, Wolfie! We travel light." This sounded good to Wolfie, too. The other was unimaginable, like being forced to wear layers of heavy clothing on a warm day, or eating ten times as much food as you wanted.

It was part of cemetery-visiting to bring lunch, & we had peanut butter on whole grain bread, hardboiled eggs, yogurt & wheat germ & McIntosh apples & Cokes, sitting amid the Heartwellville Lutheran dead, eating like pigs, especially Wolfie, for cemeteries whetted the appetite & it was a bright damp-sunny October day. Me's idea, Wolfie hadn't gone to school that morning, for what (Me would explain in her note to the school principal) were family-religious reasons. Later we stood on a crumbling stone wall behind the church looking out toward the lake, & what more beautiful sight, how happy we were we got to laughing, seeing the lake that, though we'd been living by it for weeks, was nameless to us, not a lake but an inland sea, stretching out west & east beyond our eyesight, & a hazy floating horizon, said to be the Canadian shore, where we'd never yet traveled, just visible to the north.

THE GIRL WITH THE BLACKENED EYE

THIS BLACK EYE I had, once! Like a clown's eye painted on. Both my eyes were bruised and ugly but the right eye was swollen almost shut, people must've seen me and I wonder what they were thinking, I mean you have to wonder. Nobody said a word, didn't want to get involved, I guess. You have to wonder what went through their minds, though.

Sometimes now I see myself in a mirror, like in the middle of the night getting up to use the bathroom, I see a blurred face, a woman's face I don't recognize. And I see that eye.

Twenty-seven years.

In America, that's a lifetime.

THIS WEIRD THING that happened to me, fifteen years old and a sophomore at Menlo Park High, living with my family in Menlo Park, California, where Dad was a dental surgeon (which was lucky: I'd need dental and gum surgery, to repair the damage to my mouth). Weird, and wild. Ugly. I've never told anybody who knows me now.

Especially my daughters. My husband doesn't know, he couldn't have handled it. We were in our late twenties when we met, no need to drag up the past. I never do. I'm not one of those. I left California forever when I went to college in Vermont. My family moved, too. They live in Seattle now. There's a stiffness between us, we never talk about that time. Never say that man's name. So it's like it never did happen.

Or, if it did, it happened to someone else. A high school girl in the 1970's. A silly little girl who wore tank tops and jeans so tight she had to lie down on her bed to wriggle into them, and teased her hair into a mane. That girl.

When they found me, my hair was wild and tangled like broom sage. It couldn't be combed through, had to be cut from my head in clumps. Something sticky like cobwebs was in it. I'd been wearing it long since ninth grade and after that I kept it cut short for years. Like a guy's hair, the back of my neck shaved and my ears showing.

I'D BEEN FORCIBLY abducted at the age of fifteen. It was something that could happen to you from the outside, *forcibly abducted,* like being in a plane crash, or struck by lightning. There wouldn't be any human agent, almost. The human agent wouldn't have a name. I'd been walking through the mall parking lot to the bus stop, about 5:30 P.M., a weekday, I'd come to the mall after school with some kids now I was headed home, and somehow it happened, don't ask me how, a guy was asking me questions, or saying something, mainly I registered he was an adult my dad's age possibly, every adult man looked like my dad's age except obviously old white-haired men. I hadn't any clear impression of this guy except afterward I would recall rings on his fingers which would've caused me to glance up at his face with interest except at that instant something slammed into the back of my head behind my ear knocking me forward, and down, like he'd thrown a hook at me from in front, I was on my face on the sun-heated vinyl upholstery of a car, or a van, and another blow or blows knocked me out. Like anesthesia, it was. You're out.

This was the *forcible abduction*. How it might be described by a witness who was there, who was also the victim. But who hadn't any memory of what happened because it happened so fast, and she hadn't been personally involved.

IT'S LIKE THEY say. You are there, and not-there. He drove to this place in the Sonoma Mountains, I would afterward learn, this cabin it would be called, and he raped me, and beat me, and shocked me with electrical cords and he stubbed cigarette butts on my stomach and breasts, and he said things to me like he knew me, he knew all my secrets, what a dirty-minded girl I was, what a nasty girl, and selfish, like everyone of my *privileged class* as he called it. I'm saying that these things were done to me but in fact they were done to my body mostly. Like the cabin was in the Sonoma Mountains north of Healdsburg but it was just anywhere for those eight days, and I was anywhere, I was holding onto being alive the way you would hold onto a straw you could breathe through, lying at the bottom of deep water. And that water opaque, you can't see through to the surface.

He was gone, and he came back. He left me tied in the bed, it was a cot with a thin mattress, very dirty. There were only two windows in the cabin and there were blinds over them drawn tight. It was hot during what I guessed was the day. It was cool, and it was very quiet, at night. The lower parts of me were raw and throbbing with pain and other parts of me were in a haze of pain so I wasn't able to think, and I wasn't awake most of the time, not what you'd call actual wakefulness, with a personality.

What you call your personality, you know?—it's not like actual bones, or teeth, something solid. It's more like a flame. A flame can be upright, and a flame can flicker in the wind, a flame can be extinguished so there's no sign of it, like it had never been.

My eyes had been hurt, he'd mashed his fists into my eyes. The eyelids were puffy, I couldn't see very well. It was like I didn't try to see, I was saving my eyesight for when I was stronger. I had not seen the man's face actually. I had felt him but I had not seen him, I could not have identified him. Any more than you could identify yourself if you had never seen yourself in a mirror or in any likeness.

In one of my dreams I was saying to my family I would not be seeing them for a while, I was going away. *I'm going away, I want to say good-bye.* Their faces were blurred. My sister, I was closer to than my parents, she's two years older than me and I adored her, my sister was crying, her face was blurred with tears. She asked where was I going and I said I didn't know, but I wanted to say good-bye, and I wanted to say *I love you.* And this was so vivid it would seem to me to have happened actually, and was more real than other things that happened to me during that time I would learn afterward was eight days.

It might've been the same day repeated, or it might've been eighty days. It was a place, not a day. Like a dimension you could slip into, or be sucked into, by an undertow. And it's there, but no one is aware of it. Until you're in it, you don't know; but when you're in it, it's all that you know. So you have no way of speaking of it except like this. Stammering, and ignorant.

WHY HE BROUGHT me food and water, why he decided to let me live, would never be clear. The others he'd killed after a few days. They went stale on him, you have to suppose. One of the bodies was buried in the woods a few hundred yards behind the cabin, others were dumped along Route 101 as far north as Crescent City. And possibly there were others never known, never located or identified. These facts, if they are facts, I would learn later, as I would learn that the other girls and women had been older than me, the oldest was thirty, and the youngest he'd been on record as killing was eighteen. So it was speculated he had mercy on me because he hadn't realized, abducting me in the parking lot, that I was so young, and in my battered condition in the cabin, when I started losing weight, I must've looked to him like a child. I was crying a lot, and calling *Mommy! Mom-my!*

Like my own kids, grown, would call *Mom-my!* in some nightmare they were trapped in. But I never think of such things.

The man with the rings on his fingers, saying, There's some reason I don't know yet, that you have been spared.

Later I would look back and think, there was a turn, a shifting of fortune, when he first allowed me to wash. To wash! He could see I was ashamed, I was a naturally shy, clean girl. He allowed this. He might have assisted me, a little. He picked ticks out of my skin where they were invisible and gorged with blood. He hated ticks! They disgusted him. He went away, and came back with food and Hires Diet Root Beer. We ate together sitting on the edge of the cot. And once when he allowed me out into the clearing at dusk. Like a picnic. His greasy fingers, and mine. Fried chicken, french fries, and runny cole slaw, my hands started shaking and my mouth was on fire. And my stomach convulsing with hunger, cramps that doubled me over like he'd sunk a knife into my guts and twisted. Still, I was able to eat some things, in little bites. I did not starve. Seeing the color come back into my face, he was impressed, stirred. He said in mild reproach, Hey: a butterfly could eat more'n you.

I would remember these little pale-yellow butterflies around the cabin. A swarm of them. And jays screaming, waiting to swoop down to snatch up food.

I guess I was pretty sick. Delirious. My gums were infected. Four of my teeth were broken. Blood kept leaking to the back of my mouth making me sick, gagging. But I could walk to the car leaning against him, I was able to sit up normally in the passenger's seat, buckled in, he always made sure to buckle me in, and a wire wound tight around my ankles. Driving then out of the forest, and the foothills I could not have identified as the Sonoma hills, and the sun high and gauzy in the sky, and I lost track of time, lapsing in and out of time but noticing that highway traffic was changing to suburban, more traffic lights, we were cruising through parking lots so vast you couldn't see to the edge of them, sun-blinded spaces and rows of glittering cars like grave markers I saw them suddenly in a cemetery that went on forever.

He wanted me with him all the time now, he said. Keep an eye on you, girl. Maybe I was his trophy? The only female trophy in his abducting/raping/killing spree of an estimated seventeen months to be publicly displayed. Not beaten, strangled, raped to death, kicked to death, and buried like animal carrion. (This I would learn later.) Or maybe I was meant to signal to the world, if the world glanced through the windshield of his car, his daughter. A sign of—what? *Hey, I'm normal. I'm a nice guy, see.*

Except the daughter's hair was wild and matted, her eyes were bruised and one of them swollen almost shut. Her mouth was a slack puffy wound. Bruises on her face and throat and arms and her ribs were cracked, skinny body covered in pus-leaking burns and sores. Yet he'd allowed me to wash, and he'd allowed me to wash out my clothes, I was less filthy now. He'd given me a T-shirt too big for me, already soiled but I was grateful for it. Through acres of parking lots we cruised like sharks seeking prey. I was aware of people glancing into the car, just by accident, seeing me, or maybe not seeing me, there were reflections in the windshield (weren't there?) because of the sun, so maybe they didn't see me, or didn't see me clearly. Yet others, seeing me, looked away. It did not occur to me at the time that there must be a search for me, my face in the papers, on TV. My face as it had been. At the time I'd stopped thinking of that other world. Mostly I'd stopped thinking. It was like anesthesia, you give in to it, there's peace in it, almost. As cruising the parking lots with the man whistling to himself, humming, talking in a low affable monotone, I understood that he wasn't thinking either, as a predator fish would not be thinking cruising beneath the surface of the ocean. The silent gliding of sharks, that never cease their motion. I was concerned mostly with sitting right: my head balanced on my neck, which isn't easy to do, and the wire wound tight around my ankles cutting off circulation. So my feet were numb. I knew of gangrene, I knew of toes and entire feet going black with rot. From my father I knew of tooth-rot, gum-rot. I was trying not to think of those strangers who must've seen me, sure they saw me, and turned away, uncertain what they'd seen but knowing it was trouble, not wanting to know more.

Just a girl with a blackened eye, you figure she maybe deserved it.

HE SAID, There must be some reason you are spared.

He said, in my daddy's voice from a long time ago, Know what, girl?—you're not like the others. That's why.

THEY WOULD SAY he was insane, these were the acts of an insane person. And I would not disagree. Though I knew it was not so.

THE RED-HAIRED WOMAN in the khaki jacket and matching pants. Eventually she would have a name but it was not a name I would wish to know, none of them were. This was a woman, not a girl. He'd put me in the backseat of his car now, so the passenger's seat was empty. He'd buckled me safely in. O.K., girl? You be good, now. We cruised the giant parking lot at dusk. When the lights first come on. (Where was this? Ukiah. Where I'd never been. Except for the red-haired woman I would have no memory of Ukiah.)

He'd removed his rings. He was wearing a white baseball cap.

There came this red-haired woman beside him smiling, talking like they were friends. I stared, I was astonished. They were coming toward the car. Never could I imagine what those two were talking about! I thought *He will trade me for her* and I was frightened. The man in the baseball cap wearing shiny dark glasses asking the red-haired woman—what? Directions? Yet he had the power to make her smile, there was a sexual ease between them. She was a mature woman with a shapely body, breasts I could envy and hips in the tight-fitting khaki pants that were stylish pants, with a drawstring waist. I felt a rush of anger for this woman, contempt, disgust, how stupid she was, unsuspecting, bending to peer at me where possibly she'd been told the man's daughter was sitting, maybe he'd said his daughter had a question for her? needed an adult female's advice? and in an instant she would find herself shoved forward onto the front seat of the car, down on her face, her chest, helpless, as fast as you might snap your fingers, too fast for her to cry out. So fast, you understand it had happened many times before. The girl in the backseat blinking and staring and unable to speak though she wasn't gagged, no more able to scream for help than the woman struggling for her life a few inches away. She shuddered in sympathy, she moaned as the man pounded the woman with his fists. Furious, grunting! His eyes bulged. Were there no witnesses? No one to see? Deftly he wrapped a blanket around the woman, who'd gone limp, wrapping it tight around her head and chest, he shoved her legs inside the car and shut the door and climbed into the driver's seat and drove away humming, happy. In the backseat the girl was crying. If she'd had tears she would have cried.

Weird how your mind works: I was thinking I was that woman, in the front seat wrapped in the blanket, so the rest of it had not yet happened.

IT WAS THAT time, I think, I saw my mom. In the parking lot. There were shoppers, mostly women. And my mom was one of them. I knew it couldn't be her, so far from home, I knew I was hundreds of miles from home, so it couldn't be, but I saw her, Mom crossing in front of the car, walking briskly to the entrance of Lord & Taylor.

Yet I couldn't wave to her, my arm was heavy as lead.

YES. IN THE cabin I was made to witness what he did to the red-haired woman. I saw now that this was my importance to him: I would be a witness to his fury, his indignation, his disgust. Tying the woman's wrists to the iron rails of the bed, spreading her legs and tying her ankles. Naked, the red-haired woman had no power. There was no sexual ease to her now, no confidence. You would not envy her now. You would scorn her now. You would not wish to be her now. She'd become a chicken on a spit.

I had to watch, I could not close my eyes or look away.

For it had happened already, it was completed. There was certitude in this, and peace in certitude. When there is no escape, for what is happening has already happened. Not once but many times.

When you give up struggle, there's a kind of love.

The red-haired woman did not know this, in her terror. But I was the witness, I knew.

They would ask me about him. I saw only parts of him. Like jigsaw puzzle parts. Like quick camera jumps and cuts. His back was pale and flaccid at the waist, more muscular at the shoulders. It was a broad pimply sweating back. It was a part of a man, like my dad, I would not see. Not in this way. Not straining, tensing. And the smell of a man's hair, like congealed oil. His hair was stiff, dark, threaded with silver hairs like wires, at the crown of his head you could see the scalp beneath. On his torso and legs hairs grew in dense waves and rivulets like water or grasses. He was grunting, he was making a high-pitched moaning sound. When he turned, I saw a fierce blurred face, I didn't recognize that face. And nipples. The nipples of a man's breasts, wine-colored like berries. Between his thighs the angry thing swung like a length of rubber, slick and darkened with blood.

I would recall, yes, he had tattoos. Smudged-looking like ink blots. Never did I see them clearly. Never did I see him clearly. I would not have dared as you would not look into the sun in terror of being blinded.

He kept us there together for three days. I mean, the red-haired woman was there for three days, unconscious most of the time. There was a mercy in this. You learn to take note of small mercies and be grateful for them. Nor would he kill her in the cabin. When he was finished with her, disgusted with her, he half-carried her out to the car. I was alone, and frightened. But then he returned and said, O.K., girl, goin for a ride. I was able to walk, just barely. I was very dizzy. I would ride in the backseat of the car like a big rag doll, boneless and unresisting.

He'd shoved the woman down beside him, hidden by a blanket wrapped around her head and upper body. She was not struggling now, her body was limp and unresisting for she too had weakened in the cabin, she'd lost weight. You learned to be weak to please him for you did not want to displease him in even the smallest things. Yet the woman managed to speak, this small choked begging voice. Don't kill me, please. I won't tell anybody. I won't tell anybody don't kill me. I have a little daughter, please don't kill me. Please, God. Please.

I wasn't sure if this voice was (somehow) a made-up voice. A voice of my imagination. Or like on TV. Or my own voice, if I'd been older and had a daughter. *Please don't kill me. Please, God.*

For always it's this voice when you're alone and silent you hear it.

AFTERWARD THEY WOULD speculate he'd panicked. Seeing TV spot announcements, the photographs of his "victims." When last seen and where, Menlo Park, Ukiah. There were witnesses' descriptions of *the abductor* and a police sketch of his face, coarser and uglier and older than his face which was now disguised by dark glasses. In the drawing he was clean-shaven but now his jaws were covered in several days' beard, a stubbly beard, his hair was tied in a ponytail and the baseball cap pulled low on his head. Yet you could recognize him in the drawing, that looked as if it had been executed by a blind man. So he'd panicked.

The first car he'd been driving he abandoned somewhere, he was driving another, a stolen car with switched license plates. You came to see that his life was such maneuvers. He was tireless in invention as a willful child and would seem to have had no purpose beyond this and when afterward I would learn details of his background, his family life in San Jose, his early incarcerations as a juvenile, as a youth, as an adult "offender" now on parole from Bakersfield maximum-security prison, I would block off such information as not related to me, not related to the man who'd existed exclusively for me as, for a brief while, though lacking a name, for he'd never asked me my name, I'd existed exclusively for him. I was contemptuous of "facts" for I came to know that no accumulation of facts constitutes knowledge, and no impersonal knowledge constitutes the intimacy of knowing.

Know what, girl? You're not like the others. You're special.

That's the reason.

DRIVING FAST, FARTHER into the foothills. The road was ever narrower and bumpier. There were few vehicles on the road, all of them minivans or campers. He never spoke to the red-haired woman moaning and whimpering beside him but to me in the backseat, looking at me through the rearview mirror, the way my dad used to do when I rode in the backseat, and Mom was up front with him. He said, How ya doin, girl?

O.K.

Doin O.K., huh?

Yes.

I'm gonna let you go, girl, you know that, huh? Gonna give you your freedom.

To this I could not reply. My swollen lips moved in a kind of smile as you smile out of politeness.

Less you want to trade? With her?

Again I could not reply. I wasn't certain what the question was. My smile ached in my face but it was a sincere smile.

He parked the car on an unpaved lane off the road. He waited, no vehicles were approaching. There were no aircraft overhead. It was very quiet except for birds. He said, C'mon, help me, girl. So I moved my legs that were stiff, my legs that felt strange and skinny to me, I climbed out of the car and fought off dizziness helping him with the bound woman, he'd pulled the blanket off her, her discolored swollen face, her face that wasn't attractive now, scabby mouth and panicked eyes, brown eyes they were, I would remember those eyes pleading. For they were my own, but in one who was doomed as I was not. He said then, so strangely: Stay here, girl. Watch the car. Somebody shows up, honk the horn. Two-three times. Got it?

I whispered yes. I was staring at the crumbly earth.

I could not look at the woman now. I would not watch them move away into the woods.

Maybe it was a test, he'd left the key in the ignition. It was to make me think I could drive the car away from there, I could drive to get help, or I could run out onto the road and get help. Maybe I could get help. He had a gun, and he had knives, but I could have driven away. But the sun was beating on my head, I couldn't move. My legs were heavy like lead. My eye was swollen shut and throbbing. I believed it was a test but I wasn't certain. Afterward they would ask if I'd had any chance to escape in those days he kept me captive and always I said no, no I did not have a chance to escape. Because that was so. That was how it was to me, that I could not explain.

Yet I remember the keys in the ignition, and I remember that the road was close by. He would strangle the woman, that was his way of killing and this I seemed to know. It would require some minutes. It was not an easy way of killing. I could run, I could run along the road and hope that someone would come along, or I could hide, and he wouldn't find me in all that wilderness, if he called me I would not answer. But I stood there beside the car because I could not do these things. He trusted me, and I could not betray that trust. Even if he would kill me, I could not betray him.

Yes, I heard her screams in the woods. I think I heard. It might have been jays. It might have been my own screams I heard. But I heard them.

A FEW DAYS later he would be dead. He would be shot down by police in a motel parking lot in Petaluma. Why he was there, in that place, about fifty miles from the cabin, I don't know. He'd left me in the cabin chained to the bed. It was filthy, flies and ants. The chain was long enough for me to use the toilet. But the toilet was backed up. Blinds were drawn on the windows. I did not dare to take them down or break the windowpanes but I looked out, I saw just the clearing, a haze of green. Overhead there were small planes sometimes. A helicopter. I wanted to think that somebody would rescue me but I knew better, I knew nobody would find me.

But they did find me.

He told them where the cabin was, when he was dying. He did that for me. He drew a rough map and I have that map!—not the actual piece of paper but a copy. He would never see me again, and I would have trouble recalling his face for I never truly saw it.

Photographs of him were not accurate. Even his name, printed out, is misleading. For it could be anyone's name and not *his.*

In my present life I never speak of these things. I have never told anyone. There would be no point to it. Why I've told you, I don't know: you might write about me but you would respect my privacy.

Because if you wrote about me, these things that happened to me so long ago, no one would know it was me. And you would disguise it so that no one could guess, that's why I trust you.

My life afterward is what's unreal. The life then, those eight days, was very real. The two don't seem to be connected, do they? I learned you don't discover the evidence of any cause in its result. Philosophers debate over that but if you know, you know. There is no connection though people wish to think so. When I was recovered I went back to Menlo Park High and I graduated with my class and I went to college in Vermont, I met my husband in New York a few years later and married him and had my babies and none of my life would be different in any way, I believe, if I had not been "abducted" when I was fifteen.

Sure, I see him sometimes. More often lately. On the street, in a passing car. In profile, I see him. In his shiny dark glasses and white baseball cap. A man's forearm, a thick pelt of hair on it, a tattoo, I see him. The shock of it is, he's only thirty-two.

That's so young now. Your life all before you, almost.

Part Two

CUMBERLAND BREAKDOWN

TONIGHT AGAIN THERE'S that buzz-saw feel to the sky at dusk. Coming wind out of the mountains and unnatural heat for October. Like something breathing on you through its nostrils. And the poplars out back shivering. That scratchy whispering to drive you crazy. You turn scared half to death, but there's nothing.

In the kitchen she's moaning: "Jesus. Tell me nooo."

At the sink running water. Or vacuuming the goddamn house one more time till the carpets are worn through. Or playing some of his tapes brought in from the truck, not the bluegrass she can't listen to, it reminds her too much of him, and how she teased him for liking it, but Springsteen mostly, she knows by heart. Because she understands she's going to talk to herself and what sounds come out of her moaning and a noise like laughing, or a drunk person, she can't control and she wants to spare us hearing her.

"Jesus! Tell me *no!*"

Tyrell and me, we hate hearing any mention of Jesus. Especially now since the fire. Like, what good did Jesus do us? Dad died in a fire on the Temperance Vale Road seventeen days ago, and moaning to Jesus won't bring him back. I know, Mom can't help it. She's been drinking Gallo wine. Dad would be embarrassed all to hell, to hear. Even with us kids it'd be O.K. muttering fuck, shit, asshole, as long as it wasn't too loud and directed to any actual person, but if you uttered Jesus or Jesus Christ or God in any serious way Dad would get a frightened look on him, like anybody would. Because the first step to going nuts is talking to Jesus and God and the second step is them answering you back.

I AM MELORA RAWLS, I'm thirteen years old. My brother is Tyrell, sixteen. We are Raleigh Rawls's two children remaining at home. We were always close because of a certain thing that Tyrell did to me, not meaning to, when I was two years old and he was five playing with this b.b. gun belonging to one of our older brothers he hadn't ought to have touched, and crack! there's a b.b. lodged in Baby Melora's left eyeball quick and easy as a knifeblade cutting into butter. I am not blind in that eye exactly, in bright sunlight I can see blurry shapes and colors. I have pretended I don't remember a thing of that time but in fact I do. I pretend not for Tyrell's sake. He's like Dad in that way, quick to take on guilt.

Always Tyrell and me were close but since Dad has died in the Barndollar fire, that he was helping fight as a volunteer for the Ransomville Hook & Ladder, we are like twins almost. Tyrell is not one to talk much, but he will talk to me.

"If I could look those fuckers in the eye," Tyrell mumbles, in this voice so low and shamed I almost can't hear, "and hear them say they are sorry."

Meaning he'd feel a whole lot better? That's what he means?

"People say any fucken thing comes into their heads," I tell Tyrell, disgusted. "No guarantee it's true."

This just rips out of my mouth. I'm not even talking in any normal way, but with my teeth gritted tight, and my jaws like I have lockjaw.

Every day since the fire I'm getting more disgusted. I could toss kerosene and light some fires of my own. Them drunk Barndollars smoking in bed was probably the cause, and who'd want to give up his life for them? Tyrell is saying, "If they'd been worthy people. If Dad even liked them for Christ sake."

I say, "He didn't know. He couldn't judge. Firemen just go inside where it's burning, they don't expect to die."

Like our dad needed me to explain his actions. Like it was my right, and I knew what the fuck I was saying.

Tyrell says, shaking his head, "The fucken Barndollars for Christ sake."

It's like we are arguing with Dad, and getting fed up he's so stubborn. Like he traded his life on purpose for theirs, which is a wrong way of interpreting it, I know. Like Dad wants to be dead, and the newspapers printing his picture and calling him a hero. For these welfare people that don't give a shit, just pick up and go on with their worthless lives. I want to say to him now the joke's on you, see, the Barndollars are alive this minute and you are dead and what good's it do you being Raleigh Rawls the firefighter hero if you're fucken dead.

You'd think Tyrell and me would tire of this subject with the days passing but we don't. Like a dog with a copperhead coiled around its neck trying to shake the snake off, crazy and foaming at the turning in circles not getting anywhere.

Fifteen days have passed since the funeral. Seventeen, since the fire.

This month of October we have not gone to school more than a few days. Mom never goes out either. Especially when it rains this is a small-feeling house like a cave so you're in one damn room or another all the time practically. Unless you're outside keeping deliberately away. Sometimes I run, run and run across the fields not giving a damn if my heart bursts, I'm running so hard, but after a while I turn and come back all sweaty and panting because there's nowhere to go. Tyrell, too. There's something drawing us back, like we are worried about our mother though beginning to be disgusted, too. Every pure good thought I have ever had, seems like it turns sour and sarcastic and disgusted the more I turn it over in my mind, I wonder is this something special with me, Melora Rawls with the legally blind eye, or is it like everybody else?

"Jesus! Jesus! Nooooo."

A wail like somebody's turning a knife in her guts. She turns the faucets on harder, a fucken flood out there in the sink.

It'd be one thing if Mom believed in Jesus but I never heard that she did, much. Her or Dad either.

It's good that Mom stays inside. These days she's scrawny and grubby and her dark-blond hair like seaweed and she's wearing these old plaid Kmart slacks she's had a hundred years, covered in dog hairs, and a pajama top, and nothing beneath. And wool socks of Dad's on her feet, or barefoot. (Before the funeral Mom's mother and sisters came over and took charge, thank God. Nothing Tyrell and me could hope to do here.) And Mom was this pretty blond girl, you wouldn't believe her and Raleigh Rawls in their wedding photos looking like a glamor couple on TV. Now Mom looks puffy-faced drunk as Mrs. Barndollar. It's too much effort for her to answer the phone, just lets it click onto the answering tape then never plays the tape. "People have told me all they have to tell me. They can go fuck themselves, and leave me alone," Mom says but not in any angry voice just matter-of-fact. She has taken to sleeping half the day. In bed just laying there in the churned-up bedclothes. And on the sofa, and the TV on *mute.* Or she's in the kitchen running water or vacuuming the house like I said, dragging the vacuum around like a swollen leg, banging into things and moaning Jesus-words nobody wants to hear especially not Tyrell and me.

Sure we cried with Mom at first. We did all that. Plenty of that. And every relation of Dad's or whoever coming into this house and breaking down and bawling, and we did it with them, and we heard the tributes at the funeral blah-blah-blah and it wore us out. Like Mom says they can go fuck themselves just don't hang out here.

So weird. I hate it. The way Mom's eyes are bloodshot and caved-in looking and the pupils dilated but it's like she is blind, staring at me and not seeing me. Not just the Gallo is causing this but these capsule pills her sister Frannie passed on to her from her own prescription for nerves. "To help your mom sleep," Aunt Frannie informs us.

Like Mom not sleeping is the problem in this house.

WHEN HE SAID that about the Barndollars, Tyrell was cleaning his rifle. Cleaning and oiling his rifle that's a twenty-two in that tight dreamy way of Tyrell. Not like our father who'd whistle while he cleaned his guns, brisk and with an air of wanting to get the job done so he could move on to the next thing had to be done. But Tyrell since the fire he's in no hurry to get anywhere. He's nerved-up and impatient doing the same few things over and over like somebody has hypnotized him which is how I feel, too, this weird combination of nerved-up and nasty-minded but nowhere to go with it. Like a dog Dad and his brothers used to tell of, their own dog, poking in a wood-pile and suddenly it's yipping and thrashing around like crazy, a copperhead twined around its neck, and the dog desperate to shake off the snake, crazy and foaming at the mouth turning in circles not getting anywhere till one of the boys yanked off the snake, snapped it like a whip and broke its neck.

Except this time Tyrell says glancing sidelong at me from where his rifle parts are on the table, on newspaper where he's cleaning and scraping and oiling, and the smell of the cleaner sharp in the air, and the long blue-steel barrel of the rifle raised vertically, "We could change that, M'lora. That those fuckers are alive and Dad is dead, we could change that. Real easy."

WE SAW THE fire glowing against the sky like a demon pumpkin. We heard the air raid siren in Ransomville three miles away. If you're in town close by the firehouse when that thing goes off you press your hands against your ears, the noise is so loud. It's got to be loud, to summon volunteers to the station, that live outside Ransomville like Dad.

It was 11 P.M. Dad wasn't in bed but wasn't all dressed. He shoved on his shoes, threw on a shirt, and was out of the house and into his truck in about the time it takes to tell it. Tyrell and I wanted to come with him but no, we could not. We stood in the driveway and watched him drive away. The red rear lights of the Dodge pickup gone as soon as Dad turned out onto the highway. And the siren kept on at the firehouse. And after a few minutes the fire truck siren began, that sound that makes your heart race. And there was the fire itself we could see at some place two or three miles beyond the creek. The Temperance Vale Road it would turn out, the ramshackle old farm-house the Barndollars rented, with a fallen-down hay barn at the rear and a rusted Harley-Davidson motorcycle in the front yard with a hand-lettered sign FORE SALE that'd been there for a year at least.

People had to laugh, Clyde Barndollar used to ride that motorcycle like he was some kind of Hells Angel biker on TV. Black leather jacket straining across his beer gut. Boots, gloves. Crash helmet. Gold chains around his neck. He's a pipe fitter, or was. On some disability pension. Forty-three, it was printed in the paper after the fire. And Raleigh Rawls was forty-two.

When Dad left for the firehouse, he didn't know where he was headed of course. Whose house it would be. Or even if it was a house. There are not that many fires for volunteers to put out in our township, though there begin to be more once the weather turns. Mom was always scared to death something would happen to Dad but Tyrell and me, we never gave a thought to it. Not in a million years the thought would've come to me *Daddy will be killed tonight.*

Raleigh Rawls was one of those volunteers forbidding any of his family from showing up at any fire to gawk like assholes and take pictures like some did. He was more scornful of such behavior than of people causing their own fires with wood-burning stoves, sparks igniting in rugs or chimneys, smoking in bed and drunken error. Still, Tyrell was disappointed, he'd have liked to go with his father this time now he was sixteen and had his driver's license and believed he could help. He'd have taken off for the fire on foot except Mom screamed at him to get back inside.

"A fire's serious, damn you! A fire isn't for playing around."

TYRELL WOULD SAY he hated her for that. Tyrell would tell me rubbing his hands over his jaws that needed shaving that she had insulted him in saying such a thing. That he, Tyrell Rawls, would be playing by going to any fire to assist. He was not a boy to play, she should know his seriousness.

Tyrell was diagnosed as "dyslexic" at school which meant the special-ed class and he would work damn hard to learn to read which he did eventually, with two eyes so much slower than Melora with just one. But he did it. Through his growing up he'd been a serious boy.

I told Tyrell our mother didn't mean it. Any words that came out of her mouth then or now. I told him he should be easy on her, Dad would want that.

Tyrell said disgusted, "If I'd been there he might not be dead, see? I might of made some difference."

I don't say this is not likely. I don't say anything at all.

When Tyrell's in one of his moods I don't interfere. Watching like you'd watch a house ablaze.

THEY SAY THAT Raleigh Rawls didn't turn back when the other firefighters did. They say he pushed inside the falling-down house, that burned faster than anybody expected. These old farmhouses with worn-out wiring and insulation, decayed chimneys, stacks of newspapers and God knows what stored in boxes, fire traps waiting for a spark to set them going. If not for Raleigh Rawls insisting upon going in the Barndollars would both be dead of smoke inhalation where they were fallen on the burning floor of their bedroom. He'd gotten them out, or almost out, when the ceiling caved in, and Raleigh Rawls was pinned beneath. *Like that it happened, that fast. A flash fire in the kitchen after the fire began in the bedroom probably a mattress fire caused by a burning cigarette.*

TYRELL SHAKES HIS head marveling like there is something in this room floating before our eyes you can see but can't believe. "If it'd been somebody else for Christ sake. The fucken *Barndollars.*"

Tyrell fits the parts of his rifle back together. The oily swabs he tosses away. The gun cleaner smell is strong like lye soap. I like it, it makes my eyes water. Makes the inside of my nose sting.

I can see Dad cleaning his guns, his shotgun. But it's blurred like through my bad eye. I see Dad's mouth moving, he's saying something to us but I can't hear the words. Like the TV on *mute.*

Tyrell is looking at me. Like he asked me something, and I didn't hear.

I say, "If we shot them up they'd know who did it. Right away everybody'd know, see, Tyrell?"

Tyrell keeps staring at me like he never saw me before.

Tyrell says, "I sure to hell hope they do."

ALREADY TYRELL AND me have gone out. Not to where the Barndollars are staying with their married daughter and her kids but just out. It wasn't planned. Tyrell didn't take his rifle nor even think of taking his rifle. It was more just the two of us restless in the house. A wind from that direction, across the creek and the cat tail marsh we used to explore where people'd tossed their unwanted things some of it big as washing machines, kids' broke bicycles, every kind of tire and car part, and mattresses so stained it was a wonder to see them. We'd played in there until Tyrell was too old and lost interest when he was maybe twelve but before then we'd gone sometimes with other kids including Judd Barndollar who was a year or so older than Tyrell, I mean he still is that age but he's away at the Red Bank Boys' Detention for car theft, attempted armed robbery, and some other serious things. All the guys including Tyrell would joke they'd wind up at Red Bank someday. But Tyrell would never joke like this that our father could hear. Some things are too close to the bone Dad would say to be funny.

A wind from across the Mud Creek and the cat tail marsh and it's bringing the fire-smell to us. Outdoors and in. No matter how much wind, and rain on the windows peaking down the glass like a waterfall, when it's over the smell returns. A smoldering stink you don't want to think might have some burnt-human flesh in it.

Tyrell says, "Fuck let's get out of here."

It's 9 P.M. Mom never came out for supper. Tyrell and me, we found some leftovers in the refrigerator but hadn't any appetite for them. Nothing has much taste now which is O.K. with me, then I don't get a sick stomach. We've been watching TV surfing the channels. Flickering faces is what TV mostly is, voices cranked up to sound important, corny mood music and laugh tracks and dumb-ass ads. After the fire it all seems like ways of not-thinking about real things but the real things poke through anyway. What Dad liked was sports mostly baseball which Tyrell and I tried to watch with him, but got restless when nothing happened. Every season Dad had some new player he liked, it was underdog teams he favored, and up to when he died it was a six-foot-ten gangling guy with lank hair and a mustache who pitched for Arizona who Dad was just thrilled by, said this character was the twin image of some old friend of his from high school who'd died in a car crash. I would watch Dad when this pitcher was on and Dad's face was so tense, his fists closed on both his knees and his posture so straight, and the light of the TV flickering on him, and I was a little jealous I guess, and maybe Tyrell was, too, that nothing in actual life could mean so much to our father as some stranger pitching ball, and when a batter swung and missed one of these pitches it had the power to make Dad happy in a way we guessed we never could.

It was just four days after the funeral, this night Tyrell and me went outside into the night and hiked through fields to get to the interstate by the mall. This is the worst ugly dug-up place around here. I'd swear it has been under construction forever. Mom says there was all just cornfields and grazing land here when I was a baby but it's hard to believe. Just to see such ugliness makes you want to break something. Makes you want to toss a bomb. There was no plan that Tyrell had, though. We were out on the overpass kicking chunks of concrete and rocks and crap like metal rods, parts of tires, beer bottles, and cans down onto the highway and watching the stuff break, or bounce. There wasn't much traffic this time of night about 2 A.M. A sick-looking moon behind some clouds tattered and blowing like old curtains. Tyrell grinned and grunted dragging a block of concrete to the edge and pushing it over to fall and shatter below us like ice. There was a fascination to this but I said:

"Drop it on some fucken car, you want to do something."

Tyrell snorted. "Do it yourself, One-Eye."

This was harsh. I felt the sting in those words, that kids at school used to call me when I was younger. (And maybe still do behind my back.) "One-Eye" was nothing Tyrell would dare to utter at home especially in Dad's hearing he'd have had his ass kicked. That he knew this, and still he said it, and Tyrell being the one who'd blinded his baby sister himself, was something to ponder.

I said, "All right, asshole. I will."

I was fucken mad! Felt like a hornet not caring who got stung.

With my foot I pushed another chunk of concrete up onto the overpass. It was damn heavy, I'd guess the weight of two bricks at least. Tyrell didn't help me none just stood leaning over the rail smoking a cigarette. And he ain't supposed to smoke, he'd promised Dad when he was my age. By the time I got the concrete where I wanted it I was sweating inside my jacket and my oily hair I hadn't washed since the funeral was stuck to my forehead. But I liked the feel of my pulse going fast! It was like Dad's bluegrass music where the fiddles race with each other. Tyrell said, "You ain't gonna drop that on anybody, girl.

You'll kill 'em. Wind up at Red Bank Girls'. You can sleep in a bunk with Sissie Lamar." Tyrell laughed. (Sissie Lamar is this mean fat girl pleaded guilty to smothering her own baby nephew she'd been babysitting, sent away for as long as they could send her as a minor of fifteen.)

At the interstate there's not the same hilly land as there is other places outside Ransomville because when they excavated they cut through the hills to try to level the road. So you can see pretty far into the distance. Especially at night you can see headlights a long way away like at the edge of the earth. The size of fireflies when you first see them. We watched the headlights get bigger. We were excited but calm, too. Like Dad used to say telling us of hitch-hiking which nobody does now, but people did when he was a kid, even girls and women sometimes hitching all the way to Port Oriskany and Buffalo, he'd be standing at the side of the road with his thumb out and always sooner or later somebody stopped for him, male or female, old or young, somebody he knew or a total stranger, and it came to seem to him so weird that the vehicle destined to stop for him was already headed for him from miles away, and the driver with no awareness or expectation of him as he had no awareness or expectation of the driver, and yet it would happen that this person would stop for him, Raleigh Rawls; and that Raleigh Rawls would be there at the side of the road to be stopped for, and he'd have no choice who it was stopped for him because it had been ordained that way, from the beginning of the world you could argue. "When your number is up" doesn't have to be just some thing like being killed Dad would say it just means your number is "up" like in gambling, where you could win a bundle.

Tyrell and me, that was how we came to feel watching these headlights coming toward us, a rig barreling along in the night on the mostly deserted highway. Sort of dreamy-hypnotized watching. And my foot on the big block of concrete rocking it back and forth at the edge. My heart was beating really hard now like listening to "Cumberland Breakdown" or "Whirlpool" on my dad's tapes. My mouth was so dry I had to keep swallowing. It came to me slow that my dad was a trucker, too, short-haul trucking for the Ransomville Stone

Quarry, and there was the thought *What if it's somebody else's father, they're waiting to come home.* But I couldn't change my mind because Tyrell would call me One-Eye and scorn me as a coward and I was pissed at him so I waited until the truck was almost beneath the overpass and shoved the concrete off and it fell straight down hitting the side of the highway, not the truck which was already past. My right eye was shut tight so just my blind eye could witness what would happen but nothing happened, the big old rig was past and the air stank of diesel exhaust. Tyrell was relieved I knew, just like me. Sweaty and shaky like me. But he's got this nasty laugh saying, "See, you can't do shit. Missed by a mile."

I went crazy then, I hit Tyrell on the chest with both fists and he cursed and hit me back harder than maybe he meant, being so much taller than me, and not one to strike any girl. There I was on the pavement in broke glass and bawling like a baby he could not walk away from, under the circumstances.

NEXT DAY TYRELL would stammer he was sorry. He was goddamn sorry. Hurting me and near to causing some innocent man's death, he'd want to think he'd been shit-faced drunk but in fact he'd been stone cold sober.

TYRELL DOES DRINK some. All the beers and ale in the fridge left over from the funeral, it isn't just Mom but Tyrell has been depleting.

He's got a beer in hand, driving to where the Barndollars are staying since the fire gutted their house. At least, we think this is where we heard the Barndollars are staying with some relatives. Tyrell grunts, "Put in a tape, M'lora." In the glove compartment he's got Dad's old tapes and CDs, bluegrass, country and western, rock rattling around. "Cumberland Breakdown" is my first choice.

On the backseat of the car is Tyrell's smooth-oiled rifle. Loaded, and the safety on.

The more Dad is gone the more I love these tapes of his. He'd be playing them in his truck turned up high. What "breakdown" means in bluegrass is the musicians playing so fast you can hardly hear the individual notes. There's no lyrics only a wild nerved-up kind of music like somebody dancing till they drop. Like my feeling sometimes I want to run, run, run to feel my heart beat hard and the blood pound in my ears till I can't run any faster, and the voices in my head fade to just wind and that scratchy whispering of certain kinds of leaves, poplar and willow, you would swear must be human and trained upon you.

Run, run! Ceiling is ablaze, ceiling's going to fall.

They said he hadn't a chance, once it fell. Trapped there, and the others couldn't get to him in time.

Third-degree burns over 90 percent of his body they said.

Good reason for a closed casket. None of us, not even Raleigh Rawls's wife and his mother, would get to see.

Our mother had her way, she'd thrown out these precious tapes and CDs of Dad's like they were shameful. A drunk woman rubbing her sunk-in eyes. "Your father never grew up. That was his doom."

You couldn't believe these shitty things she's been saying, when she isn't bellyaching to Jesus.

It's her car Tyrell is driving. He has the use of it now he has a license and has been working part-time in town. And Mom won't go out anyway, so Tyrell just takes her keys. Nobody is going to make Tyrell go back to school. (Me, I guess I will. Sometime.) Dad's truck is for sale with a dealer in Ransomville. We cleared it out right after the funeral when we were all nerved-up and couldn't be cooped inside. Tyrell drove it under the carport and Mom still in her glamor makeup and her hair blow-dried for the funeral dragged the vacuum cleaner out, and I helped her, and we got the truck pretty clean inside, considering.

Dad's cousins wanted to play "Cumberland Breakdown" at his funeral but Mom would not hear of it. Almost screaming *No!* Like his taste in music is something to be ashamed of. I think that must be it. Like anything a man cares for, after he's dead seems like some weakness of his.

I'm thinking that being dead is a weakness. You can't speak for yourself any longer, everybody else is gabbing and yammering and making speeches over you like they are chewing you up and getting set to swallow. I hate it.

Turning onto the Carpenter Road, which is the road the

Barndollars are living at, Tyrell cuts the car headlights. Right away I say, "Hey. Your lights are out."

Tyrell laughs. "Ol' Eagle-Eye. What'd I do without you?"

I'D GONE TO school two days. Second day, I walked out and all the way home three miles in the rain.

A sick feeling comes over me like I am confronted with a math problem I can't figure out. A tall column of numbers to be added up. I'm O.K. at math but this I can't do. I feel sick like throwing up all the time. It's the smell in the air from across the creek.

Melora! I'm so sorry, dear. I feel so bad about your father, I . . . don't know what to say.

So don't say anything for Christ sake.

Your father was a very brave man . . .

Miss Urquhardt with her watery droopy eyes and sniveling voice that's too loud so everybody in homeroom can hear. *Oh! oh! She's fainted! Melora Rawls is fainted! Get the nurse, somebody! Hurry!*

Fuckers, I'm thinking. Could strap dynamite under my jacket and walk into Friday morning assembly like one of them suicide bombers no older than me. I'd do it in a heartbeat. Like Tyrell says groping his words, "Just to get it over and done. Fuck, so you wouldn't have to think about it."

It is all we think of, for sure.

Fifteen days have passed since the funeral. Seventeen, since the fire.

Each day, like today, especially staying home from school, time moves s-l-o-w as pushing a boulder uphill. You can't believe how slow the clock hand moves.

How any days have passed at all, I don't know.

I wish I could hear his voice better. Words he'd said to me, a thousand thousand times, they're fading.

At school there wasn't just Miss Urquhardt of course there was everybody else. Teachers from last year and Mr. Klinkson the principal. And this new ninth grade teacher with the scissor-cut blond hair and flashy glasses I overheard ask something of an older teacher and the reply was *Childhood accident* so I knew they were talking of my ruined eye. Like it's part of Raleigh Rawls dying like he did, that his daughter would have a ruined eye. All of them adults have got to take you aside and Talk. Like it's so fucken important they say what they have prepared to say like a politician on TV and you hear it, like you give a shit for them Feeling Bad. How many times you need to be told your daddy was a hero for Christ sake. At the memorial service no wonder half the Rawlses was drunk. In cafeteria line where I was grabbing my own scraped elbows and glowering to scare people off there came Brad Lamar and damn if Brad didn't say *Your dad went into a fire to save those Barndollars, Jesus why'd he do that? I'd of let 'em burn.*

"Cumberland Breakdown" is about finished, so I set the tape back to play over. Tyrell is driving with no headlights only just moonlight but it's a weird shifting light, clouds running over the moon so he's taking care. Suddenly he stops the car. Are we here? Where? There's a lone barn off in a field looking like it's floating. Tyrell says, "We could burn that barn. I'm prepared."

Quick I say, "We could."

I'm thinking this would be safer than shooting out windows at the Barndollar place. If that's what Tyrell is thinking of doing with the rifle.

Dreamy Tyrell finishes his beer and tosses the can out the window which I don't like, you're not supposed to do. Leaning his arms around the steering wheel. Almost I can hear his thoughts. You need so bad to *do something.*

Raleigh Rawls! Until the fire, just to say that name would be to make people smile. Dad was so well-liked.

Now somebody sees you, that name flashes to them and they get this look in their face like somebody jammed a stick up their ass. So sorry and guilty-seeming and hope to escape from you. And you can't blame them.

The older girls used to say my dad was sexy. I hated to hear this, you don't like to think that way about your own father.

What *sexy* is, is a mystery. Some people are, but most are not. Good looks has only part to do with it I guess.

(But being One-Eye would definitely exclude you. I would guess that.)

They say there will come a time, it might be years, it might be sooner. When you surrender your hurt and grief. My Grandma Rawls telling how she surrendered her son at last, Dad's older brother who'd drowned when he was nine years old in 1967, when there was the Yewville flood in 1984 and seventeen people died including five children in a single family and one of them but a baby. Grandma said she saw it then, the justice of it, that a boy of nine might drown if these others drowned. Grandma couldn't explain it but we knew what she meant.

About Dad, though. I don't think that time will ever come or that I would wish it. Mostly I don't give a shit for any future time, I'm thinking the only time is now.

"YOU COMING? Or want to stay in the car?"

Like this is a serious question! I tell him I'm coming with him for Christ sake.

Tyrell has driven slow past the Barndollar place. One of those old farmhouses that's been fixed up with asphalt siding and a shingle roof and even got a carport like our house. Still it's pretty run-down. A part-collapsed front porch and trash piled on it and in the yard and strips of torn plastic blowing in the wind from where they'd insulated the windows last winter. There's lighted windows downstairs and not all the blinds pulled down to the sills so anybody could look inside. I'm thinking Tyrell will fire some shots at these windows then get us the hell out of here but instead he parks up the road a ways and gets out carrying the rifle. I'm scared now but excited. Couldn't remain in this car for five seconds waiting for him to do whatever it is he's planning.

These fuckers are alive and Dad is dead, we could change that.

Tyrell leads us back to the house but not on the road. We're going through a cornfield that's dried stalks seven feet tall, rustling and whispering in the wind. There's a dog yipping somewhere, sounds like inside a house. We're coming up behind the Barndollar house through tall grasses. Back here, the downstairs windows are lighted clear as TV pictures we can observe out of the dark. Tyrell keeps nudging me with his elbow to keep behind him. Like I'm going to push past and fuck things up for him! Through a window we can see into a kitchen and there's somebody moving around. Two women. Maybe a man, sandy-haired. Tyrell says, "That's them." I'm squinting my good eye to see but it keeps misting over. I guess I can see this big-boned straggly-gray-haired woman that would be Clyde Barndollar's wife. My mother would not speak of this woman now but before the fire she'd shake her head in pity saying *Poor Janet*. Mrs. Barndollar was a school guard at the Ransomville grade school when I was there, one of those persons wearing a fluorescent orange vest and with a whistle who act important like they're stopping traffic for you when you cross the street, is how I recognize her. But she looks a lot older now. And there comes a man looking like Clyde Barndollar passing close by the window. His hatchet-face is about the color of baked brick. Sand-colored hair sticking up like a blue jay's crest but at his temples he's going bald.

It was just something that happened I can imagine my Dad saying. *There was no intention to it, see, that I would die in anybody's place.*

These words I can almost hear! But I can't make out the tone, if Dad is disgusted with how it turned out or matter-of-fact meaning just to explain to Tyrell and me.

While I'm thinking this Tyrell lifts the rifle slow and sights along the barrel at Clyde Barndollar not thirty feet away. Just to aim I am thinking. Not to pull any trigger just yet.

Because Tyrell is breathing kind of ragged. Like he's been running. You don't pull any trigger till your breathing is calmer than that, I know.

There's this dog barking suddenly inside the kitchen, we can't see. Clyde Barndollar comes to the window and shades his hands around his eyes trying to look out into the dark. I'm panicked thinking Tyrell is going to pull the trigger, must be I knock at his arm and ruin his aim saying, "Tyrell, no wait!" At the same time the dog's barking and yipping like crazy, and Clyde Barndollar's coming outside to see what's happening saying in this scared drunk voice, "Who's out there? Anybody out there?" There's a crash, Clyde or the dog has knocked a garbage can off the back stoop. Tyrell crouches back in the tall weeds, in the dark. I'm just standing there like my legs are paralyzed. An outside light is switched on. It's weird, I'm so scared I could piss my pants but I'm smiling. The thought has come to me *If they see me, it will be O.K. Tyrell won't shoot.*

Clyde Barndollar is shining a flashlight onto me where I'm standing in the weeds. The dog is a fat yellow retriever who's yapping and panting a few feet from me, hackles raised up his back, but it looks like he won't bite. Clyde is saying like he can't believe it, "Who the hell? Are you Raleigh Rawls's girl? Is somebody else there?" Tyrell curses me and shows himself, he's tossed the rifle into the weeds for safekeeping.

I will never know why Tyrell didn't run off and leave me, but he did not. Why he didn't fire the rifle anyway, but he did not.

The women are outside now, too. Mrs. Barndollar is talking loud and excited and the younger woman is confused asking is it Hallowe'en so early?

Clyde Barndollar keeps saying, "You two Rawls kids? Is that who you are? Je-sus."

This drunk man limping from a hurt leg like a man trying to walk with one foot in a bog comes right up to Tyrell and me where we're standing blinking in the lights. Wanting us to come inside and sit down with them for supper, we're just in time. We're saying no, no we can't, but they don't pay any attention, it's like they're deaf. I don't know why I'm allowing myself to be touched and grabbed at by these people I hate. By Janet Barndollar! Hugging me and crushing me against her big breasts slid halfway to her waist and calling me "Melora" like she actually knows me. She's saying the worst kind of crap about our father everybody's been saying but I can't push away from her, I'm feeling so weak. And she's crying, and I'm crying. Tyrell is mumbling, "We can't stay, see? We got to leave. We just came over to see how you all are getting along . . ."

Almost, hearing Tyrell say this, you'd believe it's true.

WE WILL NEVER tell anybody where we are, this night.

Eating supper with the Barndollars! We'd never have said we were hungry yet we're eating. It's like a dream of that kind that goes on and on where you're just *there.* Meatloaf, mashed potatoes, bread pudding in big sloppy servings. Hard-crusted ketchup on the meatloaf. Clyde Barndollar gives Tyrell a can of Coors ale, and Tyrell doesn't refuse. There's three young children at the table with us staring like they've never seen anybody like Tyrell and me I'm damn grateful the Barndollars don't think to explain to them who we are. It's a noisy place. Eating in the kitchen with the dog yapping and whining to be fed from the table. There's a strong smell of scorched food here, and a dog smell, and cigarette smoke, and mildew of old farmhouses. Halfway through the meal Mrs. Barndollar gives a little cry like a hurt bird saying, "Oh, hey! We forgot." Making us put down our forks and bow our heads while she says in a drunk singsong voice, "Bless us O Lord and these our gifts which we are about to accept from Your bounty Amen." Close up, Mrs. Barndollar doesn't look so old but her face is like raw meat that's been mashed by a fork and her hair is gray and oily and straggling past her shoulders. She's drinking Coors too, and there's a lighted cigarette behind her in an ash tray on the counter she keeps turning to pick up, panting and wheezing. And Clyde is talking a mile a minute like a TV turned up high in some room where nobody is watching. Something happens, Clyde's voice cracks, looks like he's going to bawl and the young woman says, "O.K., Pa. That's O.K. They know all that, Pa. They know that you don't need to tell them, Pa. These kids." I'm eating meatloaf, chewing and swallowing. It's got more onions than my mom's meatloaf. The ketchup crust is kind of burned. Tyrell is sullen eating and not saying much. I'm trying to think what to say. Mrs. Barndollar is asking about the meatloaf, I tell her it's really good. The dog nudges against my knees. Mrs. Barndollar has scars on her hands and forearms, looking like burn scars. She's saying her own kids never liked sliced onions. I tell her the meatloaf is delicious. Mrs. Barndollar starts to say something then thinks better of it. Clyde Barndollar lurches to the refrigerator to fetch two more cans of ale for Tyrell and him. I'm doing something my mom and dad would give me hell for, feeding a dog from the table. Letting a forkful of meatloaf fall to the floor and the dog scrambles under my chair so eager he almost knocks me over.

Sometime later, after we leave, Tyrell will have to double back on foot to retrieve the fucken rifle.

UPHOLSTERY

HAD RYAN VOIGT guessed that thirteen-year-old Sharon McGregor had a crush on him? Probably. Sure. Lots of girls had crushes on Ryan Voigt.

It was Sharon's older sister, Eva, who first used to hang out at the Voigt Brothers upholstery shop; her closest friend was Karen Voigt. Ryan was Karen's uncle. Ryan was a teaser. Loved to tease his brother's young children, and they loved to be teased by their boisterous good-natured uncle. Karen's pale, plain face blushed when Uncle Ryan called her "toots," "babe," "bombshell," and quizzed her about which was larger, her foot size or her bra size. The younger children ran shrieking with laughter when their uncle Ryan threatened to tickle them; if he failed to follow, they slowly crept back to his workbench. Adult women, customers, lingered at Ryan Voigt's workbench to see what his plans were for re-covering their furniture, examined dozens of sample swatches of fabric, traded flirty, just slightly risqué wisecracks with him, and went away (Sharon could see, even as a young girl) smiling and gratified. "Uncle Ryan" was a few years older than his brother Jimmy but he looked, and he certainly behaved, as if he were years younger. He lived in an apartment on Main Street downtown and he drove a new-model car, and had no wife and kids to "drag him down," as he liked to boast. When he spoke this way he glanced with a small, self-satisfied smile at his legs as if you could see feeble hands grasping at his ankles and being repelled.

He was a beefy, solid-bodied man, with heavy eyebrows like streaks of tar, good-looking in a coarse, simian way. His hands were square and spatulate. He was one to hammer with precision blows. *Whack! Whack!* He pounded nails into the undersides of chairs that, upside-down on the workbench, made you think of human legs, up-ended. He had shrewd small "X-ray eyes," as he called them. He had a quick sly insinuating smile. He liked to laugh, baring his big teeth, and he liked to provoke laughter. Especially, he liked to make you laugh against your will: his squinchy eyes gleamed with pleasure. His tone with most people, including his brother and sister-in-law, with whom he worked in the shop, was one of easy mockery: like a trailer truck rolling down a highway, Sharon thought. You were wary lest it swerve and roll over you, yet you had to admire such power.

Sharon's mother had furniture reupholstered several times by the Voigts, and seemed to be pleased with the results. Sharon now wondered if her mother had been one of those women who lingered to laugh and flirt with Ryan Voigt. If she had been, Sharon hadn't been present to see it.

AFTER COLLEGE, SHARON had moved hundreds of miles away; she rarely returned home to Yewville. It was Eva who remained. Sharon sent money when it was needed, but it was Eva who'd cared for their parents, and then, after their father died, arranged for their widowed mother to go to a nursing facility, Eastwood Manor, when it became clear that she could no longer live alone. Eva was a high school principal; she'd taught biology and general science; she was fifty-one years old and a woman of remarkable physical presence. There was something toughly radiant about her, a heat that could be intimidating yet also warm, magnanimous, protective. Sharon was three years younger, far less defined to herself or to others. Sharon had always admired Eva without especially liking her. But now that they were older, and lived at some distance from each other, she was beginning to feel a tentative, halting affection for her sister—though she still felt uneasy in Eva's presence, as if subtly handicapped.

Eva's tidy attractive house made it difficult for Sharon to breathe. Her sister's life—husband an orthodontist, children grown, graduated from good colleges—was a reproach to her own, so much messier, undefined. By the second day of her visit, she wanted to leave, though the dinner the previous night had gone well enough. Eva's lovely dinner. Their mother had been seated between her two grown daughters in a haze of—was it love for them? Surprise that she hadn't been abandoned? The table talk had been of the weather, a safe topic, yet one you could have an opinion about, even a vehement opinion. Their mother had looked from one daughter to the other, smiling a vague sweet smile that seemed to say, "Wherever this is, why ever you have brought me here, I love you."

This morning, Sharon had slipped away from the house, feeling Eva's eyes on her back. No, not breakfast, not just yet. She called out an apology, a vague excuse. She could play the role of the slapdash younger sister here, behaving oddly, you might even say rudely. That was her prerogative.

Now she was tramping through a wooded lot behind her sister's house, municipal land that opened into a residential area of older frame houses, a Methodist church, the Toll Gate Grammar School, where she and Eva had gone many years ago. Here, at the eastern edge of Yewville, Main Street was a three-lane state highway. So early in the morning, just past seven o'clock, traffic was still light.

She was thinking how it wasn't Hell people feared any longer. In her own lifetime, that fear, like the promise of Heaven, seemed to have evaporated. Instead, it was the assisted-care facility. This was the Place of Dread. You tell yourself no. Not me. And so their mother had vowed, at times emotionally, "Not me!" Their father, during the last years of his life, in a perpetual rage over his body's betrayal of him, had been adamant: "Not me. Not ever. Not your mother, either. We stay right here. This is our place. You hear? Not us!"

At dinner, their mother had said to Sharon several times, "I haven't seen Dad in a while," but it was said more in bewilderment than in sorrow. Somehow their mother had learned not to ask questions that betrayed her confusion. She wouldn't ask, Where is Dad? If you spoke to her of something requiring an act of memory, she would respond guardedly, but usually smile. You would almost think (relatives said this, leaving Eva's house, with an air of loyalty) that nothing much was wrong with her. She was so very attractive as always, and so nicely dressed, and when Eva and Sharon drove her back to Eastwood Manor at the end of the evening she hadn't protested, as she had on previous occasions.

Sharon was walking quickly, though she did not know where she was headed. Often, in Manhattan, she left her apartment and walked in this way, as if a distant music were drawing her, or a conversation just out of earshot. Here in Yewville it was memory that drew her. She had reached an old, slightly run-down residential neighborhood. Nearly each house meant a name, a classmate. Her closest friend, Inge Sorensen, had lived in a gray clapboard house, which had been converted into a karate school. One by one, the old single-family homes facing the busy road had been converted into something—a real-estate office, a dentist's office, a day-care center, a Chinese take-out. Karen Voigt had lived near here, in the barnlike shingle-board house where her father and Ryan Voigt had their upholstery shop. It, too, had been converted—into a secondhand furniture store. But it looked vacant now, derelict. A FOR SALE sign was hammered into the front yard amid weeds.

WAS THIS WHAT had drawn her here—the Voigts' old house? She circled the building, peering through begrimed windows. The Voigts had lived in the rear; the store had been in the front. Mrs. Voigt had worked in the shop, too, at a sewing machine. After Karen had left for nursing school in Buffalo, Sharon had babysat for Mrs. Voigt a few times.

In the dusty front window, there had been displays, unchanged from season to season—a high-backed carved mahogany settee with a velvet cushion, brocaded fabrics in suggestive folds like luxuriant snakes. Hanging out with Eva and her friend Karen, Sharon would drift out of their company in Karen's room and make her way out front, to the shop. There, Ryan Voigt was usually working at his cluttered bench, and if he was in the mood he might tease her, ask her questions about boys, flatter her with his apparent interest. Sharp and jabbing and indiscriminate this interest seemed to her, like the actions of a bored boy stabbing sticks into a pond in the hope of striking something living. Yet she was thrilled, excited. If a customer entered the shop, jarring the bell above the door, Ryan Voigt would forget her at once. His coarse face with its heavy eyebrows and just perceptibly mottled, singed skin took on a new expression: alert, adult, courteous, and helpful. The mockery would vanish, like a soiled handkerchief stuck into a pocket. And Sharon would think jealously, But I know who he is. Who he is with me, that's who he is.

Karen's father, Jimmy Voigt, was often on the telephone with customers, seated at a rolltop desk amid a clutter of invoices, order slips, sample swatches of cloth. Or he was out in the truck, picking up furniture, making deliveries. Ryan Voigt, by reputation the more skilled upholsterer, remained in the shop. He worked swiftly, measuring fabric and cutting it. His hands seemed to possess their own instinctive intelligence. Watching them, Sharon felt an indefinable yearning. She was thirteen, and beginning at last to grow. "Fill out"—this was the common expression. Older girls like Karen and Eva were like grown women to Sharon, with their fleshy young breasts, widening hips and buttocks; prematurely adult in a way that both intimidated and repelled Sharon. She knew men like Ryan Voigt "liked" girls' breasts: but why? She was lanky, thin, her small breasts creamy-pale with tiny nipples like rapt staring eyes. She understood that she must make herself of interest to a man like Ryan Voigt, to claim his attention. Even as she shrank from his attention. When his small squinched-up eyes moved on her, when he smiled his sly smile and called her "toots," "babe," "sweetie," her impulse was to turn and run—and yet boldly she stuck out her tongue at Ryan Voigt and told him he'd better mind his business.

He laughed, saying maybe this was his business? It was his shop, she was the one busting in.

Hotly she protested, "I am not. Karen invited me, she's my *friend*."

"Hey, and I'm not? Sure I am, toots. Ryan Voigt is your *friend*."

It was banter. It was of no more significance than the noisy rock music Ryan Voigt listened to on a portable radio. It was a diversion, at most. Yet to Sharon it was the first sexual interest any man or boy had taken in her or given the signals of taking. She wouldn't realize this for years. At the time, she'd surprised herself with peals of childish laughter, rapid-fire verbal exchanges and feints—like snatching up a lighted cigarette of Ryan Voigt's from an ashtray. Once, when Sharon dared to take up a newly opened, still icy-cold bottle of Black Horse Ale, Ryan Voigt grinned at her and told her to take a sip. "It'll do you good, sweetheart. Grow you some—" He gestured at his chest. He meant "grow you some tits."

Sharon felt her cheeks blush, and said meanly, "You're the one—you're growing a beer belly."

"Yeah?" Ryan Voigt glanced down at himself. "That ain't all I'm growing, sweetheart."

How old had Ryan Voigt been, when he'd said such things to a thirteen-year-old girl? Sharon would calculate, years later, that he must have been in his early forties. Yet he seemed a generation younger than her father, who would also have been in his mid-forties, who never teased his adolescent daughters, and seemed scarcely to look at them.

FOR A WHILE, Eva, too, had liked to be teased by Ryan Voigt.

Eva was a solid fleshy girl of sixteen with healthy olive skin and a dark downiness on her upper lip. Ryan Voigt's eyes snagged on her; you could see there was something in Eva that attracted him, though he was wary of her, for of Karen's girl friends Eva McGregor was the one least intimidated by him. He had to respect her way of standing with her hands on her hips and staring him down.

One day, when the girls were ambling about the shop, testing out sofas and chairs by lounging in them, pretending to be prissy adult females, they overheard Ryan Voigt speaking in an unnerving voice, one they'd never heard before: he must have been talking to someone who owed him money, and he was using words like weapons ("fuck," "asshole," "son of a bitch"). It was frightening to hear yet also thrilling. When Ryan Voigt hung up the phone, the girls pretended not to have heard. Karen was chattering nervously. Eva had discovered crimson velvet scraps in the discard pile, and was holding them up admiringly. She asked Karen if she could have them, and Karen said, "Sure, I guess so. They just get thrown out." Ryan Voigt lit a cigarette, came over, and asked what the hell Eva wanted with the scraps, and Eva said she wanted to re-cover a cushion she kept on her bed, this was a color that matched, and the fabric was beautiful, and Ryan Voigt pulled the scraps out of Eva's hand and said, "I'll make you a cushion, honey." He was heated, nerved up from the phone call. His eyes dropped to Eva's ankles and rose swiftly. "See, honey, I'll make you a dandy cushion if you promise me one thing."

Eva said guardedly, "What?"

Ryan Voigt said, "If you sit on it. Your sweet tender ass. I'll make the cushion if you promise you'll sit on it bare."

Eva turned away, muttering what sounded like, "I hate you." The other girls sniggered. (Though Sharon felt a stab of jealousy. She knew what Ryan Voigt's offer meant: he preferred her sister to her.) Flush-faced, Eva slammed out the front door of the shop, clanging the bell behind her.

Ryan Voigt called after, "Hey, I'm serious, hon. You'll see."

In fact, Ryan Voigt did make a cushion, covered in the splendid crimson velvet, with black silk tassels; Sharon would discover it on her sister's bed in a week or so. "Where'd you get that?" Sharon asked, shocked. Eva shrugged, with an evasive smile. It was a Yewville High affectation at the time to repel unwanted questions with the airy rejoinder, "Who wants to know?"

SHAME MAKES A haze of memory. Sharon still could not recall the precise chronology of what happened that evening at the Voigt home.

Well, he came to the rear door. Rapped on the glass with his knuckles. Grinned at her. "Hey, toots: want some company?"

Did Sharon open the door? Or had Ryan Voigt opened it? It was just past 9:30 P.M. The Voigts had driven to Buffalo to visit relatives and were due back, Mrs. Voigt had promised, around 11 P.M. Sharon had babysat for Mrs. Voigt twice before, she knew the house and felt comfortable in it. She would have locked the door from the inside (as Mrs. Voigt had instructed) but Ryan Voigt had his own key, didn't he? He was part owner, wasn't he?

It was the sequence of small moments, remarks, actions that would elude her. She felt, now, that recollecting the events was like trying to piece together a sheet of broken glass. She did remember Ryan Voigt brushing past her in the kitchen, just a little too near, and the hairs on her forearm stirring. There was a feeling of wonderment as well as excitement, of elation and alarm. He was at the "fridge," as he called it. "Hey, want an ale?" he asked, and Sharon laughed nervously and said no thanks. In fact she'd been drinking Pepsis. She had made popcorn for the Voigt children, and it was eaten except for a few greasy burnt kernels. In the living room she'd been doing math homework and watching TV, grateful to be alone and quiet, now that the children were in bed. As far as Sharon knew, even the restless four-year-old boy was asleep. Ryan Voigt grinned, pushing the bottle into her face. Practically into her mouth, bumping her teeth. "It won't kill you, it'll do you good." His eyes were red-veined and his skin was coarsely mottled as if he'd been out in the sun that day. Sharon could smell his fierce, beery breath.

Ryan Voigt wandered into the living room and stared derisively at the TV screen, switched channels, and then turned the set off—"Load of crap." He'd just dropped in to see his little nephew and niece, he said. Play with them. They were terrific kids, crazy about their uncle Ryan. Why would he want kids of his own? Why'd anybody want to get married—y'know what Elvis Presley said, Why buy your own cow when you can get milk through a fence? Ryan Voigt laughed at this witticism, staring at Sharon. He seemed not to know her name, but he knew who she was: he began to ask her about Eva, describing her as "your big sister"—"that gal with the boobs and the sweet ass." He asked if Eva had a boyfriend, and then asked if Sharon had a boyfriend, and that was when she began to feel, not frightened exactly, not yet, but disoriented. She'd been accustomed to moving in another direction, a direction she'd taken for granted. Except now she wasn't up front in the upholstery shop, it wasn't daytime, and she was alone with Ryan Voigt.

He sat heavily on the sofa, partly crushing her math textbook. He snatched it up, leafed through it, tossed it onto the floor. He patted the cushion beside him, inviting her to sit. He was wearing a pullover sports shirt through which he'd sweated across his chest, and he was in need of a shave. He smiled; his smile was boyish, lopsided, and he held onto it too long. Sharon stood smiling, too; there was a roaring in her ears, like laughter at a distance. Ryan Voigt drank from his bottle of ale in large thirsty mouthfuls. He teased Sharon, telling her she looked like she "had a stick up her ass." He asked her what his sister-in-law paid her for babysitting, and he said he'd pay her double that to babysit him, over at his place. He asked her if she was one of those girls who wanted to get married young and have babies, if she knew how babies were made, and if she thought it sounded like fun. He got up suddenly and went to get another ale from the fridge, brushing past Sharon, who took an instinctive step backward. He smiled at her, leaning close. There was a choked look to his face, as if something he'd swallowed was backing up on him, and Sharon could smell his breath, could almost taste it. He asked her which was larger, her shoe size or her bra size. He asked her if the tops of her thighs rubbed together when she walked wearing only panties. She laughed nervously, her face very hot. She hadn't the capacity to think *I don't want him to like me, I guess.* She hadn't the capacity to think, as an older girl like Eva would have thought, *I'll wake the children, he'll have to go home then.* Nor did it occur to her simply to tell him, *Go home. Leave me alone.*

She escaped to the bathroom. She had to use the bathroom, in fact. And Ryan Voigt lumbered after her, teasing and chortling like a small boy, except there was a meanness in his voice that wasn't a small boy's meanness. Sharon shut the bathroom door quickly and fumbled to lock it. Ryan Voigt sniggered on the other side. "Don't be long, I'm listening, toots. Need some help getting your panties down?" She was frightened now. She was trapped, and she was having difficulty thinking. Ryan Voigt said, "Don't be shy. You know you aren't shy. You girls."

She saw the doorknob turning, and said, "No! Leave me alone. Please." Suddenly she was begging. She didn't know what to call this man: Ryan? Mr. Voigt? A few times she'd echoed Karen, calling him "Uncle Ryan," but that was in play, and this wasn't play. Ryan Voigt laughed, bumping against the door. "Darlin', I'm waiting. You didn't fall in, did you?" The bathroom had a single window, and this window was jammed partway up; only a very small child could have squeezed through it. Yet in her panic Sharon considered the possibility. Better yet, she might smash the glass, and crawl through, where there was more room, climbing up onto the toilet, then the sink, then the windowsill. Amid slivers of broken glass she could escape. But the Voigts would be angry with her. Her parents would be angry. Ryan Voigt would claim he'd only been teasing, which was possibly true. After all, Sharon hung about the upholstery shop often, and never minded when Ryan Voigt teased her then. She would be laughed at, ridiculed. Everyone in the neighborhood and everyone at school would know. So she stood, crying. At some point she'd begun to cry. Possibly Ryan Voigt could hear her crying. He'd ceased rapping on the door. Then he turned up outside the bathroom, speaking to her through the window. There were bushes just outside the window, and the ground was lower than the floor, so he couldn't see her very well. Quickly, Sharon switched off the light.

"Please leave me alone, please go away and leave me alone," she said. She might now have left the bathroom and gone to wake the children, she might have run to the phone and dialed 911, but her brain seemed caught in knots. She was sobbing, she was pleading. Her bladder pinched with the need to pee.

The siege lasted forty minutes. Then, with no word, he was gone.

THERE STOOD EVA MCGREGOR, fifty-one years old; in her high school principal's navy-blue gabardine pants suit, frowning at her younger sister. "Sharon, you are not going back to New York tonight."

Eva spoke with the air of one accustomed to giving orders and to being obeyed. It must be an axiom, Sharon thought: adult children, especially sisters, are expected to quarrel over their parents' more valuable possessions. To be indifferent is to be unloving, unnatural. And there were plenty of these possessions—valuable and otherwise—to be sorted out before the property could be sold. That, after all, was the purpose of Sharon's visit. So she kept telling herself. It was duty, it must be done.

In the car, Eva pointedly asked Sharon what she'd done all day. Sharon murmured something vague and evasive: she'd gone for a long walk in their old neighborhood. "It must have been long," Eva said. "All those hours." Wasted hours, you could almost hear Eva say. Squandered hours.

They were headed west on Main Street in a stream of early-evening traffic. It was mid-September, a season of drought. Sharon saw out of the corner of her eye the Voigts' old house, where, a few hours before, she'd been walking. She said, offhandedly, "The Voigts. What's become of them?" Eva shrugged. Sharon said, encouragingly, "I always liked Karen. I was always jealous of you and Karen."

Eva sighed. "Karen's a nurse. We send cards. My closest friend—it all seems so long ago." The upholstery shop, she said, had gone out of business in the 1980's, as Sharon must know; they'd had to sell. "They were considered first-rate upholsterers, the Voigts. The things they did for Mom, you'll see they've really held up. Thirty years!"

Sharon was trying to remember what those things were. Ryan Voigt hammering at an upended chair. The living-room sofa: a rich winy-dark brocaded fabric that Sharon had liked to pet, like fur. She heard herself ask Eva what had become of Karen Voigt's uncle.

Eva said, "Him! Karen's crazy uncle. He was a drunk. I think he's somewhere in Buffalo, institutionalized. Alzheimer's, I think Karen said."

"Alzheimer's! But—is he that old?"

"He was an alcoholic for years. And, yes, he's that old."

Eva parked in the driveway of the old house. Sharon stared as if, for a moment, she didn't know where she was. There was the spacious white Colonial in which the sisters had grown up. Entering the house by the rear door as they'd always done, Sharon heard katydids in the tall grass, loud as cymbals, castanets. She knew she had to guard herself: the house was filled with their things—cumbersome objects and useless memories. She was thinking of Ryan Voigt, how his fingers had tugged at her hair, how he'd made a crude pinching gesture at her breasts and a joke about crab apples. Outside the bathroom, in the bushes, he'd urinated noisily. He'd wanted her to hear, and she'd heard. Sharon had never told anyone what happened that night at the Voigts'. But she never babysat for the Voigts again. She'd ceased trailing after Eva and Karen. And she'd never again entered the upholstery shop, or heard the brass bell jingle overhead.

Well, Sharon had glimpsed Ryan Voigt a few times afterward. Once, home from college, she'd seen him on the street in downtown Yewville, big-bodied, ruddy-faced, with that look of a swerving vehicle, and possibly he'd seen her, but hadn't recognized her because she'd changed so much, or hadn't let on he'd recognized her. Flushed with excitement at being home, knowing herself at the age of nineteen or twenty to be so much more than Ryan Voigt could ever have guessed, she'd actually lifted a hand to wave at him, whether in sincerity or mockery she couldn't have said. But Ryan Voigt had already been turning away, disappearing into the noontime crowd.

WOLF'S HEAD LAKE

It's an early dusk at the lake because the sky's marbled with clouds and some of them are dark, heavy, tumescent as skins of flesh ready to burst. It's an early dusk because there's been thunder all afternoon, that laughing-rippling sound at the base of the spine. And heat lightning, quick spasms of nerves, forking in the sky then gone before you can exactly see. Only a few motorboats out on the lake, men fishing, nobody's swimming any longer, this is a day in summer ending early. In my damp puckered two-piece bathing suit I'm leaning in the doorway of the wood-frame cottage, #11, straining the spring of the rusted screen door. You don't realize the screen is rusted until you feel the grit on your fingers, and you touch your face, your lips, needing to feel *I'm here! Alive* and you taste the rust, and the slapping of waves against the pebbled beach is mixed with it, that taste. Along Wolf's Head Lake in the foothills of the Chautauqua Mountains the small cottages of memory, crowded together in a grid of scrupulous plotted rows at the southern edge of the lake that's said to be shaped like a giant wolf's head, sandy rutted driveways and grassless lots and towels and bathing suits hanging on clotheslines chalk-white in the gathering dusk. And radios turned up high. And kids' raised voices, shouting in play. He's driving a car just that color of the storm clouds. He's driving slowly, you could say aimlessly. He's in no hurry to switch on his headlights. Just cruising. On Route 23 the two-lane blacktop highway, cruising down from Port Oriskany maybe, where maybe he lives, or has been living, but he's checked out now, or if he's left some clothes and things behind in the rented room he won't be back to claim them. You have an uncle who'd gotten shot up as he speaks of it, not bitterly, nor even ironically, in the War, and all he's good for now, he says, is managing a cheap hotel in Port Oriskany, and he tells stories of guys like this how they appear, and then they disappear. And no trace unless the cops are looking for them and even then, much of the time, no trace. *Where do they come from, it's like maple seeds blowing.* And you think *What's a maple seed want but to populate the world with its kind*. He's wearing dark glasses, as dark comes on. Circling the cottages hearing kids' shouts, barking dogs. He might have a companion. In the rooms-by-the-week hotel in Port Oriskany, these guys have companions, and the companion is a woman. This is strange to me, yet I begin to see her. She's a hefty big-breasted woman like my mother's older sister. Her hair is bleached, but growing out. She's got a quick wide smile like a knife cutting through something soft. She's the one who'll speak first. Asking if you know where somebody's cottage is, and you don't; or, say you're headed for the lake, in the thundery dusk, or sitting on the steps at the dock where older kids are drinking from beer cans, tossing cigarette butts into the lake, and it's later, and darker, and the air tastes of rain though it hasn't started yet to rain, and she's asking would you like to come for a ride, to Olcott where there's the carnival, the Ferris wheel, it's only a few miles away. Asking what's your name, and you're too shy not to tell. Beneath the front seat of the car, the passenger's seat, there's a length of clothesline. You would never imagine clothesline is so strong. Each of them has a knife. The kind that fold up. From the army-navy supply store. For hunting, fishing. Something they do with these knives, and each other, drawing thin trickles of blood, but I'm not too sure of this, I've never seen it exactly. I'm leaning in the doorway, the spring of the screen door is strained almost to breaking. Mosquitoes are drawn to my hot skin, out of the shadows. I see the headlights on Route 23 above the lake, a mile away. I see the slow passage, he's patient, circling the cottages, looking for the way in.

HAPPINESS

In the harsh sunlight on the pebbly southern shore of Lake Ontario. All objects are sharp and clear as if drawn with a child's crayon. Colors are bright, bold, unambiguous. Always there's wind. No shadows. Maybe the wind blows shadows away?

This story is written with a child's crayon. Matte black, or purple, with a faint oily sheen. Crayolas like the kind we played with when we were small children.

What did you see that day?

Kathlee. What did I see that day, I saw nothing. I saw the sharp edges of things. I heard a dog snarling and whining but I saw no dog. I was headed into the house because I was looking for Irish. He wasn't my fiancé then. He was not. Somehow I was in the house. And passing through the kitchen, and saying *Irish? Where are you, Irish?* because maybe it was a game, Irish was a boy for games, you couldn't look at him for more than a minute before he'd get you to smile, and there came Irish stepping out of nowhere, behind me I guess, in the hall, and catching my arm, my bare forearm, between two of his big calloused fingers, and I stopped right there on my toes on the threshold of that room (did I smell it, yes I guess: the blood: a rich dark-sickish smell and the buzzing! yes I guess it must've been flies, on the McEwan farm there were horseflies big as your thumb) like a dancer, and his arm around my waist quick to turn me toward him, and he said *Kathlee, no you don't want to see* and right there I shut my eyes like a scared little girl, pressed against his chest and he held me, oh I felt his heart beating hard and steady but what did I see that day at the McEwan farm, I saw nothing.

Irish McEwan was my first love, and my only. I would believe his innocence all my life. I was sixteen, that day at the farm.

Nedra. What did I see that day, *I don't know!* It was the start of my nervousness. My bad eyes. Even now I hate a surprise. If I'm back from school and it's winter and dark and nobody's home I'm half scared to go inside. After that day at the McEwan farm, I couldn't sleep a night through for years. And if Red, our border collie, began barking it's like *I might jump out of my skin!* People joke about things like that but what's funny? I'd go upstairs in our house and if it was dark, somebody'd have to come with me. For a long time. Almost, I couldn't use the bathroom during the night. Couldn't sleep, thinking of what I'd seen. No, not thinking: these flashes coming at me, like a rollercoaster ride. And Kathlee across the room sleeping. Or pretending to sleep. *Kathlee didn't see, she has sworn that on the Holy Bible. Her testimony at the courthouse. Her affidavit.*

These are words not a one of us knew before. Now we say them easy as TV people.

Kathlee. What did I see that day, I saw nothing. Swore to the police and then to the court ALL I KNEW EXACTLY AS I RECALLED IT. Placed my hand on the Holy Bible so help me God. I had prayed for help and guidance in remembering but when I tried there was a buzzing in my head, a fiery light like camera flashes.

Kathlee, no you don't want to see. C'mon!

Even now, it's years later. I will get sick if I try.

No, Holly will *not be told.* If I learn of anyone telling her, I will be madder than hell! That's a warning.

Nedra. What did I see, O God: I looked right into the room. I ran to the doorway, couldn't have been stopped even if Irish had grabbed me, which he did not, hadn't seen me I guess where I'd been sort of hiding behind the refrigerator. Half-scared but giggling, like this was a game? Hide-and-seek.

I'm like that. I mean, I was. A tomboy. Pushy.

At school I always had to be first in line. Or raising my hand to answer the teacher. I was quick, and smart. It wasn't meant to be selfish—well, maybe it was, but not only that—but like I was restless, jumpy. Mexican jumping bean, Grandma called me. Like a watch wound so tight it's got to tick faster than any other watch or it will burst.

How long we were driving the back country roads, I don't know. Started out in Sanborn, around 2 P.M., I mean Irish and Kathlee picked me up then. We drove to Olcott Beach, then the Lake Isle Inn where Irish was drinking beer and Kathlee and me Cokes and we played the pinball machines and Irish played euchre with some older men and it happened he won fifty-seven dollars. The look in his face! Kathlee and I counted it out in mostly ones and fives. Irish kept saying he wasn't any card player, must've been luck like being struck by lightning.

Kathlee said then we'd better go home, Nedra and her. And Irish right away agreed. We'd been with him all that afternoon. And I was worried that Grandma might've called home to tell Momma—or what if Daddy answered the phone!—how we'd gone off with somebody in a pickup truck she hadn't caught a clear glimpse of (from the front window where she was looking out) but believed it was an older boy, not Kathlee's age. And that swath of dark-red hair, maybe one of the McEwans? (The McEwans were well-known in the area. Mostly, the men had bad reputations. Not Irish McEwan, everybody liked Irish who'd played football at Strykersville High, but the others especially the old man Malachi.)

So Irish treats everybody at the Lake Isle Inn to drinks, roast beef sandwiches and french fries. Spent more than half of his winnings like he needed to be rid of it.

When we left it was a little after 5 P.M. Though I could be wrong. It's summer, and bright and glaring-hot as noon. A kind of shimmery light over the lake, and a warm briny-smelling wind, and that smell of dead fish, clams. Irish is driving us home and there's a good happy feeling from him winning at euchre, he's saying maybe his luck has changed, and it's strange to me, to hear a boy like Irish McEwan say such a thing, like his life is not perfect though he is himself perfect (in the eyes of a thirteen-year-old, I mean). In the front seat Kathlee is next to Irish squeezed between him and me and her hair that's the color of ripe wheat is blowing wild. And her skirt lifting over her knees so she's trying to hold it down. And she's sneaking looks at Irish. And him at her. They'd danced a little at the tavern, dropping coins in the jukebox. And on the beach, I'd seen him kissing her. And I'm NOT JEALOUS, I'm only just thirteen and would be scared to death I KNOW if any boy let alone Irish McEwan asked to dance with me, or even talked to me in any special way. I'm this jumpy homely girl, immature my mother would say, for my age. Maybe I like Irish McEwan too, more than I should, but I know he'd never glance twice at me, and it's a surprise even he seems interested in Kathlee who's never had a boyfriend, she's so sweet and nervous and shy and blushes when boys talk to her, or tease her, though she can talk O.K. with girls, and adults, and gets B's in school. *Simple!* some of the kids say of my sister and that is absolutely untrue. Now Irish McEwan is asking politely where do we live, exactly?—he thinks he knows, but better be sure. And Kathlee tells him. And we're on the Strykersville Road, a two-lane blacktop highway leading away from Lake Ontario where the tavern is. It would be said of Irish McEwan that he'd had a dozen beers that afternoon, the alcohol count in his blood was high, but Irish never drove recklessly all the hours we were with him and has been polite not just to Kathlee and me, but to everybody we met. He's a muscle-shouldered boy you might compare to a steer on its hind legs. He's strong, and can be a little clumsy. He's got pale skin, for a boy who works outdoors, with scatterings of freckles, and thick dark-red hair straggling over his ears and down his neck, he would've been good-looking except for his habit of frowning, grimacing with his mouth, as bad as my father who's hard of hearing and screws up his face trying to figure out what people are saying. Irish McEwan is twenty-three years old and already his forehead's lined like a man's twice that age.

Then on the Strykersville Road, Irish says suddenly he has a feeling he'd better drop by his own house first. Because his father has been sort of expecting him and he hasn't gone. Because of meeting up with Kathlee, and then with me. And his father was expecting him around noon but he'd been with Kathlee then, and lost track of time. And Kathlee says O.K., sure. So that's what we do. Where the McEwans live, or used to live, it's on the Strykersville Road about two miles closer to the lake than our house, and we live on a side road, so it makes sense to drop by Irish's house before he takes us home. The McEwan house (that would be shown in newspapers and on TV always looking better, more dignified than it is) is back from the highway about a quarter-mile. One of these bumpy rutted dirt lanes. Except the house is on a little rise, and evergreens in the front yard are mostly dead, you couldn't have seen it from the road. One of those old faded-red-brick houses along Lake Ontario that look larger from the outside than they actually are, and sort of distinguished, like a house in town, except the shutters and trim are rotting, and the roof leaks, and the chimney, and there's no insulation, and the plumbing (as my father who's a carpenter would say) is probably shot to hell. And the outbuildings in worse shape, needing repair. The McEwans are farmers, or were, but hadn't much interest in farm work, at least not Malachi and Johnny who worked odd jobs in town, but never kept them long. These McEwans were men with quick tempers who didn't like to be bossed around, especially when they'd been drinking. So we're driving up the rutted lane and on one side is a scrubby cornfield and on the other is a rock-strewn pasture, and some grazing guernseys that raise their heads to look at us as Irish bounces past raising clouds of dust. *My pa is gonna be madder than hell* Irish says with this nervous laugh *he wanted me here by noon.* Parking then in the cinder driveway. And there's an old Chevy sedan, and another pickup in the drive. And nobody around. Except scruffy chickens pecking in the dirt unperturbed, and a dog barking. This dog is a black mongrel-Labrador cringing by the rear door of the house, and when Irish climbs out of the pickup the dog shies away, barking and whining, as if it doesn't recognize him. Irish calls to the dog *Mick, what's wrong? Don't you know me?* But the dog cringes and whimpers and runs away around the corner of the house.

And that's the first strange thing.

This gaunt ugly old faded-red-brick house. Plastic strips still flapping over the windows, from last winter. Missing shingles, crooked shutters. The back porch practically rotted through. Streaks down the side of the house below the second floor windows from, it would be said in disgust, men and boys urinating out the windows. *A house with no woman living in it you can tell.* (Because Irish's mother had died a few years ago, and the family split up. In the papers and on TV it would seem so confusing, who lived in this house, and who did not. Suspicious-sounding like the way they'd identify Irish as *Ciaran McEwan* which was a name nobody knew, and always giving his age as *twenty-three.* Strange and twisted such facts can seem.)

That day, August 11, 1969, only just the old man Malachi and the oldest brother Johnny were actually living in the house. But other McEwans, including Malachi's thirty-six-year-old biker son from his first marriage, might drop by at any time or even stay the night. And there might be a woman Malachi'd bring back from a tavern to stay a few days. At one time there'd been six children in the family, four brothers and two sisters, but all except Johnny had moved away. Irish moved away immediately after his mother died to live alone, aged seventeen, in Strykersville, in a room above the barber shop, and to work at the lumberyard where my dad knew him, and liked him. Most Saturdays in August, Irish had off. And so he happened to turn up in Sanborn, a small town six miles away, near the lake, where it just happened that Kathlee was working in our aunt Gloria's hair salon like she does some Saturdays, but not every Saturday, and I was at the library for a while, and then at our grandma's. *These things just happened, like dice being shaken and thrown, or like a pinball game, no more intention than that. I can swear!*

Irish enters his father's house by the rear door saying he'll be right back. The black Lab (that Irish would say he'd known since it was a pup) is hiding beneath the porch. Kathlee says, *Oh Nedra, d'you think Irish likes me?* She's excited, can't hardly sit still, licking her lips peeping at herself in the dusty rear view mirror, and out of meanness I say guys like any girl who'll make out with them. Though I know it isn't true, an older guy like Irish would be used to kissing girls, and girls kissing him back, and plenty more beside that Kathlee, who's shocked by just words some of the boys at school yell, would never consent to.

Kathlee says, *Nedra you're not nice.* And I say, nudging her, in the waist where there's a pinch of baby fat Kathlee hates being teased over, *I guess you think you are? Kiss-kiss* I'm puckering my lips making the ugliest face I can.

Kathlee says, *Sometimes I hate you.*

So Kathlee's fired up and huffy, and climbs out of the pickup, and goes to the screen door that's rusted and has a broken spring, swinging open from where Irish has gone inside. She's wearing that blue-striped halter top sundress with the elastic waist and short skirt that makes her look like a doll, and her fluffy-wavy hair to her shoulders, and her cheeks sort of flushed and slapped-looking from the excitement. *Because Kathlee Hogan isn't the kind of nice girl you'd expect to be seen with a boy like Irish McEwan.* She's calling, *Irish? Irish?* in a breathy little voice nothing like you'd hear from her if it was just me, her sister, close by. And after a minute or so, she goes to look inside the screen door, saying, *Irish? Can I come in?* and I'm surprised, Kathlee opens the door and turns back to me and sticks out her tongue, and disappears inside like this is a house she's been inside before, and I know for sure *it is not.* And I jump down out of the pickup, too. And (not knowing how stupid this behavior is, as I'd realize later) I'm squatting by the porch trying to see the black dog that's hiding beneath it, that I can hear panting and growling, and I'm cooing *Mick! Good dog! Don't be afraid, it's just Nedra.*

Like I'm God's gift to animals. If Irish McEwan is going to be Kathlee's boyfriend, I'm not jealous for I can talk to animals, some animals at least. As I don't wish to talk to humans.

But the dog won't come to me, and I'm fed up and restless, and I follow Kathlee into the McEwan house, like this is a kind of thing I'm accustomed to doing. And stepping inside I feel shivery right away, and my heart starts kicking in my chest. That kitchen! A real old refrigerator, and a filthy gas stove, and a plastic-topped table covered with dirtied plates, and more dirtied plates in the sink, and grease-stained walls and a high ceiling that's all cobwebs and cracks. A sickish smell of old burnt food. And a darker smell like fermenting apples. And worse. And I'm wiping at my eyes, and almost can't see. You'd think I would be calling *Kathlee? Kathlee? Irish?* but it's like my tongue has gone numb. I'm wearing just a tank top and denim cut-offs and rubber-thong sandals from the discount bin at Woolworth's. Wet from Olcott Beach where we'd been running in the surf. And my straggly hair that's dishwater blond, not a soft pretty color like Kathlee's, sticking in my face. And there's Kathlee in the doorway, her back to me. She's looking into the front room (that would be called in the news stories the "parlor," not the living room) and it seems to me I can see her spine shivering, though she isn't moving just standing there, and what I'm seeing also that's unexpected is a grandfather clock in the hall, not ticking, pendulum still, a tall handsome wood-carved clock with roman numerals and afterward I will learn that the clock belonged to Irish's mother, she'd brought it with her when she married Malachi McEwan. *Of course it's broken. Like everything in this house.* And there comes Irish up behind Kathlee. From a room off the hall. The bathroom, I'm thinking because Irish is wiping his hands on his thighs like he's just washed them. Or maybe his hands are sweaty, he's sweated through his T-shirt. And there's this look on his face, hungry and scared, but when he touches my sister he's gentle, takes hold of her wrist between two of his big fingers, and Kathlee turns right away to look up at him, blank and trusting as a baby, or maybe she's stunned, in a state of shock, and and Irish slips his arm around her waist, and says words I can't hear, and Kathlee presses against him and hides her face and when Irish turns to walk her away, back through the kitchen and out of the house, I hide from them in a corner of the kitchen, and they don't see me. And I'm excited, I know there's something in the front room *I have to see.* I can smell it, I'm so scared I'm shaking, or maybe it's just excitement, like our cats excited and yellow-eyed and their tails switching when they smell their prey invisible and indiscernible to us, and irresistible. I'm Nedra, the pushy one. I'm Nedra, all elbows. Lucky your sister came first, folks teased, 'cause your mother might not've wanted a second one of *you*. I'm Nedra, I would've pushed past Kathlee in the hall if Irish hadn't stepped out of that room. So I run to the doorway in a house strange to me, pushy and nosy. And I see. I'm panting like that dog under the porch, and I see. I don't know what I am seeing, what the name or names for it might be, this sight is no more real to me than flicking through TV like I do when I'm restless and nobody's there to scold me. Maybe I'm smiling. I'm a girl who smiles when she's nervous or scared, for instance if boys look at me in a certain way and I'm alone, and nobody close by to define me, to know not *who I am* (because I would not expect that) but *whose daughter.* My nostrils are pinching with the strong smell, and I'm beginning to gag. There's something sickish-rotten like guts, and human shit, a shameful smell you recognize without putting a name to it. And I hear the flies. And see them. Where they're a buzzing cloud like metal filings on the broken heads of two men. Men I don't know. Adult men, one of them with thick white bloodstained hair. Blood and brains on the filthy carpet of this room that would be called the parlor. Like a child had smeared crimson Crayola marks across a picture. Splashed onto a worn-out old sofa and chairs. The bodies looked like they'd crawled to where they were. Blood-soaked workclothes, and blood in the ridges and crevices of what had been faces. Yet they were lying easy as sleep. The weirdness was to me, seeing adult men lying on the floor, and me standing over them almost! Thinking *Except for those horseflies they'd be at peace now.*

Kathlee. No, Irish McEwan was not my fiancé that day. Nor my boyfriend. All that, I explained.

I explained we'd been together every minute. Since late that morning around eleven, or eleven-thirty. To whenever time it was when the sheriff's men came, with their siren blasting, to the house. Irish was the one to telephone for help. He'd gone back inside the house, to use the phone. Yes: all those hours I was in his company. At first it was just Irish and me, then we went to pick up Nedra at Grandma's. Oh, all the places we drove, I don't know . . . We were talking and laughing. Listening to Tommy Lee Ryan, "Just Kiss Good-bye," and the Meadowlarks, "Sweet Lovin Time." And the Top Ten.

A dozen times I would be questioned, and always I would swear. I began to get sick, fainting-sick, in just entering one of their buildings. My parents would take me of course. But you never get used to it. People looking at you like you're not telling the truth. Like you're a criminal or murderer yourself! *Don't be afraid of them, honey* Irish would console me. *They can't do anything to you. They can't do anything to me either, I promise.* And I knew this was so, but I was filled with worry.

The last customer's hair I rinsed for my aunt Gloria was about ten o'clock, a walk-in. Then I did sweeping and cleanup and taking out trash etcetera into the alley. An hour of this, maybe. That's when I saw Irish McEwan driving past. On Niagara Street. Around eleven o'clock. A little later, I saw him parked by the bridge. Gloria said it was all right if I quit a little earlier, that time of summer is slow in the beauty salon. So I left around quarter to twelve, I'm sure. If Aunt Gloria remembers later, around one, oh she is mistaken but I never wanted to argue face-to-face. Always I was polite to older relatives, always to adults. You weren't rude, not in my family. I ran down the street to say hello to Irish McEwan whom my father knew. Yes, that was the first time. Like that. Yes, but I knew him. From Strykersville. No, I never knew his father or brother. His father they called old man McEwan. (Not that Malachi McEwan was truly old: in the paper, his age was given as fifty-seven.)

Yes, Irish knew my name. He said it—*Kathlee.* It was my baby sister's name for me from when she couldn't pronounce *Kathleen.* So everybody called me *Kathlee,* that was my special name and I liked it.

We were talking and kidding around and Irish asked if I'd like to ride a little and I said yes, so we did, then he asked how'd I like to drive to Olcott Beach, which is nine miles away, and I said yes I would except we have to take my little sister Nedra, she's at our grandma's. So we went to pick up Nedra, where she was slouched on the glider on Grandma's porch reading. What time was this, maybe twelve-thirty. That Nedra! She was a fanatic about books. Every Saturday she'd return books to the library and take out more books and she had cards for two public libraries, and still that was hardly enough for her. She would go to college and be a librarian or a teacher everybody predicted. The first in the Hogan family to go away to school. I would have been the first to graduate from high school, except marrying Irish McEwan like I did in my junior year, I had to drop out. You couldn't be married at that time and remain in school. It just wasn't done. You'd be expelled. Nobody questioned this just as nobody questioned the Vietnam War. (Remember that war?) These days a girl can be pregnant and unmarried and she'll be welcome to stay in school, nobody protests. At least, not officially. It's an enlightened time today in this new century, or a fallen time. It's a more merciful time, as a Christian might see it, or it's a time of no shame. But then in the early

1970's where we lived in Eden County in upstate New York we were the people we were, and when Irish McEwan and I married I dropped out of school, and was happy to be a wife to him, and soon a mother. Good riddance was how I felt, leaving Strykersville, people talking about us like they were. Even so-called nice people. Even my friends. Because they were jealous. Because I was so happy, and had my baby thirteen months after we were married (I know, everybody was counting months), and nobody was going to cheat me of what I deserved. I swore on the Holy Bible that Irish McEwan had been in Sanborn by eleven o'clock that morning and he'd been in my company for hours and when we drove to his father's farm he was never out of my sight for more than a few seconds, and never until then saw what was inside the house. It was a pure shock to him. But his first thought was for me. *Kathlee* he said *no you don't want to see.* He was white-faced and trembling but his first thought was of me. He pulled me from the doorway, and I didn't see. He said they'd been struck down by shotgun blasts, that was what it seemed to him. He was not excited or hysterical but calm-speaking, yet he was mistaken about this. Also, Irish said he knew who'd done it, but afterward he wouldn't repeat these words, he'd never repeat them again even to me, even after we were married. And moved away from Strykersville. And the farm (which was mostly mortgaged) was sold.

No. Nedra never went into that house. She was in Irish's pickup in the driveway. She was afraid to get out because of the dog barking. She says she followed me inside, and she saw the dead men, but that's just Nedra making things up. She was always nervous, and saw things in the dark.

Anything physical, that wasn't in a book, Nedra could not handle. For all her pushy behavior and sarcasm. Yes, she was smart, she got high grades, but there were things she didn't comprehend. She'd never have an actual boyfriend. The boys who might've liked her, she scared off with her smart-aleck remarks, and the other boys, they'd never give a plain skinny girl like Nedra a second glance. She was scornful of them too, or pretended to be. Saying to me, after Irish and I were married and living in Yewville, and Holly was about a year old, in this earnest quivering voice *Kathlee, how can you let it be done to you? What a man does? Doesn't it hurt? Or do you get used to it? And having a baby, doesn't it hurt awful?* I was so surprised at my sister saying such things, I laughed, but I was angry, too. I said *Nedra! Watch your mouth. This baby could pick pick up such talk, and remember years later.*

Nedra. And somebody comes up behind me to touch my shoulder. Where I'm just standing there. And it's Irish, and he's gentle with me like he'd been with Kathlee, saying my name, *Nedra,* which was strange on his lips, saying I'd better come outside with him, and not look any more.

Like there's danger he must rescue me from. There *is* danger, and he will rescue me from it.

Not holding me as he'd held Kathlee. But he took my hand, that was numb as ice, like I'm a little girl to be led away, he brings me dazed and blinking and stumbling back outside where Kathlee is crying and whimpering, saying *Oh! oh! oh!* but I'm not crying, and I won't cry, it wasn't real to me yet. Or, I was thinking *Who are they, nobody I know. Why should I cry.* But a hot acid mash comes boiling up out of me, my stomach, and I'm vomiting, spattering the ground at my feet and onto my yellow rubber-thong sandals from Woolworth's I would throw away forever, after that day.

I would not be a witness. I would not give a statement. I was thirteen years old and the county argued I was not a child, I was old enough to provide a statement they argued, but my parents told them yes I was too young, I was an immature girl for my age, and what I believed I might have seen wasn't necessarily to be believed. For Kathlee swore she'd seen nothing inside the house, and Kathlee insisted I had not even gone inside. *Because she was jealous. Irish McEwan leading me out of the house, holding my hand. That red-haired boy with the dark eyes, treating her sister tenderly.*

My eyes were never the same since. In the fall, I would be diagnosed as myopic in both eyes, and would have to wear glasses, and nobody can believe my eyes were perfect before what I was made to see, and my life changed. In a few years, I would "see" without glasses just vague blurry things, and partly this was my habit of reading, reading, reading all the time including late at night, with just a single lamp burning, but mostly it was because of what I saw at the McEwan farm that day, that my sister Kathlee would deny I ever saw! *Nedra you know you're imagining it. You never went anywhere near that house. Irish says he doesn't remember you inside. There was so much happening, and none of it had to do with you.*

I would wish to God I'd never gone to Sanborn that day. Or I would wish I'd stayed at Grandma's. I had my library books, and I was helping Grandma cut out a dress pattern in tissue paper, sticking in the straight pins, and holding it up against me. (A wool plaid jumper for me. That ever afterward, when I wore it, I would have a sickish feeling.) When Irish and Kathlee came by to get me, I would not know what time it was. It was after lunch, but how long, I don't know. They would inquire of Grandma, too, and she was confused and obstinate, and finally they gave up in disgust because if Grandma said one thing, next morning she would wish to change it, and finally they gave up on me. Because I could not contradict my sister who was so certain what she knew. I could not contradict my sister who swore what she believed to be true while in my state of nerves I could not swear what was true, nor even what I believed might be true. Was it past two o'clock they came for me, in the steel-colored Ford pickup with rusted grillwork, pulling up at the curb outside Grandma's house, or was it before noon, *I could not swear.* I would not say either time. For what a surprise to see my sister Kathlee with any boy, happy and waving at me, let alone that red-haired Irish McEwan everybody knew. When you're thirteen, being driven around in a twenty-three-year-old's pickup, and at Olcott Beach on the boardwalk and running along the beach laughing and squealing like girls you've seen all your life, with guys, but never dreamt it could be you, you are not able to retain a clear picture of what did, or did not, happen. Especially if it is hurtful of those close to you.

Nedra, you know. Just tell the truth.

It was before noon Irish came for me. It was only just a few minutes later, we came for you at Grandma's. You know!

He couldn't have been at the farm. When it happened. He was with me at the time they said it happened. Every minute, Irish was with me. Nedra, you know!

But I wish I didn't. Even now a long time later. Mr. McEwan and his son Johnny had been seen alive by a neighbor around noon of that day. The coroner ruled they'd been killed between that time and approximately 2 P.M. But Kathlee had seen Irish in Sanborn as early as 11:30 A.M. She would swear. So Irish could not have been the murderer, that was a fact. *Nedra, you saw him, too. Say you did. Say you did! Just say what's TRUE.*

But I could not. I became dizzy, and stammered; and shook so bad, it was speculated I might be "epileptic." That was when my eyes began to worsen. For I could not swear what I had seen, because Kathlee insisted I had not seen it, how then could I swear what I had not seen?

The look in my sister's eyes! Like mica glinting in the sun.

The change that came over my sister, and would never go away. *She is in love. She isn't Kathlee now.* So fierce, I believed she might have clawed out my eyes like a cat. But even earlier, at Olcott. A wildness in her. For no boy had ever kissed her before that day as Irish McEwan kissed her (I'm sure of it!) where they drifted off away from me. Where I stood barefoot in the smelly surf tossing broken clam shells out into the lake. Calling after them jeering *Kiss-kiss! You're disgusting! I hate you both!*

But the wind blew my words away.

Wished I hadn't gone to Olcott with them that day. And on that ride to the McEwan farm! Irish had been drinking but was not drunk I'm sure. He was excitable, and jumpy, but you could say that was only natural because he feared the old man who was known for his bad temper and his cruelty to his wife and children. For sure, Irish's father had beaten them all. It would come out in the papers. And you could say that the dog Mick who'd known Irish all its life was frightened of him that day and ran under the porch to hide had been terrified by the murders, the screaming and shouting, and by the awful smell of death that all animals can identify.

The flies! I feel them brushing my lips sometimes. My eyelashes. Wake up screaming.

The ax, no I did not see any ax. (Never would the *murder weapon* be found. People said he'd buried it or dropped it in the Yew River.) I saw no ax in the front room, but I would later learn the murder weapon was a double-edged ax, investigators concluded; and the McEwans' ax was missing from the farm, never to be found. In the first shock of seeing the bodies Irish would think his father and brother had been killed by shotgun blasts. And Irish would say to us, he knew who the murderer was. He knew! Saying in a dull slow voice *There's somebody wanted Pa dead for a long time, now it's happened.* But when the police came, Irish would not tell them this. He would tell no one these words, ever again.

I never lied, because I never gave testimony. And if I had sworn, I would not have lied because I could not remember except what was confused and rushing as a bad dream. I was a plain girl with a silly streak and I would grow into a plain woman with a melancholy heart. Except when I look at my niece Holly, then my heart swells with something like happiness. For I love this child like my own. For I have never had any daughter, and never will. It's true that I have a certain weakness for my students (I teach seventh-grade English at Strykersville Junior High) and in their eyes I am Miss Hogan, one of the no-nonsense, funny, enjoyable teachers, for I hide my melancholy from them, but my affection isn't very real or lasting and as soon as school ends in June, I cease to think of the children and will scarcely remember them in the future. Maybe I am not a happy woman but I believe that happiness is a region in which we can dwell, if only for brief periods of time. And when I am with Kathlee and Holly my niece, I dwell in such happiness. For they are my family, mostly; and when I am with them I behave like a happy woman, and so it might be so.

Kathlee. The fact is, Irish McEwan *had not been* at his father's house that morning, he *first saw the bodies past 5 P.M.* of that day, stopping at the farm with Nedra and me. But many were doubtful of him, at first. For a long time it was hard. How people want to believe the worst, oh I came to know how people are, even Christians: in your hearts mean and malicious and hurtful. And yet—meeting Irish as people did, looking into his eyes that were a warm rich brown, a burning-brown, almost black, those beautiful eyes, you would see the goodness in him, and come to believe him, too.

The police questioned so many men, why'd anybody wish to focus upon Irish? Yet there are people who wish to believe the worst: that a son would murder his father (and his older brother!) in such a terrible way. But what about Melvin Hooker who lived next door, it was known there was an old feud between him and the McEwans,

Malachi had shot one of Hooker's dogs claiming it had killed some of his chickens. And there were men Malachi owed money to, scattered about. And his son Petey he was always fighting with. And the Medinas, the family of Malachi's deceased wife Anne, who bitterly hated Malachi for his treatment of her. It was said that Malachi had ceased to love and respect his wife during her first pregnancy, and she would have six children! By the time she was wasting away with breast cancer, and bald from chemotherapy, Malachi made no secret of his revulsion for her, even to their children. And made no secret of his affairs with women.

Like the wind in the dried cornfields the whisper came to me. *If ever a man deserved death. And a hard death. If ever a man deserved God's vengeance.*

But Irish was not one to speak ill of the dead. In all things, Irish was respectful. We were married in the Methodist Church and our baby baptized in that faith. In time, my mother came to accept my husband and even, I believe, to love him. My father, being ill with diabetes, and set in his mind against us, never came to truly know Irish nor even, to that old man's shame, his beautiful granddaughter.

Irish said, *He's a good man, Kathlee. But troubled in his heart.*

Irish said, *He's an old man. It isn't for us to judge him.*

It was a fact, Irish McEwan and I were deeply in love when we got married. But it was not to be an easy marriage, with such a shadow over us, like great bruised-looking clouds over Lake Ontario you look up and see, surprised, where a few minutes before the sky had been clear. For people persisted in saying mean things behind our backs. For it was not easy for Irish to keep a job, which was why we moved so often. And there was Irish's weakness for drinking, like all the McEwan men, his only true reliable happiness he spoke of it, shamefacedly, wishing he might change, yet finding it so very hard to change, as I could sympathize, for I had such a bad habit of smoking, like a leech was sucking at me with its ugly lips, for years. Yet it was a fact: Irish was a good husband, and a good father, as far as he could be. I understood he was troubled in his mind, that the true murderer of his father and brother was never arrested. He seemed to know and to accept who it was. That first hour, at the farm, when he'd discovered the bodies, and shielded me from seeing, where I had come up behind him like a silly little fool, he'd known who it was, most likely, the murderer, but never would he say. Never, questioned by police, would he accuse another, even to defend himself.

Tell them what you know, honey. I begged him.

What do I know? Irish asked, lifting his hands and smiling. *You tell me, baby.*

Of course, all the McEwan sons were questioned by police. The thirty-six-year-old biker who lived in Niagara Falls, and had a criminal record, Irish's half-brother, was a strong suspect. But nothing was ever proven against him. Like Irish, Petey McEwan could account for where he was at the time of the murders. And it was miles away. There was a woman who claimed he was with her, and maybe this was so.

The family farm was only twelve acres. Mostly mortgaged from a Yewville bank. In time, the property would go to Malachi McEwan's surviving sons and daughters, but it would be near-worthless after taxes and other assessments, and not a one of the heirs would wish to live there, nor even to visit it, as I said to Irish we might do, one day, a crazy idea I guess it was, but an idea that came into my head, and I spoke without thinking, *Honey, why don't we drive out to the farm before it's sold, and show Holly?*

Holly was just two years old then. We were living in Yewville.

Irish said, *Show Holly what?*

The farm. Where you grew up. The land, the barn . . .

The house? You'd want to show her the house?

It's been cleaned, hasn't it?

Has it?

Well, I mean, and here I began to stammer, feeling such a fool, and Irish staring at me with this tight little smile of his meaning he's pissed, but trying not to let on—*hasn't it? Been cleaned?*

I had not looked into the front room. As Nedra claimed she had. I saw only just a blur, a dizziness before my eyes. There were vivid crimson blotches and a frenzied glinting (I would learn later these were horseflies! ugly nasty horseflies) but I saw nothing, and I did not know. And now Irish was waiting for me to answer—what? I could not even think what we'd been speaking of! My thoughts were so confused.

Then I remembered: yes, the house had been cleaned. Of course! How could such a property be sold, otherwise? After the police took away what they wished. Nobody in the McEwan family wished to do such a task, so the janitor at the high school was hired, and scrubbed the floorboards and the walls and whatever. And the filthy old blood-soaked carpet had been hauled away by police, for their investigation. So the "parlor" might now be clean. But we would never step into that place of death of course, I never meant that Holly would see that room! This I would have explained to Irish except—where had Irish gone?

Out in the driveway I heard the pickup start. He'd be gone through the night probably, and one day, some years into the future, when Holly was in junior high, he wouldn't come back at all.

That night I watched Holly sleeping in her little bed as often I did. Not in concern that she would cease breathing, as nervous mothers do, but in a trance of love for her. *Your grandfather had to die* the sudden thought came to me *that you might be born.* A great happiness filled my heart. A great calmness came over me. What I knew seemed too great for what I could comprehend in an actual thought, as a mother knows by instinct her child's need. As when I was nursing Holly, in a distant room I could feel her waking and hungry for the breast, and my breasts would seem to waken too, leaking sweet warm milk, and in my trance of love I would hurry to her.

For my life is about her, my baby. It is not about Irish McEwan after all.

Nedra. Those nights! When I couldn't sleep. When Kathlee didn't want to share a room with me any longer, saying I made her nervous, so I had to sleep in a tiny room hardly more than a closet, in the upstairs hall. When my eyes began to go bad, from so much reading. Bright-lighted pages (from a crook-necked lamp by my bed) and beyond the pages darkness. My eyes stared, stared at the print until it melted into a blur. And a faint buzzing began I would refuse to hear knowing it was not real. Sometimes then I would jump from bed to use the bathroom, or I would tiptoe to a window on the landing where some nights, by moonlight, you could see the lake a few miles away, a thin strip of mist at the horizon. Most nights there was only a thickness like smoke and no moon, and no stars.

For my niece Holly's second birthday I would give her a big box of Crayolas. Like the crayons I'd loved when I was a little girl. And we would draw together, my niece and I, and tell each other silly stories.

Holly used to laugh, and touch my cheek. "Auntie Nedra, I love you!"

The story of what I saw but had not seen. And what I had not seen, I would see and tell myself all my life.

FIRE

HAD IT BEEN arson? After the funeral she drove past the burnt-out wreck of her father's house at 819 Church Street, slowly. It was four days after the fire. But it was hard to imagine a fire where all was stillness, deadness. And a cold November wind. To her surprise she found she'd driven her car into the cul-de-sac at the end of Church, had to back the car up awkwardly, circle the block and drive past the burnt house a second time. She'd been warned not to do this. Still, she was doing it. She'd even brought a Polaroid camera from home, intending to take photos. But the sight of the ruin, which had once been her family's house, repelled her. There was death. A stink of burnt things, an odor of damp organic rot beneath. Perrysburg Township authorities had partly boarded up the doors and windows, ugly yellow tape stretched across the soot-blackened cobblestone posts of the veranda. CAUTION: DO NOT ENTER. Seen from the street, the doctor's old house still looked impressive, with its wide, squat veranda and stone facade, but from the side you could see how the bulk of the house was gone, stucco and wood collapsed in upon itself. The downstairs rear, where the fire had begun, was a blackened shell. Something whitely gauzy like a tattered flag blew in the wind from a broken window on the second floor, where Vivian's room had been. The back stairs were exposed, and skeletal. The adjoining garage, that in another era had been a stable and carriage house, was mostly destroyed. The tall splendid oaks beside the house, that Dr. West had so loved, were ravaged. The eight-foot redwood fence at the front of the property, erected as a barrier against increased traffic and noise on Church Street, had been knocked down by firefighters and lay in sections. For much of a night the fire had "raged out of control" as the local papers had reported. "Thousands of gallons of water" had been dumped on the residence by Perrysburg firefighters. The cause of the fire was "under investigation" but "faulty" electrical wiring, commonplace in older homes in the city, was suspected. An elderly retired physician, Dr. Maynard West, 83, sole occupant of the house since his wife's death in 1994, had "lost" his life in the blaze.

Lost! The poignancy of the word struck Dr. West's daughter.

She wondered: How do you *lose* a life, where do you *lose* your life to, if your life is *lost* can it ever be found? If so, by whom? Or will it remain simply *lost,* in perpetuity? Vivian smiled, considering. Maybe there's a cyberspace of *lost lives, lost souls.* Like Hades, where bodiless wraiths drift about like stroke victims, baffled by the cruelty of their fate.

"Oh, shit." Another time, she'd unknowingly driven her car into the cul-de-sac and would have to turn it around. As if she didn't recognize these familiar surroundings. As if she hadn't lived in that house, on this street, for eighteen years; as if the old, lost neighborhood of her childhood in Perrysburg, New York, wasn't more real to her than where—wherever—she lived now.

THIS SENSATION OF floating. This dryness in the mouth. Like a drug rush except no drug coursed in her veins. Maybe it meant, now both Vivian's parents were gone, she was—what? Free?

She'd stammered something like that to her brother Harvey when he'd first called. The shock of it. The wrongness. And the suddenness. "They're both gone, Harvey? Our *parents?*"

At the funeral home relatives warned Vivian not to check out her old house just yet. They knew her shaky medical history. "You'll only upset yourself, Vivian." She'd said, with the brashness of a twelve-year-old, "It's appropriate to be upset, isn't it, when your father has just died?" She spoke louder than she'd meant to speak, attracting attention. Anger flared up in her swift as flames, now she wasn't medicated against such fits of emotion, and wasn't drinking. But she hadn't said *When your father has died a horrible death, burned to death.* She'd stopped herself before uttering these words.

In fact he'd died, according to the coroner's report, of smoke inhalation which had precipitated cardiac arrest. He'd died in terror, maybe that was worse than being burned alive, unknowing in his bed.

In the *Perrysburg Journal,* it was grimly noted that the "badly charred remains" of Dr. West had been recovered from the fire. Vivian was wondering how a pathologist could examine such remains. She was wondering, staring at the closed casket, what those remains looked like. But her mind wasn't capable of such a feat. She couldn't even recall clearly what her father had looked like in life: the last time she'd seen him, six months before, and he'd hugged her good-bye and she'd involuntarily steeled herself against the new, peculiar smell of his breath that was like copper pennies held in the moist palm of a hand . . . She did think it was strange, a matter for ironic commentary, that the "badly charred remains" of an elderly man who, frail with myriad illnesses, had weighed less than one hundred forty pounds at the time of his death, required such a large, lavish, gleaming-ebony receptacle. Dr. West had ridiculed such excess. And seeing that he'd died in a fire, why hadn't Harvey and the other relatives arranged to have his remains cremated? Vivian's father had been the most practical and unsentimental of men, and he'd had a sense of humor.

Ashes to ashes, dust to dust. The poetry of death.

Vivian began trembling badly. There was something here so large she couldn't get her mind around it. The compulsive swallowing was getting worse. She knew that people were regarding her critically. Clinically. She was too thin in a shapeless black jersey dress that fell nearly to her ankles. She'd hidden her raw-aching eyes behind oversized black-plastic-rimmed very dark sunglasses that gave her, a lanky, pasty-skinned woman of fading beauty, the druggy-chic look of a rock singer of some bygone, depraved era. The seventies? She'd been born in 1966, which seemed to her, in a galaxy hurtling through space at a vertiginously fast speed, a very long time ago.

"Viv. C'mon, don't be like that. They're only trying to be nice." It was her brother Harvey, speaking in an undertone, gripping her arm. In this gathering, Harvey was the only individual, male or female, who had the right to grip her arm at the elbow and exert the pressure of authority; a pressure that hinted at coercion, actual pain. "They're in a state of shock, too. You're not the only one."

Vivian had no idea what Harvey was talking about. She whispered, "It was arson, wasn't it? In that neighborhood." For there'd been a number of suspected-arson fires in past years in the old Church Street neighborhood, which had changed, deteriorated you might say, since Harvey and then Vivian had left home in the mid-eighties. The large, handsome, single-family homes had been mostly converted to multifamily dwellings or office buildings; there were scattered vacant houses taken over by drug users and prostitutes in the grungy blocks near downtown Perrysburg and the river. After their mother's death Harvey and Vivian had urged their father to sell the house and move elsewhere, to a condominium or retirement village in a suburb, and for years he'd resisted. Harvey had arranged for a burglar and fire alarm system to be installed in the house but, perversely, their father neglected to activate it. He wasn't a paranoid old man, he said. He got along with his neighbors. And this house is the house of my happiness, he'd told them. My happiness that isn't likely to come again.

Harvey was telling her not to bring that subject up. Not here.

"Arson means murder. Somebody murdered our father."

A sudden scissor-flash of light on the ebony basket. A line of poetry drifted into Vivian's mind, as if out of that light. In times of stress, poetry was her consolation. But only stray lines, like shreds of cloud blown across the night sky. *Things as they are are changed upon the blue guitar.*

Meaning what? That the blue guitar was impervious to fire?

AFTER THE BURIAL Vivian left the cemetery without a word to anyone. Without a backward glance. Unlike Lot's wife, she wasn't going to be turned, in a heartbeat, into stone. Not Vivian West! She was observed to be unsteady in her high-heeled black shoes. Her hair that looked dyed black, too jet-black and lustrous for a woman on the down-side of thirty-five, was windblown, disheveled. Her crimson lipstick was smeared too thickly on her mouth and she was breathing through her mouth. Though she wasn't medicated, and had not been drinking. Not yet that day.

Harvey said, in explanation, "Viv's in a state of shock. Let her alone."

DRIVING ALONG CHURCH STREET, gripping the steering wheel of her car tightly . . . *I do what I want to do.* It was a brash statement of Vivian's girlhood. Now she was an adult, the boast seemed quaint.

For rarely do you know what you want. Even after you've done it you can't say clearly if that was what you'd wanted or just something that happened to you, like weather.

Three times she circled 819 Church before parking at the curb. The driveway was blocked by a sawhorse festooned in ugly yellow tape. CAUTION: DO NOT ENTER. At a nearby corner children were playing in the street, young black children shouting at one another. This had become a neighborhood of many children. And adolescents staring after Vivian's car. When she got out of the car, carrying the Polaroid camera, someone shouted in her direction.

It was a shout she decided to interpret as playful, impersonal. Something like, "Hey lady!" She acknowledged it with a quick wave of her hand, turned away. Probably they'd think she was an official photographer. The camera belonged to her husband. Don't you think I should come with you? he'd asked uncertainly.

No. Vivian wanted to be alone with this grief, and with the guilt of grief.

It was still strange to her. She was married again after years of living more or less alone. He was assistant superintendent of the Rochester public schools. Twelve years older than Vivian, with two near-adult sons. Harvey had whistled at this news when Vivian told him. How'd you meet this guy? When did all this happen? Sounds good, Viv.

Harvey had meant, this one sounds safe.

Vivian was having difficulty holding the bulky camera steady. The smell of burnt things frightened her. She was trying very hard not to become nauseated. *No medication, never again. Raw reality for me.* She'd never been a junkie, she'd taken only legally prescribed drugs and yet those drugs had nearly destroyed her so you could argue that the rawest of reality was less of a risk. This, she'd vowed to her father who had seemed to believe her.

A perverse thought came to her: Did firefighters often smell the odor of burning human flesh? Cooked flesh? Obviously, yes. You get used to it, she supposed. Like everything.

The ruin of a house loomed above her. Before prices in the Church Street neighborhood began to fall in the mid-seventies, such a property in this revered residential neighborhood of Perrysburg would have been worth hundreds of thousands of dollars. Built today on the outskirts of the city, on the Niagara River, it would be worth as much as $1,000,000. Beautiful hardwood floors, elegant moldings and wainscotting, silk wallpaper, regal ceilings, French doors opening out onto a landscaped terrace . . . Vivian thought with a shudder that if her father had survived the fire, losing the house would have killed him.

Never leave the house of my happiness, how could I.

In the past year or two Vivian's father had become an aged, ailing man. A doctor doesn't expect to succumb to the commonplace symptoms of his patients. Vivian had invited him to sell the house and move to Rochester to live with her and her husband, but of course he'd refused. And she hadn't insisted. Because of course Vivian hadn't really wanted her father with her. She loved him, but at a distance. Dr. West had been restless, easily bored. No Florida retirement for Dr. West. He'd only reluctantly retired from his practice at the age of seventy-six, for health reasons, yet he'd continued to treat neighborhood patients *gratis.* He consulted at a local women's health clinic. He would have been miserable living with Vivian, or with anyone.

Now it was too late, now he was dead, Vivian felt repentance, and she felt guilt. The luxury of guilt that sweeps over us too late.

She stumbled in the churned, grimy snow. Looking for a way in? This was madness. Everywhere were warning signs. CAUTION: DO NOT ENTER. BY ORDER OF PERRYSBURG FIRE COMMISSIONER. Charred boards swung loose overhead, creaking in the wind. Broken glass lay underfoot. If she ventured inside what had once been the kitchen, debris might fall on her head. Why the hell are you doing this, didn't I warn you, Harvey might ask. Vivian had no reply except, This is my grief.

Overhead, ghostly shreds of curtains seemed to beckon to her, coyly.

She was breathing hard, through her mouth. The first several Polaroids she'd taken were something of a disappointment. They might have been of any burnt-out house, conveying no special significance or emotion. She hadn't counted on that.

Maybe she'd expected the spirit of her dead father to be dwelling in this place? Absurd.

There would be an official investigation into the fire but, apart from that, the stately old house at 819 Church Street, residence of Dr. Maynard West for more than forty years, no longer had meaning. *Things as they are are changed.* The property, two acres of land abutting a ravine and a wooded area at the rear belonging to the township, would be sold. The burnt-out ruin would be razed. Those heavy, round cobblestones rarely used as building materials any longer would be hauled away in dump trucks. The magnificent old oaks, taller than the house, would be uprooted, chainsawed, and ground to oblivion. Vivian was thinking that, if her father had died a natural death, the house would have been left to her and Harvey, jointly. That was the provision in Dr. West's will. Neither would have wanted to live in it, even Harvey who'd remained in Perrysburg, and lived in a high-rise condominium on the river, yet neither would have wanted to sell it, either. For once the past is gone, it's gone. Vivian had not been especially happy in that past but it was *hers.* As, stricken by nightmares in her late twenties, she'd still cherished such visions, for they were *hers.*

She smiled suddenly at an old memory. How, when they were children, Harvey and two friends had terrorized other neighborhood children, playing at jungle warfare along the banks of the ravine. The boys had carried sharpened spears decorated with black turkey vulture feathers. Harvey, ten years old, the chieftain, had striped his cheeks with red clay from the ravine. He'd been a husky, sly kid. Very smart, but rebellious at school. His gang had spared little Vivie because she was his sister. The reign of terror had ended after a boy nearly drowned in ditch water in the ravine, shoved and kicked over the side by Harvey and his gang . . .

Now Harvey West, thirty-eight, was a responsible adult, an investor in the successful Shop-Rite Mall at the edge of Perrysburg, a member of the Chamber of Commerce and the Rotarians. He'd followed their father's lead in investing in real estate and, Vivian supposed, he'd made some money. Always Harvey had been close-mouthed about his private affairs, including his love affairs. So she couldn't be certain.

Now the insurance money will come to us? Jointly? The thought was an unpleasant one: she didn't want to profit from her father's death. She didn't want an ounce of happiness, of pleasure, from an elderly man's suffering and death.

She didn't want Harvey to profit from it, either.

As she was waiting for the last of the Polaroids to develop, watching as mysterious shapes, lines, faint colors emerged out of a chemical-smelling void, the thought came to her: Maybe Harvey had set the fire?

The Boathouse. The Roostertail. Davy Deezz Gent's Club. Café a Go-Go. The Starboard. Good Times. First & Ten Sports Club. Mitch's Tavern & Bowling Lanes. Cruising Perrysburg's riverfront district as dusk came swiftly on. There was a shabbily romantic cocktail lounge called *Blue Guitar* in one of the downtown hotels, she seemed to remember. She'd been taken there years ago by a man whose name she couldn't now recall or didn't wish to recall though she recalled vividly that he'd been a married man, and she'd liked that: the thrill of trespassing, of taking something belonging to another. If only temporarily.

She never found *Blue Guitar.* But there was *Firs Inn & Marina* on the river. Near downtown police headquarters, it was said to be a popular hangout for off-duty cops. Neon flashed in every window. Behind the inn was the marina. A flotilla of sailboats. Flags on their tall masts whipped in the wind. Speedboats, yachts, rocked with the waves. In the vestibule of the inn, warm, smelly air rushed at her as if out of the past. Her heart quickened. How relieved she was to be here. To have avoided the relatives. The funeral luncheon given by a younger sister of her father's. There the relatives murmured, scolding, Now where's Vivian? And Harvey would repeat, She's in shock. I told you, let her alone.

Harvey loved her. Harvey, her big brother. Harvey would protect Vivie even from himself.

Vivian stepped into the dimly lighted bar and quickly calculated where to sit: at the bar, or in one of the booths. A booth was always a prudent idea. But at the bar she could catch fugitive glimpses of her face in the mirror behind rows of glittering bottles. In her thirties, somehow she'd become a woman who looked her best in tawdry lights. Flashing neon like a fevered pulse. She was relaxed, she was prone to laughter. Even when she'd been a serious graduate student in English literature, even when she'd been a promising assistant professor at the State University of New York at Binghamton she'd rewarded herself for bad times by visiting such places.

Vivian sat at the bar. Except for an amorous couple, the girl in a leather miniskirt and fishnet stockings, bouffant hair, the other eight or nine patrons at the bar were men. She ordered a scotch on the rocks. The bartender was trying not to be curious about her, she hoped to Christ she hadn't gone to Perrysburg High with him.

Drinking clarified. Confusion dissolved. She smiled to think that from a certain perspective all of that day of her father's funeral including the vision of light flashing out from the closed casket had been leading to this moment of grace: Vivian's first serious drink in months.

She wanted to be alone, she would have said. When a husky bearded man with a familiar face, seated a few stools away, leaned over to say hello, asked if she was Vivie West, Vivian shook her head without engaging him. But a while later, when she was about to order a second drink, another man drifted past, carrying his drink, she glanced up and their eyes locked and he asked, O.K. if I join you? and Vivian indicated yes, it was O.K. The man was no one she knew, she was certain. He was about forty years old. He looked married, but he wasn't wearing a ring. He slid onto the stool beside her, brushing against her arm. He squinted at her, seeing a melancholy face. A very pale face. She'd penciled in dark boldly defined eyebrows. She'd outlined her eyes in black mascara like eyes in a Matisse painting. Her mouth was fleshy, pouting. In her car, before coming inside, she'd removed her wedding ring. Her companion was saying, "Some people, some women, don't like cops so I'll tell you right off: I'm with the PPD."

Vivian laughed. "I'm not 'some women.' "

They exchanged first names. They even shook hands. He was a plainclothes office, a detective. Desire coursed through her suddenly like an electric current.

"I DON'T KNOW him. I don't trust him. I adore him."

It was her brother Harvey she spoke of, to herself. For driving to Perrysburg on the occasion of her father's terrible death was also driving to Perrysburg to meet with Harvey. Always Vivian's heart stirred with urgency, part tenderness, part dread, when she thought of her brother.

Through childhood he'd been Vivie's protector. Through much of her girlhood. Her girlfriends had envied her an older brother; an older brother with such swaggering style. When you're a girl in public school to have a brother three years older means being spared the gauntlet of boys' rude appraising stares, sniggering remarks and innuendos, muffled laughter. When a boy took Vivie West out on a date he was taking out Harvey West's younger sister. "I was treated with respect because of you," Vivian told Harvey once they were adults, and spoke calmly of the past. "Maybe you never realized that."

Harvey said, "Sure I knew it. Any guy who looked at you cross-eyed, I'd have punched him out."

They laughed together, startled. As if excited by the prospect.

In recent years, as their widower-father aged, Vivian and Harvey, his only children, were more in contact with each other of necessity. Harvey, who lived in Perrysburg, took on responsibilities he might not have anticipated as a younger man; Vivian, living ninety miles away in Rochester, returned more frequently to Perrysburg, and spoke more frequently on the phone with her father and with Harvey. A noose tightening, she'd felt it.

But no. She loved her father. And she loved Harvey, if at a distance.

Harvey had been reporting to Vivian how forgetful their father was becoming, and how furious he was if you brought up the subject. Harvey had said, laughing over the phone, "I'm getting afraid of the old man. He's got a sting like a hornet." Vivian too had noted the accumulating dirt in the household. A smell of stale, unwashed things. And her father's personal odor, of which she would no more speak than she would have uttered an obscenity in his presence. Vivian and Harvey discussed the possibility of hiring, over their father's objections, a younger, more reliable cleaning woman, but finally decided, no. "Not just Dad would be so angry, but Mrs. Lunt"—always they spoke of the heavyset black woman by her formal name, respectfully, as they'd been taught—"would be broken up. And her sons . . ." Harvey's voice trailed off irresolutely. Vivian thought: Is he afraid of them? Of what they might do to Dad?

After the fire Vivian would wonder if Mrs. Lunt's sons had anything to do with it. While she and Harvey still lived at home there had been talk of Mrs. Lunt's several sons in trouble with police; they'd spent time in juvenile facilities, and eventually in prison.

But when Vivian brought this possibility up to Harvey he'd responded with annoyance. "Look, Viv. The police chief said he thought it was probably the wiring, or a space heater. Remember that antiquated space heater of Dad's? Don't fantasize about this accident. And don't start thinking *race.*"

Vivian felt her face burn, so rebuked.

Still she thought: Dr. West had believed that the neighborhood revered him, which may have been true, generally. But there had been break-ins, acts of vandalism, over the years. Harvey had had the burglar alarm installed after someone broke into their father's office looking for drugs and cash. "Dad wanted to think everyone loved him but maybe not everyone did. It would only have taken one. Maybe the fire was to cover up a burglary, maybe to cover up an assault . . ." Vivian spoke quietly. She refrained from saying *a murder.*

Harvey shrugged. The subject offended him, clearly. He told again of how forgetful their father was becoming, and how he'd allowed stacks of medical journals and other magazines to accumulate in the downstairs, rear rooms of the house. Harvey had questioned the wisdom of their father saving, for instance, copies of *Science* and *The New England Journal of Medicine* dating back to the seventies. The seventies! Thirty years! " 'How can I throw anything away without having read it thoroughly?' Dad asked me, like he was explaining something to a moron, 'and if I've read it, underlined and annotated it, and it's valuable, how can I throw it away?' "

They laughed uneasily together, Harvey had so perfectly mimicked their dead father's voice.

It wasn't at that moment that Vivian first thought *Did you set the fire, Harvey? I would hate you if you had. But I would never betray you.* This thought came to her afterward, as she stared at the Polaroid image of a barricaded doorway and blackened stucco materializing slowly before her eyes.

HE WAS EXPLAINING to her that arson is usually easy to detect, if set by an amateur.

"A legitimate fire is an accident. It takes time to spread. It smolders, half the time it goes out. It moves unevenly through a house, erratically. Not like a fire started with an accelerant, like kerosene, lighter fluid, that moves in a direct line, and fast. And hot. An accidental fire begins low and moves up, in a room I mean. And in a house. Of course, if it begins in an upstairs room or an attic, that's different. And if there's combustible material. But most accidental fires it's bad wiring, space heaters too near curtains or they get knocked over by kids, candles that fall over, sparks out of a chimney, somebody's smoking in bed and falls asleep, or, this happens with old people, they put a kettle on the stove, walk away and forget it . . . Each fire has its own history, they say. Like the family it happens to." He was speaking matter-of-factly, professionally. Vivian was listening in a way that might be described as professional. No interruptions, no evident emotion. She'd told him why she was in Perrysburg: a relative's death by fire. That terrible fire on Church Street. Sure, he knew about it. Possibly he guessed that Vivian was the elderly doctor's daughter but he was a tactful man, he let that go. If they saw each other again, she'd tell him then. Or maybe.

They'd moved from the bar to one of the booths. Where their conversation could be more private. They were on their third drinks. He was paying, somehow he'd finessed the move. Vivian who'd told him only her first name was thinking she wanted to take the man's dense, curly hair in her hands; wanted to embrace him, tight; because she didn't know him, he was all potential, mystery. His first name was Arnold—his friends called him Arne. "Arne." Vivian spoke the name as if testing it. *Arne. I want to make love with you.*

No, it wouldn't work. Vivian didn't want to make love with any man, even a plainclothes detective with the Perrysburg PD, whose name was Arne.

His last name, she'd later learn, was Malinski, Malinowski. She wouldn't ask him to repeat it or spell it. She wouldn't ask if he was married. Probably yes, but he was separated from his wife and feeling the strain, the loneliness, heavy-hearted, anxious about his children (for obviously there'd be children), and she hoped he wouldn't be bitter, angry at women because he was angry at a woman. Though if that was true she couldn't blame him, could she?

Roll a drum upon the blue guitar. Vivian smiled.

Her companion told her that there were fires, every winter especially, in the Church Street neighborhood, because of the old houses, and too many people living in some of them. "Usually it's small children who die. Single mothers, and they can't save them." Vivian nodded as if subtly rebuked. She liked this man's manner. He had authority but he wasn't a bully. He had knowledge inaccessible to her but he didn't flaunt it. He was allowing her to know: accidents happen, people die in fires, and some of these are young children, not elderly men.

And maybe he hadn't wanted to live, maybe at the end of his life that had been his secret. Vivian didn't want to think so.

Vivian asked the detective how he'd come to be such an expert on fires, it was the kind of remark a woman made to a man for whom she felt an attraction, not a serious remark entirely, though the man could take it seriously, as this man did, saying he wasn't an expert, what he'd been telling her was common knowledge. He didn't add *I'm a detective, are you bullshitting me, lady?*

Here was a man who didn't want flattery from a woman. Maybe that meant he'd be honest with her, too.

Which Vivian wasn't sure she wanted.

The point of picking up a man in a bar, the evening of your father's funeral, hadn't that much to do with wanting honesty, sincerity. She'd seen the detective glance at her ring finger, and wondered uneasily now if it was obvious she'd only just removed a ring; and what that signalled.

From time to time men passed by their booth, and Vivian's companion smiled and waved at them but didn't encourage them to linger, his friends, fellow cops. Vivian knew they must be curious about her. Who is Arne with? That woman averting her eyes, casually shielding her face with an uplifted hand. She dreaded someone recognizing her. Harvey had PPD friends. High school buddies. They'd know her as Harvey West's kid sister, all grown up.

She said, "If it's arson, then. You're saying it's easy to detect?"

Her words weren't so clearly enunciated as she'd wished. The alcohol coursing warmly through her veins, she felt illuminating her veins like Christmas lights, but now there was a swerve to the motion, like white water rapids in a river. A giddy sensation, she had to fight an impulse to laugh and grip the edge of the booth's table to steady herself.

He said, " 'Easy' to detect? I didn't say that. Not if the fire's done by a pro."

" 'Pro'—?"

"Professional arsonist."

Vivian stared at her companion. In the bar light his skin had appeared coarse, a sliver of scar tissue above his left eye. But he'd been smiling then, and he'd looked almost boyish, hopeful. Now, in this more refracted light, partly obscured by smoke from his own cigarette, his features were less distinctive, and she wasn't sure of the expression in his eyes. Did he think she was a fool? Was he calculating his chances with her, sexually? And what would be the consequence, if any? Or maybe, a detective now by instinct as well as training, he saw that she was in a state of something like shock, numbed, uncertain what she wanted from him, or from this conversation; a woman intent upon getting drunk, not by herself.

Faintly Vivian said, "I guess I didn't realize. That there are professional arsonists."

"Vivian, there's a professional everything."

Rebuked another time, feeling her face burn, Vivian excused herself and went to the women's rest room, a grimy pink-walled cubicle like the interior of a womb, and there was her skillfully made-up face in the mirror, startlingly young-looking and defiant. She fumbled for her cell phone in her bag, dialed Harvey's number. No answer. And no answering machine. "God damn you, Harvey. Where are you!" She used the lavatory and washed her hands and reapplied lipstick like a schoolgirl mashing it on. She wondered if he had a condom, obviously yes. Never would Vivian carry anything so incriminating, or so hopeful, in her bag. Now she was married, of course not.

Then she thought suddenly, He isn't waiting for me. He's gone. That will make it easier.

So convincing was this thought, when she saw that the detective who called himself Arne was waiting for her in the booth, with the patience of a lover, arms crossed, smoking a cigarette and squinting toward her, she was surprised. He had dark, thick hair trimmed high around his ears. He wore a nondescript dark coat, a white shirt, and no tie. She hoped to hell it wouldn't turn out he'd gone to school with Harvey, he was about that age. For a moment she saw desire in his face, too. The rawness of it, that registers as a kind of surprise, wholly unpremeditated. And something yearning, vulnerable. It was rare to see such an expression in a man's face, in such circumstances. What this man must know of women. What ugly truths no skill at makeup, charm, female subterfuge could disguise.

She must have appeared uncertain, wavering. A wan half-smile on her face. He was on his feet beside her, lightly touching her arm.

"Should we leave? Go somewhere? Is that what you'd like, Vivian?"

He spoke quietly. He wasn't trying to coerce her. Her name on his lips made her feel weak, fated.

"Yes," Vivian said. "That's what I'd like."

So that's life then. Things as they are.

She tried to recall the rest of it. *Picks its way on the blue guitar.*

HARVEY WAS ASKING where she'd been. In that mode of brotherly disgust that signalled he didn't expect a truthful answer. Like Vivian he carried himself cautiously, not wanting the crystalline honeycomb of his brain to shatter in this too-vivid daylight. Vivian wondered where Harvey had been drinking the night before, and with whom. "I tried to call you last night at the motel. No answer," he said.

Vivian had insisted upon staying at a motor inn in Perrysburg. Not with any of the relatives. Nor even with Harvey, who had a spare room. If she couldn't stay in her old room in the house at 819 Church Street she wanted to be alone with her grief, in neutral territory; the relatives could sympathize, even Harvey wouldn't have guessed how before she'd set out on her journey from Rochester she'd vaguely imagined, in the way of a fever patient fantasizing some measure of relief in which in fact she can't force herself to believe, cruising those downtown bars, finding a man.

Had it been in the *Blue Guitar* she'd found him? Vivian would try to remember it that way.

She said, defensively, "I called you, Harvey. Several times. No answer."

Harvey wasn't going to ask *Were you out drinking?* He wasn't going to remove her dark glasses to expose her eyes.

There was this unexpected tact, this delicacy of manner, in her brother. Not wanting to expose Vivian, or embarrass her. Or humiliate her. He didn't appear to be the type. He spoke of himself as a light-heavyweight, meaning in the vicinity of one hundred ninety pounds, he had a retired boxer's confidence in his body, a shrewd impassive face blunt as a shovel upon which he fitted wire-framed glasses with mother-of-pearl nosepieces. This side of Harvey, almost you might call it a feminine side, made him attractive to women, not always with good results for the women. He complained now he'd been damned worried about her, under the circumstances.

"Harvey, I'm sorry. I needed to be alone . . ."

It was mid-afternoon of the day following their father's funeral. They were in Harvey's seventh floor apartment overlooking the choppy, wind-tormented Niagara River. A treacherous river, especially above the Falls some miles away. A magnet for the melancholy, the self-punishers. You might imagine a swift easy death except death by Niagara Falls is so brutal, the dead are often unrecognizable. Vivian wasn't going to say *I'm not suicidal.*

High overhead Canadian geese flew in a precise V-formation, south. Always that was a pleasing sight. Like a compass pointing true north.

Vivian understood that her shrewd older brother saw something in her face this afternoon, a memory of the previous night, and the long dreamy hours of that night, he hadn't expected to see. But he couldn't know. As it turned out, Arne was acquainted with Harvey West but didn't know him well, and Vivian knew he had no reason to call Harvey. Not if he wanted to see Vivian again.

Harvey said accusingly, "Viv. What are you smiling at?"

He was teasing. But Vivian was smiling, staring after the geese.

She said, quickly, "Imagining Aunt Ida's luncheon yesterday. What they said of me. 'Poor Vivie! So *thin*'—the old biddies. Dad was well out of it, yes? He'd have been bored to death."

"Vivie."

She hadn't meant to say that. They laughed together like deranged children.

They sat at a table beside a sliding glass door, floor to ceiling, that led out to a balcony. Glaring sunshine, Vivian had a good excuse to keep on her dark glasses. Harvey had spread their father's legal documents and other papers on the table. He had practical things to inform her, ask her. Vivian had forgotten how tedious death can be. The aftermath, the tidying-up. Now we have no ritual dressing of the dead, no solemn washing, ointments, winding cloths, only just legal documents. The will, insurance policies. But there was also furniture, a few things spared from the fire ("But stinking of smoke") and many things in storage, inherited furniture from both their parents' families Vivian had forgotten. Some of these items were valuable antiques, maybe. Vivian had the idea that Harvey wanted her to ask for some of them, a sentimental gesture. But she wanted nothing. The Polaroid snapshots, which she'd shown her lover of the night before, revealed nothing, contained no suggestion of emotion, mere objects to break the heart in the raw light of day. Vivian nodded as Harvey spoke. He had a droning, punishing voice for such occasions. *This is fucking boring, I know. So you won't be spared, either.* Vivian interrupted to ask, "Did you know there are professional arsonists, Harvey? Men whose living is setting fires that can't be detected?" Vivian watched her brother sidelong. He was staring at her. "Well, of course you'd know. There's a professional everything, I guess."

Vivian could hear Harvey draw in his breath slowly. She wondered what he would say. But he said only, after a moment, "There isn't an arson that can't be detected by someone. I'm sure. I wish you'd get off the subject, O.K.? The fire is being investigated. If the insurer doesn't trust the verdict, the insurer will investigate, too. There's a lot of money involved. But we have other things to talk about."

"Arson would mean murder, Harvey. If our father was murdered, we would want to talk about that."

Harvey was tapping a pen against his glasses. He said meanly, "Maybe it was suicide, Viv. But we won't go into *that.*"

Vivian said excitedly, "Daddy wouldn't have wanted to die in such a way! He didn't believe in needless suffering. He had other options—barbiturates, morphine."

"Which can be detected. He'd know that."

Vivian said, stung, "Did Dad talk about things like that with you?"

Harvey said curtly, "He had to have someone to talk to. He was an old, sick man. I'm his son, see? I live here."

Vivian stammered, "I—loved him, too. I came to see him. I talked with him on the phone . . ."

Harvey shook his head impatiently, he'd had enough of the subject.

He had documents for Vivian to peruse. Legal forms she'd have to sign in the presence of their father's attorney. Vivian tried to concentrate but was feeling faint. The estate was larger than she'd expected. The property insurance, the life insurance. Real-estate investments. Several million dollars. But then she hadn't wanted to expect anything. She fumbled in her handbag for a tissue. In the handbag was the detective's card. The name was "Arnold Joseph Malinowski." He'd scrawled his home number in pencil below his PD number. She'd been right, he was separated from his wife. And from his children. His heart had been lacerated, she knew. But he spared her details. She'd spared him. They'd held each other through what had remained of the night. He was an ardent lover, hungry and desperate as Vivian herself. She'd experienced sharp, intense sexual pleasure, that echoed now in her memory. Her female body that possessed its own secret memory. She foresaw that her life would become mysterious again, rich and corrupt.

Death is the mother of beauty. The line of poetry floated to her like music. Never before had she taken it as true, only as paradoxical and annoying in the way that poetic paradoxes are annoying; now she saw that it might be true. In the right circumstances. She hadn't been able to cry for her father's death. His terrible suffering and death. Not until her lover had brought her to the point of breakage, collapse. Then she'd clutched at him like a drowning woman, she'd cried, she'd screamed and cried as she hadn't cried in years. In a delirium she murmured how she loved him, she loved him, a man whose name at that moment she could not have said. Near morning he told her if she wanted to see him again, call him. He gave her the card. He hoped she would call, very much. He'd drive to Rochester to see her. He wouldn't call her, wouldn't put pressure on her. He could love her, he said. Hearing these tender, absurd words Vivian bit her lower lip to keep from laughing. *But how can I love you, I'm dead inside. I'm a dead woman.*

Now, by day, watching geese fly in formation above the river, seeing scissor-flashes in the choppy waves, she felt differently. It was so simple: her life would take a new turn.

Vivid, florid, turgid sky.

"Vivie? You're listening to this, aren't you?"

"No. Yes. I'm sorry, Harvey."

"This is hell for me too, Vivie. I could use a drink, too."

"It's too early, Harve. We can't."

Harvey went to fetch them drinks. Splashed Johnnie Walker into two shot glasses. His, he downed smoothly, neatly. Vivian sniffed at hers like a doubtful child.

"He was so frightened, Vivie. I never expected it of him. He'd say, 'Don't tell your mother, I'm losing control of my bladder. Even during the day. I'd be so ashamed if she knew.' He'd say, grabbing my arm, 'Harvey, put me out of my misery. You'd do it for a dog.' "

Vivian said quickly, "Harvey, no."

"He said, 'Are you and your sister'—it was like he'd forgotten your name, Vivie—'waiting for me to go? You'd like that wouldn't you, you little shit.' "

Vivian wanted to press her hands against her ears. She wanted to slap Harvey's face and send those prissy glasses flying. "We don't don't have to have this conversation, Harvey."

"All right, then, Vivie," Harvey said, adjusting his glasses on his nose, "have it your way. We won't."

THE INSTRUCTOR

1.

SHE WOULD LONG remember: she'd taken no notice of him at first.

Kethy, Arno C. One of thirty-two names on the computer print-out. After the name was an asterisk and at the bottom of the page the asterisk was decoded: Special Student, Night Division. But most of the students enrolled in Composition 101 were in the Night Division of the university. They were all adults; some were conspicuously older than their twenty-seven-year-old instructor E. Schegloff who was a petite, smiling, tense woman looking much younger than her age. Her voice was husky and tremulous. "I realize that my name—Schegloff—" she pronounced it slowly, as a spondee, "—is difficult to pronounce and yet more difficult to spell, but please try. Any reasonable approximation will do." Was this meant to be humor? A few of the more alert, sociable students in the class laughed appreciatively while the rest sat staring at her.

Erma Schegloff would wonder afterward, with a stab of chagrin, if *Kethy, Arno C.*, had been one of those staring at her in silence.

I am not what I appear to be! I am so much more.

To be a young woman of hardly more than five feet in height, weighing less than one hundred pounds, is a disadvantage like disfigurement. Erma Schegloff's size had always seemed to her a rebuke to her ambitions and pretensions. Hadn't her parents reproached her years ago when she'd told them she hoped to teach *You! you're not strong enough! too shy! used to stammer!* She wore leather boots with a medium heel to give her a little height and a little authority. Temporary height and spurious authority but wasn't that often the case, in civilization? Her face was a striking, sculpted face like a cameo; plain and fierce as that likeness of Emily Dickinson, waif-woman with a secret, implacable will. Erma parted her fine dark wavy hair severely in the center of her head, Dickinson-style, and brushed it back and plaited it into a single thick bristling braid like a pony's mane thumping between her delicate shoulder blades. Her eyes were large and intelligent and inclined, when she was excited or nervous, to mist over. In the early morning, walking in the cold to the university swimming pool a quarter-mile from her rented apartment, Erma brushed repeatedly at her eyes, which wept without her volition; tears threatened to freeze on her cheeks. She wore no makeup and there were times when her pale skin glowed, or glared, as if she'd been scrubbing it with steel wool to abrade its predominant, feminine features. She had a dread of her male students gazing upon her with sexual interest, or indeed with any interest other than the academic.

Please respect me! I must succeed with you, I can't fail.

Erma Schegloff was a poet, though not writing poetry at the present time, an emotionally complicated time in her life; she was, more practicably, a Renaissance scholar, completing a Ph.D. with a dissertation on seventeenth-century visionary poetry (John Donne, Richard Crashaw, Henry Vaughan, George Herbert) at the elite main campus of the state university sixty miles away. She'd applied for this modestly paying teaching position because, she told her friends, she needed the money: she was helping to support her aging, ailing parents back in Pennsylvania. She'd wanted to test herself outside the rarified atmosphere of a graduate program of seminars and endless research projects. She'd wanted to become *adult*.

That first evening, her voice quavering with drama, Erma read the class list for Composition 101, enunciating the names (and what unusual names) with care; as if she were reading not a miscellany of sounds but a mysterious surrealist poem. She was young and romantic enough to believe it must mean something that these strangers, enrolled seemingly by chance in a remedial writing course, had been assigned to her, E. Schegloff, and would be in her care for twelve weeks. She meant to teach them everything she knew! *Brielli, Joseph. DeVega, Alban. Eldridge, E. G. Hampas, Felice. Hasty, Lorett V.* As she read off these names she glanced about the room, smiling and nodding as individuals murmured "Here" or "Yes, ma'am" or shyly raised their hands in silence. The classroom was oddly proportioned, wider than it was deep, with a high ceiling of hammered tin peeling pale green paint; antiquated fluorescent tubing hummed, as in a clinical setting; there was a faint hollow echo. *Inglas, Sylvan. Jabovli, Nada. Kethy, Arno C. Marmon, Andre. Poak, Simon. Portas, Marta. Prinzler, Carole.* And so to the end of the alphabetized list. An incantatory poem! But she'd taken no special notice of *Kethy, Arno C.*

Except, several hours later, in her apartment, restless still from the excitement of her first class, Erma began to read through the papers her students had written in response to an impromptu assignment—"Who Am I? A Self-Portrait in Words"—and was stunned by the unknown Kethy's composition.

WHO AM I

First thing is when your on Death Row long enough you don't ask WHO AM I because you have learnt nobody would be there anyway. And not seeing any face in the mirrer (because there is no mirrer trusted to you) you accept not having a face and so could be anybody.

I would say I saw you before tonight. Not knowing your name till now. INSTRUCTOR E. SCHEGLOFF. You were a beacon to me. You were shining all that time.

On Death Row where Id been condemned like an animal I swear the face I would see was yours. Not that long ago—5 weeks, 16 days. You were a sign MISS SCHEGLOFF that my luck would change. There was a lockup thru the facility (Edgarstown) becuse thered been trouble earlier. (Not on Death Row I mean, we were in our cells.) 1 hour of 24 for outdoor exercise.

Next day a guard took me to Visitors. Hed handcuffed my wrists tight to give pain. They hope for you to beg but I never did. He took me to Visitors. My lawyer was there I had not seen in a long time. Your conviction is overturned he says. I am not even sitting down yet, I tell him God damn I knew I was innocent. I tried to tell you all *eight years.*

It was your face E. SCHEGLOFF I beleive I saw in my cell that day. You knew me though I did not (yet) know you. You were saying, Arno dont give up hope. Arno, I am awaiting you. Never give up hope thats a sin.

But, I did not die. Its absolute truth I was innocent all those years. That was my plea.

Erma read and reread this composition. Indeed, it didn't seem like a composition, composed, but a plea from the heart; as if Arno Kethy were in the room with her, speaking to her. She'd begun to breathe quickly. She tried to recall Kethy from class: a smiling youngish black man with a pencil-thin mustache, at the back of the room? Or a blunt-faced Caucasian, in his late thirties, in black T-shirt and soiled work pants, hair in a ponytail? In the last row, by a window? She seemed to recall how when she'd called his name, this man had raised his hand furtively, only a few inches, and quickly lowered it, wordless.

Kethy had written his self-portrait in a tight, cramped hand on a single sheet of lined tablet paper. His sentences ran out to the edges of the paper. The letters of his words were clearly formed and yet the words were so crowded together, the effect was claustrophobic, crazed. That voice! Erma set the paper aside, shaken.

How different Kethy was from his fellow students:

Hello! My name is Carole Prinzler and I am 32 years old. Returning to school now that my youngest is started school (at last) and I have a chance to breathe now and then! My hope is to improve my writing skills and acquire work in Public Relations.

My name is Dave Spanos, 29 years old. I am a Post Office employee (downtown branch). I am a born resident of this city. I am also enrolled in Intro. to Computers (Wed. night). I am hoping to improve my skills to "upgrade" my statis at the P.O. where I have been selling stamps for 7 years at the counter. Though I enjoy such work, for I like people . . .

There was Eldridge, E. G., a round gleaming butterball of a black man in his fifties who wore a suit and tie and gave off a powerful fragrance of cologne. Turning his self-portrait in to Erma, he'd shaken her hand vigorously.

May I itroduce myself, I am the REVEREND E. G. ELDRIDGE of the Disciples of Jesus Christ. I am a proud resident of this city and of the City of God. I am a father of nine children and eleven grandchildren and a husband of many years. I am blessed with good health and a desire to improve my fellow man. Already you have given us faith, Miss Schegloff, with your opening words that we will write, write, and write like pratising a musical instrument—PRACTISE MAKES PREFERT.

Erma set these aside, and reread Arno C. Kethy's composition. What did he mean, he'd seen her face? In his cell? She smiled nervously. But it wasn't funny, of course. Kethy was serious. (She didn't want to consider he might be mentally unbalanced.) Why not interpret such extravagant thinking as poetry of a kind? Poetry in prose. A stranger's anguished yet intimate voice.

I seem to know him, too.

She smiled. Her heart was beating quickly. For the spring term she'd rented the cramped, austerely furnished upstairs of a run-down Victorian house near the university hospital grounds; the sound of sirens frequently filled the air, a wild, yearning cry that grew louder and louder and ceased abruptly, like lovers' cries. To hear, as a neutral observer, is to feel both involved and excluded. Erma wondered at the prospect before her. An unwilling witness to crises she couldn't control. But her landlady had assured Erma that she'd get used to the sirens—"We all have."

That night, she woke repeatedly hearing a man's yearning voice mixed with the sound of sirens real or imagined. Sitting up, not knowing at first where she was, Erma was panicked that someone might have broken into the apartment. But there was silence. Not even a siren.

On the door to her three-room apartment, as on the downstairs front door to the house, there was a reassuring Yale lock. And she could bolt her door, too, when she was inside.

THURSDAY EVENING, her second class, E. Schegloff resisted the impulse to look for *Kethy, Arno C.*

E. Schegloff, Instructor. What a mystery that, as soon as she stepped inside the classroom, her nervousness began to lift. Since Tuesday night she'd been anticipating this moment. *Too shy! Used to stammer! Remember how you'd cry!* But now, in the busyness of the classroom, so many faces, all that faded. Erma knew she had helpful information to impart and she knew, from their self-portraits, that these adults were motivated to learn. They were not adolescents of the kind enrolled as undergraduates in the daytime university. These were adults with responsibilities. They had full-time jobs, and families; some were divorced with children; some were newly naturalized American citizens; a few were retired; a few were mysteriously afflicted (a woman with multiple sclerosis in remission, an ex-Marine "legally blind" in one eye). Their common hope was that Composition 101 taught by E. Schegloff would somehow improve their lives. Erma's Ph.D. advisor had expressed concern that such elementary teaching would exhaust her and delay the completion of her dissertation; her intelligence and her sensibility were too refined, he feared, for remedial English; she was destined to be a university professor and a poet. Erma had been flattered but unswayed. She'd risked the man's disapproval by pressing ahead anyway and taking the job, without apology. Years before, Erma's parents had tried to discourage her from moving to the Midwest, a thousand miles from home, as if such a move were a personal betrayal. (Which possibly, in the secrecy of Erma's heart, it was.) But Erma was a young woman with a quiet, implacable will. *My life is my own. You'll see!*

Midway through the class Erma handed back the students' self-portraits and asked for volunteers to read their work aloud, which induced a flurry of excitement and drama. On their papers she'd commented in detail, but without grading. (She dreaded the prospect of grading! How do you grade adult men and women who've spilled their guts to you, in utter trust?) When she handed back Arno Kethy's paper she was shocked to see, rising stiffly from his seat at the rear of the room, coming reluctantly forward, a scowling man in his late thirties with a sunken, shadowed face and downturned eyes. His face was mysteriously ruined as if stitched together, a mass of scars. Razor scars, acne? His voice was an embarrassed mumble—"Thank you, ma'am." In his self-portrait he'd spoken of Erma Schegloff's face as a beacon of light and it seemed now he might be blinded by her, approaching her, refusing to meet her gaze, even as Erma smiled forcefully, determined to behave as normally as possible. She'd rehearsed this moment but Kethy took the paper from her fingers with no further acknowledgment, folding it at once, turning away and lurching back to his desk like an agitated child. So this was *Kethy, Arno C.* Not the handsome black man with the thin mustache who smiled at her so readily during class, but the Caucasian with the slovenly ponytail straggling down his back. He was tall but limp-boned like a snake gliding on its tail. His greasy hair was receding at the crown of his head, a coarse gingery-gray. His jaws had a steely unshaven glint. His eyes were evasive, in bruised, hollowed sockets. Yet he wore a cheaply stylish sport coat of simulated suede, fawn-colored, that gave him an incongruous sexy swagger; beneath it a black T-shirt with the logo of an obscene grinning skull out of whose mouth a floppy pink tongue protruded. A man who'd spent eight years of his life on Death Row, and might have been executed . . .

Erma wondered if others could sense the intensity of emotion, the tension, in Kethy's body. It seemed to radiate from his pallid skin like waves of electricity.

Kethy returned to his seat without having looked the instructor in the face. His mouth was twitching. Erma steadfastly looked away. She'd planned to say to him *Mr. Kethy . . . Arno? . . . this is very strong, compelling writing . . . If you'd like to speak with me after class . . .* but the words stuck in her throat.

At the end of the class, as a number of students gathered around the instructor wanting to talk to her, Arno Kethy left quickly by a rear exit. Erma saw that he didn't glance back at her, nor was he walking with any of the others. A loner. A very strange man. Erma was light-headed with exhaustion after the lengthy class but determined to speak with the students as if she were delighted they wanted to speak with her. Later she would wonder if she'd been disappointed in the ex-convict's eccentric behavior, or relieved that he'd kept his distance from her.

ERMA HAD MADE a photocopy of Kethy's self-portrait, and her detailed comments on it, for safekeeping. She was eager to see what he might write next. (Or did she halfway hope he might drop the course?) When a friend from graduate school called to ask how her first week of teaching had gone, Erma said vehemently, "I love it. I mean—I've never had such an experience before." She could not have said what these tremulous words meant.

You were a beacon to me. E. SCHEGLOFF.

Your face I beleive I saw.

In her office on the third floor of Greer Hall, at a temporarily assigned desk, Erma glanced up at a hesitant knock on the opened door, or a murmured approximation of her name. But, through the remainder of January, it was never Arno Kethy.

Because she was only an adjunct instructor with a single-term contract, Erma Schegloff had no permanent office. She shared a battered aluminum desk, large and vaguely military in appearance, like a tank, with two or three other instructors who taught at other times, and whom she never saw. The desk drawers were stuffed with old, yellowed papers by students long since vanished, syllabi and memos and university print-outs. She'd neatly taped to a waterstained wall a reproduction of a beautifully austere painting by Georgia O'Keeffe—a steer's skull floating in a pellucid-blue sky. *Only just a coincidence, its resemblance to Kethy's ugly T-shirt.* On sagging bookshelves in the office, crammed and untidy, were aged books abandoned by their owners; hardcovers, paperbacks; textbooks, outdated dictionaries and university directories. On the uneven floor was a grimy carpet faded to the color of dishwater by the sun which, on clear days, flooded the office through a ceiling-high, ill-fitting window. The room smelled of dust, mouse droppings, forlorn desires. Lost or worn-out hope. Above the door, confronting Erma as she sat at the desk, was an old-fashioned clock that was not only no longer functioning but had somehow lost its minute hand.

Except that Erma's office was three steep flights up from her classroom in the basement of Greer Hall, and therefore discouraging to visitors, she liked it very much. *My first office! Until I'm expelled.* She hadn't had a particularly happy childhood back in Erie, Pennsylvania, amid a family of older brothers but she often recalled random moments when she'd stepped into an unexpected, magical space, indoors or out, but usually in, a space mysteriously waiting for her; for her alone; warm and dazzling with light. And even if the space was small, she felt a sense of amplitude. And this office was large, even cavernous; especially at night, when the windowpanes reflected only the interior.

Instructors in the Night Division were required to keep two office hours a week, preferably before each class, and Erma's were 6 P.M. to 7 P.M. Tuesdays and Thursdays; but she'd added an extra hour each evening, following class, for she wanted to give her students every opportunity to meet with her. "Come see me, please. I'll be in my office upstairs." After her initial euphoria over their self-portraits, Erma had come to a more realistic assessment of their writing skills. Two-thirds of the class performed at about the eighth-grade level, a few were virtually illiterate. And there were two or three, in addition to Arno Kethy, who weren't turning in any work at all, for what motive Erma didn't know.

Yet she was feeling optimistic. Reckless!

A mysterious strength suffused her days and even her nights. She rose, in the dark, at 6:30 A.M. to swim in the university pool, amid strangers; she spent hours each day at her scholarly work in the university library and in her apartment; she prepared diligently for Composition 101, choosing exemplary essays from their text to teach and scanning newspapers and magazines for clippings to bring to her students of good, forceful writing. She loved her solitude. She was never lonely. *So physically lonely! Of that, I can't speak.* In fact she'd come to this aging post-industrial city on a famously polluted river partly to put distance between herself and a man for whom she'd felt a complex of emotions and she was discovering (contrary to what poetic sentiment might suggest) that the blunt fact of distance, sixty snowswept miles of interstate highway and monotonous, level countryside, was a remedy. Far from the intellectual and cultural center of the state, at the university's main campus, Erma felt like a renegade from a proper, approved life. She felt illicit, and renewed.

Not a man to be pushed, obviously. He's suffered.

Arno Kethy had not handed in the next two assignments ("description of a setting," "description of an action or process") and he'd offered Erma no excuse. She was determined not to call him to account, just yet. She would wait another week or so, before asking to speak with him privately.

Am I afraid of him?

I am not!

Those eyes. Wounded, haunted. Ever-shifting. Fixed upon the instructor covertly, hidden behind his raised, big-knuckled hands.

Often in the library, in the midst of researching the myriad religious schisms of the vanished seventeenth century, Erma found herself thinking of *Kethy, Arno C.* His deformed-seeming yet swaggering body. His ravaged face. And those eyes. He was standing in the cheap stylish coat and black T-shirt, not before her, but at the periphery of her vision, like an imperfectly recalled dream. His behavior was a riddle she would one day solve.

In the meantime she'd become a true teacher. An instructor. She was discovering the very real satisfactions of teaching motivated adults who yearn to know skills elemental to the lives they envision leading; not luxury skills of an affluent civilization, but skills of necessity. How impassioned Erma Schegloff felt, speaking to her students: "Many of you have these skills by instinct, and now you'll be formalizing them. You'll be revising your papers for me which means you'll be steadily improving. That's our goal!" Strange and wonderful, Erma's students seemed to believe her. They seemed to like her. They must have forgiven her her youth and inexperience and were beginning to appreciate her oblique sense of humor. (Did Arno Kethy smile at her jokes? Erma didn't dare look.) Other adjuncts in the Night Division warned Erma not to spend too much time on her course, these were low-paying, dead-end jobs in the university, but Erma thought stubbornly what was too much time when you were crucially involved with others? "They need me. Someone like me. Who will help them, and not judge harshly."

Since she'd become an instructor, it seemed to her that the flaws of her personality, as she saw them—shyness, self-consciousness, insecurity, an excessive concern with detail and precision—evaporated as soon as she stepped into the classroom. As soon as her students saw her. As if the humming flickering fluorescent lights of the undistinguished room had the power to magically transform her.

She was determined that Arno Kethy would not distract her. No one would have guessed (Kethy himself could have not guessed) that she was aware of him at all. The fact that he slouched in his seat at the back of the room, staring fixedly at her. She told herself *That man is on my side.* In three weeks Kethy hadn't missed a single class but he never participated in the frequently lively discussion. So far as Erma could gather he shunned all contact with his fellow students. (As they shunned contact with him.) Often, as Erma spoke, he began to scribble rapidly in his notebook. He was left-handed, and writing involved some contortion of his body. *A man imprisoned in a tight space.* Her heart welled with pity for him.

She meant to commiserate with Arno Kethy when at last he spoke with her. She rehearsed her words, even her facial expressions. She would be quietly sympathetic, she would urge him to speak. If he wanted to speak. She would say nothing (of course) about his fantasy of her; his conviction that he'd somehow known her before meeting her. *Arno don't give up hope. Arno I am awaiting you.* She couldn't help but wonder how close he'd come to being executed. Months, weeks? She believed that, in time, he would tell her.

And she wondered what he'd done, or had been wrongly convicted of doing, to warrant a death sentence. It could only have been murder. Murders. In this Midwestern state executions had been rare for decades but were being reinstated under a Republican governor and legislature. Erma had made inquiries and learned that the state no longer electrocuted men but killed them by lethal injection.

Yet when class ended at 8:15 P.M., Arno Kethy left abruptly. He didn't drift forward to speak with her, nor even to say goodnight like the others. There he was gathering up his duffel bag, shrugging on an overcoat that looked too large for him, and with a practiced gesture flicking his gingery-gray hair over his collar. He departed swiftly by the rear exit. Erma saw how others moved out of his way.

He can't be judged by ordinary standards. A man who has survived Death Row.

ONE NIGHT IN early February, Erma was in her office after her last student left. It was nearly 9:30 P.M. Greer Hall felt deserted as a mausoleum. She'd had conferences with several students, one of them the ebullient charmer Reverend Eldridge, and now she was alone, and realized that the corridor outside her office was unlighted. She felt the first tinge of concern, preparing to leave. During the preceding hour a custodian had been working in the main corridor, perpendicular to this corridor; when he'd finished he had evidently switched out all the lights on the floor, assuming everyone had left for the night.

So Erma stood hesitantly in her office doorway. The overhead light in her office was still on; the switch was near the door. Some distance away, perhaps fifty feet, was a dimly lighted stairwell that led off the main corridor of Greer Hall. This was the stairwell she would take when she left; her car was parked close by, just behind the building. Heavy double doors with inserted windows divided the stairway from the corridor so that light falling back into the corridor was murky; between Erma's office and the stairwell was an alarming darkness. Erma could barely make out the walls. There were office doors, bulletin boards, a drinking fountain, a custodian's closet, all lost in darkness. Erma swallowed hard. She didn't know Greer Hall well enough yet to remember where the light switch for her corridor was, though she assumed it must be near the double doors. On this large urban campus there were frequent assaults and attempted assaults against students, especially lone women; Erma knew this was a risky situation. She could telephone one of the university proctors, as they were called, to come escort her to her car . . . "God damn! I won't be intimidated." Asking for help when there was no discernible danger would only underscore a woman's weakness. Erma Schegloff's weakness.

What Erma might do: leave her office door open so that she could see into the corridor for a few yards, make her way quickly to the light switch (if she could locate it); turn on the lights, and return to her office to darken it and lock the door, behaving with caution, though if anyone were waiting to attack her it wouldn't make much difference except of course she could see her assailant, and could scream, and screaming might scare him off . . . But yes, it would make a difference: lights would discourage an assailant even if no one else was in Greer Hall. A sane, reasonable assailant.

Erma's mind was racing. She heard her own quickened breath.

She decided against such over-scrupulosity. The building was absolutely silent. There could be no one here. She switched off her office light and shut the door, acting as if the corridor were adequately lighted, not pitch-black, and she wasn't terrified. She could see the stairwell ahead, dimly. She had only to get there. She wouldn't run, for she might collide with something and hurt herself. She walked like a blind woman, groping one hand against the wall. *Breathe naturally. Like swimming. Inhale on a stroke, exhale in the water. Don't inhale water!* She was reminded of the numerous times her brother Lyle had lain in wait for her . . . She pushed away all thoughts of Lyle, they were inappropriate here, never did she think of Lyle any longer, or the others, she was no longer the trapped girl who'd had to think of Lyle, and of her family. By the time she got to the stairwell her heart was beating so rapidly she felt faint. But she got there, safely. Clearly no one was waiting for her. Erma pushed through the double doors with a smile of relief, and there, squatting on the stairway landing, smoking a cigarette, like a nightmare figure calmly coming to life, was the stitched-faced, ponytailed Arno Kethy.

Erma screamed. She'd never been so frightened in her life.

Stammering, "W-What—what do you want—" knowing Kethy was there for her, unable to pretend in the crisis of the moment that he was not; that this an accidental encounter. Kethy rose out of his crouch at once. How tall he was, towering over Erma. He was a nocturnal creature blinded by light. He muttered something Erma couldn't decipher, turning away from her and running down the stairs.

She was faint with shock. She leaned against the railing weakly. Listening to a man's footsteps echoing in the dim-lit stairwell until he was out of the building, and gone.

2.

"HE'S MAD."

But was it so simple? Could she dismiss him, and what he represented, with a blunt, ugly term?

ASSIGNMENT #2: DESCREPTION

Descreption of Edgarstown Death Row.
The cell measures 6 feet 11 inches by 9 feet.
There is the cot. The toliet. The locked door.
There is the air which you have breathed and fouled
and must breath again. Or suffocate.

There is the concrete-block wall which is
one wall on three sides.

First, you are in the cell. Then, the cell
is in you. If I shut my eyes (like now)
I am there. When sleeping, I am there.
But every time words are put to it,
they are not the exact words.
This descreption has been writen so many times.
I would say that I have failed.

They say that there are grounds for suing,
for false incarceration. But to recall that other time
(before Edgarstown Death Row) you would have to be
that other person again. But he is gone.

I confessed to what they said was done,
for I did not know certainly that I had not done it.
Later it was known to me, I was INNOCENT.
I was 31 yrs old when put like an animal in a cage.

He was #DY4889. But that person is gone.
They sliced his face with a razor.
He could not look to see the wounds. But,
he could feel with his fingers.
What you try to descrebe, a long time later,
the words are false.

E. SCHEGLOFF your name is please understand
I was not born a beast. I said I was INNOCENT
and they laughed. Thats what a beast
always says they told me.

If I hurt those people I was said to hurt,
there would be a memory of their blood,
I beleive. But it is my own blood I remember.
Your face told me, always have hope.
I had no knowledge of how you would be waiting.

Descreption of Room #417 Greer Hall.
It is three times larger than a cell on Death Row.
There is a smell of mildue and time here.
The window is very high, to the cieling.
The panes do not fit well. There is leakage.
The desk is a large one, and old.
There are bookshelfs with many books looking
old and used.
There is a swivil chair behind the desk.
The Instructor E. SCHEGLOFF is seated in this chair.
The Instructor E. SCHEGLOFF shares this desk with
other instructors.
There is a skull in a blue sky on the wall!
The Instructor E. SCHEGLOFF put this picture on
the wall. Reaching to above her head, and
her hands trembled with the strain.
I did not have a tape to measure the room but beleive
it is maybe 20 feet by 30.

And the cieling maybe 12 feet high.
There is an overhead light and a light on the
desk.
The clock above the door is broken, the hour hand gone.
It is strang to see a clock broken in that way.
You look at it a long time wondering, what is wrong.
When the Instructor remains here late the windowpanes darken.
You cant see outside.
When the Instructor remains here late there is danger.
A woman by herself is in danger. In danger of beasts.

I would protect E. SCHEGLOFF I promise.
I beleive I am summoned for that purpose.
Her face I could not see in my cell clearly.
It is a very beutiful face like an angels.
Seeing you then at your desk, when you did not see
me (and your hair like mine!) I wanted to say
I would protect you I promise forever.
I wanted to say I am not a beast
for if even my hands did what they said,
which I beleive was not so,
I did not give up HOPE.

Erma read Arno Kethy's "Descreption" several times. She was in a haze of alarm and sympathy. Surely the man was mentally unbalanced, and yet . . . "He's speaking from the heart. He isn't stopping to think how it must sound." She was alone in the bedroom of her small apartment, it was midnight. That morning in the pool she'd gotten chlorine in her eyes and through the long day her eyes had been stinging and watering and it was difficult for her to read Kethy's small cramped words, crowded and urgent, on a lined sheet of tablet paper without margins.

Erma was upset, that Kethy had somehow watched her at her desk in Greer Hall. He'd certainly been waiting for her in the stairwell. To protect her? *Summoned for that purpose.*

She knew she should show Kethy's compositions to someone else.

The program director in the Night Division. "But he trusts me. I can't betray him."

Erma was agitated, on her feet to stare at herself in the oval mirror of her bureau beside the bed. *Your hair like mine!* She plucked at the braid, quickly unraveling strands of hair. From now on, she would wear her hair loose. Better yet, she would get it cut. How could Kethy imagine her hair resembled his! Her cheeks burned with the insult.

Beutiful face like an angels.

Arno Kethy was in love with Erma Schegloff. Was that it?

"But he doesn't know me. It's his delusion."

Arno Kethy was stalking her. In the guise of protecting her.

Yet truly he believed he was protecting her. He would not wish (Erma was certain) to harm *her.*

(Or was this, Erma wondered, a delusion of her own? To be so convinced.)

He'd known that evening that Greer Hall was deserted and Erma's corridor was darkened and he'd remained after their class, to protect her. In case there was danger, she needed him.

Seeing herself as in a hallucinatory flash pushing again through the double doors into the stairwell and there was that figure of nightmare Arno Kethy with his stitched-looking face and staring eyes, squatting on the landing and smoking a cigarette. *I beleive I am summoned.*

"He might have hurt me then, if he wanted. We were alone."

The incident had happened on a Tuesday night. On Thursday, Kethy handed in the second assignment, "Descreption." It was weeks late. He'd passed it up to the instructor, several times folded, by way of another student. When Erma received it, she saw Kethy slouched in his seat, as if hiding; his ropey-muscled forearms lifted to shield his face. Since the other night, they were known to each other. There was the connection between them, irrevocable. He'd seen her face, her terror of him she'd tried to hide. She'd seen his face, the shock and adoration in his eyes. During class, as she taught, Erma was aware of Kethy as she hadn't been previously. While speaking she lost the train of her thought several times and noticed students looking at her quizzically.

It was midwinter malaise on the campus. Many students had flu.

She was disheartened, a little. Seven students of thirty-two were absent that night.

When class ended, Erma didn't go upstairs to her office. She could not. She remained in the classroom to speak with those several students who'd arranged for conferences with her. "This will save us all a hike up those stairs. Those steep stairs." When she left the building in the company of another student, a woman, she had the idea that Kethy might be close by, watching.

You see? I don't need you to protect me.

But that night, in her apartment, the door locked and bolted and the telephone off the hook (in case her former lover should call, for he'd been calling, late, several times that week) and no sirens to interrupt her solitude, Erma read and reread Arno Kethy's "Descreption" and could not decide: was it a voice of madness, or a voice of radiant insight? Might the two be conjoined?

Nor could she decide if it was a declaration of love, or a subtle threat.

A woman by herself is in danger. In danger of beasts.

She wondered what would happen if her former lover drove to see her. As she'd forbidden him. If Arno Kethy saw them together.

She went to bed, turned off the light, at 2 A.M. Though knowing she couldn't sleep. In this unfamiliar bed, in this unfamiliar place. She shut her eyes. There was Kethy, squatting. Gazing at her with hurt, hopeful eyes. And in the swimming pool. Was that why her eyes had been bleeding all day? *Glimmering of a ponytailed man in the pool's choppy aqua water in the instant before Erma Schegloff drew breath, to dive in.*

THESE WERE SNOWY blinding-bright Midwestern days. Flat land, enormous sky. Erma's eyes wept behind dark glasses.

She was remembering (she hated remembering!) how back in Erie, Pennsylvania, in the squat ugly asphalt-sided house near the railroad tracks where she'd lived a captive for eighteen years, her parents, sullen and demoralized by life, debilitated by physical ailments and alcohol, had ignored her brothers' relentless teasing of her. *Erma! Er-ma where're you hiding! Little bich.* There was Judd, six years older than Erma; there was Tommy, three years older; and there was Lyle, eighteen months older. Who'd most resembled Erma. Lyle with dark features, thick-lashed intelligent eyes glistening with hatred. Lyle with a speech impediment he'd exaggerated out of spite. *Little bich. C-c-cunnnt. You in here?* Kicking at the bathroom door with its notoriously loose lock. Giggling when the door flew open and Erma was revealed, frightened, embarrassed, rising from the toilet and trying to adjust her clothing. Lyle who chased her, tickled and pinched her, one Hallowe'en night in a Batman mask squeezing, squeezing, squeezing his fingers around her neck until Erma fell unconscious to the floor.

"You kids. What're you kids doing, God damn you."

Much of it, the "teasing," had been in or near the bathroom. At the top of the stairs. A single poorly heated bathroom for the six of them. Filthy toilet, filthy sink and tub. There'd been a year when Erma's mother, recovering from a gallbladder operation, hadn't done any housework. Erma's father was often gone from the house. Downstairs, watching her daytime TV, Erma's mother had been indifferent to cries and thuds overhead. Once, aged thirteen, Erma had desperately slapped Lyle as Judd and Tommy looked on laughing and Lyle had flown into a rage and punched her in the back so hard she fell stunned, unable to breathe. Their mother yelled at them hoarsely, up the stairs, "Shut up! I'll get your father to beat the shit out of you! You kids make me *sick.*"

ARNO KETHY WOULD have protected her from Lyle. From all her brothers.

Unless (she didn't want to consider this!) Arno Kethy was one of her brothers.

NOW, A DECADE later, Erma was gone from Erie, Pennsylvania, and guiltily plotted never to return. Not for her father's angina and alarming weight loss, not for her mother's swollen joints, blackouts, and "nerves." Not for Judd's wedding, and his fatal car crash barely a year later. Not for Lyle's mysterious "trouble with the police." Speaking two or three times a month on the phone with her parents, she liked it that the line crackled with distance. You could hear the howling cleansing wind of the prairies. You could hear stinging particles of snow. Before each of her calls home Erma was nervous, anxious, but she called dutifully, and she put a smile into her voice. For now they were older, seriously ailing, and their meanness as curtailed as vicious dogs on leashes. "When am I coming home, I'm not sure, Mom. My term doesn't end until . . . After that, I have a summer research grant . . ." But she sent them checks. Considering her poverty, generous checks.

She was a captive paying her kidnappers ransom in order to remain free.

Oh, gratefully! That was why she smiled.

ASSIGNMENT #3: ARGUEMENT

Sometimes its just simple, you want to improve
your Life to where it is worthwhile as a citizen.
Its hard to argue what would be my exact hope
as I did not gratuate from high school.
I had trouble with all my subjects especally
English where the teacher hated me. Even gym,
I failed. The coach hated me!
They think if you are quiet, you are hating them.
You are thinking of ways to hurt them.

My arguement would be, what does the US expect
if you treat us like shit? Eight years, on
Death Row and saying they are sorry afterward,
sorry I am alive they mean. That the appeal
went so slow. (A man in the block, his appeal
went faster and was rejected, and so he was
put to death, and the new law applied to me,
that would have saved him, was not on the books
yet. A laugh on him.)

I drive my car at night, for I am lonely.
There are so many houses in this city.
Sometimes, you don't pull your shades
to the window sill, Im thinking.
Could toss a bomb through any lighted window.
People watching TV, or having supper.
What about us out here in the Night.

I quit Mayflower movers. Its not a life
to plan for. I cant beleive—I am 39 yrs old.
Where is my life taken from me, I dont know.
My arguement is to return to schooling, where
I took a wrong turn. If I had sertain skills
as with computers. I started Accounting too
but have not done too good. My mind is fixed on
sertain issues. There is the wrongness of putting
a man to death, if he is innocent or even if
he is not. I would wish to marry one day
but at Edgarstown I was injured in sertain ways
and (I beleive) contacted diseases, but
the insurance will not cover it. They said
it was before I went in, in another State.
There records but no records (they say) of this.

My conviction was overturned and so I was free,
still I would wish sometimes to murder you them all.
I was not born a beast, that is my arguement.

3.

It's time. It can't be avoided. Erma went to consult with the program director. Mr. Falworth was an earnest, harassed-looking old-young man of about forty who didn't seem to recognize her until she told him her name twice. "My hair," she said apologetically. "I've cut my hair." Her long braid had vanished. Her hair was wavy and insubstantial as feathers, framing a winter-pale, scrubbed-looking face. Falworth smiled a quick but vague social smile, saying his hair, too, had departed in the service of remedial composition; he made a fluttering gesture with his fingers across the dome of his near-bald head. Such a gesture meant simply *I like you, I'm a decent guy. But don't bring me trouble.* Erma had brought with her a number of student compositions to show Falworth, a sampling of the range of her grades; among them were Arno Kethy's three ungraded compositions which she intended to show him matter-of-factly, as if Kethy were an academic problem merely, and not a personal problem. As they conferred, Erma began to doubt the wisdom of what she'd planned. She had rehearsed saying to Falworth *What do you make of these, I can't grade them by any standards I know, it's like prose poetry isn't it, or is it just illiterate, unacceptable, this student isn't following the guidelines is he, what do you advise, Mr. Falworth?* She supposed the program director would be shocked. But possibly he wouldn't be shocked. The Night Division, Erma had been told by other, more experienced instructors, accepted virtually all applicants who were residents of the state. The legislature looked at numbers, not academic records. No doubt there were mentally disturbed patients among the Night Division's clientele, even criminals. No doubt there were frequently problems for new instructors, especially women. Falworth might have just the answer. He might call in Arno Kethy to see him. He might speak severely with Kethy, he might suggest that Kethy drop out of school. Since Kethy's third composition seemed to contain a threat of violence, Falworth might report him to authorities.

Or, what was equally likely, he might be annoyed with the inexperienced young woman instructor who'd come to him with such a problem. Would a male instructor have had this problem? As they conferred, through most of an hour, Erma realized that she couldn't betray Arno Kethy; he was emotionally disturbed, but he trusted her; he would never hurt her. *I would protect you I promise.* Erma slipped Kethy's handwritten papers into her brief case; if Falworth noticed them, he wasn't about to ask for more compositions to examine. He said briskly, "You appear to be doing very well, Erma. This is good work." This was meant sincerely and Erma felt a wave of relief. Some guilt, but mostly relief. The consultation was ending on a positive note. Falworth saw her to the door of his office, a gesture she guessed he didn't ordinarily make with visitors. He asked if she would like to teach in the program in the fall, possibly two courses, for more than double her current salary, and Erma heard herself say yes, possibly she would. "I've never had an experience like this before."

"Our most successful instructors always say that," Falworth said with a smile. "It's the others, the ones with problems . . ." His voice trailed off into disapproving silence.

Erma Schegloff had said the right thing.

NEXT DAY, she made inquiries after *Kethy, Arno C.* in the registrar's office. But Kethy had no transcripts predating that semester when he'd enrolled, as a special student in the Night Division, in Composition 101 and Accounting 101. No high school transcripts or letters of recommendation seem to have been required. Erma went to the office of the dean of the Night Division and was allowed to look through a similarly meager file for Kethy there. (Aluminum filing cabinets filled most of a room, containing thousands of students' files, since 1947! It was a daunting vision, like looking into a vast mortuary.) Here there was a poorly photocopied letter dated September 1989 from a county parole officer attesting vaguely to Arno C. Kethy's punctuality, willingness to cooperate with authorities, and "adoptive nature," which Erma supposed must mean "adaptive nature." Yet the letter was only a form letter addressed to To Whom It May Concern; it concluded with a disclaimer—

> Arno C. Kethy is of above average intelligence it is believed, but not easy to communicate with. The report of the court psychiatrist is that he is a "borderline" personality capable of knowing right from wrong and therefore sane under the law. He has always claimed total innocence for his actions even those of which he has been found guilty on the testimony of witnesses and circumstantial evidence.

Whatever Kethy had done, or had been convicted of doing, in this instance, had been before 1989. And 1989 was a long time ago.

Erma saw that Kethy's address was 81 Bridge Street.

But how is he borderline? Dangerous?

He reveals himself in words like a poet.

MAYBE (ERMA CONCEDED!) she'd regret it. But she showed Kethy's most recent, most disturbing composition to no one. She lay the single, much-folded sheet of tablet paper on top of the bureau in her bedroom, a primitive piece of Shaker furniture painted robin's egg blue and decorated with tiny pink rosebuds, a girl's bureau with a romantically fogged oval mirror in which Erma's own face, girlish, rather pale, somber yet often smiling, floated; and after a week she'd read and reread it so many times, it no longer seemed threatening. It was a poem in prose. She could hear Kethy's anguished voice reciting it. And it was written for her, Kethy's instructor. *I was not born a beast, that is my arguement.* Erma thought of Shakeseare's Caliban. Milton's rebellious Satan in *Paradise Lost.* She still hadn't attempted to grade him for how could she grade a man's soul?

He reveals himself to me. Alone.

THERE CAME THURSDAY evening, their next class. When Erma hurried into the room breathless and invigorated from the cold, already Kethy was hidden in his corner, remote and downlooking. Among so many other individuals, Kethy might be ignored even as the instructor was sharply aware of him; his searching eyes. She knew he would be struck by her hair. The thick braid between her shoulder blades, suddenly missing.

Now it was late February in this snowswept Midwestern city and the winter term was beginning to wear. Flu was locally rampant; nine students were absent. Erma had looked forward to teaching Zora Neale Hurston's self-portrait "How It Feels to Be Colored Me"—a choice she assumed would meet with enthusiasm since it was zestfully written yet a serious glimpse into the soul of a brilliant black woman writer; but to her surprise and chagrin, Reverend E. G. Eldridge loudly objected on the grounds of Hurston's "mocking tone" and "ignorance of the place of Jesus Christ" in the lives of black Americans. In turn, others objected to the reverend's bold, blustery statements. Students who'd been silent all term joined in. But Eldridge dominated, clearly accustomed to being the authority in any gathering. Erma found herself in the instructor's perilous position of disagreeing strongly with a student yet wanting to respect his opinion and wishing to be, or to appear to be, neutral. As others, mostly women, black and Caucasian, defended Hurston, and the Reverend and a few others attacked her, Erma stood uncertainly before them, no longer in control. She might have been observing, from a few yards away, a suddenly raging brushfire. When a black woman said to Eldridge with withering scorn, "This Hurston a genius, man, and you a sorry asshole," Erma was shocked, stammering, "Oh, Lorett! That isn't very—polite." Eldridge shot back, baring his teeth in fury, "*You,*

woman, are just plain *ig-nor-ant.*" Erma said, trying to re
tention, "Mr. Eldridge, please—" Eldridge turned t
woman instructor to whom, for weeks, he'd been exces
ous, his usually benign face creased with disdain, "M
me! You are not qualified to speak on this subject!"

The instructor's nightmare epiphany. *This has all been a game. He doesn't respect me at all. Do any of them . . . ?*

Erma's face burned. She must have looked like a slapped, publicly humiliated child. Eldridge, having gone too far, realized his blunder and began to make amends. Others, who hadn't taken part in the noisy discussion, looked on like observers at an auto wreck. Some were shocked, a few hid smiles and smirks. Arno Kethy had risen partway from his desk, peering over heads. His stitched-looking Caucasian face shone with indignation. Eldridge was apologizing profusely, having reverted to his usual benevolence. Erma said, smiling, "It's quite all right, Reverend Eldridge. I stand corrected." She meant to turn the unpleasant confrontation into a good-natured joke, though Eldridge's hard round face gleamed with oily beads of sweat, and Erma was still trembling. Lorett said with pursed, pouty lips, "See, Miz S'heg'off, what we women got to contend with? The black male ego revealed." Eldridge managed to laugh at this remark, barely, dabbing at his face with a handkerchief. Erma guided the class onto another, safer essay. She didn't glance back at Arno Kethy. Everyone would be on good behavior for the remainder of the class and of course, at the end, Reverend Eldridge would hurry forward to further apologize. *He's worried. He showed me his true face. He'd been hoping for a high grade.* Erma was disillusioned, but behaved graciously with Eldridge. She wasn't upset with him in the least, she said; in fact, she was pleased that their discussion had been so animated. "That's the aim of strong writing, isn't it? To provoke thought."

By this time Kethy had vanished by the rear exit. Erma had wanted to hand back his "Arguement" and ask him to speak with her about it, but when she looked up, exhausted and demoralized, Kethy was gone.

NEXT CLASS MEETING, and the next, E. G. Eldridge was absent. Erma felt the sting of a public rebuke. She wondered if Eldridge had opped the course, or was just staying away temporarily to punish her. She wanted the man back, to make amends; though she'd been disgusted with him, she couldn't bear it that he might be disgusted with her. She made inquiries in the dean's office and was told only that Eldridge's wife had called to say he was hospitalized, and would probably not be returning to school. Erma was astonished. "But he seemed to be in good health. He's a strong, vigorous man . . ."

She wondered guiltily if, in any way, she was to blame.

ASSIGNMENT #4: OBSEVATION AND ANYLSIS

The house is two floors, brown shinglewood with a
look of soft rotted wood. There is a front porch
and a side porch. The roof is black tarpaper.
It is just an ordinary house you would think
from the outside. It is near the hospital.

Her place she lives in, is on the second floor.
The stairs are squeezed in. There is a smell
of cooking from the downstairs. There is linolum
tile on the floor. The mailboxes are downstairs.
The lock on the front door is not a serious lock.

Her skin was very white even in the shadow.
There was radio music playing, very soft.
She has wrapped a white towel around her hair.
When she brushes it out, it is strange to her,
it has become shorter. It makes her younger.
There is a swatch of bush-hair, a lighter color
between her legs. It is curly and if you
sallowed a hair, it would tickle!

There are only three rooms in the apartment,
this is a surprise. Not what a college teacher
deserves. Except for the blue bureau
and some pictures of trees she has taped to her walls
there is not enough beauty in this place.

The blinds are drawn but you can see through.
Maybe they are not drawn to the window ledge.
The lock on the door is the same lock as downstairs.
From the hospital, there are sirens.

She came out from the steamed bathroom drying
her hair, and another towel wrapped around her.
His hands helped her. He was holding the big towel,
she felt his hands through the clothe and shivered.
She would look up though she did not SEE him then.
Yet she smiled. For she knew he was there.

Hed painted the bureau for her. A little wood bureau
with pink rosebuds and the knobs made of glass.
He explained to her he would like to marry
and have children except they have tired to discorage
him. Its their hope to discorage you from life.
They laugh if you try to hang yourself, they provide
the clothes. They pretend they dont see spoons,
for you to sharpen. They hope for the lower class
to die out like dogs.

Before he knew her name ERMA SCHEGLOFF
he was granted knowledge of her face.
If you love somebody that is all there is.
If you anylise it you will fail.
You knew each other before it happened.
Always he would recall her face
that brought him hope.
For you cant live without hope.
He would protect her from all enemies.
He would cut away their faces and their hearts.
To protect her he would not be afraid
to use all his strength.

He would not live without her, he felt.

"'BORDERLINE.' BUT 'BORDERLINE' to *what?*"

She had a vision of a single, isolated nation-state floating in darkness, its borders touching upon nothing.

IN THE ALL-but-deserted reference room of the downtown public library there was Erma Schegloff scrolling through back editions of the city newspaper on microfilm. Anxious, dreading what she might find in these rows upon rows of shimmering print. Headlines of national and international crisis juxtaposed with area news and all of it reduced to history. Time past. The extraordinary set beside the commonplace. It was *County News* she focused upon, the second section of the paper. Scrolling through weeks of campaign and election coverage, photos of smiling politicians, town meetings, sewer bond issues, school board debates, schoolbus safety, fires, arson, arrests for robbery, theft, drunken driving, armed assault. Ladies' charity bazaars, church news, archbishop dies, scholarship winners, lottery winners, arson suspected, arson-suspect arrested, embezzlement of bank funds, school superintendent dies, dean of business school at the university retires, honorary degrees conferred upon, arrests in drug raids, and suddenly there was

EDGARSTOWN DEATH ROW PRISONER, 39
FREED AFTER 8-YEAR ORDEAL

The date was December 2 of the previous year. She'd been staring at a photo of Arno Kethy aged thirty-one, young-looking, with hurt narrowed eyes and the shadow of a beard and brutally short-trimmed hair, without recognizing him.

Kethy had been convicted of raping and murdering a woman and her thirteen-year-old daughter in a state park in July 1990; he'd been identified by witnesses as being near the scene of the crime, there was "evidence" linking him to the crime site, he'd made a confession to police, a police informant testified at his trial he'd boasted of committing the crimes. Kethy had subsequently recanted the confession, alleging he'd been beaten by police. He had a "drug history." He'd spent time in rehabilitation, in Iowa. He'd also spent time in Iowa State Penitentiary on a charge of armed robbery. At his trial he'd taken the witness stand but became "catatonic" and could not testify. During his two-week trial he became violent and had to be placed under restraint in the courtroom. A jury found him guilty of two counts of murder and two counts of rape, and he was sentenced to death by lethal injection. His case was automatically appealed. His conviction was overturned when a county man, arrested by police for drug dealing, told police that the rape-murders had been committed by another man, not Kethy; subsequent DNA evidence proved that Kethy had not been the rapist, and linked the other suspect to the crimes. When Kethy was released after eight years on Death Row TV reporters had asked him to comment on his ordeal but Kethy "shook his head wordlessly and walked away."

Erma wiped at her eyes. *Shook his head, walked away.* What more manly gesture!

It was when Erma was returning the rolls of microfilm to the librarian that she happened to see, on a table, scattered pages of the city paper. Immediately her eye leapt to a photo of a familiar face. Reverend E. G. Eldridge. And the headline MINISTER BRUTALLY ATTACKED IN ROBBERY ATTEMPT.

Appalled, Erma read that E. G. Eldridge, fifty-one years old, had been attacked with a razor while getting into his car in the parking lot behind his church, the Disciples of Jesus Christ, on Friday of the previous week. The attack had occurred at 7 P.M., after dark but in a lighted area. Eldridge had not seen his assailant. He'd been severely lacerated in the face and hands and was in stable condition in the hospital. The unknown assailant had removed Eldridge's wallet from his coat pocket but dropped it near him without taking money or credit cards. Police believed he'd been frightened off by someone on the street, but no witnesses to the crime had yet come forward.

"For me. He did it, for me."

For several minutes she sat stunned. Then she folded up the newspaper carefully, inserting pages in their proper order, and returned it to the librarian's desk where current issues of the local paper were kept.

SHE LIFTED THE telephone receiver. She would call the police, she would say carefully: "I think I know who might have assaulted Reverend Eldridge. His name is . . ."

So long she held the receiver in her sweaty hand, the dial tone turned to an irritated mechanical squawking in her ear. Somewhere close by, a siren wailed. It had begun to snow again, windborne sleet. Not yet March, this winter of Erma's life seemed to have gone on forever with the fascination of one of those mad works of adoration *The Faerie Queene, The Romance of the Rose* . . . By the time she replaced the receiver the mechanical squawking had ceased. There was no dial tone, no sound, as if the line had been cut.

This can't be happening can it? I am not truly here.

Through the ice-stippled side window of her car Erma saw the dimly lighted windows of 81 Bridge Street. A shabby red-brick townhouse in a neighborhood of similar run-down rowhouses near the ramp of the enormous bridge. Human life was dwarfed here, human habitations like caves, hives. Though close by, the polluted river was invisible.

She wondered if Kethy was home. If he was alone.

I can't love you. You mustn't love me. You don't know me: my face is not me.

You must not hurt others on my account . . .

Yet their connection was forged too deep for such words, now.

No words Erma uttered would matter to Kethy, no words could deflect his adoration.

He'd stayed away from class. He wouldn't come again, Erma understood. So she must go to him, if they were ever to meet again. He would injure and even kill on her account but he believed himself unworthy of her.

Uncertain what to do, Erma drove on. She was morbidly excited, exhilarated. She'd brought Kethy's last composition with her, to give to him personally. What madness! Yet she would do it, if she could force herself. She'd become, she believed, a stronger person: willful, resolute. Like the man who adored her, reckless.

The last time she'd called home, for instance. The duty-bound daughter. Gentle all-forgiving never-judging daughter. Her mother was saying in a hurt whining voice why are you so far from us Erma, why have you left us in our old age, like your brothers, no better than your brothers, why do you imagine you can "teach," you're not the type, never were, you're shy, you used to stammer so badly remember how you came home crying, the other children teased you so—and Erma quietly hung up the receiver on her mother's voice. Smiling, thinking *The connection was broken. No one's fault.*

Within the hour she'd arranged for her telephone number to be changed, unlisted.

She would tell Kethy, maybe. They'd laugh together. She would tell Kethy such things she'd never told anyone in this raw new life of hers in the Midwest or in the old lost life back east. She would tell him *None of them ever knew me, I'm so lonely.*

Erma was circling the block, evidently. She perceived that that was what she was doing. One-way streets, and narrow. And vehicles were parked on the streets, some of them abandoned. There was trash dumped on the pavement, overturned trash cans. In this setting Kethy's "Obsevation and Anylsis" acquired a touching, comical significance. Remedial English, taught to inhabitants of such a world. The strategies of prose, persuasive prose, prose to save one's life, taught to Death Row prisoners. Erma hadn't graded Kethy's compositions, out of respect. Out of fear for him, yes; but out of respect, too. She would return the composition to him in person as an act of homage but she hadn't committed herself to any action beyond that. She was one who wished to believe that human motives precede actions for she was (she had always been) a rational individual yet clearly there were times (was this one of those times?) when actions might precede motives and even render them useless.

The one-way streets made this part of the city a maze. Erma had been forced to drive several blocks out of her way. *Go home! Continue on home, no one will ever know you've been here.* She passed beneath another ramp of the old ugly Victorian-era bridge. In warmer weather it would be dangerous for Erma to drive in this part of the city, a lone white woman in a compact car, but tonight no one was on the street. Though her heart was pounding, she knew the symptoms of anxiety. Exhilaration! She saw that she was driving again on Bridge Street, heading south. Street numbers were diminishing: 231, 184, 101 . . . She approached Kethy's house another time. She was fairly certain someone was home. That bluish undersea TV glimmering. She braked her car at the curb: a shadowy figure was passing by the window, behind the carelessly drawn shade. *I drive my car at night, for I am lonely. Could toss a bomb through any lighted window.* Erma turned off the ignition. She saw that, while the porches of other rowhouses on the street were cluttered with objects, chairs, bicycles, trash cans, the porch at 81 Bridge was empty except for a single trash can.

He lived alone. He was in there, alone.

Carefully, Erma walked up the icy sidewalk. Stepped onto the porch. Through the thin, cracked shade she had the impression of a male figure moving swiftly toward the door by the time she pressed the bell. The door was opened within seconds like an inhalation of breath: Arno Kethy stood there, staring at her.

He wore a clean black T-shirt. Work pants, hiker's boots. A long spidery blue tattoo covered much of his left forearm. His eyes were deep-set, shocked. As if he'd been expecting a visitor he'd shaved so recently that tiny beads of blood shone on the underside of his jaw. And he'd cut his hair with a scissors, now the gingery-graying hair fell just below his ears, newly washed, limp and thin.

Erma heard her prepared words. "Mr. Kethy, may I speak with you? Arno."

Part Three

THE SKULL: A LOVE STORY

THEY BROUGHT HIM the skull in a plastic bag, in pieces. Like broken crockery it was. A human skull smashed into approximately two hundred fragments, a few large enough to be immediately identified (a three-inch section of the lower jaw containing several teeth, a portion of the largest bone of the cranium), and the smallest about the size of his smallest fingernail. Contrary to popular belief, the human cranium isn't a single helmet-shaped bone but eight bones fused together, and the facial mask is fourteen bones fused together, and these, in the victim, had been smashed with a blunt object, smashed, dented, and pierced, as if the unknown killer had wanted not merely to kill his victim but to obliterate her very being. There was the almost palpable wish here that the dead should cease to exist even as matter: should never have existed. No hair remained on any skull fragments, for no scalp remained to contain hair, but swaths of sun-bleached brown hair had been found with the skeleton, and had been brought to him in a separate plastic bag. Since rotted clothing found at the scene was a female's clothing, the victim had been identified as female. A woman, or an older adolescent girl.

"A jigsaw puzzle. In three dimensions."

He smiled. Since boyhood he'd been one to love puzzles.

He was not old. Didn't look old, didn't behave old, didn't perceive of himself as old. Yet he knew that others, envious of him, wished to perceive him as old, and this infuriated him. He was a stylish dresser. Often he was seen in dark turtleneck sweaters, a wine-colored leather coat that fell below his knees. In warm weather he wore shirts open at the throat, sometimes T-shirts that showed to advantage his well-developed arm and shoulder muscles. When his hair began to thin in his mid-fifties he simply shaved his head, that tended to be olive-hued, veined, with a look of an upright male organ throbbing with vigor, belligerence, good humor. You couldn't help but notice and react to Kyle Cassity: to label such a man a "senior citizen" was absurd and demeaning.

Now he was sixty-seven, and of that age. He would have had to concede, as a younger man he'd often ignored his elders. He'd taken them for granted, he'd written them off as irrelevant. Of course, Kyle Cassity was a different sort of elder. There was no one quite like him.

A maverick, he thought himself. Not to be labeled. Born in 1935 in Harrisburg, PA, a long-time resident of Wayne, NJ: unique and irreplaceable.

Among his numerous relatives he'd long been an enigma: generous in times of crisis, otherwise distant, indifferent. True, he'd had something of a reputation as a womanizer until recent years, yet he'd remained married to the same devoted wife for four decades. His three children, when they were living at home, had competed for their father's attention, but they'd loved him, you might have said they'd worshipped him, though now in adulthood they were closer to their mother, emotionally. (Outside his marriage, unknown to his family, Kyle had fathered another child, a daughter, whom he'd never known.) Professionally, Dr. Kyle Cassity was something of a maverick as well. A tenured senior professor on the faculty of William Paterson College of New Jersey, as likely to teach in the adult night division as in the undergraduate daytime school, as likely to teach a sculpting workshop in the arts school as a graduate seminar in the School of Health, Education, and Science. His advanced degrees were in anthropology, sociology, and forensic science; he'd had a year of medical school, and a year of law school. At Paterson College he'd developed a course titled "The Sociology of 'Crime' in America" that had attracted as many as four hundred students before Professor Cassity, overwhelmed by his own popularity. had retired it.

His public reputation in New Jersey was as an expert prosecution witness and a frequent consultant for the New Jersey Department of Forensics. He'd been the subject of numerous media profiles, including a cover story in the *Newark Star-Ledger* Sunday Magazine bearing the eye-catching caption SCULPTOR KYLE CASSITY FIGHTS CRIME WITH HIS FINGERTIPS. Was such publicity embarrassing? Or did it, in a way, gratify his sometimes childish vanity, his wish to be not merely known but well-known, not merely liked but well-liked? In his heart he wasn't an ambitious man.

He gave away many of his sculptures, to individuals, museums, schools. He gave lectures for no fee throughout the state.

As a scientist he had little sentiment. He knew that the individual, within the species, counts for very little; the survival of the species is everything. But as a forensic specialist he focussed his attention upon individuals: the uniqueness of crime victims, and the uniqueness of those who have committed these crimes. Where there was a victim, there would be a criminal or criminals. There could be no ambiguity here. Kyle had no patience for the proviso . . . "Innocent until proven guilty." You were guilty, guilty as hell, as soon as you committed a crime.

As Dr. Kyle Cassity he worked with the remains of victims. Often these were were badly decomposed, mutilated, or broken, seemingly past reconstruction and identification. He was good at his work, and had gotten better over the years. He loved a good puzzle. A puzzle no one else could solve except Kyle Cassity. He perceived of the shadowy faceless as-yet unnamed perpetrators of crime as human prey whom he was hunting, and was licensed to hunt.

"POOR GIRL. IT ended for you sooner than it should have, eh?"

This skull! What a mess. Never had Kyle seen bones so broken. How many powerful blows must have been struck to reduce the skull, the face, the living brain to such broken matter, Kyle tried to imagine:

twenty? thirty? fifty? A frenzied killer, you would surmise. Better to imagine madness than that the killer had been coolly methodical, smashing his victim's skull, face, teeth to make identification impossible.

No fingertips—no fingerprints—remained, of course. The victim's exposed flesh had long since rotted from her bones. The body had been dumped sometime in the late spring or early summer in a field above an abandoned gravel pit near Toms River in the southern part of the state, a half-hour drive from Atlantic City. Bones had been scattered by wildlife but most had been located and reassembled: the victim had been approximately five feet two, with a small frame, a probable weight of one hundred to one hundred ten pounds. Judging by the hair, Caucasian.

Here was a grisly detail, not released to the press: Not only had the victim's skull been beaten in, but the state medical examiner had discovered that her arms and legs had been severed from her body by a "bluntly sharp" weapon like an ax.

Kyle shuddered, reading the report. Christ!—he hoped the dismemberment had been after, not before, the death.

Strange it seemed to him: the manic energy the killer had expended in trying to destroy his victim in the most literal way, he might have used to dig a deep grave and cover it with rocks and gravel so that it would never be discovered. For of course a dumped body will eventually be discovered.

Yet the killer hadn't buried this body. Why not?

"Must have wanted it to be found. Must have been proud of what he did."

What the murderer had broken, Dr. Cassity would reconstruct. He had no doubt that he could do it. Pieces of bone would be missing of course, but he could compensate for this with synthetic materials. Once he had a plausible skull, he could reconstruct a plausible face for it out of clay, and once he had this, he and a female sketch artist with whom he'd worked in the past would make sketches of the face in colored pencil, from numerous angles, for investigators to work with. Kyle Cassity's reconstruction would be broadcast through the state, printed on flyers, and posted on the Internet.

Homicides were rarely solved unless the victim could be identified. Kyle had done a number of successful facial reconstructions in the past, though never working at such a disadvantage. This was a rare case. And yet, it was a finite task: the pieces of bone had been given to him, he had only to put them together.

When Kyle began working with the skull in his laboratory at the college, the victim had been dead for approximately four months: through the near-tropical heat of a southern New Jersey summer. In his work place, Kyle kept the air conditioning at 65° F. He played CDs: Bach's *Well-Tempered Clavier* and *Goldberg Variations,* performed by Glenn Gould, most suited him. Music of brilliance and precision, rapid, dazzling as a waterfall, that existed solely in the present moment; music without emotion, and without associations.

Someone's daughter. Missing four months. By now they must know. Must be resigned.

THE HAIR! It was fair, sun-bleached brown with shades of red, still showing a distinct ripply wave. Six swaths had been gathered at the crime scene and brought to his laboratory in a separate plastic bag. Kyle placed them on a windowsill where, when he glanced up from his exceedingly close work with tweezers and bits of bone, he could see them clearly. The longest swath was seven inches. The victim had worn her hair long, to her shoulders. From time to time, Kyle reached out to touch it.

Sun-warmed on the windowsill. Lustrous burnished-brown. Clinging to his fingers with static electricity, as if alive.

EIGHT DAYS: It would take longer than Kyle anticipated. For he was working with exasperating slowness, and he was making many more small mistakes than he was accustomed to.

His hands were steady as always. His eyes, strengthened by bifocal lenses, were as reliable as always.

Yet it seemed to be happening that when Kyle was away from the laboratory, his hands began to shake just perceptibly, as in the aftermath of tension, or terror. And once he was away from the unsparing fluorescent lights, his vision wasn't so sharp.

He would mention this to no one. And no one would notice. No doubt, it would go away.

Already by the end of the second day he'd tired of Bach performed by Glenn Gould. The pianist's humming ceased to be eccentric and became unbearable. The intimacy of another's thoughts, like a bodily odor, you don't really want to share. He tried listening to other CDs, piano music, unaccompanied cello, then gave up to work in silence except of course there is no silence: traffic noises below, airplanes taking off and landing at Newark International Airport, the sound of his own blood pulsing in his ears.

Strange: the killer didn't bury her.

Strange: to hate another human being so much.

Hope to Christ she was dead by the time he began with the ax . . .

"KYLE, WHAT IS this new project? You seem so . . ."

Distracted, Vivian might have wished to say. Her voice was hesitant and mild and in no way confrontational. For these two had been married for more than forty years and Kyle's wife had long ago learned how to gauge his moods, how to interpret his ominous silences. Seeing him now pause on the stairs, frowning, running an impatient hand over his smooth, darkly flushed and veined head as if a thought had suddenly struck him.

". . . seem so distressed. Kyle?"

Kyle looked toward her, and paused. Then he seemed to wake from his trance and smiled, saying, "Am I? I don't mean to be."

In this way, polite, pleasant, he deflected her question. His immediate response to an interruption of his thoughts was often a smile.

"Is it . . . anything we can talk about?"

"Is what 'anything we can talk about'?"

He wasn't angry with Vivian, he was protective of Vivian. But he did rather resent her use of the word *distressed*.

Not very likely, that Kyle Cassity would be distressed.

He had no interest in discussing his forensic work with his wife, or with anyone except fellow professionals. Her naive questions and invariably emotional responses bored him. If he confided in Vivian about the skull, her soft face would stiffen. Her fingers would flutter at her throat and her eyes would register alarm, dread, even hurt.

Oh Kyle, how can you work with such ugly, such hideous . . .

Why do you ask, then?

You're my husband, I want to know. I want to share . . .

No. You don't.

In his domestic life, Kyle made every effort to be good-natured. As a younger man, he'd been difficult: but those days were gone. He no longer allowed his frustrations with his work to erupt into displays of temper with his family. He no longer saw other women, he no longer became involved with sexually attractive, needy, manipulative women. He'd outgrown not passion exactly, for often he felt still the wayward pangs of sexual desire, but the capacity for taking passion seriously. Among those closest to him Kyle had cultivated his good nature like a paper mask. Not a rubber mask that clung to his face and might have interfered with his breathing, not a gargoyle-mask that called attention to itself. Kyle Cassity's mask was smiling, affable, kindly, patient. He'd been a charismatic lecturer at the college, and he maintained some of that spotlit affability around the house. Through the mask's mouth he could even kiss, sometimes. Brushing his lips against the lips of the woman who was his wife. Brushing his lips against the cheeks of the adults who were his grown children, and now the young children, scarcely known to him, who were his grandchildren. Through the mask's smiling eye-holes he regarded the world, that region of infinite chaos, sorrow, and cruelty, with a sunny equanimity.

Vivian was saying, not accusing but simply saying, in the manner of one naming a mystery, that he hadn't seemed to be sleeping very well lately, and he didn't have much appetite, and she wondered if he was working on something stressful . . . "I wish you would tell me. If there's anything you can talk about?"

"Vivian, yes. Of course."

He was on his way out. Though it was nearly 10 P.M., he wanted to return to work. Through dinner he'd been distracted by thoughts of the skull, that was now about one-quarter re-assembled. Once he reached a critical point in the reconstruction, the remainder would go quickly: like completing a jigsaw puzzle. His heart yearned for that moment with the avidity of a young lover.

His lips brushed against the woman's cheek, in passing.

IN PROFESSOR CASSITY'S spacious high-ceilinged office adjacent to his laboratory there was a sofa. Old, battered, but comfortable, having been put to variegated pragmatic uses over the years. If needed, he could sleep there.

"NOW YOU HAVE a friend, dear. 'Kyle' is your friend."

The victim had been between eighteen and thirty years old, it was estimated. A size four, petite, they'd estimated her rotted clothing to have been. Size six, a single open-toed shoe found in the gravel pit. She'd had a small rib cage, small pelvis.

No way of determining if she'd ever been pregnant, or given birth.

No rings had been found amid the scattered bones. Only just a pair of silver hoop earrings, pierced. The ears of the victim had vanished as if they'd never been, only the earrings remained dully gleaming.

"Maybe he took your rings. You must have had rings."

The skull had a narrow forehead and a narrow, slightly receding chin. The cheekbones were high and sharp. This would be helpful in sculpting the face. Distinctive characteristics. She'd had an overbite. Kyle couldn't know if her nose had been long or short, a pug nose, or narrow at the tip. In the sketches they'd experiment with different noses, hair styles, gradations of color of the eyes.

"Were you pretty? 'Pretty' gets you into trouble."

On the windowsill, the dead girl's hair lay in lustrous/sinuous strands. Kyle reached out to touch it: so soft.

MARRIAGE: A MYSTERY.

For how was it possible that a man with no temperament for a long-term relationship with one individual, no evident talent for domestic life, family, children can nonetheless remain married, happily it appeared, for more than four decades?

Kyle laughed. "Somehow, it happened."

He was the father of three children within this marriage, and he'd loved them. Now they were grown—grown somewhat distant—and gone from Wayne, New Jersey. The two eldest were parents themselves.

They, and their mother, knew nothing of their shadowy half-sister.

Nor did Kyle. He'd lost touch with the mother twenty-six years ago.

His relationship with Vivian had never been very passionate. He'd wanted a wife, not a mistress. He wouldn't have wished to calculate how long it had been since they'd last made love. Even when they'd been newly married their lovemaking had been awkward, for Vivian had been so inexperienced, sweetly naive and shy, that had seemed part of her appeal. Often they'd made love in the dark. Few words passed between them. If Vivian spoke, Kyle became distracted. Often he'd watched her sleep, not wanting to wake her. Lightly he'd touched her, stroked her unconscious body, and then himself.

Now he was sixty-seven. Not old: he knew that. Yet, the last time he'd had sex had been with a woman he'd met at a conference in Pittsburgh, the previous April; before that, it had been with a woman one-third his age, of ambiguous identity, possibly a prostitute.

Though she hadn't asked him for money. She'd introduced herself to him on the street saying she'd seen him interviewed on New Jersey Network, hadn't she? At the end of the single evening they spent together she'd lifted his hand to kiss the fingers in a curious gesture of homage and self-abnegation.

" 'Dr. Cassity.' I revere a man like you."

THE CRUCIAL BONES were all in place: cheeks, above the eyes, jaw, chin. These determined the primary contours of the face. The space between the eyes, for instance. Width of the forehead in proportion to that of the face at the level of the nose, for instance. Beneath the epidermal mask, the irrefutable structure of bone.

Kyle was beginning to see her now.

Yet not clearly, for her face was in shadow. That hazy-gray shadow where fluorescent lighting doesn't reach. A perverse and sickly sort of shadow like a gauzy forgetful mind. Nor was her voice clear. She stood about fifteen feet from Kyle in the doorway leading to his office. Turned slightly at the waist as if she'd only just noticed him, or if she meant to show her small but pointed breasts, her slender waist. A man's hands could fit around that waist. In her ears glittered silver hoop earrings. Her smile was sweetly shy, hesitant. Her chin was narrow as a child's, her nose was small and snubbed. Her skin was pale, smooth, luminous. Her hair in a wavy, lustrous tangle fell past her shoulders and looked as if it had just been brushed.

Dr. Cassity! Dad-dy. See, I revere you?

Kyle woke, startled. His head had slumped forward onto his crossed arms, he'd slept at his workbench beneath glaring fluorescent lights. Against his warm forehead, an impress of bone fragments. He rubbed his face, his dazzled eyes.

Wanting to protest, nothing like that had ever happened to him before.

THE EYE-HOLES OF the skull regarded him with equanimity. Whatever question he would put to it, Kyle would have to answer himself.

Dr. Cassity. He had a Ph.D., not an M.D. To his sensitive ears there was always something subtly jeering, mocking, in the title "Doctor."

He'd given up asking his graduate students to call him "Kyle." Now he was older, and had his reputation, none of these young people could bring themselves to speak to him familiarly. They wanted to revere him, he supposed. They wanted the distance of age between them, an abyss not to be crossed.

Dr. Cassity. In Kyle's family, this individual had been his grandfather. An internist in Harrisburg, Pennsylvania, whose field of specialization was gastroenterology. As a boy Kyle had revered his grandfather, and had wanted to be a doctor. He'd been fascinated by the books in his grandfather's library: massive medical texts that seemed to hold the answers to all questions, anatomical drawings and color plates revealing the extraordinary interiors of human bodies. Many of these were magnified, reproduced in bright livid color that had looked moist. There were astonishing photographs of naked bodies, bodies in the process of being dissected. Kyle's heart beat hard as he stared at these, in secret. That such things should be! That such things should be allowed! Someone, a man like Kyle's own grandfather, had the privilege of taking up a sharp instrument and making an incision in human flesh and beginning to cut . . . Decades later, Kyle sometimes felt a stirring of erotic interest, a painful throb in the groin, reminded by some visual cue of those old forbidden medical texts in his long-deceased grandfather's library.

Beginning at about the age of eleven he'd secretly copied some of the drawings and plates by placing tracing paper over them and using a pencil. Later, he began to draw his own figures without the aid of tracing paper. He would discover that, where fascination gripped him, he was capable of executing surprising likenesses. In school art classes he was singled out for praise. He became most adept at rapid charcoal sketches, executed with half-shut eyes. And later, sculpting busts, figures. His hands moving swiftly, shaping and reshaping clay.

"My hands just move, I guess. They have their own way of thinking."

This emergence of "talent" embarrassed him. To obscure his interest in the human figure *in extremis,* he learned to make other sorts of sculptures as well. His secret interests were hidden, he believed, inside the other.

It would turn out, he disliked medical school. The dissecting room had revulsed him, not aroused him. He'd nearly fainted in his first pathology lab. He hated the fanatic competition of medical school, the almost military hegemony of rank. He would quit before he flunked out. Forensic science was as close as he would get to the human body, but here, as he told interviewers, his task was re-assembling, not dissecting.

THE SKULL WAS nearly completed. Beautifully shaped it seemed to Kyle, like a Grecian bust. The empty eye-sockets and nose-cavity another observer would think ugly, Kyle saw filled in, for the girl had revealed herself to him. The dream had been fleeting yet remained with him, far more vivid in his mind's eye than anything he'd experienced in his own recent life.

Was she living, and where?

His lost daughter. His mind drifted from the skull and onto her, who was purely abstract to him, not even a name.

He'd seen her only twice, as an infant, and each time briefly. At the time her mother, manipulative, emotionally unstable, hadn't yet named her; or, if she had, for some reason she hadn't wanted Kyle to know.

"She doesn't need a name just yet. She's mine."

Kyle had been deceived by this woman who'd called herself "Letitia," an invented name probably, a stripper's fantasy name, though possibly it was genuine. Letitia had sought out Kyle Cassity at the college where he'd been a highly visible faculty member, thirty-nine years old. Her pretext for coming into his office was to seek advice about a career in psychiatric social work. She'd claimed to be enrolled in the night division of the college which turned out to be untrue. She'd claimed to be a wife estranged from a husband who was "threatening" her which had possibly been true.

Kyle had been flattered by the young woman's attention. Her obvious attraction to him. In time, he'd given her money. Always cash, never a check. And he never wrote to her: though she left passionate love notes for him beneath his office door, beneath the windshield of his car, he never reciprocated. As one familiar with the law he knew: never commit yourself in handwriting! As, in more recent years, Kyle Cassity would never send any e-mail message he wouldn't have wanted to see exposed to all the world.

He hadn't fully trusted Letitia but he'd been sexually aroused by her, he liked being in her company. She was a dozen years younger than he, reckless, unreliable. Not pretty, but very sexual, seductive. After she vanished from his life he would suppose, sure, she'd been seeing other men all along, taking money from other men. Yet he accepted the pregnancy as his responsibility. She'd told him the baby would be his, and he hadn't disbelieved her. He had no wish to dissociate himself from Letitia at this difficult time in her life, though his own children were twelve, nine, five years old. And Vivian loved him, and presumably trusted him, and would have been deeply wounded if she'd known of his affair.

Though possibly Vivian had known. Known something. There was the evidence of Kyle's infrequent lovemaking with her, a fumbling in silence.

But in December 1976 Letitia and the infant girl abruptly left New Jersey. Even before the birth Letitia had been drifting out of her married lover's life. He'd had to assume that she found another man who meant more to her. He had to assume that his daughter would never have been told who her true father was. Twenty-six years later, if she were still alive, Letitia probably wouldn't have remembered Kyle Cassity's name.

"NOW: TELL US your name, dear."

After a week and a day of painstaking work, the skull was complete. All the bone fragments had been used, and Kyle had made synthetic pieces to hold the skull together. Excited now, he made a mold of the skull and on this mold he began to sculpt a face in clay. Rapidly his fingers worked as if remembering. In this phase of the reconstruction he played new CDs to celebrate: several Bach cantatas, Beethoven's Seventh and Ninth Symphonies, Maria Callas as Tosca.

EARLY IN OCTOBER the victim was identified: her name was Sabrina Jackson, a part-time community college student studying computer technology and working as a cocktail waitress in Easton, Pennsylvania. The young woman had been reported missing by her family in mid-May. At the time of her disappearance she'd been twenty-three, weighed one hundred fifteen pounds, her photographs bore an uncanny resemblance to the sketches Kyle Cassity and his assistant had made. In March she'd broken up with a man with whom she'd been living for several years and she'd told friends she was quitting school and quitting work and "beginning a new life" with a new male friend who had a "major position" at one of the Atlantic City casinos. She'd packed suitcases, shut up her apartment, left a message on her answering service that was teasingly enigmatic.

> Hi there! This is Sabrina. I sure am sorry to be missing your call but I am OUT OF TOWN TILL FURTHER NOTICE. Can't say when I will be returning calls but I WILL TRY.

No one had heard from Sabrina Jackson since. No one in Atlantic City recalled having seen her, and nothing had come of detectives questioning casino employees. Nor did anyone in Easton seem to know the identity of the man with whom she'd gone away. Sabrina

Jackson had disappeared in similar ways more than once in the past, in the company of men, and so her family and friends had been hesitant at first to report her missing. Always there was the expectation that Sabrina would "turn up." But the sketches of the Toms River victim bore an unmistakable resemblance to Sabrina Jackson, and the silver earrings found with the remains were identified as hers.

" 'Sabrina.' "

It was a beautiful name. But Sabrina Jackson wasn't a beautiful young woman.

Kyle stared at photographs of the missing woman, whose blemished skin was a shock. Nor was her skin pale as he'd imagined but rather dark, and oily. Her eyebrows weren't delicately arched as he'd drawn them but heavily penciled in, as the outline of her fleshy mouth had been exaggerated by lipstick. Still, there was the narrow forehead, the snubbed nose, the small, receding chin. The shoulder-length hair, wavy, burnished-brown, as Kyle had depicted it. When you looked from the sketches drawn in colored pencil to the actual woman in the photographs, you were tempted to think that one was a younger, sentimentally idealized version of the other; or that the two girls were sisters, one very pretty and feminine and the other somewhat coarse, sensuous.

"You? Always, it was you."

Strange it seemed to him, difficult to realize: the skull he'd reconstructed was the skull of this woman, Sabrina Jackson, and not the skull of the girl he'd sketched. Always, Sabrina Jackson had been the victim. Kyle Cassity was being congratulated for his excellent work but he felt as if a trick had been played on him.

He contemplated for long minutes the girl in the photographs who smiled, preened, squinted into the camera as if for his benefit. The bravado of not-knowing how we must die: how our most capricious poses outlive us. The heavy makeup on Sabrina Jackson's blemished face made her look older than twenty-three. She wore cheap tight sexy clothes, tank tops and V-neck blouses, leather miniskirts, leather trousers, high-heeled boots. She was a smoker. She did appear to have a sense of humor, Kyle liked that in her. Mugging for the camera. Pursing her lips in a kiss. The type who wouldn't ask a man for money directly;

but if you offered it, she certainly wouldn't turn it down. A small pleased smile would transform her face as if this were the highest of compliments. A murmured *Thanks!* And the bills quickly wadded and slipped into her pocket and no more need be said of the transaction.

The skull was gone from Kyle's laboratory. There would be a private burial of Sabrina Jackson's remains in Easton, Pennsylvania. Now it was known that the young woman was dead, the investigation into her disappearance would intensify. In time, Kyle didn't doubt, there would be an arrest.

Kyle Cassity! Congratulations.

Amazing, that work you do.

Good time to retire, eh? Quit while you're ahead.

There was no longer mandatory retirement at the college. He would never retire as a sculptor, an artist. And he could continue working indefinitely for the State of New Jersey since he was a freelance consultant, not an employee subject to the state's retirement laws. These protests rose in him, he didn't utter.

He'd ceased playing the new CDs. His office and his laboratory were very quiet. A pulse beat sullenly in his head. Disappointed! For Sabrina Jackson wasn't the one he'd sought.

"I RESENT THIS. You mooning over the dead."

Startled, Kyle glanced up from the *Newark Star-Ledger* he was holding before him. He'd been reading of Sabrina Jackson, new leads in the investigation into her murder. It was a week since he'd shipped back the skull. He'd been staring at the young woman's jauntily smiling photograph prominent on the first page of the second section of the newspaper. Vivian must have come up behind him, silently.

Kyle was astonished by the bitterness in his wife's voice, and by the clumsy violence with which she struck the newspaper, as a child might do. "A man your age! Making a fool of himself over a girl young enough to be your—granddaughter."

"Vivian, for God's sake. I'm only just reading the paper. This is—"

"I know what it is! Always the dead! You never cared so much for Jacky. You never cared so much for any of us."

"Vivian—"

"No. Don't touch me. Your clammy hands *disgust me.*"

In the years of their marriage Vivian had never spoken to Kyle Cassity like this.

He couldn't have been more shocked than if she'd struck him with her fists. She left the room, and her footsteps were heavy and graceless on the stairs. Kyle knew he must follow her, though he dreaded it.

In the woman's face he had seen no love for him. No respect.

Upstairs in their bedroom that smelled of the lavender sachets she kept in the bureau drawers Vivian was crying, but tears glistened like hot acid on her face. When Kyle tried to touch her she pushed away his hands. "Your 'fetishes'—that's what they are. Skulls. Bones. Drawings of dead people. Dead women. I've seen them, they disgust me." Another time Kyle was shocked, and deeply embarrassed. Had Vivian been going through the file drawers in his study? He had a collection of explicit anatomical drawings and color plates hidden away, at which he hadn't glanced in years. Choked with indignation Vivian said, "You never could touch me in the light, could you! Never could make love to me knowing it was *me.* I knew about your other women. Everybody knew. Our children knew, that's why they didn't respect you when they were growing up—that's why they don't respect you now. I wasn't going to give my husband up to those women, I wanted you then. I thought I loved you. But now—"

There were no words for Kyle to stammer except flat banal unconvincing words in which he couldn't himself believe. "Vivian, you don't mean it. What you're saying—"

"I'm speaking the truth for once. This last time, the way you've been behaving, gone most of the time, prowling the house in the night, rude, selfish, mooning over her, whoever she is, another one of the dead. A man your age!" Vivian spoke with the liquidy passion of Callas, her voice rising to madness. "You disgust me, I've decided I don't want to live with disgust any longer. Not at my age. I deserve better. I'm going to stay with Jacky. I've called her, it's been decided. I don't know when I'll be back." Jacky was their married daughter, now forty years old; she lived with her family in Evanston, Illinois.

Kyle was having difficulty absorbing what he heard. There was a roaring in his ears. Decided? Something had been decided.

"Vivian, don't be ridiculous. You can't possibly—"

"I can. I can, and I will. I *am*."

Kyle stood smiling as a man might smile who has been struck a mortal blow. *It's over. She knows my heart.* He tried to reason with Vivian but she would not be dissuaded. In her fiery face shone the valor of revenge. When Kyle fumbled to embrace her she pushed him away with an expression of contempt.

"We're too old for love. We make ourselves ridiculous."

IN THE MORNING when Vivian was preparing to leave, Kyle said good-bye to her quietly and without rancor. He took her limp hand that felt so soft and so vulnerable in his, and he would have closed his arms around her in a clumsy farewell except with a little cry of hurt she stepped aside, her face averted. She was fearful of leaving, Kyle saw. But he would not attempt another time to dissuade her. As she'd seen into his heart so he had seen into hers. Though he knew he wouldn't be home to take the call, he said, "Call me tonight. Keep in touch." After forty years he could not bring himself to speak her name another time.

Before the taxi arrived to take Vivian to Newark Airport, Kyle was gone. He would drive to Easton, Pennsylvania, as he'd been planning irresolutely for days. His heart beat with the avidity of a young lover.

"OFFICER. COME IN."

The face of Sabrina Jackson's mother was tight as a sausage in its casing. She made an effort to smile like a sick woman trying to be upbeat, but wanting you to know she was trying for your sake. In her dull-eager voice she greeted Kyle Cassity, and she would persist in calling him "Officer" though he'd explained to her that he wasn't a police officer, only just a private citizen who'd helped with the investigation. He was the man who'd drawn the composite sketch of her daughter that she and other relatives of the missing girl had identified.

Strictly speaking, of course this wasn't true. Kyle hadn't drawn a sketch of Sabrina Jackson but of a fictitious girl. He'd given life to the skull in his keeping, not to Sabrina Jackson of whom he'd never heard. But such metaphysical subtleties would have been lost on the forlorn

Mrs. Jackson who was staring at Kyle as if, though he'd just reminded her, she couldn't recall why he'd come, who exactly he was. A plainclothes officer with the Easton police, or somebody from New Jersey?

Gently, Kyle reminded her: the drawing of Sabrina? That had appeared on TV, in papers? On the Internet, worldwide?

"Yes. That was it. That picture." Mrs. Jackson spoke slowly as if each word were a hurtful pebble in her throat. Her small warm bloodshot eyes, crowded inside the fatty ridges of her face, were fixed upon him with a desperate urgency. "When we saw that picture on the TV . . . We knew."

Kyle murmured an apology. He was being made to feel responsible for something. His oblong shaved head had never felt so exposed and so vulnerable, veins throbbing with heat.

"Mrs. Jackson, I wish that things could have turned out differently."

"She always did the wildest things, more than once I'd given up on her, I'd get so damn pissed with her, but she'd land on her feet, you know?—like a cat. That Sabrina! She's the only one of the kids counting even her two brothers, made us worry so." Oddly, Mrs. Jackson was smiling. She was vexed at her daughter, but clearly somewhat proud of her too. "She had a good heart, though, Officer. Sabrina could be the sweetest girl when she made that effort. Like the time, it was Mother's Day, I was pissed as hell because I knew, I just knew, not a one of them was going to call—"

Strange and disconcerting it was to Kyle, the mother of the dead girl was so young: no more than forty-five. A bloated-looking little woman with a coarse, ruddy face, in slacks and a floral-print shirt and flip-flops on her pudgy bare feet, hobbled with a mother's grief like an extra layer of fat. Technically, she was young enough to be Kyle Cassity's daughter.

Well! All the world, it seemed, was getting to be young enough to be Kyle Cassity's daughter.

"I'd love to see photographs of Sabrina, Mrs. Jackson. I've just come to pay my respects."

"Oh, I've got 'em! They're all ready to be seen. Everybody's been over here wanting to see them. I mean not just the family, and Sabrina's friends, you wouldn't believe all the friends that girl has from just high school alone, but the TV people, newspaper reporters. There's been more people through here, Officer, in the last ten–twelve days than in all of our life until now."

"I'm sorry for that, Mrs. Jackson. I don't mean to disturb you."

"Oh, no! It's got to be done, I guess."

The phone rang several times while Mrs. Jackson was showing Kyle a cascade of snapshots crammed into a family album, but the fleshy little woman, seated on a sofa, made no effort to answer it. Even unmoving on the sofa she was inclined to breathlessness, panting. "Those calls can go onto the answering service. I use that all the time now. See, I don't know who's gonna call any more. Used to be, it'd be just somebody I could predict, like out of ten people in the world, or one of those damn solicitors I just hang up on, but now, could be anybody, almost. People call here saying they might know who's the guilty son of a bitch did that to Sabrina but I tell them call the police, see? Call the police, not me. I'm not the police."

Mrs. Jackson spoke vehemently. Her body exuded an odor of intense excited emotion. Hesitantly Kyle leaned toward her, frowning at the the snapshots. Some were old Polaroids, faded. Others were creased and dog-eared. In family photos of years ago it wasn't immediately obvious which girl was Sabrina, Mrs. Jackson had to point her out. Kyle saw a brattish-looking teenager, hands on her hips and grinning at the camera. As a young adolescent she'd had a bad skin, which must have been hard on her granting even her high spirits and energy. In some of the close-ups, Kyle saw an almost-attractive girl, warm, hopeful, appealing in her openness. *Hey: look at me! Love me.* He wanted to love her. He wanted not to be disappointed in her. Mrs. Jackson sighed heavily. "People say, those drawings looked just like Sabrina, that's how they recognized her, y'know, and I guess I can see it, but not really. If you're the mother you see different things. Sabrina was never pretty-pretty like in the drawings, she'd have laughed like hell to see 'em. It's like somebody took Sabrina's face and did a makeover, like cosmetic surgery, y'know? What Sabrina wanted, she'd talk about sort of joking but serious, was, what is it, 'chin injection'? 'Implant'?" Ruefully Mrs. Jackson was stroking her chin, receding like her daughter's.

Kyle said, as if encouraging. "Sabrina was very attractive. She didn't need cosmetic surgery. Girls say things like that. I have a daughter, and when she was growing up . . . You can't take what they say seriously."

"That's true, Officer. You can't."

"Sabrina had personality. You can see that, Mrs. Jackson, in all her pictures."

"Oh! Christ. Did she ever."

Mrs. Jackson winced as if, amid the loose, scattered snapshots in the album, her fingers had encountered something sharp.

For some time they continued examining the snapshots. Kyle supposed that the grief-stricken mother was seeing her lost daughter anew, and in some way alive, through a stranger's eyes. He couldn't have said why looking at the snapshots had come to seem so crucial to him. For days he'd been planning this visit, summoning his courage to call Mrs. Jackson. He'd nearly forgotten the painful episode with Vivian the night before: had scarcely thought of Vivian at all. No doubt, she would return to their marriage. No doubt, their marriage would endure. The time for a breakup was past: Vivian was right, people their age made themselves ridiculous very easily. Mrs. Jackson said, showing him a tinted matte graduation photo of Sabrina in a white cap and gown, wagging her fingers and grinning at the camera, "High school was Sabrina's happy time. She was so, so popular. She should've gone right to college, instead of what she did do, she'd be alive now." Abruptly then Mrs. Jackson's mood shifted, she began to complain bitterly. "You wouldn't believe! People saying the cruelest things about Sabrina. People you'd think would be her old friends, and teachers at the school, calling her 'wild'—'unpredictable.' Like all my daughter did was hang out in bars. Go out with married men." Mrs. Jackson's ruddy skin darkened with indignation. Half-moons of sweat showed beneath her arms. She said, panting, "If the police had let it alone, it'd be better, almost. We reported her missing back in May. Over the summer, it was like everybody'd say, 'Where's Sabrina, where's she gone to now?' A bunch of us drove to Atlantic City and asked around, but nobody'd seen her, it's a big place, people coming and going all the time, and the cops kept saying 'Your daughter is an adult' and crap like that like it was Sabrina's own decision to disappear. They listened to her tape and came to that conclusion. It wasn't even a 'missing persons' case. So—we got to thinking maybe Sabrina was just traveling with this man friend of hers. The rumor got to be, this guy had money like Donald Trump. He was a high-stakes gambler. They'd have gotten bored with Atlantic City and went to Vegas. Maybe they'd driven down into Mexico. Sabrina was always saying how she wanted to see Mexico. Now—all that's over." Mrs. Jackson shut the photo album, clumsily; a number of snapshots spilled out onto the floor. "See, Officer, things maybe should've been left the way they were. We were all just waiting for Sabrina to turn up, any time. But people like you poking around, 'investigating,' printing ugly things about my daughter in the paper, I don't even know why you're here taking up my time or who the hell you *are.*"

Kyle was taken by surprise, Mrs. Jackson had suddenly turned so belligerent. "I—I'm sorry. I only wanted—"

"Well, we don't want your sympathy. We don't need your goddamn sympathy, Mister. You can just go back to New Jersey or wherever the hell you came from, intruding in my daughter's life."

Mrs. Jackson's eyes were moist and dilated and accusing. Her skin looked as if it would be scalding to the touch. Kyle was certain she wasn't drunk, he couldn't smell it on her breath, but possibly she was drugged. High on crystal meth, that was notorious in this part of Pennsylvania, run-down old cities like Easton.

Kyle protested, "But, Mrs. Jackson, you and your family would want to know, wouldn't you? I mean, what had happened to . . ." He paused awkwardly, uncertain how to continue. Why should they want to know? Would he have wanted to know, in their place?

In a voice heavy with sarcasm Mrs. Jackson said, "Oh, sure. You tell me, Officer. You got all the answers."

She heaved herself to her feet. A signal it was time for her unwanted visitor to depart.

Kyle had dared to take out his wallet. He was deeply humiliated but determined to maintain his composure. "Mrs. Jackson, maybe I can help? With the funeral expenses, I mean."

Hotly the little woman said, "We don't want anybody's charity! We're doing just fine by ourselves."

"Just a—token of my sympathy."

Mrs. Jackson averted her eyes haughtily from Kyle's fumbling fingers, fanning her face with a *TV Guide.* He removed bills from his wallet, fifty-dollar bills, a one-hundred-dollar, folded them discreetly over, and placed them on an edge of the table.

Still, the indignant Mrs. Jackson didn't thank him. Nor did she trouble herself to see him to the door.

WHERE WAS HE? A neighborhood of dingy wood-frame bungalows, rowhouses. Northern outskirts of Easton, Pennsylvania. Mid-afternoon: too early to begin drinking. Kyle was driving along potholed streets uncertain where he was headed. He'd have to cross the river again to pick up the big interstate south . . . At a 7-Eleven he bought a six-pack of strong dark ale and parked in a weedy cul-de-sac between a cemetery and a ramp of the highway, drinking. The ale was icy-cold and made his forehead ache, not disagreeably. It was a bright blustery October day, a sky of high scudding clouds against a glassy blue. At the city's skyline, haze of the hue of chewing tobacco spittle. Certainly Kyle knew where he was: but where he was mattered less than something else, something crucial that had been decided, but he couldn't recall what that was, that had been decided, just yet. Except he knew it was crucial. Except so much that seemed crucial in his younger years had turned out to be not so, or not much so. A girl of about fourteen pedaled by on a bicycle, ponytail flying behind her head. She wore tight-fitting jeans, a backpack. She'd taken no notice of him as if he, and the car in which he was sitting, were invisible. With his eyes he followed her. Followed her as swiftly she pedaled out of sight. Such longing, such love suffused his heart! He watched the girl disappear, stroking a sinewy throbbing artery just below his jawline.

THE DEATHS: AN ELEGY

1.

"CRISSIE? HELLO."

The call came out of the void. That nasal voice so like her own. She could not have expected it, who had not thought of him in years. Instinctive now, unthinking, in the way in which we maintain our balance if we begin to slip on ice, was her response to well-intentioned queries about her family: she had none.

Her mother had died of breast cancer when she, Crista, was six years old, and her father and nine-year-old brother had died in an automobile accident in Olcott, New York, her hometown, only a few weeks after her mother's death.

Such explanations, when she felt obliged to make them, she made, quietly. The dignity of her manner—even as a child Crista had cultivated dignity, out of repugnance for its opposite—forestalled pity. More important for Crista, it forestalled further questions.

How terrible for you . . .

Well, I was very young. I was taken in by an aunt. I didn't lack for love.

All of this was both true and not-true. Certainly Crista had lacked for love, but she wasn't one to have expected love. Her original family had not been loving. Her father, maybe. At times. When not drinking. Her mother, Crista could not remember clearly.

For memory is a moral action, a choice. You can choose to remember. You can choose not.

Now the call. "Crissie? It's Henry."

As if he'd needed to identify himself.

For there was his voice, nasal, reedy, disagreeable to her ears, the unmistakable accent of western New York State she'd long tried to obliterate from her own speech. At once she'd recognized that voice. And there was "Crissie": no one had called her "Crissie" in the life after Olcott, New York. Meaning no one had called her that childhood name in more than twenty years.

Rapidly she calculated, even as she held the receiver to her ear trying to make sense of his imploring urgent words: it was June 2002 now, the deaths had occurred in June 1981. This meant, Henry was thirty years old. Thirty!

She tried to envision him: a spindly-limbed nine-year-old with eyes dark and luminous as their father's, and their mother's fair, carroty-brown hair. Henry, an adult. In a way, it was not possible. Her brain clamped down, against it.

Crista herself was twenty-seven. This seemed to her fully possible, probable. In fact, she felt older. Never would she become one of those tiresome individuals who profess, and perhaps actually feel, disbelief at their age. As a child of six she'd become an adult, and she had liked it. To be an adult—even as a child—is to exercise judgment, control. It's to successfully resist self-pity and to forestall pity, the most despicable of human responses, in others.

No one, not even a lover, in a succession of lovers, had been encouraged to call her "Crissie."

Yet there was the name, repeated. Punctuating her brother's conversation. Forcing her to acknowledge, yes she was the sister he could think of only as "Crissie," for indeed it would have been unnatural for him to have called her "Crista," as it would have been unnatural, impossible, for either of them as children to have called their parents by their first names.

Young parents they'd been. Married young, and having their babies young. Very young to have died: in their early thirties.

Crista was "Crista Ward." Her aunt had adopted her. Henry remained "Henry Eley," the old surname. She would wonder how he'd looked her up but supposed their aunt had informed him, where Crista had moved. She resented it, but would never speak of it to their aunt who had only meant well.

Henry was asking, "Can we see each other? I think it's time."

Crista's response was instinctive, unthinking. "Why?"

An unexpected response, and unanswerable. Henry was silent for a moment. If their conversation was a Ping-Pong game, Henry had failed to return his opponent's fiercely placed ball, he'd failed even to see it flying at him.

Henry said, not so much arguing as presenting his case, and the logic of his case, "Because I'm here, in the northeast, Crissie. And it's been so long. Mostly I live in the Bay Area. San Francisco. I was thinking I'd like to rent a car, and drive to see you, and the two of us could drive up to Olcott together, to the lake. We could do that."

Crista could not believe the words she was hearing.

"You haven't been back, have you?" Henry paused, as if hearing Crista's murmured reply, though in fact she said nothing, nor even framed words of reply. "I haven't, either. Of course."

Crista said, "I'm going to hang up now."

"Wouldn't you want to? Revisit Olcott? After so long? June nineteenth, 1981."

Crista hung up.

No. Never.

Though she understood that, through her life, she'd been awaiting such a call. From her lost brother Henry, or from someone. (In that twilight consciousness between sleep and waking, surely it was her parents she awaited. Their voices, their hands on her. Where their young attractive faces had been, Crista's memory could provide only blurs, like faces seen through wavy glass, or underwater. In the worst of the dreams, Crista opened her eyes wide and was blind. The wider she opened her eyes, the more helplessly blind.)

Possibly some of the belligerence in her character originated in this: she'd been awaiting a call, an explanation. She was owed this. A revelation. It was like waiting for a phone to ring—the phone would not ring. Except if you left, the phone would ring, and you would miss your opportunity, if only to repudiate the call and the caller and to replace the receiver. Thank you. No.

Now the phone had rung. The call had come. But it was her brother who knew no more than she, why what had happened to them had happened. Her brother who could not know more than she knew. (For how could he? She refused to believe this might be possible, though he was three years older.) Her brother who could not tell her what she wanted to hear. *Your father did not kill your mother. Another person killed her on the beach. Your father died because he couldn't bear the loneliness. His death was an accident.*

Yet that call, that revelation, had never come. She was ready, long she'd been ready to hear it. But it had not come. Another call had come in its place, unwanted.

Aloud she vowed, "No. Never."

YET: THREE DAYS later, there was Crista Ward waiting on the front stoop of her apartment building for her brother Henry Eley whom she had not seen in twenty-one years. He'd called back, and Crista must have weakened and changed her mind. Somehow, this had happened.

It wasn't like Crista, such a reversal. Still, it had happened.

She was dressed casually yet elegantly. Pale linen trousers, a silk blouse, and a fine-knit cotton sweater. These were designer sports clothes of understated quality, not conspicuous. She wore her hair that was a faded red-brown, prematurely threaded with silver, trimmed very short and curled against her head tight as a cap, needlessly clamped in place with a rod-like silver barrette behind her left ear. This was Crista Ward's distinctive look: calculated, stylish, nothing left to chance.

She was bringing a single overnight bag. For they had to stay overnight, the drive was too far otherwise. Crista supposed they would find a motel at Olcott Beach. She seemed to remember motels in that area, a middle-income resort area. Along the pebbly southern shore of Lake Ontario, numerous small motels. They'd made no definite plans beforehand, at least Crista didn't know of any plans her brother Henry might have made. They would revisit the old cottage on the lake—from a distance, probably, since strangers would be living in it now—and they would walk along the beach. They would talk together, become reacquainted. Why? Crista wondered. It was just as well, Crista had no lover at the present time. She could not have explained to him, why.

My lost brother. I must love him.

Olcott Beach retained in her memory an aura of festivity, excitement. There was a boardwalk overlooking the lake, there were amusement rides: Ferris wheel, merry-go-round, bumper cars. High-pitched tinkly music. Food smells, hot and greasy. She and Henry had been taken on the rides by—who? The adult figures were blurred. One was meant to be Mommy, the other had to be Daddy. When she tried to see, she could not. Vividly she recalled the taste of pink cotton candy, though. Root beer, chocolate Tastee-Freez in cones. She never ate sweets now, disliked the taste of sugar. Rather swallow a mouthful of ground glass than a mouthful of sugar.

Henry had planned to arrive by 11 A.M. He was driving north to Albany from New York City where he'd been staying for several days. Yet it was 11:20 A.M. when at last he drove up to the curb. By which time Crista was feeling fierce, indignant. Her first words to the man she took to be her brother were: "You're late. I've been waiting out here, and you're late." Why she'd chosen to wait outside, instead of in her apartment on the sixth floor, she had no idea.

The bearded man, grayer-haired than she'd envisioned, and thinner-faced, stared at her for a long moment as if disbelieving. Then he smiled, a smile that struck her as both boyish and aggressive, and said, "Crissie? *You?* Climb in."

She did. She would think afterward she'd had her choice of telling him she wasn't going with him after all, she'd changed her mind, but instead, face smarting as if she'd been slapped, she climbed into the car. Cheap compact rental car, she'd bumped her head on the door-frame. She could have wept. *This isn't Henry. I don't know this man.* She fumbled to take the hand extended to her. For a moment she was fearful of crying. Her heart beat in fury, refusing to cry. The bearded man was marveling, "Well. Crissie. Look at you." His eyes may have glistened with tears. His teeth shone with smiling. He was trying to embrace her, while Crista held herself stiff, not pointedly resisting yet not acquiescing, holding her breath against the sudden smell of him, unkempt hair, straggly beard, T-shirt and denim vest that needed laundering, if she'd retreated somewhere inside herself, that familiar place, a light becoming smaller, ever smaller, close to extinction.

Look at you. It was an adult voice yet immediately recognizable. The voice of Crista's lost brother, she had not seen since she was six years old.

AFTER *the deaths,* the children were taken in by relatives. Crista went to live with her mother's older sister whom she knew as Aunt Ellen and Henry went to live with his father's parents. There may have been a wish expressed by the children—Crista seemed to remember this, for she'd loved her brother very much—that they might live together. But neither Aunt Ellen nor Grandma and Grandpa Eley wanted both children. There was the expense. There was the responsibility. There was the belief that, so long as the children were raised apart, they would cease to remember *the deaths* more readily.

The deaths: this was what it was called. The cataclysmic event of June 19, 1981 when Rick Eley killed his wife Lorraine with a claw hammer, smashing her skull as she ran screaming from him on the beach at Olcott, and when Rick Eley subsequently killed himself by driving his car into a highway abutment later that night.

Logical to think then, as Crista grew to do, that *the deaths* had occurred at the same time. Not one death on the beach down beyond the Eleys' cottage on Lake Ontario, and, about forty minutes later, and fifteen miles away, the other.

The deaths. The deaths. Not *murder, suicide* but *the deaths.*

In time, in Crista's reasoning, her brother would be absorbed into *the deaths,* too. Exactly when this happened, how old, or young, Crista was, she wouldn't afterward recall. For Aunt Ellen never spoke of Henry, it was as if he'd vanished. If vanished, died. Telling her account of her childhood to others, which was always brief, seemingly impersonal, Crista would say that her mother had died of breast cancer (for so many women, mothers of school friends and acquaintances, seemed to die of or be stricken by cancer, this was a logical explanation), and that her father and nine-year-old brother Henry had died in an automobile accident only a few weeks afterward.

How terrible for you . . .

Well. I was very young.

Sometimes, not often but sometimes, Crista felt a pang of guilt for having killed Henry off. In the car crash with their father south of Lockport that same night. And why had she done it? She hadn't wanted to talk about him. She hadn't wanted to think about him. She hadn't wanted strangers to her life to inquire too closely into her life. She dreaded the inevitable prying query. *You and your brother must be very close, you must see each other often?*

Crista's mother's older sister Ellen Ward had been a public schoolteacher in Utica, New York. Unmarried, which was convenient. Her father's parents, devastated by what their son had allegedly done to his wife and to himself, moved from the small city of Lockport where they'd been living and resettled in Cincinnati. The driving distance between the households was less than six hundred miles but would seem to have been six thousand miles. Never were the children taken to see each other, and they were not encouraged to write or to speak on the phone. The adults became estranged from one another, as well. What had Aunt Ellen to do with the Eleys? *She* had not married into that family.

Strange how, at first Crista cried herself to sleep every night, she'd missed her Mommy and her Daddy and her brother Henry so badly, but then suddenly, overnight it seemed, she was forgetting. Since Aunt Ellen refused to speak of *the deaths* it was natural to begin to forget. Where there are no words, there memory cannot take root. By the first heavy snowfall in November, the child was well into forgetting. By the turn of the year, numbness had taken hold. Numbness like the falling snow. Numbness like sinking into sleep, in snow. Numbness that crept into her mittened hands, and into her booted feet. Wool mittens, wool socks, and waterproof rubber boots were not sufficient to keep out this numbness. For it was a delicious numbness, too.

No family? None?

I was taken in by an aunt. I didn't lack for love.

2.

THEY WERE SPEEDING westward across the hilly underpopulated breadth of New York State. On the map, their destination was a pinprick on the southern shore of Lake Ontario. Crista kept checking the map as if fearful of losing it: Olcott. Henry talked.

"Are you surprised to see me, Crissie? I mean, to see *me.* As I am."

"No. Not really."

"I look the way you'd imagined me? Really?"

Her brother was right to doubt Crista: for of course she wasn't telling the truth. It wouldn't have occurred to her to speak the truth, for that wasn't her practice. As a lawyer, in the hire of a large Albany firm, one of a team of lawyers, she was accustomed to dealing in expediencies, not truths.

In fact she was shocked by her brother's appearance. Shocked and disconcerted. She was wishing she'd never agreed to see him. She was wishing he'd never called her, she'd hung up the phone on both his calls. She was wishing he didn't exist.

Henry, her brother she'd adored. He could not have weighed more than one hundred thirty-five pounds. He was tall, perhaps five feet ten, yet emaciated. Willfully so, you could see. His beard was unkempt as an old brush, and prematurely graying. His hair was thinning at the crown of his head, falling to his shoulders. A sly skinny ferret-face out of which ghoul eyes shone. Shallow chest, a maddening Christly manner. His skin was sallow, and, on the cheeks, acne-scarred. His voice grated like sandpaper. Every utterance was a tease. Within five minutes Henry had identified himself to his sister he hadn't seen in twenty-one years as a Citizen of the World, but nominally a Citizen of the United States. He was a vegetarian, a licensed practitioner/instructor of Yoga. He'd been living in northern California since the age of seventeen when he'd "fled" Cincinnati. He was manager and part-owner of a "locally renowned" organic food store/restaurant in Oakland and he was "on TV, sometimes, cable, discussing the Yoga way of life." He'd been in Manhattan, in fact, being filmed for a documentary, and delivering a second manuscript to his publisher. He said, "That's my first book, Crissie, on the backseat. I mean, it's for you. It's gone into eight printings since last September."

Crista was surprised: the book was an attractive paperback published by Ballantine. *Yoga: The Art of Living Life* by H. S. Eley. On the dedication page was inscribed in red ink *For My Beloved Sister, Crissie E. After Long Absence. Always, Your Brother Henry. 18 June 2002.*

Crista murmured, "Thank you."

She leafed through the book's pages without seeing a word. She would never read it. Yoga! Ridiculous. She was feeling cheated: her brother had had his life apart from her. A northern California life. A wholly invented life. Her older brother who should have protected her had forgotten her, obviously. He'd obliterated her, as she had obliterated him. Easier to imagine the child Crissie dead. One of *the deaths.*

Henry said, in that grating-teasing way of his, casting her a sidelong ferret look, "*You* look terrific, Crissie. You're beautiful like Lorraine was. Except your hair . . ."

Lorraine! Crista felt a small shock.

"What's wrong with my hair?"

"It's so, somehow, sculpted. It doesn't seem real. Is it?"

Before Crista could prevent him, Henry actually reached out and touched—fingered—her hair. She recoiled from him, offended.

"Sculpted things are real." Crista spoke adamantly, in her logical-lawyer voice. "Sculpted things are no less real than non-sculpted things."

She was surprising him, she saw. Good! If Henry had been thinking of her as his baby sister, the one who'd been permanently traumatized by *the deaths,* he would have to modify his thinking.

Henry said, gently, "But your eyes, Crissie."

"What about my eyes?"

"Lorraine's eyes. I saw that immediately."

"No."

"Certainly, yes. You have her features."

"That's ridiculous. I do not."

"Crissie, you do."

"I do *not.*"

Crista was staring at the map. Throbbing with indignation.

"And I wish you wouldn't call me 'Crissie,' do you mind? No one else does."

"But no one else is your brother."

He meant this jokingly. He was trying to make her laugh. Tickle her as long ago she'd been tickled, the baby of the family. They had all loved her. Crissie, the sweetest prettiest little girl. All that was finished now, of course. Yet, Henry would remember. "You're a lawyer, Aunt Ellen said?"

Crista shrugged. On the map she was moving her neatly filed unpolished fingernail along the Thruway, westward past Syracuse, the Finger Lake Region, Rochester. They would exit beyond Rochester, and take a country highway north to Lake Ontario. In twenty-one years she had never returned. As an adolescent of fifteen, sixteen, she'd thought briefly of returning, but had not. *To walk along the beach. To run. In the direction she'd run.*

As in adolescence we torment and comfort ourselves with thoughts of suicide. A punishment to expiate all sins: our own, and those that have been perpetrated upon us.

"A lawyer. 'Corporate.' In Albany?" Henry laughed, that sandpaper sound. He had no idea how abrasive and disagreeable the sounds that issued from him were, there was a curious sexual complacency to him. A man to whom women were attracted? What sort of women? Crista saw with repugnance his fingers gripping the steering wheel, like talons. "You like that life-style, do you, Crissie?"

Crista was tempted to say *No. I hate it. I've made it my life because I hate it, asshole.*

Aloud she said, "You know nothing about my 'life-style,' Henry."

"You're not married, eh."

This wasn't even a question. Crista didn't trouble to respond.

"I'm not, either. Never will be." Henry laughed. "Not *me.*"

He knew where she'd gone to college, and where to law school, their aunt had told him. He'd dropped out of San Francisco State after three semesters, know why?

His voice was smug, insufferable. "Information isn't knowledge. Knowledge is deeper than facts."

Crista said, annoyed, "You don't learn just facts in college. Not a good college. You learn methods. You learn how to think. You learn wisdom."

" 'Wisdom'!" Henry laughed heartily.

Crista knew better than to quarrel, she was not one to be drawn into idiotic quarrels, yet she heard herself say, "I *did.* I read philosophy, I read Shakespeare. I read the tragedies. I read everything I could. Our parents were uneducated but I was determined that I would be educated, and I'm far from coming to the end of all that I need to know."

Crista was breathless. As a lawyer she often made such spirited speeches on behalf of a client, yet never had she made such a speech on her own behalf. But Henry was unimpressed.

"What you need to know, Crissie, is with*in.*"

" 'Within'—what? My skull? My navel? What do yogins meditate on, isn't it their navels?"

Crista spoke with shocking hostility, but Henry laughed.

" 'Attention is the appeal of the soul to itself.' Meditation is many things, Crissie. You could do worse than begin with your navel."

His manner was so jokey, so unpleasantly intimate, Crista steeled herself halfway expecting him to throw out his hand and grab and tickle at her belly. Instead, Henry did something yet more maddening: he began to hum to himself. Pushing his lank graying Christly hair out of his eyes and humming until the very car vibrated. They were passing exits for MEDINA, CHILDS.

Crista stared out the window, clutching at the map. How she despised whoever this was, this ridiculous man masquerading as her brother she'd adored.

Crissie! Come here.

He was screaming at her. Dragging her somewhere. Beneath the porch? She tried to fight him but he had hold of her wrists, her wrists would be bruised, he was so much stronger. The sweaty palm of his hand clamped over her mouth.

Had she seen what had happened farther up the beach, she had not because it was too dark. There was no moon, it was too dark. Waves breaking at the shore, rolling up hissing onto the packed sand, froth and foam and seaweed and the small lifeless gleaming-silver bodies of fish.

She was just a little girl, no one scolded her for shrieking and giggling when the chilly foamy water washed over her bare toes like nibbling fish.

Had she seen, she had not. Hadn't seen, and hadn't heard. Had not heard the woman who was her mother screaming for help.

"MY BROTHER? He died when he was nine."

There was never anyone to whom she could speak of Henry. Shrewdly she'd erased him from all accounts of herself. While she'd lived in Utica with her fussy schoolteacher aunt she had not been encouraged to remember that she had a brother, still less to beg to see him. "All that," her aunt said, with an annoyed flutter of her hands, as you might wave away flies, "all that is finished." Aunt Ellen was one who could not even bring herself to refer to *the deaths.*

Hard to believe now, Crista had initially loved that woman. Desperately. A teacher of junior high English who gave Crista books to read, books and books, helped her with arithmetic. A stocky-bodied twitchy-faced woman with eyes like nickels who took satisfaction in her niece's good grades at school, which reflected well upon her.

In early adolescence, Crista decided she hated her aunt.

Why? Why not.

Once she left Utica, and began the process of forgetting, she'd ceased to feel much emotion of any kind for the woman. *All that is finished.* She saw the logic of such a statement, it was only a fact. Yet, as a sentimental gesture, she invited her aunt to her law school commencement in Ithaca, for there were no other relatives to invite, and when the woman arrived, a woman of late middle age, frankly fat by this time, panting and overdressed and bearing spots of rouge on her sallow cheeks like a deranged clown, Crista had behaved coolly and politely as if she scarcely knew her. When her aunt said, clutching at Crista's hands, eyes suddenly leaking tears, "Your mother would be so proud of you, dear, if—if only—" Crista turned away unhearing. And afterward when her lover of that time asked her about her aunt, Crista explained that the old woman wasn't an "actual" aunt, only just a friend of the family.

She would never make a sentimental gesture again. That, she'd learned.

As a boy at Olcott, Henry had run with a pack of boys his age. Some of them were summer residents at the beach and others, like Crista's family, were year-round residents who lived in bungalows and "winterized" cottages overlooking the lake. (Their father worked for Niagara County: road repair, snow removal. He was paid to watch over cottages owned by summer residents.) Henry had been a happy-seeming boy. He'd been loud, pushy, aggressive. A rough boy, with other boys. By nine he'd seemed to her one of the older boys: he rode a bicycle, he swam, dived off the wharf at Olcott Beach. He seemed to her physically fearless. In his play with other boys he was frequently dominant. Carroty-brown hair and a stocky sturdy tanned body, and strong. Only around their father had Henry been quiet, watchful. Deferential. If Henry gave their father what their father called "lip" the air crackled with excitement. ("Give me any of your lip, you little cocksucker, and your ass will be warmed, got it?") The danger increased when their father had been drinking, but you couldn't always tell when he'd been drinking. It was like easing out onto the frozen lake: you couldn't tell when the ice would begin to crack and buckle beneath your feet.

Rarely was there a warning from their father, and never an apology afterward. Their mother tried to intervene, in her weak pleading voice. *Honey, please! He didn't mean it . . .*

For some reason, Crista would always remember, it was crucial among all the households of that stretch of road above the lake that children be respectful to their fathers. You were risking catastrophe, like tossing lighted matches at spilled gasoline, to invite misunderstandings. Boys especially. Boys were vulnerable. Boys were apt to talk back, to give their fathers "lip." Sometimes, a boy like Henry had only to squirm and to scowl in his father's presence, to incur his father's wrath. *Little bastard. I saw that, think I'm blind? C'mere.*

Crissie was such a little girl, and such a big-eyed pretty little girl, naturally she was Daddy's favorite. Daddy never punished his favorite little girl who was so pretty and shy in his company, adorable as a doll.

Crista recalled some of this. Faces flicking past like rapidly dealt playing cards. The faces of her father and mother (so young! it was heartbreaking to realize how young) she didn't retain, as she did not retain the sight of the bloodied claw hammer in her father's fist. But the face of her boy-brother she saw clearly. She saw it, inside the face of this ridiculous bearded man with the acne-scarred cheeks. A child-face, trapped inside the other. She wanted to accuse him.

You turned out like this to spite us. You did it on purpose. You aren't even a man, the way our father was a man. You're more like a woman. Like our mother.

"STORM CLOUDS, SEE? Like old times at the lake."

He spoke with wry satisfaction. One of those who welcomed things turning out badly, to demonstrate his equanimity in the face of disappointment.

For by the time they approached the lake at Olcott in the late afternoon, the sky overhead was layered in gauzy strips of cloud. Above the almost invisible farther shore, in Ontario, Canada, were white, wind-braided mares'-tails stretching for miles. Storm clouds.

At the lake, weather changed with notorious swiftness. You could take nothing for granted. Sudden chill winds out of the north, thunderstorms and dangerous summer squalls. A pelting of rain turning to sleet like nails against the roof of their cottage was an old memory of Crista's. The storm-ravaged lake. Angry waves breaking on the littered sand.

Once you lived on the lake, people said, all that empty space to look out on, you never wanted to live anywhere else.

As Henry approached Olcott Beach on the county highway, Crista was beginning to see that things were wrong. Not right. A boarded-up gas station, a run-down Days Inn. Businesses along the highway didn't look very prosperous. Where was the Tastee-Freez stand? Where were the summer residents? Crista said guardedly, "Maybe—we shouldn't be here."

For a long moment Henry didn't reply, as if he too were disoriented. Then he said, with an older brother's annoying insouciance, "Where else? Where else should we be?"

"That isn't the point." Crista was becoming nervous. Children on bicycles were pedaling on the wrong side of the highway, very near the right fender of Henry's car. She saw no sign of the Ferris wheel. The roller coaster. Unless the amusement park was in the other direction, and she'd forgotten.

Well, the old school was still there: Olcott Elementary. Weatherworn and drab but still there, on the corner of . . .

Their old road, Post Road, running parallel to the lake, was still just gravel and dirt, unpaved. But there was a trailer park on a stretch of what had been vacant land, about a block from the beach. And the beach at this end of town, what Crista could see of it, was looking badly eroded.

This was the poorer side of Olcott. The larger houses and summer cottages were in the other direction. Post Road hadn't prospered in the intervening years. Far from being built up and developed, as Crista had dreaded, it was becoming derelict. A number of the cottages were boarded-up, abandoned. FOR SALE signs looked as if they'd been stuck in the ground for years.

Crista said, for Henry's benefit, "It's the economy. We're in a recession upstate. There aren't any jobs."

Henry protested, "But it's the *lake.* Look at the *view.*"

Their house. The "winterized" cottage. Someone had added a carport and painted the clapboards dark green, but this hadn't been recent, for the paint was peeling and the roof looked rotted. There was a gas drum behind the kitchen area, badly rusted. There was a pile of debris. Broken things. "It's empty," Henry said, relieved.

Locked up, the windows sealed over with duct tape and polyethylene sheeting. Crista said, with lawyerly attentiveness, "It isn't for sale, though. I don't see a sign."

She was trying to speak calmly. This was an ordinary conversation they were having.

Henry parked the car. Neither made a move to get out.

Henry said, "Here we are."

Henry said, making an effort not to sound accusing, "Strange—you never came back here, Crissie. When you live so close."

"Albany isn't close. Albany is all the hell away across the state."

All the hell. Away across the state. Crista was shocked, she never spoke like this.

They got out. No one was near. In the distance, children were shouting. Though the wind on the lake was picking up, and white caps were visible, still there were sailboats some distance from shore. But no one on the ravaged beach below the road. Cottages adjacent to their old cottage appeared to be in no better condition. Crista breathed in the fresh air, hoping to clear her head. She was having difficulty breathing, as if tiny seeds or bits of lint had accumulated in her lungs.

Henry said, pointing. "The old TV antenna."

"It wouldn't be ours. After so long."

"Why not? I bet it is."

Crista was tempted to peer through a window. But the ugly plastic sheeting was a deterrent. "The carport is new, though."

"No. Dad built that carport."

"He did? He . . . I don't think so."

"We kept our bikes under it. You had a, what do you call it, a little kid's bike, three wheels . . . "

"Tricycle."

"Right. And my bike, we kept back here."

The carport had no foundation, only just chunky gravel through which weeds had grown. At the rear of the carport was another mound of debris including sheets of plasterboard sprouting nails. Needlessly Crista said, "No car. They're not home."

"They haven't been home for a while. See the crap in the mailbox."

It was on the floor of the sagging porch, too. Waterstained advertising fliers, torn brochures. Henry stepped cautiously onto the porch, which creaked beneath his weight. Beneath the porch was a narrow, shadowy space. Crista was remembering that space: as a child, she'd crawled under the porch. She'd peered out from the shadows into the bright sunshine. She'd seen the feet and bare legs of adults. *Crissie? Where are you?*

Before Crista could prevent him, Henry tried the door of the cottage. Luckily, it was locked. He said, "This was where it began. Just inside the door. He'd just come home. It was late. She came to unlock the door because she'd locked it against him, he was yelling at her to let him in. He was drunk. I was still in bed, I didn't see him get the hammer from the closet. Or maybe he brought it in from outside. The carport."

Crista said, "There wasn't any carport. It didn't exist."

"Or out of a drawer. In the kitchen. He had it." Henry paused, stroking his straggly beard. His voice was strangely thrilled, tremulous. "I heard her scream before she was hit. Because she knew what was going to happen."

Crista said, "No. She struck him first. She had the hammer. I saw."

Henry stared at her. *"You* saw? How?"

"I was awake. I was watching. I heard the car. I heard him calling for the door to be unlocked."

"*I* was awake, I was standing behind Mom. You weren't even out of bed."

"She struck him first. She had the hammer, out of the closet. She had it ready, she had it raised, when he broke the door in."

"He didn't break the door. It was just the screen door."

"The screen door. It was latched, and he kicked it in."

"But he had the hammer, Crista. He came in with it. She was wearing just a nightgown. A short nightgown, with lace straps. She was afraid of him. She'd been on the phone with somebody, then she'd gone to bed. We were all in bed. You were sleeping when it began, you were just a baby."

"Oh, no. I saw it." Crista stepped onto the porch and took hold of the screen door and shook it. The screen was badly rusted. Both the screen door and the inner door were locked. "She was awake, and waiting for him. She'd been drinking, too. Nobody wanted to say, how our mother drank. It was just beer, but she drank. She'd been on the phone with somebody she knew, some man. You never knew, but I knew. I'd seen them together. They'd meet places, like at the 7-Eleven. Nobody wanted to say, afterward. She'd been crying, carrying on. When he came home, she came at him with the hammer. She hit him, he got it away from her—"

"Crissie, you're wrong. You never saw that."

"He wrenched the hammer out of her hand, because she was going to kill him. He got it from her—"

"It wasn't like that, God damn it. He dragged her outside. He had the hammer, and he dragged her outside and was hitting her. She was already screaming. She broke away from him, and he chased her down onto the beach. She was barefoot, in just her nightgown. He tore it off her. I saw."

"*I* saw. I was awake, and I was watching. She had the hammer, he took it from her. She said things to him. She provoked him. She laughed at him, she was always laughing at him. She wanted to kill him."

"He was the one who was drunk. He'd come home drunk."

"She was drunk. He swung at her, to scare her off. He didn't mean to hit her."

Henry laughed angrily. "Of course he meant to hit her! He'd hit her plenty of times before. He hit me, and he even hit you. For wetting the bed."

"He did not. My father never touched me."

"Lots of times he did. It wasn't just her and me."

"He loved me. He loved me best."

"Maybe he did. So what! He was a drunk, and he was an asshole, and I'm glad he killed himself, he should have killed himself a long time before. Mom was the one who tried to protect us."

"She provoked him. There was this man who'd come over, when Daddy was away . . . "

"They were all friends. There were lots of people. They drank out on the beach. They were young."

Crista, stepping from the porch, was demonstrating the hammer swing. There was no hammer in her hand but she could see it, and she could feel its weight. Henry was staring at her as if he could see it, too. Crista said, "Like this! She came at him swinging. She came at him, like this."

Crista swung the invisible claw hammer back behind her head, and over, in a swift deadly arc. Henry leapt out of the way of the blow.

"Crista! You're crazy."

"Because I didn't see what you saw? I know what I saw."

"You saw nothing. You were back inside the house. *I* saw."

"I saw her swing at him, and I saw him take the hammer from her. She ran away from him, and he followed her, and I—I didn't see anything after that, it was too dark."

Henry said, "Look, there were witnesses. Even if they didn't see, they could hear. All along the road. He was shouting at her, he was going to kill her. People would tell police, Rick Eley had been hitting and threatening his wife for months. We all knew he'd hurt her seriously one day. We thought he'd hurt the children, too."

Crista said stubbornly, "Daddy meant just to scare her off. That was all he meant."

"He broke her skull! But that wasn't enough, he kept hitting her with the hammer. I wish I'd been big enough and strong enough to stop him but I wasn't. He was sobbing, and cursing. He called her all the names. She was dying, and he called her all the names. That's the kind of asshole murderer he was. Son of a bitch fucker murderer. *You* weren't here. You were hiding up at the house."

"I heard it. I heard her screaming at him, how she hated him."

"He left her down by the water. He left her half naked—our mother. Her skull was smashed, there was blood all over, a trail of blood. He smashed her brains out. Then he came for us."

"She was the one who'd started it, Henry. She provoked him."

"He was the one with the woman friends."

"I heard them arguing—"

"I heard them arguing—"

"She accused him—"

"He accused her—"

"She caused it."

"He was the murderer."

They were speaking sharply to each other. Henry gripped Crista's shoulders, and shook her. Crista shoved him away: she wasn't a weak young woman, her shoulder and arm and legs muscles were small but hard, well developed. They were on the beach, Crista stumbling from Henry. Their feet sank into the wet packed sand. A sudden stench of rotted kelp, fish, clam shells. Everywhere were shards of glass, beer cans, Styrofoam cups. Higher up, on a gravel road perpendicular with Post, several children straddling bicycles were watching. Henry said, furiously, "He wanted us to go with him. He came back to get us, there was blood on his hands and that's why there was blood on us. Know what he said?"

Crista was pressing her hands against her ears. She hadn't heard a word her brother had said.

"He said, 'How'd you kids like some Tastee-Freez?' He tried to grab us. You were out of bed by now, and outside, you were in just pajamas, and he grabbed you. It was around 1 A.M. He wanted to take us with him in the car, the son of a bitch wanted to kill us, too."

"He did not. I don't remember any of that."

"Look, he tried to drag you into the car with him. That's why there was blood on you. You were screaming. You knew what he was going to do. You were only six, but you knew."

"I—didn't know. I didn't see any of it."

"I pulled you away from him. I got you out of his hands. I dragged you with me under the porch. We hid under the porch. That's what saved us. We were hiding under the porch in the dirt and he was too drunk and crazy to get hold of us, he drove away in the car and left us and that's why we were saved, that's the only fucking reason we're alive today."

Crista laughed. This was so ridiculous.

"I hate you! I wish you were dead, too."

"You're hysterical."

Henry would have grabbed her except Crista was too quick for him. Her hand leapt out, her nails raked his face. Blood appeared on his pitted cheeks like astonished cries. Henry swore, and shoved Crista hard, and she stumbled but didn't fall, thinking *The children are watching: witnesses.* Even in her fear and confusion she was thinking like a lawyer. She backed off, seeing the fury in his face. Who was this ghoul-eyed bearded man, advancing upon her? She ran, her feet sinking in the sand. Ran along the littered beach in the rain, her elbows at her sides, sobbing and laughing to herself.

When had it begun to rain? Within minutes the sky was dark, the lake had become choppy and agitated.

Instinctively she knew where to run: that sandy spit of land thick with saplings. There was a decayed log that had been there for decades. Crista crouched behind the log, hoping to hide. It was raining harder. Rain on the heaving surface of the lake like machine-gun bullets, sprayed. She heard someone calling *Crissie? Crissie?* headed in her direction.

JORIE (& JAMIE): A DEPOSITION

WHICH ONE AM I, people used to try to guess. But no longer.

Are you Jamie, or are you Jorie? they would ask smiling. As if we had a choice which we could be. As if there is something to make you smile, just seeing twin little girls.

I hate talking about this! My mom, she isn't to blame. I used to hate Jorie but I don't now. Nobody's to blame but especially not my mom. *I want to see my mom now* . . . O.K., if I tell you how it was can I see my mom? I hate people lying to me, I don't trust anybody any more, like at school my teacher saw me crying and the nurse told me she would keep any secret, she promised, then right away I told her about Jorie she was on the phone, and everything changed after that. I hate how everybody treats me like a young kid when I am thirteen years old.

No we are not identical twins. We are what is called "fraternal" twins. ("Fraternal" meaning brothers, boys. Like there is no clinical term for twin sisters like us.)

Are you Jamie, or are you Jorie? Daddy would ask teasing and pretending not to know. But that was a long time ago when we were little and you could mix us up, before Jorie began to change.

FIRST IT WAS the back bedroom which anyway she shared with me who was her twin sister people said was the "normal" one. Just to have a place for her that was set off from the place for us. Because the house is small, and there were four of us. And then when the screams and kicking were too loud and the neighbors called to complain and too much damage was inflicted it was the clothes closet in the hall with everything taken out, and then the cellar, not the whole cellar but the storage room where water leaked sometimes, after a heavy rain, and the lightbulb swung on a chain Mom removed out of a fear that Jorie would leap up and seize the bulb in her teeth, bite the glass, and swallow it.

Neurological impairment were the words we came to learn *frontal lobes, cerebral cortex* just naming these scared me *dyslexia, attention deficit disorder.* Just the sounds, the syllables as in a foreign language. And I said to Mom, will it happen to me, too, I'm like Jorie aren't I, I'm Jorie's twin aren't I, I was crying saying to Mom how scared I was, don't lock me in the cellar with her, Mom, you won't Mom, will you? and Mom hugged me, and my little brother Calvin, we were both crying and Mom hugged and kissed us and her face was wet with tears saying, Oh never.

Can I see my mom now? When can I see my mom?

I miss my mom. I hate it here, I'm so lonely.

The beds smell here. The mattresses! Kids my age, you'd think they wouldn't be wetting the bed! Bad as Jorie. But Jorie meant to be bad, wetting the bed, and that's different.

AT FIRST IT was just the bedroom when Mom gave Jorie her medication so she'd sleep. The door didn't lock so Mom tied a cord around the knob and I helped her fix it on both sides tied tight and sometimes we'd push a heavy table against it and mostly that worked if Jorie didn't fly into a rage and push out. Because in her rages she's *strong.* You'd be scared of her, too. She scratches, and she bites. These marks on my arm, see? Mom said to say it was just cat scratches which was what I told the nurse but she examined them, she said, These are teeth-bites, human. Right away the nurse saw, there was a look in her face like she was scared, herself. And I knew there was danger, and I tried not to cry. But I was weak, I gave in. I hate myself for giving in!

It wasn't Mom anyway, it was me. That's what I told before but nobody would believe me. It was *me.*

The back bedroom was where we slept anyway. There was nothing wrong with making Jorie stay in there sometimes so Mom could have some peace, she said. She'd take one of Jorie's tranquillizers herself, she was so nervous. The pills didn't always work with Jorie so Mom would take them. There was nothing wrong with that room till Jorie trashed it. Smashed the window with her bare fist, bled all over the windowsill, the rug, the bed. My bed, too! And she was laughing, like it didn't hurt her at all. Like she didn't feel anything, and Mom almost fainted. I hate seeing blood, it makes me go weak and sick but Jorie just laughed waving her hands and splattering blood where she could. *Jam-ie! Jam-ie!* she shouted at me laughing and running at me like it was a game of tag, smearing her bloody hands on me.

And she'd wet the bed, our bed, in the night. How many times she did this I don't know. When Daddy was still with us he'd make a face, crinkle his nose, and walk away saying *Bad! Bad girls* like there was no difference between us. But Mom always knew.

You wouldn't expect a girl of ten, eleven, twelve years old to wet the bed, you'd know she was doing it on purpose. More than once Jorie did this giggling to wake me, and torment me. And when Mom came stumbling and groggy Jorie said in this hateful singsong voice *It wasn't me it was Jam-ie! Jamie went pee-pee in the bed! Shame-shame Jame-Jame!* like she was five years old.

I knew: Jorie was not to be judged by normal standards. We all knew, even Calvin. And yet.

Sometimes I hated her, wished she'd never been born. Or that she wasn't my twin. So that people look at her, and look at me. And think *Is she crazy too? She must be!*

One thing about Jorie, she never lies. Maybe she doesn't know how. Maybe that part of the brain that lets you tell lies is part of her brain that is damaged. *I never lie, either.*

"SPELLS" MOM CALLED them. "Spells" was Mom's word for everything from Jorie spitting out her food and gagging like it was some reflex, like she couldn't help it, when she was little, to the way she was this past year screaming at us like she hated us so veins stood out in her forehead and her eyes bulged like a wild animal's that has been trapped and is dangerous. "Spells" were when Jorie's face went dead-white and she fell to the floor kicking, thrashing, convulsing (*epileptoid* these convulsions were called though Jorie was never diagnosed with actual epilepsy). Mom would know that Jorie hadn't swallowed her pills only pretended to, when these "spells" came on.

Mom wanted to believe that there was "good" Jorie and there was "bad" Jorie and it was "spells" that were the cause for her being bad, and would pass. Like a spell of lousy weather. A spell of lousy luck. Mom would say *Honey c'mon! Please honey c'mon snap out of it* like it was something Jorie could shake off like a dog shaking water off its fur.

Well, sometimes this did seem to be so. When we were younger, I think. Jorie wasn't so sick then, maybe. She'd be "acting up" to get her way, trying to get Daddy's attention, teasing Mom, taking my toys, snatching food out of my fingers she didn't even want but threw on the floor. If anybody was around like visitors (Mom used to have visitors then), Jorie would clown and squeal and act up to get attention, she was jealous if anybody talked to me for just a minute and nudged me aside or pulled my hair. *Jam-ie! Ug-ly!* She'd be biting her lower lip and laughing and her dark-honey eyes sly and so beautiful you wanted Jorie to be good, and to be well, you wanted to think she was just playing a little rough, she didn't mean it. You'd forgive Jorie anything, she was so pretty.

Obsessive-compulsive. Nonverbal learning disability. Hyperactivity. Mild autism. These are words they gave us. Scary words that made Mom cry. Pressing her hands over her ears.

A beautiful angel child everyone believed her, when she was little. And this was true. I am not beautiful but am an ordinary girl. When we were little I cried when Jorie cried like a single skin enclosed us but Jorie could not be trusted, she'd kiss and cuddle and wrap her snaky arms around my neck then (for instance) bite my ear, and wouldn't let go when I screamed in pain, or (for instance) she would get me to tell her some little thing and go running to Mom with it, shouting, laughing, repeating it so the words were nonsense, but so loud, Mom had to rush her into the bathroom, try to quiet her down, later it would be the closet, and later still the storage room in the cellar. *The neighbors will call the police. Jorie, no!*

Mom loves me, and Mom loves Calvin, but Mom would love Jorie best if Jorie got over her "spells." Everybody could love Jorie best. (Even me.) We wonder, does Jorie know this? *Wants to break my heart* Mom would say. So exhausted sometimes she would lie down on the sofa saying *What did I do to deserve this, how is this my fault.* After Daddy left a few years ago. *It is not my fault. I know!* Mom would say. *It is nobody's fault.* To Calvin and me she would say *It isn't your sister's fault, you know that don't you* and Calvin and I would say *Yes Mom.*

At first Daddy wouldn't believe how bad Jorie could be, Jorie hid her badness from him. She was his angel, so pretty and sly-eyed like she was winking, teasing, playing a game with just Daddy alone. *Angel-baby* Daddy called her, then seeing me watching, my thumb in my mouth, Daddy would say quickly, *You too, Jamie. You're Daddy's angel-baby, too.* But Daddy was gone a lot. Daddy did not know.

It got so that Mom could not take us to the playground, or would have to go to different playgrounds in different parts of the city, for there was the danger of Jorie hitting other children, taking away their toys, or sneaking up to scare them like she was hunting them, it was a game to make her squeal with laughter. The other mothers tried to be nice to Jorie but it was no use. You could see they felt sorry for Mom and for me who was the twin sister of the strange little girl who could not be trusted for five minutes not to misbehave, they felt sorry for Calvin in his baby buggy but finally they did not want us anywhere near. They took their children away from the swings, the teeter-totter, the monkey bars, the sand boxes. They took their children away from the wading pools. As if these places were contaminated. As if Jorie, squealing and screeching and jabbering in her high-pitched way at (for instance) some little girl's left-behind doll in the sand like it was an actual baby, could contaminate an entire playground, an entire park. In the beginning Mom would plead *Please forgive me, I am so sorry. I guess you can see that my daughter is—is not—well.* But later Mom could say nothing for the other mothers fled from us, and at this time there was trouble at school, even in the special class that Jorie was in. And Daddy was gone more and more, and Mom was on the telephone a lot, and crying, or trying not to cry.

Almost it's worse when your mom is trying not to cry than when she's crying. Because when she's trying not to, you think you can help her not to cry, somehow. You can hug her, or kiss her, you can cuddle against her. But if she's crying it's too late, like a window that has been smashed. And so you start crying, too.

Jorie laughed at Mom, at such times. Jorie called me *Silly-baby ugly-Jamie* and pinched me like I was to blame for Mom's weakness. Jorie has always had an instinct for weakness in others, even adults. Even her teachers. Jorie is scornful of weakness, especially she hates Mom when Mom is weak and so Jorie provokes Mom into becoming angry with her, carrying her kicking and screaming with laughter down into the cellar, Mom panting, red-faced, her arms wrapped tight around Jorie's arms to hold her, for if Jorie refuses to take her medication, Jorie will only get worse, her skin burning with fever, it's only a matter of time until Jorie lapses into one of her spells, thrashing and convulsing. And sometimes these seem deliberate, and sometimes not.

It started that way. Just to have some peace in the house. Just for a while. So Mom could rest. So Calvin could nap. So I could do my homework. It wasn't more than an hour, or two hours. Later it might be longer. Four hours. Five. Because the house was so peaceful without Jorie. *Your sister is safe. Under lock and key, and safe* Mom told Calvin and me, trying to smile but her eyes were scared.

Because the quiet of the house was so good! Because when you have such quiet you want it to go on, and on. And Mom knew this, and was scared of what this could mean.

You could not hear Jorie in the cellar, with the doors closed. The neighbors could not hear. And maybe the TV on, or the radio in the kitchen. So quiet! You could hear airplanes taking off and landing (our house is near Newark Airport) and children shouting in the neighborhood, dogs barking, cars and trucks passing and sometimes sirens, but inside the house it was quiet, peaceful like a dream.

My heart was not beating fast and anxious and there was not the strain beween my shoulder blades I felt when I sensed Jorie behind me. In the kitchen, I helped Mom make meals. We laughed and joked together like normal people. There was not the risk of Jorie rushing into the kitchen, humming and chattering to herself, smirking at us or ignoring us, rummaging through the refrigerator, dropping and breaking things. There was not the risk of Jorie turning the TV up loud in the other room, high as it could go. Of Jorie teasing Calvin till he cried, then laughing at *Cal-vin Cal-vin bab-by bab-by* so Mom would have to intervene. There was not the risk of some neighbor telephoning us, or pounding on the front door because Jorie had slipped out without Mom knowing and had been throwing stones at children playing up the block, or tormenting somebody's dog, or frightening somebody by peering in her window, or running in front of cars passing on the street, seeing how close she could come to being hit. There was not the risk of one of Jorie's spells ruining our dinner-time together, Jorie making gagging noises because she didn't like the food, or suddenly collapsing out of her chair onto the floor, kicking, thrashing, choking, "convulsing."

And you wouldn't know was this real, or pretend. Was Jorie truly sick from not taking her pills, or was Jorie playing one of her games.

Like a dream the house was without Jorie.

Four hours, or five. Maybe six.

If Mom had to take Calvin or me to the doctor, maybe it would be longer.

Or Mom might take us to the mall. Riding the escalators. Staring at the big sparkling fountain lighted for Christmas, and into the store windows. Maybe Mom would take us to a movie. And maybe for a snack at Taco Bell afterward. We loved Taco Bell. We didn't forget Jorie, she was not neglected. We would bring food back for her. But this was the quiet time.

And when Mom unlocked the storage room door, and Jorie came out walking like she was half-asleep, she would be quiet, too. Blinking and rubbing her eyes. Because the ordinary light would hurt her eyes, there was no light in the storage room. Because Jorie would need to be hugged by Mom, and would consent to be hugged, and kissed as she would never at any other time. *Mom-my do-you love-me* Jorie would ask like a little girl and Mom would say *Honey yes. Mommy loves you a lot.* In the beginning Jorie would throw herself against the door, pound and kick till she was bruised, bleeding, but after a while she would give up and lie down, probably she slept because it was so dark there was nothing to see. She'd be weak from not eating which made her quiet, too. And grateful to be fed.

Mom said *Now will you be good, Jorie?* and Jorie said *Yes, Mommy. I will be good.* And so Jorie was, for a while.

DADDY WENT AWAY. I can remember Daddy but Jorie can't. She says she can't. Sometimes she can't remember yesterday, or a few minutes ago. One of the doctors told Mom that Jorie's brain is wired different from other people so now I can (almost) see thin filaments like in a lightbulb inside Jorie's head and some of these are broken and snagged together. I feel sorry for Jorie who can't remember Daddy except to know that he's gone. Jorie says *I don't give a damn for anybody's Daddy they can all go to hell.* She laughs, and sniffs, and wipes her nose with the back of her hand in that way that drives Mom crazy. I don't tell Jorie that Daddy used to rock her in his arms and whisper in her ear because he loved her best. I could tell Jorie *Daddy loved me best!* and maybe she would believe it.

In kindergarten Jorie began to act strange. She never wanted to go to school as I did. She'd throw a tantrum, make herself feverish and sick to her stomach and Mom would have to keep her home. Always Jorie had been different from me. She was the lively twin. I knew people called her the "pretty" twin. It would seem that Jorie was the "smart" twin too except she could not sit still and concentrate for more than a few minutes, sometimes seconds. You could feel the heat lifting from her skin. You could see her eyes jerking and rolling. It was easier for Jorie to break a doll than to play with it. It was easier for Jorie to tear all the pages out of a book than to read it. There was no use buying a little computer for Jorie and Jamie because Jorie would crack the screen with her head or break into the back and tear out the wires. At first Dad went with Mom to the clinics, to take Jorie to be examined. After a while Mom took Jorie by herself. There were many "tests." There were "brain scans." There were doctors, therapists, dieticians, special teachers. Daddy was gone away from home a lot. I missed Daddy, but Jorie hummed and chattered to herself not needing Daddy so when he did come home, Jorie looked right through him like he wasn't there. *Hey: Angel-Baby? Jorie?* Daddy was hurt I could see. He loved Calvin and me but not like he loved Jorie who walked past him with this look on her beautiful feverish face like she was in another world, not even Daddy could enter. And once Daddy saw Jorie in one of her spells, maybe he hadn't believed Mom what these could be like, poor Daddy backed off staring at Jorie quaking and gagging and falling to the floor to thrash and "convulse" like she was dying . . .

The more Daddy was gone, "traveling," "on business," as Mom told us, the crazier Jorie behaved. Suspended from school, expelled from school, had to be bussed to a special school for "disturbed learning disability children" and eventually suspended from that school, too. She'd pick up dog shit outside and bring it into the house to throw it around laughing wildly at the looks on our faces. She stopped sleeping through the night, any night. At 4 A.M. she'd be out in the kitchen rummaging through the refrigerator eating anything she could find, for sure Mom couldn't keep ice cream very long in the freezer, Jorie would eat it out of the containers with her fingers, walk away and leave the freezer door wide open. She'd wander into the living room and turn on the TV loud and so if Daddy happened to be home, he was furious, disgusted, and blamed Mom that she couldn't control Jorie.

Saying to Mom *I am trying. You want too much. This is nobody's fault. This is not my fault. I have to support you. I have to support this household. Her medical costs. I never asked for this. You smoked when you were pregnant with the girls, no I'm not blaming you and I know you didn't smoke for the full nine months but you did smoke, there must have been damage done. Don't raise your voice with me, I'm not from people who raise their voices and live in pigstys like this. I said God damn you don't raise your voice with me—*

Jorie and I were ten when Daddy moved out.

THERE WAS A confused time then. Mom on the telephone. Or sometimes Mom talking to herself. Groggy from Jorie's pills she'd taken to calm her nerves. Or worn out from crying. Saying *You can't! You can't leave me.* Mom was desperate, pleading. Mom's voice like something hurt, dying. *What have I done to deserve this, I love you, I want to love you, but I love her, too, I love my children, what can I do, you can't leave us, I used to be a happy person, I want to be a happy person again, I'm only thirty-one, that isn't old!*

AT THE CLINIC in another city. Where they tested Jorie, again. And there were the ugly words again. *Neurological impairment. Frontal lobes, cerebral cortex. Autism.* A woman doctor told Mom this is your child, you can learn to live with a disabled child. Mom asked how long would this be and the doctor did not understand, how long? how many years? and Mom tried to explain she has two other children, she has Jorie's twin sister and Calvin who is five years younger and he too has mild dyslexia, a slight speech impediment, he's a quiet boy, very shy, withdrawn, she was concerned that Jorie's presence in the household was making Calvin worse, she was concerned that Jorie might physically injure her little brother, and the doctor interrupted to say that Mom would have to oversee Jorie, protect her little brother, maybe when Jorie is an adolescent maybe then if she is considered "dangerous" she might be institutionalized, and right away Mom said no, I will never put my daughter in an institution, I will not give up. *I will not.*

Leaving the clinic, Jorie jumped down a flight of concrete steps, fell and twisted her ankle, sprained it. Shrieking with pain which was rare for Jorie.

IN THE CELLAR, in the night. Do you hear her?

Jamie! she is crying. *Jam-ie! Help me.*

It was not Mom's fault, Jorie spat out her pills. Jorie would not use the pot to pee in. Jorie would not eat her food. Screaming and throwing herself against the wall, bloodying her nose and mouth like a Hallowe'en pumpkin. I felt so bad to see Jorie's face swollen, it was like my own face, contorted and ugly. If you are a twin you want your twin to be beautiful like an angel. If you are not beautiful yourself you want your twin to be beautiful. We were fearful that somebody would come and take our mom from us, Mom was not well, migraine headaches, so dizzy she couldn't walk across the room without stumbling, on the sofa with one of her strong-smelling bottles, smoking, the cigarette ash would fall into the cushions and we couldn't wake her, beating out the smoldering little flames with our fists. *Mom! Mommy! Wake up.*

Mom said there are people who believe that a child like Jorie is a punishment that the mother must deserve. Mom said that Daddy and his family blamed her. Would have nothing to do with her. *I love my daughter. I don't wish to harm my little girl. I know she can't help it. This is just to get some rest. Some peace. To protect the others. For a little while.* But in the night, in the cellar, if Jorie continued to rage and could not be let out, Mom said there came her own heartbeat, her deranged and murderous heart she dared not free to do injury upon others. *That would be evil. True evil.*

IT WAS NOT what they say. Mom left food for Jorie. Mom did.

If Mom forgot, I took food to Jorie. Sometimes she was so weak, she couldn't fight me. Wouldn't wish to fight me. I shared what I ate with Jorie, my sister. I would not let her starve to death and neither would my mom. But Mom was sick sometimes, too. Calvin and me, we stayed home from school to take care of her.

Mom has a college degree, or almost. She dropped out to get married she says, she wanted her twin girl-babies. She didn't want an abortion. She was in love, she loved Daddy and wanted to marry him and now Daddy has "severed all ties" with her. It is because of Jorie but Jorie is not to blame, Jorie can't help herself. *Yes but if Jorie took her pills. If Jorie went to therapy. If Jorie did not bite, kick, scream, rage. Throw herself into convulsions.* Mom says *I don't hate my daughter, I don't want to hate my daughter. Because I love my daughter.*

It's a lie, what they say about Mom. In the papers. What the neighbors say. If Jorie weighed only fifty-nine pounds, it was because she refused to eat. Or she ate, and made herself sick and vomited it up. *Jorie* I said *Please eat this* I was shining the flashlight onto the plate, I squatted there beside her till I saw her begin to eat. Then Mom called down to me. *Jamie! Get back up here, lock that door.* Jorie grabbed my arm, grinned, and sank her teeth into my wrist. That fast, I could not believe it.

NO. MY MOM did not do that. I was the one.

No! My mom did not know about that. Calvin and me, we were responsible.

Because—why? Mom was so tired, and had to sleep. And Jorie would not let her sleep. In May it began. What Mom calls *evil in Jorie.* So we—I guess that was when—we locked her in the storage room almost all the time.

I don't know! But it was me, not my mom.

I love my mom, I would do anything for her. She isn't like people say. Calvin and me, we belong together, too. We don't want some "new home." We don't want some "foster family." We want each other, and we want Mom. And we want Jorie too, when Jorie is well.

No, I would not lie for my mom. I am not lying. I am telling the truth.

Jorie will tell the truth, when she is well enough. They won't let me see her yet. They say she is "malnourished"—"mute." They say that she is "traumatized." She wouldn't look at me, the last time I saw her. Her eyes were strange and blurred like they were sleeping. I whispered *Jorie c'mon! Jorie wake up!* but she would not.

The school nurse asked why I was crying, why I was so nervous, what were the bite marks on my wrist, she would keep my secrets if I had secrets she promised. But she lied.

I know, it's better for Jorie now. It's better for all of us.

Mom said *Thank God. It's over, thank God.*

But in the jail Mom is on "suicide watch." I want to see my mom, and so does Calvin. Today. Right now!

You promised.

MRS. HALIFAX AND RICKIE SWANN: A BALLAD

It has all happened before. A thousand thousand times. Like drowning, your life flashing in front of your eyes. Something like that.

WHY RICKIE SWANN was only just in eighth grade at his age of almost fifteen towering over younger classmates was he'd been kept back twice and each time unjustly Rickie believed. The first time, so long ago he could barely remember, his mother hadn't been married yet to Dexter Swann and he'd been "temporarily placed" in a foster home in Jersey City so he'd had two years of first grade and the second time, fifth grade in East Orange, he'd had to take the year over for reasons of *tension decifit disease* or some bullshit like that. So by junior high at Grover Cleveland Rickie was the tallest boy in all his classes and by eighth grade he was as tall as some of his teachers who were uneasy in his presence and tended to assign him a seat at the very rear of the classroom. Also Rickie was skinny and twitchy as a snake balanced on its tail. His eyes often glittered with fury and obscure hurt like chips of mica. His jaws glittered with a silvery fawn-colored stubble. His hair looked like broom sage straggling past his collar. He had an Adam's apple like something stuck midway in his throat. He had few friends at Grover Cleveland and his teachers rarely called upon him in class because he had a disconcerting habit of staring blankly at them as if unhearing, and if he did manage to mumble an answer it was likely to be wrong. Nor did his teachers discipline him when suddenly he might unwind his long legs from beneath his desk and walk out of the room wiping his nose on the edge of his hand.

Rickie's grades were unpredictable. Sometimes he did surprisingly well in math. He wrote slowly in upward-slanting sentences with large balloon-like letters. Teachers encouraged him but often he gave up midway in a test, crumpled up his paper, and lurched out of the room muttering to himself.

In Mrs. Halifax's fourth-period social studies class Rickie Swann had been assigned a seat at the rear of the room. Rarely did Mrs. Halifax call upon him. Not that she was afraid of him. (Mrs. Halifax wasn't afraid of any student!) Before their love affair his grades were C, C-. None of Mrs. Halifax's colleagues at Grover Cleveland would recall her having mentioned Rickie Swann in their hearing when in the teachers' lounge they spoke of their students and compared notes.

What do you think of Rickie Swann?

Disturbed kid. Waiting to explode.

Ever seen his mother?

In fact Mrs. Swann never came to Grover Cleveland to meet with her son's teachers though she'd been so advised. Never came to PTA meetings. She had a distrust of anything to do with the government and this included public schools. Yet Mrs. Swann had her own standards of decency and these were exacting. Often she commented on Rickie's failure to adequately wash and the fact that his underarms, newly bristling with hairs, swam in slime. His *boy-equipment* as Mrs. Swann quaintly phrased it was growing, she knew, and would soon cause problems. By eighth grade, Rickie had begun to shrink from mirrors. His face was often broken out in flaming rashes. Though since he'd shot up to five feet ten there were shameless females who winked at him in the street murmuring in his wake what sounded like *Sexy boy kiss-kiss!* making him want to howl and pound his fists and tear at somebody's throat with his teeth.

You had to admire Rickie's mom. The few friends Rickie had in the neighborhood thought she was some character. Not bad-looking for a woman so old (she was maybe thirty-five) and funny like some TV comedian. She'd toss a wash cloth at Rickie: "Wash." When a patina of grime had been building up on Rickie's hands, forearms, neck of that sickly gray hue of the air of industrial New Jersey she'd toss a steel wool pad at him: "Scrub." The same high-potency deoderant she purchased for her husband Dexter Swann she was likely to shove at Rickie: "Use this. Now." Before Rickie grew taller than his mother and outweighed her by twenty pounds Mrs. Swann would dare to seize his chin in her hand and examine his teeth as you'd examine a horse's teeth: "Brush." Now that Rickie towered over his mom and flared up sometimes in bad temper, she'd ceased this practice.

Whoever Rickie's mom once was, she was now Mrs. Dexter Swann. Rickie called her *Mom* and her husband Dexter Swann (who was Rickie's step-dad, not his actual dad, but had adopted Rickie as his own son) called her *hon*. She had a shrewd ferret face and elbows sharp as hammer prongs. Many times during the nine years they'd been alone together, a family of "two survivors," she'd told Rickie of how she had been abandoned by her unknown mother as a week-old infant, left to be eaten alive by rats in a Dumpster behind a Taco Bell in Jersey City, New Jersey—"But I sure as hell didn't abandon *my kid*." Rickie was made to know that she'd had the opportunity and possibly the wish to abandon him not once but many times. Mrs. Swann's eyes were glittery like her son's, vigilant and derisive. Growing up an orphan with no "siblings" or anybody in the world who "gave a shit" about her had given her an air of suspicion tinged with mirth. Her customary stance was hands on her hips, palms up in mockery.

Rickie tried to love his step-father who spent most of his time now indoors in a Barcalounger noisily sucking oxygen through tubes in his nose and flicking through ninety-nine TV channels. Mr. Swann suffered from emphysema caused by years of inhaling the toxic stink of hogs bound for slaughter. Mr. Swann said the hogs, unlike cows, knew where they were headed and so shat in a continuous diarrhetic stream you could smell not only in the cab of his truck but everywhere in the truck's wake. Something of the brooding diarrhetic melancholy of the doomed hogs clung to Mr. Swann even in his retirement years with his "new family" which he'd hoped would have been a happy time. Over the years Rickie had grown accustomed to the smell of his step-dad and hardly ever noticed it any longer.

What was weird was: how Rickie loved his mother but was so nervous of her he couldn't sit still for more than two or three minutes at mealtimes for instance. Couldn't watch TV with his step-dad because his mom was likely to be present not watching TV herself but seeing it through Rickie's eyes so if for instance a sexually provocative female appeared on screen Rickie's mom would know exactly how this looked to Rickie and would tease: "Eyes wide *shut,* kiddo." Mrs. Swann seemed to be on intimate terms with Rickie's *boy-equipment* and sensed its every quiver and throb. Rickie had come to think he'd have to murder his mom just to stop her X-ray eyes on him, her disgust and her derision which he knew was warranted, or to protect her from disappointment in him when he brought home the kind of report cards Rickie Swann hadn't any choice but to bring home for her signature. Not just low grades for his studies but *poor* for such mysterious categories as *deportment, citizenship, peer interaction.* They were like Siamese twins, Rickie thought, him and his mom, that kind of twin where one is growing out of the spine of the other like a misshapen tree, or, the scariest sight Rickie had ever seen, one night on the Discovery Channel, one twin growing upside-down out of the other's skull.

Rickie loved his mom but if he had to kill her it would be her skull he'd smash, with maybe a hammer. His step-dad kept tools in the basement and among them a claw hammer. Not something sharp. Not a knife. It made him queasy to think of stabbing and of blood. Rickie guessed a skull could be smashed like crockery and without pain. You come up behind the unsuspecting victim and bring the hammer down hard and the person would fall unconscious in an instant like a struck steer and would be dead and never know what had happened, still less who'd done it.

Rickie would never do such a thing, though. Rickie loved his mom too much.

SOME OF HER pupils hated and feared her. Some of her pupils loved her. Mrs. Halifax was cool, they had to agree.

What she was mostly was a *tease.* She teased her favorite pupils but she teased pupils who pissed her off. So you never knew where you stood with her. If Mrs. Halifax winked at you that was usually a good sign, though not always. If she winked at the class over your head that was definitely not a good sign. What sounded like praise at first—"Why, Jimmy, did you write this report *all by yourself?*"—had a way of turning sarcastic with a sly slippage of her voice and a downward pucker of her mouth.

Though she wasn't much taller than most of her students, Mrs. Halifax exuded the authority of a giantess. She was a compact little woman with a bosom that looked, in profile, like nubs of extra limbs protruding from her body. Her face gave off a perpetual dramatic heat though her skin was pale as cold cream. Her eyes were a warm glistening brown. She licked her lips that were full and shinily red like plastic cherries. Often she stroked her bare, downy forearms and her bosom as she might pet a cat. The least mature boys in her classes staring at Mrs. Halifax's sensuous caressing hands were made to feel anxious. The more mature boys were made yet more anxious, antsy. Her rust-colored hair was sometimes twisted into some kind of teacher top-knot on her head but at other times fell loose and wavy to her shoulders. Though her official subject was social studies, Mrs. Halifax sometimes read poetry to her classes, and there was the belief that, though she credited these poems to actual poets, they were her own efforts, mysterious to even the brightest students. When Mrs. Halifax read these poems, which were laced with such words as *tempest—sorrow—destiny—soul—soul-mate—beyond the grave*—her beautiful brown eyes filled not with mockery but with tremulous tears.

Because we were fated. What a soul-mate is, is fate.

Which is why I am not guilty. Never will anyone convince me in any way I AM GUILTY.

SO IT FIGURED: Rickie Swann was fated, too. In that habit of drifting downtown after school instead of returning home where his step-dad Dexter Swann who wasn't a bad guy was wheezing through plastic tubes in his nose and surfing the TV and his mom was—well, but you never knew, did you? Maybe Mrs. Swann would be waiting for her son to drift back home or maybe, which was happening more frequently lately, Mrs. Swann wouldn't be home herself but at the grocery store so she'd return sometimes after dark with that icepick look signaling to her men *You two mouths are hungry? Me, too.* If they were lucky they got TV dinners heated up in the microwave. To avoid these encounters in the fall of his fifteenth year Rickie fell into the habit of hanging out at the 7-Eleven or he'd prowl a nearby mini-mall hanging out at Wendy's, Taco Bell, Shamrock Lounge & Bowling Lanes where older guys who were friends of his, sort of, had jobs. And one evening back of the Shamrock Rickie saw a car like his mom's secondhand Mazda including the license plate number beginning *TZ* and he thought, What the fuck? and entered the bowling alley by a rear door little knowing how this was destiny, as Mrs. Halifax would later explicate to him, his life was to be changed forever for a reason.

"Mom?"

Like it was a movie scene where edgy music comes up Rickie stood staring and gaping at Mrs. Swann in a gold lamé turtleneck and tight-fitting black nylon trousers as she was laughing, drinking beer, bowling, and obviously having a terrific time in the company of a coarse-skinned man of about her age with a chunky ferret face and icepick eyes like her own except this guy was muscled and tattooed and wore his graying ginger hair tied back in a ponytail, and he had sideburns that looked gouged into his cheeks, and a beery belly laugh as with a swaggering rush he sent a black bowling ball sliding, slipping, careening down the alley to crash squarely into the pins and send them all flying—"Stri-ike!" Mrs. Swann protested, "Hey! How'd you do *that?*" swiping at the guy's bared bicep with her fist like she seriously doubted he'd rolled a perfect strike legitimately except: how can you cheat in bowling? In plain view of any spectator? Rickie saw through a shimmering haze that the ponytail guy wasn't alone with his mother but there was a fattish girl of about eleven with them, her sturdy right leg in a brace, and the girl's face was so soft and pie-shaped and her mouth so slack, you had to figure she was mentally disadvantaged as you were taught to say at school not retarded or a moron. Who were these people? Why was Mrs. Swann hanging out with them? Rickie figured the girl was the daughter of the ponytail guy judging by how tenderly he regarded her clumsy antics as she took her turn at bowling, tottering and lurching forward dragging her stiff leg, swinging and releasing her ball (child-sized, speckled orange) to drop onto the alley like a rock that rolled forward slowly—slowly!—toward the pins and after several slow seconds the orange-speckled ball veered into the gutter failing to knock down a single pin. Which Rickie was thinking scornfully was fucking hard to accomplish.

Yet the girl was loved, you could see. Her second ball too she threw like the first, and it rolled into the gutter. *Yet her daddy grinned and applauded her.*

"My turn!"

Now came Mrs. Swann all elbows and bared gums. Whom Rickie had never seen bowling in all their life together and who'd for fucking sure never taken him bowling. Mrs. Swann in her gold lamé turtleneck reckless and show-offy as a teenaged girl for the benefit of the ponytail guy, yet with unexpected skill gave her ball a twist of the wrist as she released it so that it rolled swiftly and unerringly down the alley to strike the pins with such force that eight of them went flying; and with her second ball she knocked out the remaining two to score what's called a split, pretty damned good, Rickie had to concede, though Rickie was upset, and Rickie was resentful, seeing how the ponytail guy and the fat girl with her leg in a brace were applauding his mom. *His* mom! The guy called her "Lenore" and the girl called her "Aunt Lenore." *Was that his mom's fucking name, Lenore?* She'd never told Rickie her own son.

Noise in the Shamrock was deafening. Not just the bowlers but country rock music blaring overhead. Or was it a roaring in Rickie's ears. Not knowing if he should duck out of there before his mom saw him or should he saunter over and say "Hi, Mom!" and let the bitch know he knew, and as Rickie hesitated Mrs. Swann glanced around to see him and her face froze and for a terrible moment—Rickie would remember this all his life, he knew—it seemed almost as if his mother would not acknowledge him. Then she relented. In a kind of guilty voice, but grinning—"Kiddo, hey. Long as you're here, this is my big brother Stan and my sweet little niece Cleopatra."

Big brother? Little niece? *What?*

It was like that, who was it that Bible person turned to a pillar of salt for seeing something forbidden by God, how Rickie stood rooted to the spot blinking at his mother who was smiling so widely at him her pale pink barracuda gums were exposed like some private part of her body. Rickie was too shocked to protest *But Mom: you always said you were an orphan! No family!* Like a TV switched off his brain had gone blank. "Stan"—the tattooed muscle-guy with the ponytail who must've been Rickie's uncle—nodded at him and muttered a greeting. "Cleopatra"—the fattish girl who must've been Rickie's cousin, the only cousin known to him—smiled shyly sticking a finger in her mouth. But Rickie couldn't croak out any kind of greeting. Oh shit, was he tongue-tied. Mrs. Swann was advancing toward him with a warning icepick look, "This is our secret, Rickie, okay? No need to rat to your dear old dad." In the next alley a bowling ball black as pitch rushed into pins with a deafening clatter. Rickie felt as if he'd been hit in the gut backing out of that hellish place stammering what sounded like, "Sure, Mom. I guess . . ." though his words were lost amid bowlers' shouts and hyena laughter.

Run, run! Running into the night Rickie was panting and sobbing in a marshy field somewhere near the Turnpike where he ran until the soles of his sneakers were layered in mud the size of elephants' hooves and what came into his dazzled head was lines of a poem his social studies teacher had recited to them that day *Run run though I await you run little rabbit run from your fate, you* but he couldn't remember the rest of the words, he sank to his knees, filled with a murderous rage for that woman who was his mother he'd trusted who'd betrayed him but mostly Rickie was bawling like a baby, oh Christ he wanted to *die.*

NOW RICKIE WAS staying out of school, didn't give a fuck if they sent a notice to his mom. His mom! And when he did show up, he was sullen-faced and disheveled like some kid with a gun in his backpack you wouldn't want to cross. (There was no metal detector checkpoint at Grover Cleveland. The school was only a junior high!) Rickie's teachers nervously took note of him, and were secretly relieved when he cut their classes. Except Mrs. Halifax, Rickie's fourth-period teacher, began at last to notice him. *That woundedness in the boy's face . . .*

Seeing how the skinny gangly boy she'd never paid much attention to previously sat slumped in his desk at the back of the room staring into space with hooded eyes and his boy-face haggard as a skull. She was tempted to tease him, to wake him up, but something held her back. He was one of those Mrs. Halifax who hadn't an ounce of liberal sentimentality in her veins and was color blind on the issue filed away under *lost cause.* But now she became distracted by him. His presence. A tragic presence it began to seem. Among the ordinary boys and girls who were her pupils. And how ordinary, how banal, the day's lesson, the textbook in her hand, how ordinary Mrs. Halifax's own life she'd borne bravely like a burning candle aloft in wayward winds determined it should not be blown out, it should not be extinguished until she'd come to a fulfillment of her destiny thinking *That Swann boy, he's beautiful* shocked at what she was seeing at the rear of her familiar fluorescent-lighted classroom on the second floor of Grover Cleveland Junior High in East Orange, New Jersey, as in the monumental works of Caravaggio a holy redeeming light radiates not from celestial sources but from the potent Mystery of the inner spirit. Dazed by this vision Mrs. Halifax stood for a moment speechless at the front of the classroom slowly stroking her downy forearms and the undersides of her heavy breast in a white angora sweater and and there came a sting of moisture in her eyes now tender, not-mocking and she said, "Rickie Swann. *Please see me immediately after class.*"

And after class Mrs. Halifax instructed Rickie Swann to *please see her after school.*

THAT WAS EARLY November. Their affair would continue for eleven months. *As soon as our eyes melted together we knew. We were each helpless in our fate.*

For what Mrs. Halifax saw in Rickie Swann's face was the old-young eyes of her soul-mate. Her lover. Oh, not the lover—not the lovers—she'd actually had, in her life; not her husband Dwayne Halifax, for sure! *What a soul-mate is, is your destiny. In an instant you know.* Not that Mrs. Halifax understood what the trauma was, in Rickie Swann's heart. (One day, he would tell her. He would tell her all his secrets as she would tell him all her secrets, or almost all.) On that November afternoon darkening early with storm clouds and smelling more virulently than usual of sulfurous chemicals there sat Rickie Swann before her, fists jammed into his armpits in the most hostile of boy-postures. His jaws, covered in a soft silvery down, trembled. His eyelids trembled. Mrs. Halifax was inspired to switch off the overhead lights. She was one to dislike fluorescent lights at any time knowing how they cast shadows down upon her girlish face. "You can speak to me, Rickie. Open your heart." Mrs. Halifax was feeling tender as a fresh sliced-open melon. Spilling seeds, juice. She who'd long hardened her soul against the disillusions of her life as a woman; as, as a young idealistic teacher with an education degree from Rutgers at New Brunswick she'd had to harden her soul against the bureaucracy and stiffling intellectual mediocrity of the East Orange, New Jersey, school district. In the shadows, the walls of the classroom dissolved. The bulletin board, the floating clock face. There was just enough dimming light from the windows to see Rickie Swann staring at her. Mrs. Halifax was beginning to feel faint. Oh, what was happening to her! What was happening to this boy! "There is something locked in your heart, Rickie. You must open it to me. I am your friend . . . " Her hand reached out boldly to stroke his hair. His limp greasy tattered-looking hair. Her cool fingers stroked his warm forehead. Rickie squirmed, shivered like a frightened animal, swallowed hard. *That first touch. A flame between us.* Mrs. Halifax was deeply moved, the boy had not shrunk from her. Never had she touched any pupil so intimately in her nine years of teaching and this boy had not shrunk from her. She asked him again what was wrong, urged him to speak his heart to her, and he began to stammer that he was "so afraid"—"something was going to happen soon"—and Mrs. Halifax asked what would happen soon and Rickie said, as if the words were being pulled from him, "Something! Like lightning that can't be stopped." Mrs. Halifax moved carefully, as you might move to comfort a shivering German shepherd. She pulled up a chair close beside Rickie Swann, and she framed the boy's face between her hands, and she looked him in the eyes so close, it was like bringing your own face up against a mirror, seeing your breath steam on the mirror and so close you can't see yourself but can only feel. Gently she asked, "Who would this happen to, Rickie?" and Rickie shook his head vehemently as if he didn't know, or if he knew he could not say, and a single tear distinct and pristine as a glittering gem spilled out of his eye and ran slowly down his cheek and Mrs. Halifax *not knowing what I did I swear in that instant knowing only that this had happened between us before, in another lifetime long ago* stopped the tear with her lips. And all this while the boy was unmoving and now not breathing waiting *for what had to be, had to be.*

Following this, things happened swiftly between Mrs. Halifax and Rickie Swann.

NEVER WOULD HE betray her. Never would he speak a word in corroboration of her felonious behavior. Never would he accuse her, never would he refer to her as other than "Mrs. Halifax"—or, sometimes, more formally, "Mrs. Halifax my teacher."

His own guilt, whatever he'd done, he would accept. But not that Mrs. Halifax his teacher had conspired with him to commit it.

ENTERING THE REAR, kitchen door of her two-story wood-frame and brick home on Cedar Drive, East Orange Mrs. Halifax heard muffled laughter in the TV room. Scarcely daring to breathe she came to the doorway seeing only shifting TV shadows. A hulking silhouette on the Barcalounger. It was nearly 10 P.M. A weekday evening! Mrs. Halifax would tell her husband Dwayne she'd been—where?—at a PTA meeting at the school. Her swollen, pale mouth would insist, yes she'd told him she wouldn't be home until late, he should order a pizza for himself, wasn't pizza Dwayne Halifax's favorite favorite food? It was! Greasy Italian sausage, melted mozzarella cheese in yard-long sticky skeins, inch-thick chewy-dough crust that would set Mrs. Halifax's sensitive bowels aflame, such was Dwayne Halifax's favorite food which she was hoping he'd ordered so she'd feel less guilty. Not that she felt guilt for loving Rickie Swann! Never would Mrs. Halifax feel guilt for loving Rickie Swann, her love for the boy was the single pure clean selfless and innocent love of her life. There was only innocence between them. She was preparing to defend her love for Rickie Swann when she heard the moist rattle of snoring. Dear Dwayne had fallen asleep in the recliner. Thank God! As increasingly Dwayne was doing in the evenings since he'd lost his last job and his mysterious health symptoms had emerged. Poor Dwayne who'd once been a tight end on the Rutgers football team, with a head of shaggy curly hair, now nearly bald, pot-bellied and with a strangely shriveling right leg at the age of only thirty-seven, only five years older than Mrs. Halifax but looking at least fifteen years older, almost overnight it seemed Dwayne had become the type of man you might love but wouldn't be *in love* with, not if you were a normal very intensely female woman like Mrs. Halifax. Noooooo. Also Dwayne Halifax had been a vigorous alpha-type male in his earlier life but of late he'd become one of that category of left-behind Americans you might say. A high-tech computer whiz straight out of college hired at a six-figure salary then in the mid-1990's abruptly "downsized" and with no choice but to re-enter the work force on a far lower level of income and distinction, he'd taken a course in real-estate at the local community college and was hired by the region's largest realtor then again abruptly downsized with plummeting real-estate sales in the wake of a recession, next, still robust and hopeful, vowing not to be discouraged he'd taken first aid, lifesaving and lifeguard training and showing up for his first day as a lifeguard at Jersey City Beach he was met by State of New Jersey health officials armed with documents shutting the beach for reasons of *toxic chemical and cloacal bacterial* contamination. It was following this new disappointment that Dwayne Halifax began to turn inward upon himself, increasingly brooding and withdrawn, and his right leg began to *atrophy* as a local doctor tentatively diagnosed, it was possibly the onslaught of amyotrophic lateral sclerosis ("Lou Gehrig's disease") or a milder sclerosis, though perversely, and Mrs. Halifax supposed this must be a positive sign, Dwayne's appetite was wholly unaffected, you should see Dwayne Halifax *eat.* Well, let him have his pleasures at least. What remained to him. She was smelling pizza-smells, and beer. In her stocking feet, holding her shoes she tiptoed to the snoring, open-mouthed man on the Barcalounger and gave him a breathy kiss on the forehead. Blessed with the love of Rickie Swann, Mrs. Halifax felt a surge of affection for her husband. She would take care not to wake him. Often he slept in the TV room now. Long groggy bouts of sleep, sometimes as many as fourteen hours at a stretch. Not for an instant did it occur to Mrs. Halifax *God I hate him, wish he would die die DIE* and certainly she did not think *The boy will kill him for me,* instead she pulled a quilt up over his bulky body and switched off the TV and lights that he might sleep undisturbed through the night. In her loins that still throbbed in the aftermath of passion, staining her black stretch panties was the boy's silky semen seeping out of her, the hot deep secret core of her being, her eyeballs shuddered in their sockets as on tiptoe she ascended the stairs *Oh Ricki-ie. Rick-ie Swann. I love you so.*

"KIDDO. Where the hell've you been?"

At 10 P.M. Mrs. Swann had begun to worry about her son, yes and she was suspicious of the way he pushed past her avoiding her eyes and with his greasy hair swinging in his face like he was hiding behind it, and his mouth looked swollen and raw (had he been kissing some hot-chick little cunt?) and the scent of his underarms made even her practiced nostrils pinch. Over his shoulder he growled, "Go to hell, Mom. *I got homework.*"

Never would Mrs. Swann acknowledge their meeting in the bowling alley. Never would Rickie allude to it. Fuck if he would. Fuck if he gave a fuck about that shit. He didn't need his scrawny old mom now. He'd learned not only his heart was in the possession of somebody who would never never break it, *it had already happened before a thousand years ago.* It was, what Mrs. Halifax called it, *sacrosanct.*

THOSE MONTHS! Madness.

They could not keep from each other. They could not bear being apart not knowing exactly where the other was. Mrs. Halifax bought Rickie Swann a cell phone for his (secret) use. In Mrs. Halifax's fourth-period class Rickie sat now attentively at the rear of the classroom staring at Mrs. Halifax with a look of dreamy stunned boy-desire. Often his mouth grew slack and damp. *He loves me. Adores me.* Mrs. Halifax made every effort to keep her eyes from drifting onto Rickie Swann for if she allowed herself to acknowledge him she was in danger (she, Mrs. Halifax!) of stammering and blushing and losing her concentration. In Rickie's proximity she felt a tugging sensation in her body, in her breasts and belly, a sweet helpless slipping-down sensation like the moon's tide; she had all she could do to keep from moaning aloud in sexual need. Her classroom teasing was less cruel, more noticeably playful. She was looking flushed and youthful and gave off a new lilac fragrance. Never now did she twist her hair into a knot, always she wore it loose and sensuous on her shoulders. To her pupils' surprise, she even brought them home-baked peanut butter cookies to celebrate Columbus Day: "To honor the fact that the New World yet exists, boys and girls, to be discovered by each and every one of us in our own way."

HERE IS A FACT. That first time together in the front seat then the backseat of Mrs. Halifax's Chevy station wagon immediately the lovers knew they'd kissed before with such eagerness and desperation. Immediately they knew they'd many times declared their love. Clutching at each other in the vehicle parked in the dark-dripping interior of Edison Township Park. "Oh Mrs. Halifax, I—I guess I l-love you," Rickie Swann stammered, and Mrs. Halifax said, in a swoon of joy, "I love you too, Rickie. My darling!" Mrs. Halifax pressed her cheek against the boy's head and rocked him in her arms. They were partly unclothed. Where their skins touched, they scalded. Mrs. Halifax was the one to lead. Their damp yearning mouths, hands. Alternately they were shy and emboldened with each other. Almost at once Mrs. Halifax ceased to think of herself as a married woman; she would never again think of herself as Mrs. Dwayne Halifax. Rickie in a paroxysm of need pushed his groin against Mrs. Halifax's belly. Madness overcame her like warm lava in which she might drown. Kissing the boy, tonguing and stroking him, that beautiful lanky boy-body, the lean stubbled cheeks, hard flat flank of his thighs, and between his legs his boy-penis suddenly quivering and hard and larger in her fingers than she would have expected, and no sooner in her fingers than a violent shudder ran through the boy's body drawn tight as a bow and he groaned and shook against her and his penis erupted in a silky liquid that made Mrs. Halifax weep, it was so exquisite. The moment so perfect. They would be lovers for the remainder of their lives. *Now there is no going back.*

THOSE MONTHS. In Mrs. Halifax's station wagon. In motels on Route 1. Rarely the same motel twice. *Days Inn, Bide-a-Wee, Econo-Lodge, Sleep E Hollow, Holiday Inn* (Rahway, Metuchen), *Travellers Inn, Best Western.* Mrs. Halifax and her teenaged son (Brian/Jason/Troy/Mark). Only Mrs. Halifax entered the motel lobbies, but her adolescent son was sometimes glimpsed in the parking lot, or in the video arcade, or, if there was an indoor heated pool, there. Once they were safe inside their cozy locked room they luxuriated in lovemaking, Jacuzzi bathing, take-out McDonald's, Taco Bell, Chinese and Italian food, giant Pepsis (for Rickie) and six-packs of beer (for Mrs. Halifax). In poems Mrs. Halifax would grope to express their happiness. *Our souls we surrender. There is no I, no thee. A thousand thousand years ago for all Eternity.* Though knowing it was reckless Mrs. Halifax couldn't resist giving Rickie presents for his fifteenth birthday in January. Music videos of his favorite bands, a Hugo Boss T-shirt, Nike jogging shoes. He'd have to find some way to hide them from his mother's sharp eyes. (Maybe tell her he'd found money somewhere? A wad of bills, on the sidewalk? He could say it was behind the Shamrock bowling alley, see how Mrs. Swann reacted.)

Sometimes their lovemaking was so profound, it was almost scary.

Other times, they tumbled together, breathless and squealing and playful as lascivious puppies.

This beautiful boy Rickie Swann who might've been Mrs. Halifax's son. But he wasn't her son and that, Mrs. Halifax knew, was the very best luck. For if he'd been her son he wouldn't have adored her the way he did. And she couldn't have adored him, every square centimeter of his perfect boy-body, Even pimples, skin eruptions on his back she kissed. Never did she allow Rickie to say he was ugly, never *never.* Never that he was stupid, he was *not stupid.* Both Rickie and Mrs. Halifax were in awe of Rickie's indefatigable boy-penis, so very different from the pathetic limp skinned-looking penis of Dwayne Halifax Mrs. Halifax shrank from glimpsing by chance with the mortication of self-disgust you feel for an old discredited ridiculous and humiliating crush you'd had for somebody now glimpsed on the street and hardly recognizable, he's so *old.*

On the occasion of Rickie's fifteenth birthday. In a top-floor suite of the Rahway Hilton. As Mrs. Halifax toweled Rickie dry after their languorous Jacuzzi and restyled his hair in what she called the *Elvis look,* slicked back from his forehead in a sexy pompadour. There in a careful voice she inquired what birthday presents had he received from Mrs. Swann, and Rickie sniggered, "Are you kidding? Not a goddamn thing."

"You don't mean your mother . . . forgot? Oh, Rickie."

"Think I give a shit, Mrs. Halifax. I don't."

She saw, in the bathroom mirror, that her lover spoke the truth.

Though sensing that Mrs. Swann was her deadly enemy. And that, one day, well—

But Mrs. Halifax was determined not to think of that day. Not yet.

HERE IS A FACT. Rickie was receiving higher grades at school. For Mrs. Halifax tutored him as they lay naked together nuzzling and tickling and kissing and doling out rewards to him for each correct answer he gave. And of course Mrs. Halifax helped him with his homework in all his courses. Sometimes taking his hand in hers and pretending to guide his pen as he wrote. And what came out in Rickie's large looping handwriting was unexpectedly smart, made sense, and Rickie's grades in English began to be B-, even B. Mrs. Halifax also tutored him in "deportment"—"winning friends and influencing people." Her model was ex-President Bill Clinton who could charm the pants off, well—anyone! You smile you make eye contact you speak clearly and never mumble and never never appear sullen or slouch-shouldered. Rickie had to admit, he looked pretty cool when Mrs. Halifax groomed him. The *Elvis look* plus the Hugo Boss T-shirt and Nike shoes. Rickie had to admit he hadn't liked himself much, in fact he'd kind of despised himself before falling in love with her. He didn't tell Mrs. Halifax, though, of his crazy plan to murder his mother with a hammer. Not that it had been an actual plan. Now he had other, better things to think about. Lots better things. So, fuck Lenore Swann. Though that woman scared him sometimes sniffing around him like a dog including even his crotch if he was careless enough to pass by her so he'd push away—"Christ sake, Mom! That's disgusting." And Mrs. Swann would say, "There's some hot high school chick getting into my kid's pants, I just know it." But what could Mom prove? Not a thing. She never went to PTA meetings and would never meet Mrs. Halifax. *She can't smell Mrs. Halifax on me after the Jacuzzi so fuck her!*

THE PLAN WAS, they would wait until Rickie was out of school. They would wait until he graduated from high school at least. Then they would elope. He'd be eighteen, a legal age. They would move away to the Southwest where Rickie'd never been and was dying to go. Lying in their king-sized bed in the Travellers Inn their twenty bare toes wriggling together beneath the sheet as they leafed through *U.S. Road Maps: A Scenic Guide* marveling at color photos of the Grand Canyon, Death Valley, Yosemite, Red Rock Canyon, plotting their escape from the prying suffocating world that surrounded them in East Orange, New Jersey. Drifting to sleep in each other's arms thinking of dogs' names—Gallant, Greywolf, Duke, Cleopatra—for the greyhounds they hoped to adopt from the dog tracks, and the palomino ponies they hoped to buy at auction to spare these beautiful doomed creatures, as Mrs. Halifax spoke vehemently of them, the slaughter-house.

God help us. God who has sanctified our love, help us now.

It was not Mrs. Halifax's fault! As somehow in the late winter and early spring of the new year, things began to go tragically awry.

Not Mrs. Halifax's fault that the driver of an uninsured pickup speeding above the limit at 69 mph in a 55 mph zone lost control of his vehicle and careened across two lanes of traffic on Route 1 in Metuchen to sideswipe her station wagon at dusk of a rainy weekday in March when Mrs. Halifax was driving her lover home after a snatched hour of happiness in the Metuchen Holiday Inn. Lucky for Mrs. Halifax and Rickie they hadn't been killed in a head-on collision but not so lucky they were so abruptly *exposed*.

"Ma'am, this boy is your son, you say?"

"I . . . didn't say."

"His I.D. says his last name is 'Swann.' What's his relationship to you, your name's 'Halifax'?"

"Officer, is this . . . necessary? I mean, is it necessary for you to ask . . . ?"

"Don't get your back up, lady. Either this 'Rickie' is, or is not, your son. Which?"

"Rickie is my . . . student."

"Student, ma'am?"

"I am his eighth-grade teacher."

"Teacher? What's he doing with you in your car, ma'am?"

"I was . . . driving him home from school, Officer."

"After 6 P.M.? What kind of school would that be, ma'am?"

"I was . . . you see, I was tutoring him. He's behind in his studies. I was tutoring him after school, Officer."

"Tutoring! What kind of tutoring would that be, ma'am?"

Mrs. Halifax was feeling faint. Her neck was aching from whiplash. A migraine headache had begun behind her teary eyes. Yet under duress in the presence of burly Jersey cops eyeing her with the alerted interest of fishermen who've netted a mermaid amid their catch of smelly wriggling fish she had lapsed into the stylized gestures of desperate female coquetry: lowered rapidly blinking eyelids, seductive/shy gaze, soft husky suggestive voice.

"Social studies, Officer."

It was then that Rickie intervened. All she'd taught him of *winning friends and influencing people* came into sudden improvised practice. He told the Jersey cops in a courteous frank voice that Mrs. Halifax lived in his neighborhood and often drove him home when he stayed after school for sports so his mom wouldn't have to pick him up.

And so they were spared. And so they were allowed to leave Metuchen. Mrs. Halifax hadn't been the cause of the accident but her car had to be towed off the highway and she'd had to give a police report; she hoped to God the accident wasn't significant enough to be written up in the local papers. (It wasn't.) But she had to call a taxi to take her and Rickie Swann to East Orange, and she had to call her husband. Rickie had to call his mother. Excuses were fumblingly made. Rickie didn't get home until 10:30 P.M. that night, and Mrs. Halifax didn't get home until later. As soon as she entered the house there was Dwayne Halifax waiting for her, up from his Barcalounger and limping about the kitchen with fierce eyes and a hurt, bruised mouth. "Tutoring some kid? What kid? What the fuck's going on here? Where've you been all this week? Where's my station wagon? *What the fuck've you done with my station wagon?*"

This was the first time Mrs. Halifax had reason to believe her husband might be deranged, and might be dangerous. For the station wagon wasn't his, not any longer. How could it be *his?* Maybe it was registered in his name but that was just a technicality. She was the one who had a job, she was the one bringing in a paycheck she was the one who required transportation, *it was her station wagon.*

"Whore! Think I can't smell you!"

Dwayne Halifax's fist leapt out to strike Mrs. Halifax's already lacerated face. She uttered a short sharp cry of pain. She thought, dazed *It's TV. It isn't real.* But there was Dwayne Halifax's face contorted with rage. Mrs. Halifax turned, and ran heavily upstairs. Locked herself in the bathroom. Oh, she was bleeding again: where the nurse at the medical center had put Band-Aids on her face, blood was seeping out. Yet she knew she was lucky even so. The worst had not yet happened. Rickie Swann had not been taken from her. And lucky too that Dwayne Halifax wasn't the strapping husky youth he'd been when she had first fallen in love with him. The blow he'd given her with his atrophied right hand hadn't broken her nose or loosened any of her teeth.

He knows. But he can't know.

Can he?

NOW CAME THE time of renunciation. Now, the bittersweet time of chastity. Mrs. Halifax had long anticipated it.

Explaining to Rickie who stared at her disbelieving that they must stop seeing each other. Until he was eighteen.

Rickie protested, no! No no no.

Mrs. Halifax spoke quietly. The world was preparing to destroy them, she feared. "My husband, your mother . . ."

Rickie protested, no! His mom didn't know *a fucking thing.*

"But my husband, Rickie. He suspects."

Rickie knew nothing of Dwayne Halifax. His eyes registered blank at the mention of a *husband.* The very concept seemed to elude him. Mrs. Halifax hadn't decided whether she would tell Rickie how Dwayne had struck her already lacerated face.

"Those vulgar Jersey cops, Rickie. You heard them. If they hadn't believed you. If they'd called your parents. Our love would be exposed, now. I would lose my job, and . . ." Mrs. Halifax paused. She had no wish to ponder what would be her fate, professionally and legally; though she must have known that having sexual relations with a minor constituted statutory rape, and being involved with any of her students intimately constituted grounds for immediate dismissal, yet she hadn't thought of these matters, for it seemed to her that such sublunary things didn't apply to her. Gently she said, "No one can understand our love but us, Rickie. You know that, darling, don't you?"

Rickie nodded, yes! He knew.

Rickie had come round to believing as Mrs. Halifax did, they'd been lovers a thousand years ago. In more than one lifetime they'd been lovers. He didn't understand it completely, as Mrs. Halifax understood it, but he knew it had something to do with "incarnation"—or maybe "reincarnation"—and "transmigration of souls." It was a fact, how their eyes had met and sort of melted into each other that afternoon in Mrs. Halifax's classroom. And the way each time they made love Rickie felt safer in Mrs. Halifax's arms like her white soft body was a big balloon floating in warm water and as long as he clung to the balloon he was safe, he wouldn't drown. But at the same time—he knew this was weird, even kind of freaky—he felt stronger, too, like he was empowered to kill, to take any life, the way a god is empowered.

Mrs. Halifax was saying terrible words. Yet so calmly, gently.

"It's the only way, Rickie. For now. To preserve our love, we must say good-bye temporarily."

" 'Temporarily'—what's that?"

"Until you're eighteen, darling."

"Three fucking years—isn't it?"

"Those years will pass swiftly, darling. I promise."

"I could kill him! Your h-husband."

"Excuse me, Rickie? What?"

"I could! I have the power."

Mrs. Halifax felt a thrill of almost sexual pleasure. *He does love me. Adores me. Here's proof.*

But she insisted no, no. Better that they never see each other again than that Rickie commit so reckless an act. Better to renounce their love. They must say good-bye, and they must not seek each other out. They must not even call each other on their cell phones. At school, they must not make eye-contact. This, they must *vow.*

IN HIS STEP-DAD'S tool box covered in cobwebs Rickie located the claw hammer. Heavy! In his mind the hammer had been more of some kind of idea of a hammer but in actual life, it was heavy, and bigger than he'd expected. Must've weighed ten pounds. He swung it in his hand. He wondered, would it fit into his backpack?

IT WAS RICKIE who weakened. He called Mrs. Halifax on his cell phone. His voice was so raw, at first he couldn't speak. Mrs. Halifax had been drinking (at midday, not like her!) and immediately she succumbed. The Chevy station wagon had been repaired, she swung by to pick her eager young lover up behind Home Depot and they drove to one of their secret places, a marshy area off the Turnpike north of Newark Airport where an access road led to a cul-de-sac amid six-foot rushes that rustled romantically in the wind and dank pools of standing water in which part-submerged tires crouched like alligators.

It was then and in that place that they knew: their love was hopeless and yet it was hopeless to resist their love.

WHEN THAT EVENING Mrs. Halifax returned to her wood-frame and brick home on Cedar Drive in which she continued to live with Dwayne Halifax she steeled herself for her husband's accusatory or caustic or threatening remarks but a surprise awaited her: it was Dwayne's new strategy to ignore *her.* In the Barcalounger in the TV room the balding pot-bellied man did not deign to glance around at her as if she, the sole breadwinner in the family, the one to pay their insurance premiums, were nothing but a servant! Still, Mrs. Halifax murmured an excuse. Where she'd been, and why. For always she had an excuse. And in her arms a stack of student folders. "Guess I'll be up late tonight." Mrs. Halifax spoke earnestly, innocently. Her nipples were still erect from her lover sucking at them and the soft white flesh of her inner thighs chafed as if on fire.

"MRS. HALIFAX, I have the means."

Have the means. Such a strange phrase from the boy's lips.

"Oh, Rickie. Noooo."

Kisses to stop his mouth. But he wrenched his mouth away. He was panting, stubborn. "A hammer. That's all you need."

A hammer? What was Rickie talking about? Mrs. Halifax pressed her hands against her ears, her brain was blanking out.

Uncanny how she'd been so absolutely the dominant one at the first, by degrees Rickie Swann was taking on a new ardent urgent role. His voice cracked less frequently. It was becoming a man's voice. He'd gained weight. He called her on her cell phone at all hours though weakly she'd asked him not to call her at home, at night.

"Like, 'household accident.' I was reading some statistics."

"Rickie, what statistics? Where?"

Dwayne was insured for $90,000. Not much, with inflation. But wasn't there double indemnity or something, accidental death? A man in his physical condition, atrophying limb, slipping in the bathtub. Falling down the stairs. Falling down the cellar stairs. There were diverse *means.*

"They always suspect the spouse, Rickie. On TV."

"You wouldn't be there, Mrs. Halifax. You'd be, like, at school."

"Even so . . ."

"Let me! Mrs. Halifax, *I want to.*"

She'd told him about Dwayne striking her that night. Other times, before he'd decided to give her the cold shoulder, shoving her and threatening her. Maybe she shouldn't have told Rickie. The boy was so excitable and protective where Mrs. Halifax was concerned.

"Oh, Rickie. Sweetie. I don't think so."

That was one evening. Another time, maybe ten days later, Rickie showed up wearing the black backpack she'd bought him at the Nickel and a look in his young fierce face warned her *He's got the hammer. He'll kill you then somehow himself* and she felt a sensation of drowning, but this turned out to be ridiculous paranoid thinking for all Rickie wanted to do that evening was go bowling! At the Shamrock, he suggested, but Mrs. Halifax said definitely no, she drove them to the Starlite Lounge & Bowling Alley in New Brunswick. Whatever would happen, would happen. She was resigned by this time. She'd had a pregnancy scare, and she was all right now but during the scare she'd been resigned. She seemed to know they'd had children together in the past. Of course, they'd had children together in the past. And it had happened not once but many times. Better for them to know nothing of what's to come. Her colleagues at Grover Cleveland were watching her covertly she knew. Entering the teachers' lounge, she'd hear them go suddenly quiet. She'd see the exchange of glances. She knew. Though no one would confront her. No one dared accuse her.

Better for her not to imagine: lurid news headlines, tabloid TV. Possibly she'd be arrested. Possibly, arrested, she would be several months pregnant with Rickie Swann's child. *She would have the baby in the women's prison.* Or maybe, her sentence would be suspended by the court, she'd be on probation. An injunction not to see her former student ever again. Or maybe—oh God, this was scary!—Rickie Swann would hammer out Dwayne Halifax's brains and track through the house incriminating prints from his Nike jogging shoes in blood, tissue, brains, and splintered skull fragments while she, Mrs. Halifax, was at a teachers' conference in Trenton! Or maybe, and she was leaning in this direction, they would another time and more permanently renounce their love. They would become celibates, saints.

But tonight was bowling. Tonight they drove to New Brunswick to the Starlite Lounge & Bowling Alley. Where nobody knew them, nor gave them more than a fleeting glance. A still-young mother and her teenaged son, they looked like. Except these two got along really really well. Laughing and teasing, even kissing. Naturally Rickie was the better bowler, long-limbed, fast, giving the ball a deft twist of his wrist as he released it, but Mrs. Halifax wasn't bad considering she hadn't bowled since she'd been a girl. Gripping the heavy ball against her breasts she hurried forward in quick mincing steps like a shore bird, breathless, blushing, stooping to release the ball without giving it much momentum so amid the brutal festive sounds of other balls striking pins her own made its slow way forward only to *thunk!* in the gutter. Mrs. Halifax sighed, "Oh damn!" but Rickie told her, "It's okay, Mrs. Halifax, try again. You get a second chance."

Part Four

THREE GIRLS

IN STRAND USED BOOKS on Broadway and Twelfth one snowy March early evening in 1956 when the streetlights on Broadway glimmered with a strange sepia glow, we were two NYU girl-poets drifting through the warehouse of treasures as through an enchanted forest. Just past 6:00 P.M. Above light-riddled Manhattan, opaque night. Snowing, and sidewalks encrusted with ice so there were fewer customers in the Strand than usual at this hour but *there we were.* Among other cranky brooding regulars. In our army-surplus jackets, baggy khaki pants, and zip-up rubber boots. In our matching wool caps (knitted by your restless fingers) pulled down low over our pale-girl foreheads. Enchanted by books. Enchanted by the Strand.

No bookstore of merely "new" books with elegant show window displays drew us like the drafty Strand, bins of books untidy and thumbed through as merchants' sidewalk bins on Fourteenth Street, NEW THIS WEEK, BEST BARGAINS, WORLD CLASSICS, ART BOOKS

50% OFF, REVIEWERS' COPIES, HIGHEST PRICE $1.98, REMAINDERS

25¢—$1.00. Hard-cover/paperback. Spotless/battered. Beautiful books/cheaply printed pulp paper. And at the rear and sides in that vast echoing space massive shelves of books books books rising to a ceiling of hammered tin fifteen feet above! Stacked shelves so high they required ladders to negotiate and a monkey nimbleness (like yours) to climb.

We were enchanted with the Strand and with each other in the Strand. Overseen by surly young clerks who were poets like us, or playwrights/actors/artists. In an agony of unspoken young love I watched you. As always on these romantic evenings at the Strand, prowling the aisles sneering at those luckless books, so many of them, unworthy of your attention. Bestsellers, how-tos, arts and crafts, too-simple *histories of.* Women's romances, sentimental love poems. Patriotic books, middlebrow books, books lacking esoteric covers. We were girl-poets passionately enamored of T. S. Eliot but scornful of Robert Frost whom we'd been made to memorize in high school—slyly we communicated in code phrases from Eliot in the presence of obtuse others in our dining hall and residence. We were admiring of though confused by the poetry of Yeats, we were yet more confused by the lauded worth of Pound, enthusiastically drawn to the bold metaphors of Kafka (that cockroach!) and Dostoevsky (sexy murderer Raskolnikov and the Underground Man were our rebel heroes) and Sartre ("Hell is other people"—we knew this), and had reason to believe that we were their lineage though admittedly we were American middle class, and Caucasian, and female. (Yet we were not "conventional" females. In fact, we shared male contempt for the merely "conventional" female.)

Brooding above a tumble of books that quickened the pulse, almost shyly touching Freud's *Civilization and Its Discontents,* Crane Brinton's *The Age of Reason,* Margaret Mead's *Coming of Age in Samoa,* D. H. Lawrence's *The Rainbow,* Kierkegaard's *Fear and Trembling,* Mann's *Death in Venice*—there suddenly you glided up behind me to touch my wrist (as never you'd done before, had you?) and whispered, "Come here," in a way that thrilled me for its meaning *I have something wonderful/unexpected/startling to show you.* Like poems these discoveries in the Strand were, to us, found poems to be cherished. And eagerly I turned to follow you though disguising my eagerness, "Yes, what?" as if you'd interrupted me, for possibly we'd had a quarrel earlier that day, a flaring up of tense girl-tempers. Yes, you were childish and self-absorbed and given to sulky silences and mercurial moods in the presence of showy superficial people, and I adored and feared you knowing you'd break my heart, my heart that had never before been broken because never before so exposed.

So eagerly yet with my customary guardedness I followed you through a maze of book bins and shelves and stacks to the ceiling ANTHROPOLOGY, ART/ANCIENT, ART/RENAISSANCE, ART/MODERN, ART/ASIAN, ART/WESTERN, TRAVEL, PHILOSOPHY, COOKERY, POETRY/MODERN where the way was treacherously lighted only by bare sixty-watt bulbs, and where customers as cranky as we two stood in the aisles reading books, or sat hunched on footstools glancing up annoyed at our passage, and unquestioning I followed you until at POETRY/ MODERN you halted, and pushed me ahead and around a corner, and I stood puzzled staring, not knowing what I was supposed to be seeing until impatiently you poked me in the ribs and pointed, and now I perceived an individual in the aisle pulling down books from shelves, peering at them, clearly absorbed by what she read, a woman nearly my height (I was tall for a girl, in 1956) in a man's navy coat to her ankles and with sleeves past her wrists, a man's beige fedora hat on her head, scrunched low as we wore our knitted caps, and most of her hair hidden by the hat except for a six-inch blond plait at the nape of her neck; and she wore black trousers tucked into what appeared to be salt-stained cowboy boots. Someone we knew? An older, good-looking student from one of our classes? *A girl-poet like ourselves?* I was about to nudge you in the ribs in bafflement when the blond woman turned, taking down another book from the shelf (e. e. cummings' *Tulips and Chimneys*—always I would remember that title!), and I saw that she was Marilyn Monroe.

Marilyn Monroe. In the Strand. Just like us. And she seemed to be alone.

Marilyn Monroe, alone!

Wholly absorbed in browsing amid books, oblivious of her surroundings and of us. No one seemed to have recognized her (yet) except you.

Here was the surprise: this woman was/was not Marilyn Monroe. For this woman was an individual wholly absorbed in selecting, leafing through, pausing to read books. You could see that this individual was a *reader.* One of those who *reads.* With concentration, with passion. With her very soul. And it was poetry she was reading, her lips pursed, silently shaping words. Absent-mindedly she wiped her nose on the edge of her hand, so intent was she on what she was reading. For when you truly read poetry, poetry reads *you.*

Still, this woman was—Marilyn Monroe. And despite our common sense, our scorn for the silly clichés of Hollywood romance, still we halfway expected a Leading Man to join her: Clark Gable, Robert Taylor, Marlon Brando.

Halfway we expected the syrupy surge of movie music, to glide us into the scene.

But no man joined Marilyn Monroe in her disguise as one of us in the Strand. No Leading Man, no dark prince.

Like us (we began to see) this Marilyn Monroe required no man.

For what seemed like a long time but was probably no more than half an hour, Marilyn Monroe browsed in the POETRY/MODERN shelves, as from a distance of approximately ten feet two girl-poets watched covertly, clutching each other's hands. We were stunned to see that this woman looked very little like the glamorous "Marilyn Monroe." That figure was a garish blond showgirl, a Hollywood "sex-pot" of no interest to intellectuals *(we* thought, we who knew nothing of the secret romance between Marilyn Monroe and Arthur Miller); this figure more resembled us (almost) than she resembled her Hollywood image. We were dying of curiosity to see whose poetry books Marilyn Monroe was examining: Elizabeth Bishop, H.D., Robert Lowell, Muriel Rukeyser, Harry Crosby, Denise Levertov . . . Five or six of these Marilyn Monroe decided to purchase, then moved on, leather bag slung over her shoulder and fedora tilted down on her head.

We couldn't resist, we had to follow! Cautious not to whisper together like excited schoolgirls, still less to giggle wildly as we were tempted; you nudged me in the ribs to sober me, gave me a glare signaling *Don't be rude, don't ruin this for all of us.* I conceded: I was the more pushy of the two of us, a tall gawky Rima the Bird Girl with springy carroty-red hair like an exotic bird's crest, while you were petite and dark haired and attractive with long-lashed Semitic sloe eyes, you the wily gymnast and I the aggressive basketball player, you the "experimental" poet and I drawn to "forms," our contrary talents bred in our bones. Which of us would marry, have babies, disappear into "real" life, and which of us would persevere into her thirties before starting to be published and becoming, in time, a "real" poet—could anyone have predicted, this snowy March evening in 1956?

Marilyn Monroe drifted through the maze of books and we followed in her wake as through a maze of dreams, past SPORTS, past MILITARY, past WAR, past HISTORY/ANCIENT, past the familiar figures of Strand regulars frowning into books, past surly yawning bearded clerks who took no more heed of the blond actress than they ever did of us, and so to NATURAL HISTORY where she paused, and there again for unhurried minutes (the Strand was open until 9:00 P.M.) Marilyn Monroe in her mannish disguise browsed and brooded, pulling down books, seeking what? at last crouched leafing through an oversized illustrated book (curiosity overcame me! I shoved away your restraining hand; politely I eased past Marilyn Monroe murmuring "excuse me" without so much as brushing against her and without being noticed), Charles Darwin's *Origin of Species* in a deluxe edition. Darwin! *Origin of Species!* We were poet-despisers-of-science, or believed we were, or must be, to be true poets in the exalted mode of T. S. Eliot and William Butler Yeats; such a choice, for Marilyn Monroe, seemed perverse to us. But this book was one Marilyn quickly decided to purchase, hoisting it into her arms and moving on.

That rakish fedora we'd come to covet, and that single chunky blond braid. (Afterward we would wonder: Marilyn Monroe's hair in a braid? Never had we seen Marilyn Monroe with her hair braided in any movie or photo. What did this mean? Did it mean anything? *Had she quit films, and embarked on a new, anonymous life in our midst?*)

Suddenly Marilyn Monroe glanced back at us, frowning as a child might frown (had we spoken aloud? had she heard our thoughts?), and there came into her face a look of puzzlement, not alarm or annoyance but a childlike puzzlement: *Who are you? You two? Are you watching me?* Quickly we looked away. We were engaged in a whispering dispute over a book one of us had fumbled from a shelf, *A History of Botanical Gardens in England*. So we were undetected. We hoped!

But wary now, and sobered. For what if Marilyn Monroe had caught us, and knew that we knew?

She might have abandoned her books and fled the Strand. What a loss for her, and for the books! For us, too.

Oh, we worried at Marilyn Monroe's recklessness! We dreaded her being recognized by a (male) customer or (male) clerk. A girl or woman would have kept her secret (so we thought) but no man could resist staring openly at her, following her, and at last speaking to her. Of course, the blond actress in Strand Used Books wasn't herself, not at all glamorous, or "sexy," or especially blond, in her inconspicuous man's clothing and those salt-stained boots; she might have been anyone, female or male, hardly a Hollywood celebrity, a movie goddess. Yet if you stared, you'd recognize her. If you tried, with any imagination you'd see "Marilyn Monroe." It was like a child's game in which you stare at foliage, grass, clouds in the sky, and suddenly you see a face or a figure, and after that recognition you can't not see the hidden shape, it's staring you in the face. So too with Marilyn Monroe. Once we saw her, it seemed to us she must be seen—and recognized—by anyone who happened to glance at her. If any man saw! We were fearful her privacy would be destroyed. Quickly the blond actress would become surrounded, mobbed. It was risky and reckless of her to have come to Strand Used Books by herself, we thought. Sure, she could shop at Tiffany's, maybe; she could stroll through the lobby of the Plaza, or the Waldorf-Astoria; she'd be safe from fans and unwanted admirers in privileged settings on the Upper East Side, but—here? In the egalitarian Strand, on Broadway and Twelfth?

We were perplexed. Almost, I was annoyed with her. Taking such chances! But you, gripping my wrist, had another, more subtle thought.

"She thinks she's like *us.*"

You meant: a human being, anonymous. Female, like us. Amid the ordinary unspectacular customers (predominantly male) of the Strand.

And that was the sadness in it, Marilyn Monroe's wish. To be *like us.* For it was impossible, of course. For anyone could have told Marilyn Monroe, even two young girl-poets, that it was too late for her in history. Already, at age thirty (we could calculate afterward that this was her age) "Marilyn Monroe" had entered history, and there was no escape from it. Her films, her photos. Her face, her figure, her name. To enter history is to be abducted spiritually, with no way back.

As if lightning were to strike the building that housed the Strand, as if an actual current of electricity were to touch and transform only one individual in the great cavernous space and that lone individual, by pure chance it might seem, the caprice of fate, would be the young woman with the blond braid and the fedora slanted across her face. Why? Why her, and not another? You could argue that such a destiny is absurd, and undeserved, for one individual among many, and logically you would be correct. And yet: "Marilyn Monroe" has entered history, and you have not. She will endure, though the young woman with the blond braid will die. *And even should she wish to die, "Marilyn Monroe" cannot.*

By this time she—the young woman with the blond braid—was carrying an armload of books. We were hoping she'd almost finished and would be leaving soon, before strangers' rude eyes lighted upon her and exposed her, but no: she surprised us by heading for a section called JUDAICA. In that forbidding aisle, which we'd never before entered, there were books in numerous languages: Hebrew, Yiddish, German, Russian, French. Some of these books looked ancient! Complete sets of the Talmud. Cryptically printed tomes on the cabala. Luckily for us, the titles Marilyn Monroe pulled out were all in English: *Jews of Eastern Europe; The Chosen People: A Complete History of the Jews; Jews of the New World.* Quickly Marilyn Monroe placed her bag and books on the floor, sat on a footstool, and leafed through pages with the frowning intensity of a young girl, as if searching for something urgent, something she knew—knew!—must be there; in this uncomfortable posture she remained for at least fifteen minutes, wetting her fingers to turn pages that stuck together, pages that had not been turned, still less read, for decades. She was frowning, yet smiling too; faint vertical lines appeared between her eyebrows, in the intensity of her concentration; her eyes moved rapidly along lines of print, then returned, and moved more slowly. By this time we were close enough to observe the blond actress's feverish cheeks and slightly parted moist lips that seemed to move silently. *What is she reading in that ancient book, what can possibly mean so much to her? A secret, revealed? A secret, to save her life?*

"Hey you!" a clerk called out in a nasal, insinuating voice.

The three of us looked up, startled.

But the clerk wasn't speaking to us. Not to the blond actress frowning over *The Chosen People,* and not to us who were hovering close by. The clerk had caught someone slipping a book into an overcoat pocket, not an unusual sight at the Strand.

After this mild upset, Marilyn Monroe became uneasy. She turned to look frankly at us, and though we tried clumsily to retreat, her eyes met ours. *She knows!* But after a moment, she simply turned back to her book, stubborn and determined to finish what she was reading, while we continued to hover close by, exposed now, and blushing, yet feeling protective of her. *She has seen us, she knows. She trusts us.* We saw that Marilyn Monroe was beautiful in her anonymity as she had never seemed, to us, to be beautiful as "Marilyn Monroe." All that was makeup, fakery, cartoon sexiness subtle as a kick in the groin. All that was vulgar and infantile. But this young woman was beautiful without makeup, without even lipstick; in her mannish clothes, her hair in a stubby braid. Beautiful: her skin luminous and pale and her eyes a startling clear blue. Almost shyly she glanced back at us, to note that we were still there, and she smiled. *Yes, I see you two. Thank you for not speaking my name.*

Always you and I would remember: that smile of gratitude, and sweetness.

Always you and I would remember: that she trusted us, as perhaps we would not have trusted ourselves.

So many years later, I'm proud of us. We were so young.

Young, headstrong, arrogant, insecure though "brilliant"—or so we'd been led to believe. Not that we thought of ourselves as young: you were nineteen, I was twenty. We were mature for our ages, and we were immature. We were intellectually sophisticated, and emotionally unpredictable. We revered something we called *art,* we were disdainful of something we called *life.* We were overly conscious of ourselves. And yet: how patient, how protective, watching over Marilyn Monroe squatting on a footstool in the JUDAICA stacks as stray customers pushed past muttering "excuse me!" or not even seeming to notice her, or the two of us standing guard. And at last—a relief—Marilyn Monroe shut the unwieldy book, having decided to buy it, and rose from the footstool gathering up her many things. And—this was a temptation!—we held back, not offering to help her carry her things as we so badly wanted to, but only just following at a discreet distance as Marilyn Monroe made her way through the labyrinth of the bookstore to the front counter. (Did she glance back at us? Did she understand you and I were her protectors?) If anyone dared to approach her, we intended to intervene. We would push between Marilyn Monroe and whomever it was. Yet how strange the scene was: none of the other Strand customers, lost in books, took any special notice of her, any more than they took notice of us. Book lovers, especially used-book lovers, are not ones to stare curiously at others, but only at books. At the front of the store—it was a long hike—the cashiers would be more alert, we thought. One of them seemed to be watching Marilyn Monroe approach. Did he know? Could he guess? Was he waiting for her?

Nearing the front counter and the bright fluorescent lights overhead, Marilyn Monroe seemed for the first time to falter. She fumbled to extract out of her shoulder bag a pair of dark glasses and managed to put them on. She turned up the collar of her navy coat. She lowered her hat brim.

Still she was hesitant, and it was then that I stepped forward and said quietly, "Excuse me. Why don't I buy your books for you? That way you won't have to talk to anyone."

The blond actress stared at me through her oversized dark glasses. Her eyes were only just visible behind the lenses. A shy-girl's eyes, startled and grateful.

And so I did. With you helping me. Two girl-poets, side by side, all brisk and businesslike, making Marilyn Monroe's purchases for her: a total of sixteen books!—hardcover and paperback, relatively new books, old battered thumbed-through books—at a cost of $55.85. A staggering sum! Never in my two years of coming into the Strand had I handed over more than a few dollars to the cashier, and this time my hand might have trembled as I pushed twenty-dollar bills at him, half expecting the bristly bearded man to interrogate me: "Where'd you get so much money?" But as usual the cashier hardly gave me a second glance. And Marilyn Monroe, burdened with no books, had already slipped through the turnstile and was awaiting us at the front door.

There, when we handed over her purchases in two sturdy bags, she leaned forward. For a breathless moment we thought she might kiss our cheeks. Instead she pressed into our surprised hands a slender volume she lifted from one of the bags: *Selected Poems of Marianne Moore.* We stammered thanks, but already the blond actress had pulled the fedora down more tightly over her head and had stepped out into the lightly falling snow, headed south on Broadway. We trailed behind her, unable to resist, waiting for her to hail a taxi, but she did not. We knew we must not follow her. By this time we were giddy with the strain of the past hour, gripping each other's hands in childlike elation. So happy!

"Oh. Oh God. Marilyn Monroe. She gave us a book. Was any of it real?"

It was real: we had *Selected Poems of Marianne Moore* to prove it.

That snowy early evening in March at Strand Used Books. That magical evening of Marilyn Monroe, when I kissed you for the first time.

THE MUTANTS

SHE'D BEEN A dreamy beautiful child who had become, by imperceptible degrees, a dreamy beautiful young woman of that genre American Midwestern Blond which indicates not so much a physical as a spiritual type. Now a New Yorker—downtown, Battery Park City on South End Avenue, 10280—she yet carried with her a dreamy-golden aura as lightly borne as a cloak of Athena tossed over a favored mortal for protection on the battlefield, and she carried it unaware, believing that the myriad daily glances of admiration she encountered in the city, the smiles and lingering-eyed exchanges with strangers, and certainly the intense good fortune of her professional and personal life, were part of a general bounty shared by all, like the warm autumn air.

She was of an indeterminate age. Whether in her mid-thirties, or in her early twenties. By the age of perhaps forty-five she would begin to look perhaps twenty-nine, but only in the harshest lights, which no one would force upon her.

She was not only loved, which is a commonplace experience, but beloved. There is a distinction.

In the heartland, she was beloved by her family; in Manhattan, she was beloved by her fiancé, an editor with a distinguished midtown publishing house. They were to be married at the romantic turn of the year. Now they lived together in an aerie of tall plate-glass windows and understated off-white furnishings on the thirty-sixth floor of one of the sparkling towers of lower Manhattan and their view—to which the exclamatory adjective "breathtaking!" was invariably applied—was partly of the sparkling towering city and partly of New York Harbor an exquisite seagreen like washed glass on these clear autumn mornings.

As always on weekday mornings her fiancé left the apartment early. She'd gone out shortly after 8 A.M. to a nearby Kinko's to pick up a color-xeroxed manuscript (of a children's book) and she was crossing South End Avenue as the signal flashed WALK when she heard a droning noise at first annoying and then alarming as of a gargantuan hornet and when she looked up squinting she saw a sight so unnerving her eyes at first refused to decode it: an airplane, a commercial airliner, enormous, flying unnaturally low, careening out of the sky and out of her stunned vision behind a bank of buildings as, in the next instant, she was thrown to her knees on the pavement by a colossal explosion, and she thought *There has been a ghastly accident* though so formal and archaic a word as *ghastly* was not common in her vocabulary. She fell, she struck her knees on the pavement, it seemed to her that shards and slivers of glass were pelting her exposed skin like maddened insects yet in virtually the same instant, for she'd been an excellent basketball player in high school in Illinois, her reflexes were still rapid, unthinking, in the same instant in which she fell and in nearly the same instant in which she heard the explosion somewhere close by and overhead she was on her feet, and running into the building, her building, her place of sanctuary; she was running hunched over, still clutching the xeroxed manuscript; she was running past individuals stunned and uncomprehending as figures in a dream, now in the elevator and rapidly ascending to the thirty-sixth floor able to think calmly *If I can do this, if the elevator is working I'm all right. The accident will be taken care of.*

Fumbling with the lock to her door she would have the confused memory afterward that the second deafening explosion had to do with her forcing her key, forcing the door open, even as a vast burgeoning noise as of a volcano erupting eclipsed the very echo of the first explosion, and she would remember the building beneath and around her rock, shudder, sway, and yet remain firm as if rooted deep in the earth. Now she was inside the apartment hunched and panting like an animal though knowing herself safe. And she would be safe, locking and double-bolting the door. The slender colored-xeroxed manuscript she set carefully on a table where she would discover it five weeks later encrusted with ashy grit. She was listening for sirens from the street thirty-six floors below, she was preparing for the noise of sirens which she so disliked, for in Manhattan there are so many of these, preparing for jangled nerves. Thinking *I'll wear something different from what I'd planned today. Low heels.* For she assumed that she would be going out to work as usual: but perhaps a little later.

Like her fiancé she worked in midtown. East Fifty-third Street. She was a children's book editor. She took the subway from the World Trade Center. She would say that she loved her work, loved her colleagues. She would say . . .

She was coughing. She was beginning to breathe strangely. Her mouth was coated with a fine dry dust. Her nostrils, eyeballs. What was this? And why was it so dark? She was astonished to see that the breathtaking view from the living room windows had vanished. The living room windows had vanished. The sky had vanished. There was a quivering haze of ashes and dust and minute swirling particles (snowflakes? shreds of paper? tiny broken bits of pasta?) that pressed close, and at the bedroom windows facing east a similar haze pressed against the glass except here it was reflecting an eerie giddy dance of flame. She thought *But this building isn't on fire. This is a safe building.*

She switched on the TV in the bedroom but there was no power. The radio in the kitchen, no power. She switched on lights, and there was nothing. The telephone? No dial tone. She wasn't frightened but she was panicked as an animal is panicked. She was choking, coughing into a sink. She ran water, and cupped her hands to catch the water, rinsing her eyes, drinking in thirsty lunges as an animal might drink. Yet her heart was pounding with a kind of exhilaration, for she had never been so alert and clear-minded. Never so *wakened*.

She had kicked off her shoes. Her shoes were an encumbrance.

She would move from one window to the next, restless, ever eager yet seeing only the ash-cloud thicker than before, obscuring the sun. She'd been smelling smoke for a long time without wishing to acknowledge it. A fire somewhere, possibly fires. And so this curious churning funnel of ashes reaching to the thirty-sixth floor: astonishing. It was possible that a cyclone had struck. Whipped through lower Manhattan? Yet the careening object in the sky had looked like an airplane. There were beginning to be sirens now. (Sirens in this building?) She lifted the telephone another time, to call 911 but there was no dial tone. She located her cell phone and tried to activate it but the thing was dead. Wanting desperately now to call her fiancé but in her agitation she was forgetting his cell phone number, and she was forgetting his name. His face, she knew she would recognize if she saw it. If he appeared before her, speaking her name.

She switched on the second TV not entirely remembering that the power was out. The blank gunmetal-gray screen confronted her. She thought *There is no news, yet.* This seemed to her comforting.

She busied herself stuffing wetted paper towels around the edges of the windows and the door. The door was securely locked, double-bolted. She pressed the palm of her hand against it: yes, it was warm. But all things now were warm. The air was warming to a boil. In the living room, dining room, and kitchen as well as in the bedroom now the dust was reflecting minuscule flames so perhaps after all the building was on fire, she would die in what the media called a raging inferno, or she would die of smoke inhalation.

The thought came to her *The fire extinguisher!*

Her fiancé whose name she would recall if she had time to think calmly had purchased for their apartment a small portable fire extinguisher from Home Depot out in Jersey where they'd driven one Sunday afternoon the previous spring and she'd never taken the fire extinguisher seriously, she'd perhaps laughed at its ugliness and at her fiancé's sobriety in purchasing it, and now she hauled the surprisingly heavy object out of a closet and set it on the kitchen counter to be inspected. Her fiancé would be proud of her, she thought. That she'd remembered, as he would have hoped she might. The fire extinguisher was a vivid red cylinder with a complicated nozzle. It was covered in dust. At the top was an indecipherable gauge with a red background and a tiny yellow arrow at which she stared as her eyes filmed over. The fire extinguisher was described as a "dry chemical" extinguisher "for wood, paper, cloth, plastic, rubber, flammable liquids, grease, gasoline, and electrical fires" which seemed to her to include all possible fires. Her heart filled with love for her fiancé. She was immensely grateful to him. The operating directions were white letters on a red background arranged like a poem.

STAND BACK 6 FEET
PULL OUT RING PIN
HOLD UPRIGHT
AIM NOZZLE AT BASE OF FIRE
SQUEEZE HANDLES
USE SIDE TO SIDE MOTION

She hoped, if the fire swept suddenly upon her, she would be clear-eyed enough to locate its base. And she must remember to stand back six feet. She'd never been good at estimating distances.

She left the fire extinguisher in the kitchen where it would be discovered five weeks later upright and unmoved and encrusted with a thick film of ash like a relic of Pompeii. It was darkening now as in a solar eclipse.

She supposed she was waiting for a bullhorn voice as on TV, or a loud knocking at the door. The building would be evacuated if there was actually a fire, or even the danger of fire. She knew this, and was consoled.

Time was passing in an unnatural manner.

Clearly hours had gone by since she'd been thrown to her knees on the sidewalk yet by her watch it was only 9:20 A.M. (Unless it was 9:20 P.M. and in her panic she'd lost an entire day.) The sky outside the building was a whirlwind of darkness. She located the flashlight in a kitchen closet. Never had she switched on this flashlight before and was startled and pleased that it worked. It worked! The beam was impressive and steady. She ran water in the bathroom again, laying the flashlight on its side on the counter. Unknowingly now she'd begun to repeat a small repertory of actions and she would repeat them many times. She washed her face that seemed to be throbbing with heat, she rinsed her eyes, thirstily lapped up lukewarm water. She felt the building sway beneath her but thought sternly *This is imagination. There are no earthquakes in Manhattan.* She was beginning to smell something new, corrosive, chemical. Nerve gas: her nerves were being paralyzed. Hours would pass in a haze of pacing the dimming rooms of the apartment with the flashlight beaming into corners as she held wetted towels against her nose and mouth. This terrible smell which she believed to be the smell of chemical warfare.

Whoever their enemies were, these enemies had struck. Perhaps there would be more explosions. In other cities. She would never see her parents again. Trying to call their number in Illinois but the palm-sized phone was dead as any plastic, useless! She was very tired now. Her knees were stippled with cuts. Her forearms, her face. Yet she was very wakeful. This was no dream, this was *wakefulness* in which she couldn't help but rejoice. She ran hot water into the bathtub but the water ceased when the tub was hardly half full. Nonetheless she bathed. She smiled thinking *If this is a final bath I must enjoy it.* She was covered in a sticky ashy grime. Her hair was stiff with it. She spat into her hand. There was a pleasant surprise, her bath oils were still fragrant, that her soap still made suds. Soap suds! She shampooed her shoulder-length hair and combed it out carefully. It was no longer blond, but what color it was she could not have said: it had the look of undersea hair, seaweed hair, adrift in ash-water, the color of her sullied Caucasian skin.

Yet she dressed in fresh clothes, and regarded herself in the steamy bathroom mirror. She was hollow-eyed and gaunt yet wakeful, no longer the dreamy-eyed blond. A mutant being, primed to survive. Were there not undersea creatures that acquired extra sets of gills, eyes on stalks on either side of their blade-thin heads, cunning in the desperation of survival . . .

At the same time she was waiting for a knock on the door. A summons on the intercom.

Hours passed in oblivion. She lost consciousness, but did not sleep. She wakened suddenly. Where was the flashlight? It had rolled onto the floor. There were candles on the dining room table, fragrant hand-dipped candles so beautiful (and so expensive) you were reluctant to light them. But this was a special occasion, she would light them now. There were more candles in drawers, she groped for them and brought them out. She thought *The city is gone.* Fires raged somewhere that should have been extinguished by now. She felt their terrible heat and smelled their billowing smoke. It was volcano smoke, Armageddon smoke. She washed her face, rinsed her mouth, swallowed unsweetened grapefruit juice from a container. Suddenly she was ravenously hungry. She thought, heartened *It's absurd, I'm not important enough to be the sole survivor.* She dared to open the door to the corridor, and shone the flashlight into darkness. She called out Hello? Hello? in a quavering voice. The air of the corridor was unnaturally warm. She was terrified of being locked out of her apartment in such darkness. She cried Hello? Does anyone hear me? Is anyone there? She was anxious suddenly, that the building had been evacuated during her sleep, no one had come to her. Thirty-six floors above the street. Were the fire stairs safe? Did she dare try to leave? *And if the city is gone, what then?*

If she left the apartment, no one would know where to find her. Her fiancé would not know where to find her. Amid the rubble of the street and the churning dust, no one would know her name.

Quickly she locked the door behind her. She lighted several candles. She lighted all her candles! Arranged them on the windowsills of all her windows. Like Christmas: there was an innocence to this. She thought *This is the right thing to do at this time.* If her fiancé looked up from the street he would see her lighted candles and know that she was alive. By her watch it was two-fifteen. Not afternoon but night. For she'd lost the day. Never would she recover the day. But always she would remember her shock, and the happiness of her shock, when, out of the shifting smoke and ashes separating her apartment windows from the windows of apartments in an adjacent tower of Battery Park City, she began to see candlelight there, glimmering like distant stars. Several candles, a half-dozen candles, floating in the dark, brave and festive in the dark.

ACKNOWLEDGMENTS

Many thanks to the editors of the following magazines and anthologies in which the stories in this volume originally appeared, often in slightly different forms.

"Curly Red" in *Harper's*

"In Hiding" in *Michigan Quarterly Review*

"I'm Not Your Son, I Am No One You Know" in *Witness*

"Aiding and Abetting" in *Playboy*

"Fugitive" in *Yale Review*

"Me & Wolfie, 1979" in *Agni*

"The Girl with the Blackened Eye" in *Witness*; reprinted in *The O. Henry Awards: Prize Stories 2001* and *The Best American Mystery Stories 2001*

"Cumberland Breakdown" in *Boulevard*

"Upholstery" in *The New Yorker*

"Wolf's Head Lake" in *Salmagundi*

"Happiness" in *Ellery Queen Mystery Magazine* and reprinted in *The World's Finest Crime and Mystery II*

"Fire" in *TriQuarterly*

"The Instructor" in *Salmagundi;* reprinted in *Pushcart Prize: Best of the Small Presses 2003*

"The Skull: A Love Story" in *Harper's;* reprinted in *The Best American Mystery Stories 2004*

"*The Deaths:* An Elegy" in *Ellery Queen Mystery Magazine*

"Jorie (& Jamie): A Deposition" in *New Statesman* (U.K.) and *Yale Review*

"Mrs. Halifax and Rickie Swann: A Ballad" in *Boulevard*

"Three Girls" in *Georgia Review;* reprinted in *Pushcart Prize: Best of the Small Presses 2004* and in *The Best American Magazine Writing 2003*

"The Mutants" in *The Observer* (U.K.) and *Fiction*

© MARION ETTLINGER

JOYCE CAROL OATES is a recipient of the National Book Award and the PEN/Malamud Award for Excellence in Short Fiction. She has written some of the most enduring fiction of our time, including the national bestsellers *We Were the Mulvaneys* and *Blonde,* which was nominated for the National Book Award. She is the Roger S. Berlind Distinguished Professor of the Humanities at Princeton University and has been a member of the American Academy of Arts and Letters since 1978. In 2003 she received the Common Wealth Award for Distinguished Service in Literature.

These and other books by JOYCE CAROL OATES:

THE FALLS: *A Novel*
ISBN 0-06-072228-2 (hardcover) • ISBN 0-06-074188-0 (audio)
A haunting story of the powerful spell Niagara Falls casts upon two generations of a family, leading to tragedy, love, loss, and, ultimately, redemption.

I AM NO ONE YOU KNOW: *Stories*
ISBN 0-06-059288-5 (hardcover)
A collection of nineteen startling stories that bear witness to the remarkably varied lives of Americans of our time. These vividly rendered portraits of women, men, and children testify to Oates' compassion for the mysterious and luminous resources of the human spirit.

THE TATTOOED GIRL: *A Novel*
ISBN 0-06-053107-X (paperback)
A celebrated but reclusive author reluctantly admits that he can no longer live alone and decides to hire an assistant. Considering at first only male applicants, he is dissatisfied with everyone he meets . . . then he encounters Alma.

I'LL TAKE YOU THERE: *A Novel*
ISBN 0-06-050118-9 (paperback)
Pitiless in exposing the follies of the time, *I'll Take You There* is a dramatic revelation of the risks—and curious rewards—of the obsessive personality, as well as a testament to the stubborn strength of a certain type of contemporary female intellectual.

MIDDLE AGE: *A Romance*
ISBN 0-06-093490-5 (paperback)
Joyce Carol Oates portrays a contemporary phenomenon rarely explored in literature and popular culture: the affluent middle-aged in America reinventing themselves romantically after the energies of youth have faded or become disillusioned.

FAITHLESS: *Tales of Transgression*
ISBN 0-06-093357-7 (paperback)
As Joyce Carol Oates penetrates the formidable psyches of her characters—ordinary people who go about their ordinary lives—Oates weaves tales that are unrelenting and frightening in their awareness of the all-too-human potential for good and evil.

BLONDE: *A Novel*
ISBN 0-06-093493-X (paperback)
Joyce Carol Oates reimagines the inner, poetic, and spiritual life of Norma Jeane Baker. Rich with psychological insight and disturbing irony, this mesmerizing narrative illuminates Baker's lonely childhood, wrenching adolescence, and the creation of "Marilyn Monroe."